## More Praise for *Let the Devil Sleep*

"A genuine pleasure . . . [like] being on a runaway train."
—*Florida Times-Union/Jacksonville.com*

"A brilliant and absorbing mystery . . . I love this series, as much for its thoughtful social commentary (on the media this time) as for its mysteries. *Let the Devil Sleep* is even better than *Shut Your Eyes Tight* . . . Highly recommended."
—Bookloons

"Tightly woven . . . will keep readers guessing until the very end."
—*Parkersburg News and Sentinel*

"This is another perfect summer read full of twists, mystery, action, danger, good guys, bad guys, fires, blood trails, and of course, the FBI!"
—*Harbor Light Newspaper*

"Provocative . . . A triumphant work of mystery-fueled fiction, *Let the Devil Sleep* is a big, bold book that will have you sleeping with the lights on."
—*Free Lance–Star*

"*Let the Devil Sleep* is John Verdon's best book so far."
—*House of Crime and Mystery*

# Let the Devil Sleep

# John Verdon

# Sleep Let the Devil

*A novel*

B\D\W\Y

*Broadway Books*

NEW YORK

Copyright © 2012 by John Verdon

Published in the United States by Broadway Books, an imprint of the Crown Publishing Group, a division of Random House LLC, a Penguin Random House Company, New York. www.crownpublishing.com

Broadway Books and its logo, B \ D \ W \ Y, are trademarks of Random House LLC.

Originally published in hardcover in the United States by Crown Publishers, an imprint of the Crown Publishing Group, a division of Random House LLC, New York, in 2012.

Library of Congress Cataloging-in-Publication Data
Verdon, John.
Let the devil sleep / by John Verdon.—1st ed.
p.   cm.
The third novel in the Dave Gurney mystery series.
1. Detectives—New York (State)—New York—Fiction.
2. Serial murderers—Fiction.   3. Criminal behavior, Prediction of—Fiction.
4. Cold cases (Criminal investigation)—Fiction.   I. Title.
PS3622.E736L48 2012
813'.6—dc22      2012018564
ISBN 978-0-307-71793-1
eISBN 978-0-307-71794-8

Printed in the United States of America

Book design: Lynne Amft
Cover design: Mumtaz Mustafa
Cover photography: Katya Evdokimova/Arcangel Images

*For Naomi*

# Let the Devil Sleep

*Part One*

# The Orphans
## of Murder

# Prologue

She had to be stopped.

Hints had not worked. Subtle nudges had been ignored. Firmer action was called for. Something dramatic and unmistakable, accompanied by a clear explanation.

The clarity of the explanation was crucial. It could leave no room for doubt, no room for questions. The police, the media, and the naïve little meddler herself must be made to understand his message, to agree on its significance.

He stared down thoughtfully at the yellow pad in front of him and began to write:

> *You must abandon your ill-conceived project immediately. What you are proposing to do is intolerable. It glorifies the most destructive people on earth. It ridicules my pursuit of justice by exalting the criminals I have executed. It creates undeserved sympathy for the vilest of the vile. This cannot happen. This I will not permit. I have slept for ten years in the peace of my achievement, in the peace of my message to the world, in the peace of my justice. Force me to take up arms again and the price will be terrible.*

He read what he had written. He shook his head slowly. He was not satisfied with the tone. He tore the page from the pad and slipped it into the slot of the document shredder by his chair. He began again on a fresh page:

> *Stop what you are doing. Stop now and walk away. Or there will be blood again, and more blood. Be warned. Do not disturb my peace.*

That was better. But not quite good enough.

He'd have to work on it. Sharpen the point. Leave no doubt. Make it perfect.

And there was so little time.

## Chapter 1

# Spring

The French doors were open.

From where Dave Gurney was standing by the breakfast table, he could see that the last patches of winter snow, like reluctant glaciers, had receded from the open pasture and survived now only in the more recessed and shadowed places in the surrounding woods.

The mixed fragrances of the newly exposed earth and the previous summer's unmowed hay drifted into the big farmhouse kitchen. These were smells that once had the power to enthrall him. Now they barely touched him.

"You should step outside," said Madeleine from where she stood at the sink, washing out her cereal bowl. "Step out into the sun. It's quite glorious."

"Yes, I can see that," he said, not moving.

"Sit and have your coffee in one of the Adirondack chairs," she said, setting the bowl down in the drying rack on the countertop. "You could use some sun."

"Hmm." He nodded meaninglessly and took another sip from the mug he was holding. "Is this the same coffee we've been using?"

"What's wrong with it?"

"I didn't say anything was wrong with it."

"Yes, it's the same coffee."

He sighed. "I think I'm getting a cold. Last couple of days, things haven't had much taste."

She rested her hands on the edge of the sink island and looked at him. "You need to get out more. You need to *do* something."

"Right."

"I mean it. You can't just sit in the house and stare at the wall all day. It will make you sick. It *is* making you sick. Have you called Connie Clarke back?"

"I will."

"When?"

"When I feel like it."

He didn't think it was a feeling he was likely to have in the foreseeable future. That's just the way he was these days—the way he'd been for the past six months. It was as though, after the injuries he'd suffered at the end of the bizarre Jillian Perry murder case, he had withdrawn from everything connected with normal life—daily tasks, planning, people, phone calls, commitments of any kind. He'd gotten to the point where he liked nothing better than a blank calendar page for the coming month—no appointments, no promises. He'd come to equate withdrawal with freedom.

At the same time, he had the objectivity to know that what was happening to him wasn't good, that there was no peace in his freedom. He felt hostile, not serene.

To some extent he understood the strange entropy that was unwinding the fabric of his life and isolating him. Or at least he could list what he believed to be its causes. Near the top of the list he'd place the tinnitus he'd been experiencing since he emerged from his coma. In all likelihood it had actually begun two weeks before that, when three shots were fired at him in a small room at nearly point-blank range.

The persistent sound in his ears (which the ear, nose, and throat specialist had explained wasn't a "sound" at all but rather a neural anomaly that the brain misinterpreted as sound) was hard to describe. The pitch was high, the volume low, the timbre like a softly hissed musical note. The phenomenon was fairly common among rock musicians and combat veterans, was anatomically mysterious, and, apart from occasional cases of spontaneous remission, was generally incurable. "Frankly, Detective Gurney," the doctor had concluded, "considering what you've been through, considering the trauma and the coma, ending up with a mild ringing in your ears is a damn lucky outcome."

It wasn't a conclusion Dave could argue with. But it hadn't made it any easier for him to adjust to the faint whine that enveloped him when all else was silent. It was a particular problem at night. What in daylight might resemble the harmless whistling of a teakettle in a distant room became in the darkness a sinister presence, a cold, metallic atmosphere that encased him.

Then there were the dreams—claustrophobic dreams that recalled his hospital experiences, memories of the constricting cast that had held his arm immobile, the difficulty he'd had in breathing—dreams that left him feeling panicky for long minutes after awakening.

He still had a numb spot on his right forearm close to where the first of his assailant's bullets had shattered the wrist bone. He checked the spot regularly, sometimes hourly, in hopes that its numbness was receding—or, on bleaker days, in fear that it was spreading. There were occasional, unpredictable, stabbing pains in his side where the second bullet had passed through him. There was also an intermittent tingling—like an itch impervious to scratching—at the center of his hairline where the third bullet had fractured his skull.

Perhaps the most distressing effect of being wounded was the constant need he now felt to be armed. He'd carried a gun on the job because regulations had required it. Unlike most cops, he had no fondness for firearms. And when he left the department after twenty-five years, he left behind, along with his gold detective's shield, the need to carry a weapon.

Until he was shot.

And now, each morning as he got dressed, the inevitable final item he put on was a small ankle holster holding a .32 Beretta. He hated the emotional need for it. Hated the change in him that required the damn thing to always be with him. He'd hoped the need would gradually diminish, but so far that wasn't happening.

On top of everything else, it seemed to him that Madeleine had been watching him in recent weeks with a new kind of worry in her eyes—not the fleeting looks of pain and panic he'd seen in the hospital, or the alternating expressions of hopefulness and anxiety that had accompanied his early recovery, but something quieter and deeper—a half-hidden chronic dread, as if she were witnessing something terrible.

Still standing by the breakfast table, he finished his coffee in two large swallows. Then he carried the mug to the sink and let the hot water run into it. He could hear Madeleine down the hall in the mud-room, cleaning out the cat's litter box. The cat had recently been added to the household at Madeleine's initiative. Gurney wondered why. Was it to cheer him up? Engage him in the life of a creature other than himself? If so, it wasn't working. He had no more interest in the cat than in anything else.

"I'm going to take a shower," he announced.

He heard Madeleine say something in the mudroom that sounded like "Good." He wasn't sure that's what she said, but he didn't see any point in asking. He went into the bathroom and turned on the hot water.

A long, steamy shower——the energetic spray pelting his back minute after minute from the base of his neck down to the base of his spine, relax-ing muscles, opening capillaries, clearing mind and sinuses——produced in him a feeling of well-being that was both wonderful and fleeting.

By the time he'd dressed again and returned to the French doors, a jangled sense of unease was already beginning to reassert itself. Mad-eleine was outside now on the bluestone patio. Beyond the patio was the small section of the pasture that had, through two years of fre-quent mowings, come to resemble a lawn. Clad in a rough barn jacket, orange sweatpants, and green rubber boots, she was working her way along the edge of the flagstones, stamping enthusiastically down on a spade every six inches, creating a clear demarcation, digging out the encroaching roots of the wild grasses. She gave him a look that seemed at first to convey an invitation for him to join in the project, then dis-appointment at his obvious reluctance to do so.

Irritated, he purposely looked away, his gaze drifting down the hillside to his green tractor parked by the barn.

She followed his line of sight. "I was wondering, could you use the tractor to smooth out the ruts?"

"Ruts?"

"Where we park the cars."

"Sure . . ." he said hesitantly. "I guess."

"It doesn't have to be done right this minute."

"Hmm." All traces of equanimity from his shower were now gone, as his train of thought shifted to the peculiar tractor problem he'd discovered a month ago and had largely put out of his mind—except for those paranoid moments when it drove him crazy.

Madeleine appeared to be studying him. She smiled, put down her spade, and walked around to the side door, evidently so she could take off her boots in the mudroom before coming into the kitchen.

He took a deep breath and stared at the tractor, wondering for the twentieth time about the mysteriously jammed brake. As if acting in malignant harmony, a dark cloud slowly obliterated the sun. Spring, it seemed, had come and gone.

## Chapter 2

# A Huge Favor for
# Connie Clarke

The Gurney property was situated on the saddle of a ridge at the end of a rural road outside the Catskill village of Walnut Crossing. The old farmhouse was set on the gentle southern slope of the saddle. An overgrown pasture separated it from a large red barn and a deep pond ringed by cattails and willows, backed by a beech, maple, and black-cherry forest. To the north a second pasture rose along the ridgeline toward a pine forest and a string of small abandoned bluestone quarries that looked out over the next valley.

The weather had gone through the kind of dramatic about-face that was far more common in the Catskill Mountains than in New York City, where Dave and Madeleine had come from. The sky had become a featureless slaty blanket drawn over the hills. The temperature seemed to have dropped at least ten degrees in ten minutes.

A superfine sleet was beginning to fall. Gurney closed the French doors. As he pulled them tight to secure the latches, he felt a piercing pain in the right side of his stomach. A moment later another followed. This was something he was used to, nothing that three ibuprofens couldn't suppress. He headed for the bathroom medicine cabinet, thinking that the worst part of it wasn't the physical discomfort, the worst part was the feeling of vulnerability, the realization that the only reason he was alive was that he'd been lucky.

Luck was not a concept he liked. It seemed to him to be the fool's substitute for competence. Random chance had saved his life, but random chance was not a trustworthy ally. He knew younger men who believed in good luck, relied on good luck, thought it was something they owned. But at the age of forty-eight, Gurney knew damn well

that luck is only luck, and the invisible hand that flips the coin is as
cold as a corpse.

The pain in his side also reminded him that he'd been meaning to
cancel his upcoming appointment with his neurologist in Binghamton.
He'd had four appointments with the man in less than four months,
and they seemed increasingly pointless, unless the only point was to
send Gurney's insurance company another bill.

He kept that phone number with his other medical numbers in his
den desk. Instead of continuing into the bathroom for the ibuprofen,
he went into the den to make the call. As he was entering the number, he was picturing the doctor: a preoccupied man in his late thirties,
with wavy black hair already receding, small eyes, girlish mouth, weak
chin, silky hands, manicured fingernails, expensive loafers, dismissive
manner, and no visible interest in anything that Gurney thought or
felt. The three women who inhabited his sleek, contemporary reception area seemed perpetually confused and irritated by the doctor, by
his patients, and by the data on their computer screens.

The phone was answered on the fourth ring with an impatience
verging on contempt. "Dr. Huffbarger's office."

"This is David Gurney, I have an upcoming appointment that
I'd—"

The sharp voice cut him off. "Hold on, please."

In the background he could hear a raised male voice that he thought
for a moment belonged to an angry patient reeling off a long, urgent
complaint—until a second voice asked a question and a third voice
joined the fray in a similar tone of loud, fast-talking indignation—and
Gurney realized that what he was hearing was the cable news channel
that made sitting in Huffbarger's waiting room insufferable.

"Hello?" said Gurney with a definite edge. "Anybody there? *Hello?*"

"Just a minute, please."

The voices that he found so abrasively empty-headed continued in
the background. He was about to hang up when the receptionist's voice
returned.

"Dr. Huffbarger's office, can I help you?"

"Yes. This is David Gurney. I have an appointment I want to
cancel."

"The date?"

"A week from today at eleven-forty A.M."

"Spell your name, please."

He was about to question how many people had appointments on that same day at 11:40, but he spelled his name instead.

"And when do you wish to reschedule it?"

"I don't. I'm just canceling it."

"You'll need to reschedule it."

"What?"

"I can reschedule Dr. Huffbarger's appointments, not cancel them."

"But the fact is—"

She interrupted, sounding exasperated. "An existing appointment can't be removed from the system without inserting a revised date. That's the doctor's policy."

Gurney could feel his lips tightening with anger, way too much anger. "I don't really care much about his system or his policy," he said slowly, stiffly. "Consider my appointment canceled."

"There will be a missed-appointment charge."

"No there won't. And if Huffbarger has a problem with that, tell him to call me." He hung up, tense, feeling a twinge of chagrin at his childish twisting of the neurologist's name.

He stared out the den window at the high pasture without really seeing it.

*What the hell's the matter with me?*

A jab of pain in his right side offered a partial answer. It also reminded him that he'd been on his way to the medicine cabinet when he'd made his appointment-canceling detour.

He returned to the bathroom. He didn't like the look of the man who looked back at him from the mirror on the cabinet door. His forehead was lined with worry, his skin colorless, his eyes dull and tired.

Christ.

He knew he had to get back to his daily exercise regimen—the sets of push-ups, chin-ups, sit-ups that had once kept him in better shape than most men half his age. But now the man in the mirror was looking every bit of forty-eight, and he wasn't happy about it. He wasn't happy about the daily messages of mortality his body was sending him. He wasn't happy about his descent from mere introversion into isolation. He wasn't happy about . . . anything.

He took the ibuprofen bottle from its shelf, tapped three of the little brown pills into his hand, frowned at them, popped them into his mouth. As he was running the water, waiting for it to get cold, he heard the phone ringing in the den. Huffbarger, he thought. Or Huffbarger's office. He made no move to answer it. *To hell with them.*

Then he heard Madeleine's footsteps coming down from upstairs. A few moments later, she picked up the phone, just as the call was switching over to their ancient answering machine. He could hear her voice but couldn't make out the words. He half-filled a small plastic cup with water and washed down the three pills that were starting to dissolve on his tongue.

He assumed that Madeleine was dealing with the Huffbarger problem. Which was fine with him. But then he heard her footsteps coming across the hall and into the bedroom. She walked through the open bathroom door, extending the phone handset toward him.

"For you," she said, handing it to him and leaving the room.

Anticipating some unpleasantness from Huffbarger or one of his malcontent receptionists, Gurney's tone was defensively curt. "Yes?"

There was a second of silence before the caller spoke.

"David?" The bright female voice was certainly familiar, but his memory failed to attach a name or a face to it.

"Yes," he said, more pleasantly this time. "I'm sorry, but I can't quite place—"

"Oh, how could you forget? Oh, I am so hurt, *Detective Gurney*!" the caller cried with jokey exaggeration—and suddenly the laughing timbre and inflection of the words conjured up the person: a wiry, clever, high-energy blonde with a Queens accent and a model's cheekbones.

"Connie. Jesus. Connie Clarke. It's been a while."

"Six years, to be exact."

"Six years. Jesus." The number didn't mean much to him, didn't surprise him, but he didn't know what else to say.

He remembered their connection with mixed feelings. A freelance journalist, Connie Clarke had written a laudatory article about him for *New York* magazine after he'd solved the infamous Jason Strunk serial-murder case—just three years after he'd been promoted to detective first grade for solving the Jorge Kunzman serial-murder case. In fact, her article was a little too laudatory for comfort, dwelling as it did on his record number of homicide arrests and referring to him as the "NYPD Supercop"—a sobriquet that lent itself to scores of amusing variations created by his more imaginative colleagues.

"So how are things up there in peaceful retirement land?"

He could hear the grin in her question and assumed she knew about his unofficial involvement in the Mellery and Perry cases. "Sometimes more peaceful than other times."

"Wow! Yeah! I guess that's one way of putting it. You retire from the NYPD after twenty-five years, you're up in the sleepy Catskills for about ten minutes, and all of a sudden you're in the middle of one murder case after another. Seems to me you're kind of a major-crime magnet. Wow! How does Madeleine feel about that?"

"You just had her on the phone. You should have asked her."

Connie laughed as though he'd said something wonderfully witty.

"So between murder cases what's your typical day like?"

"There's not much to tell. It's pretty uneventful. Madeleine stays busier than I do."

"I'm having such a hard time picturing you in the middle of some kind of Norman Rockwell America. Dave making maple syrup. Dave making apple cider. Dave getting eggs from the henhouse."

"I'm afraid not. No syrup, cider, or eggs." What came to his mind was quite a different scenario describing the past six months. *Dave playing the hero. Dave getting shot. Dave recovering too goddamn slowly. Dave sitting around listening to the ringing in his own ears. Dave getting depressed, hostile, isolated. Dave viewing every proposed activity as an infuriating assault on his right to remain in a paralyzing funk. Dave wanting to have nothing to do with anything.*

"So what *will* you be doing today?"

"To be absolutely truthful with you, Connie, damn little. At most I'll walk around the edges of the fields, maybe pick up some of the branches that blew down during the winter, maybe rake some fertilizer into the garden beds. Stuff like that."

"Doesn't sound so bad to me. I know people who'd give a lot to trade places with you."

He didn't answer, just let the silence drag out, thinking it might force her to get to the point of the call. There had to be a point. He remembered Connie as a cordial and talky woman, but she always had a purpose. Her mind, under that windblown blond mane, was always working.

"You're wondering why I called you," she said. "Right?"

"The question did cross my mind."

"I called you because I want to ask you for a favor. A *huge* favor."

Gurney thought for a moment, then laughed.

"What's the joke?" She sounded momentarily off balance.

"You once told me that it's always better to ask for a big favor than a small one, because small ones are easier to refuse."

"No! I can't believe I said that. That sounds so *manipulative*. That's *awful*. You're making that up, aren't you?" She was full of cheerful indignation. Connie never remained off balance for long.

"So what can I do for you?"

"You did make it up! I knew it!"

"As I said, what can I do for you?"

"Well, now I'm embarrassed to say it, but it really is a huge, huge favor." She paused. "You remember Kim?"

"Your daughter?"

"My daughter who adores you."

"I beg your pardon?"

"Don't tell me you didn't know."

"What are you talking about?"

"Oh, David, David, David, all the women love you, and you don't even notice."

"I think I was in the same room with your daughter once, when she was . . . what, maybe fifteen?" His recollection was of a pretty but very serious-looking girl at lunch with him and Connie at Connie's house, hovering at the periphery of their conversation, hardly saying a word.

"Actually, she was seventeen. And okay, maybe 'adore' is too gushy a word. But she thought you were really, really smart—and to Kim that means a lot. Now she's twenty-three, and I happen to know she still has a very high opinion of Dave Gurney, Supercop."

"That's very nice, but . . . I'm getting a little lost here."

"Of course you are, because I'm making such a mess of asking you for the super-huge favor. Maybe you ought to sit down—this could take a few minutes."

Gurney was still standing by the sink in the bathroom. He walked out through the bedroom and across the hall into the den. He had no desire to sit. Instead he stood by the back window. "Okay, Connie, I'm sitting," he said. "What's going on?"

"Nothing bad, really. It's overwhelmingly good. Kim has an incredible opportunity. Did I ever tell you she was interested in journalism?"

"Following in her mother's footsteps?"

"God, don't ever say that to her, she'd switch careers overnight! I think her greatest goal is total independence from her mother! And forget about *footsteps*. She's on the verge of a major *leap*. So let me get down to the nitty-gritty here, before I lose you completely. She's completing a master's program in journalism at Syracuse. That's not far from you, right?"

"It's not exactly in the neighborhood. Maybe an hour and forty-five minutes away."

"Okay, not too terribly far. Not much worse than my commute to the city. So anyway, for her final degree project she came up with an idea for a kind of reality miniseries about murder victims—well, actually, not the victims themselves, but the families, the children. She wants to look at the long-term effects of having a parent murdered, without any resolution."

"Without—"

"Right—they'd all be cases where the killer was never caught. So the wound would never really have healed. No matter how much time passes, it remains the single biggest emotional fact in their lives—a giant force field that changes everything forever. She's calling the series *The Orphans of Murder*. Is that great or what?"

"Sounds like an interesting idea."

"*Very* interesting! But I'm leaving out the dynamite part. It's not just an *idea*. It's actually going to *happen*! It started out as an academic project, but her thesis adviser was so impressed that he helped her develop her outline into an actual proposal. He even got her to nail down some of her intended participants with exclusivity agreements so she'd be protected. Then he passed the proposal along to a production contact of his at RAM-TV. And guess what? The RAM guy wants it! Overnight this thing has been transformed from a frigging term paper into the kind of professional exposure that people with twenty years' experience would kill for. RAM is the hottest thing out there."

In Gurney's opinion RAM was the organization most responsible for turning traditional news programming into a noisy, flashy, shallow, poisonously opinionated, alarmist carnival—but he overcame the temptation to say so.

"So now you're wondering," Connie went on excitedly, "what all this has to do with my favorite detective, right?"

"I'm waiting."

"Couple of things. First, I need you to look over her shoulder."

"Meaning what?"

"Just meet with her? Get a sense of what she's doing? See if it reflects the world of homicide victims as you know it? She's got this one big chance. If she doesn't make too many mistakes, the sky's the limit."

"Hmm."

"Does that little grunt mean you'll do it? Will you, David, please?"

"Connie, I don't know a damn thing about journalism." What he did know mostly disgusted him, but again he kept quiet.

"She's got the journalism part down pat. And she's as smart as anyone I know. But she's still a kid."

"Then what do I bring to the table? Old age?"

"Reality. Knowledge. Experience. Perspective. The incredible wisdom that comes from . . . how many homicide cases?"

He didn't think that was a real question, so he didn't try to answer it.

Connie continued with even more intensity. "She's super capable, but ability isn't the same as life experience. She's in the process of interviewing people who've lost a parent or some other loved one to a murderer. She needs to be in a realistic frame of mind for that. She needs a broad view of the territory, you know what I mean? I guess what I'm saying is that so much is at stake, she needs to know as much as she possibly can."

Gurney sighed. "God knows there's a ton of stuff out there on grief, death, loss of a loved—"

She cut him off. "Yeah, yeah, I know—the pop-psych stages of grief, five stages of horseshit, whatever. That's not what she needs. She needs to talk to someone who knows about *murder,* who's seen the victims, talked to the families, looked in their eyes, the horror—someone who *knows,* not someone who wrote a frigging book." There was a long silence between them. "So will you do it? Just meet with her once, just look at what she's got and where she plans to go with it. See if it makes sense to you?"

As he stared out the den window at the back pasture, the idea of meeting with Connie's daughter to review her entry ticket into the world of trash television was one of the least appealing prospects on earth. "You said there were a *couple* of things, Connie. What's the second one?"

"Well . . ." Her voice weakened. "There may be an ex-boyfriend problem."

"What kind of problem?"

"That's the question. Kim likes to sound invulnerable, you know? Like she's not afraid of anything or anybody?"

"But . . . ?"

"But at the very least, this asshole has been playing nasty little tricks on her."

"Like what?"

"Like getting into her apartment and moving things around. There was something she started to tell me about a knife disappearing and later reappearing, but when I tried to get her to tell me more about it, she wouldn't."

"Then why do you think she brought it up?"

"Maybe she wants help, and at the same time she doesn't want it, and she can't make up her mind which it is."

"Does the asshole have a name?"

"Robert Meese is his real name. He calls himself Robert Montague."

"Is this somehow connected with her TV project?"

"I don't know. I just have a feeling that the situation is worse than she's willing to admit. Or at least admit to me. So . . . please, David? Please? I don't know who else to ask."

When he didn't respond, she went on. "Maybe I'm overreacting. Maybe I'm imagining things. Maybe there's no problem at all. But even if there isn't, it would still be great if you could listen to her talk about her project, about these homicide victims and their families. It means so much to her. It's the opportunity of a lifetime. She's so determined, so confident."

"You sound a little shaky."

"I don't know. I'm just . . . concerned."

"About her project or about her ex-boyfriend?"

"Maybe both. I mean, on the one hand, it's fantastic, right? But it just breaks my heart to think that she might be so determined and so confident and so independent that somehow she'd get in over her head without telling me, without my being able to help her. God, David, you have a son, right? Do you know what I'm feeling?"

Ten minutes after they'd ended the call, Gurney was still standing at the large north-facing den window, trying to makes sense of Connie's uncharacteristically scattered tone, wondering why he'd finally agreed to talk to Kim and why the whole situation made him so uncomfortable.

He suspected that it had something to do with her last comment about his son. That, as always, was a sensitive area—for reasons he had no intention of examining right then.

The phone rang. He was surprised to find that he'd distractedly been holding it in his hand, having forgotten to hang it up. *This time it really will be Huffbarger,* he thought, *calling to defend his idiotic cancellation policy.* He was tempted to let it ring, let it go to the answering machine, let Huffbarger wait. But he also wanted to be done with it, didn't want to be thinking about it. He pressed the TALK button.

"Dave Gurney here."

A young female voice, clear and bright, said, "Dave, I want to thank you so much! Connie just called and told me that you'd be willing to talk to me."

For a second he was confused. He always found it jarring when a parent was called by his or her first name.

"Kim?"

"Of course! Who did you think?" When he didn't answer, she raced on. "Anyway, here's why this situation is so cool. I'm headed up to Syracuse from the city. Right now I'm just where Route 17 meets I-81. Which means I can shoot across I-88 and be in Walnut Crossing in like thirty-five minutes. Is that okay with you? It's super-short notice, I know, but it's such serendipity! And I'm dying to see you again!"

## Chapter 3

# The Impact of Murder

Routes 17, 81, and 88 converge in the neighborhood of Binghamton, which is a good hour from Walnut Crossing. Gurney wondered if Kim's optimistic time estimate had arisen from a lack of information or an abundance of enthusiasm. But that was the least of the questions on his mind as he watched the perky little red Miata making its way up the pasture trail to the house.

He opened the side door and stepped out onto the matted grass and gravel where his Outback was parked. The Miata pulled in next to it, and a young woman emerged, holding a slim briefcase. She was wearing jeans, a T-shirt, and a stylish blazer with the sleeves turned up.

"Would you recognize me," she asked with a grin, "if I hadn't told you I was coming?"

"Maybe if I had time to study your face," he said, studying it now in its soft frame of shining brown hair, parted loosely in the middle. "It's the same face, but it's brighter and happier than it was that day I had lunch with you and your mother."

She frowned thoughtfully for a moment, then laughed. "It wasn't just that day, it was *those years*. I was definitely not very happy back then. It took me a long time to figure out what I wanted to do with my life."

"You seem to have figured it out quicker than most people."

She shrugged, looking around at the fields and woods. "This is beautiful. You must love it here. The air feels so clean and cool."

"Maybe a little too cool for the first week of spring."

"My God, you're right! I have so much going on I can't remember anything. It's already spring. How could I forget that?"

"It's easy," he said. "Come on in. It's warmer in the house."

• • •

Half an hour later, Kim and Dave were sitting across from each
other at the small pine breakfast table in the nook by the French
doors. They were finishing the omelets, toast, and coffee that Madeleine
had insisted on making when she learned that Kim had been traveling
all morning with nothing to eat. Madeleine had finished first and was
cleaning off the stove. Kim was telling her story from the beginning,
the story behind her visit.

"It's an idea I've had for years—examining the horror of murder
by examining its impact on the victim's family—I just never knew
what to do with it. Sometimes I wouldn't think about it for a while, but
it would always come back, stronger than ever. I became obsessed with
it—I *had* to do something with it. At first I thought it could be like
a scholarly thing—maybe a sociology or psychology monograph. So I
sent query letters out to a lot of the university presses, but I didn't have
the right academic degrees, so they had no interest in me. So I thought
maybe a regular nonfiction book. But for a book you need an agent,
which meant more query letters. And guess what? Zero interest. Like
I'm twenty-one, twenty-two, who the hell am I? What have I written
before? What are my credentials? Basically I'm just a kid. All I have
is an idea. Then it finally dawns on me. Duh! *This is not a book, this is
television!* From that point on, things started to fall into place. I saw it
as a series of intimate interviews—'reality television' in the best sense
of that term, which I realize has a pretty scuzzy sound these days, but
it doesn't have to be that way—*not if it's done with emotional truth!*"

She stopped, as though suddenly affected by her own words, flashed
an embarrassed smile, cleared her throat, and went on. "So anyway, I
put it all together in the form of a detailed outline for my master's
thesis and submitted it to Dr. Wilson, my adviser. He told me it was
a great idea, that it had real potential. He helped me put it in a commercial proposal format, made sure my legal bases were covered to
give me some protection in the real world, and then he did something
he said he never does: He passed it along to a production executive he
knows personally at RAM-TV—a guy by the name of Rudy Getz. And
Getz got back to us like a week later and said, 'Okay, let's do it.' "

"Just like that?" asked Gurney.

"I was surprised, too. But Getz said that's the way RAM operates. I'm not going to question it. The fact that I can make this idea real, that I can explore this subject . . ." She shook her head, as if trying to ward off some volatile emotion.

Madeleine came to the table, sat down, and said what Gurney was thinking. "This is important to you, isn't it? I mean, *really* important, beyond being a career booster."

"Oh, God, yes!"

Madeleine smiled softly. "And the *heart* of the idea . . . the part that matters so much to you . . . ?"

"The families, *the children* . . ." Again she stopped for a second or two, evidently overcome by some image that her own speech was evoking. She slid her chair back from the table, stood, and walked around the table to the French doors that looked out over the patio, the garden, the pasture, and the forest beyond.

"It's sort of silly, I can't explain it," she said, speaking with her back to them, "but I find it easier to talk about this standing up." She cleared her throat twice before beginning in a barely audible voice. "I believe that murder changes everything forever. It steals something that can never be replaced. It has consequences that go way beyond what happens to the victim. The victim loses his life, which is a terrible thing, an unfair thing, but for him it's over, the end. He's lost everything that might have been, but he doesn't know it. He doesn't go on *feeling* the loss, *imagining* what might have been." She raised her hands and placed her palms against the glass panes in front of her, a gesture that conveyed both great feeling and great effort at control.

She went on, a little louder. "It's not the victim who wakes up to a half-empty bed, a half-empty house. He isn't the one who dreams that he's still alive, only to wake up to the pain of realizing that he's not. He doesn't feel the sickening rage, the heartache his death causes. He doesn't keep seeing the empty chair at the table, hearing sounds that sound like his voice. He doesn't keep seeing the closet full of his clothes . . ." Her voice was growing hoarse. She cleared her throat. "He doesn't feel the agony—*the agony of having the heart of your life torn out.*"

She leaned against the glass for several long seconds, then pushed herself slowly away from it. When she turned around toward the table, her face was streaked with tears. "You know about phantom pain? The amputation phenomenon? Feeling pain in the place where your arm or your leg used to be? That's how murder is for the family left behind. Like the aching in a phantom limb—an unbearable pain in an empty place."

She stood perfectly still for a little while, staring at some inner landscape. Then she wiped her face roughly with her hands, emerging from behind them with a matter-of-fact determination in her eyes and voice. "To understand what murder really is, you have to talk to the families. That's my theory, that's my project, that's my plan. And that's what Rudy Getz is excited about." She took a deep breath and exhaled slowly. "If it's not too much trouble, could I have another cup of coffee?"

"I think we can manage that." Madeleine smiled pleasantly, went to the sink island, and refilled the coffeemaker.

Gurney was leaning back in his chair, his hands steepled reflectively under his chin. No one said anything for a minute or two. The coffeemaker made its initial sputtering sounds.

Kim looked around the big farmhouse kitchen. "This is very nice," she said. "Very homey, warm. Perfect, really. It looks like everyone's dream of a house in the country."

After Madeleine brought Kim's coffee to the table, Gurney was the first to speak. "It's clear that you have a lot of passion about this subject, that it means a great deal to you. I wish I were as clear about how I can help you."

"What did Connie ask you to do?"

" 'Look over your shoulder'—I think that's one of the phrases she used."

"No mention of ... any other problems?" It sounded to Gurney like she was making a childishly transparent effort to have the question sound casual.

"Does your ex-boyfriend qualify as a 'problem'?"

"She brought up Robby?"

"She mentioned a Robert Meese ... or Montague?"

"Meese. The Montague thing is ..." She trailed off, shaking her head. "Connie thinks I need protection. I don't. Robby is pathetic and extremely annoying, nothing I can't handle."

"Is he connected to your TV project?"

"Not anymore. Why do you ask?"

"Just curious."

*Just curious about what? What the hell am I getting involved in? Why am I bothering to sit here listening to some overwrought graduate student with nutty-boyfriend problems expound on her sentimental ideas about murder and her big chance at glory on America's trashiest cable network? Time to start backing away from the quicksand.*

Kim was staring at him as though she had Madeleine's gift for reading his mind. "It's not all that complicated. And since you've been generous enough to offer to help me, I should be more forthright."

"We keep coming back to that part about my *helping* you, but I don't see——"

Madeleine, who was squeezing out a sponge at the sink after washing off their omelet plates, interjected gently, "Why don't we just listen to what Kim has to say?"

Gurney nodded. "Good idea."

"I met Robby in the drama club a little less than a year ago. He was easily the handsomest guy on campus. Like a young Johnny Depp. About six months ago, we moved in together. For a while I felt like the luckiest person in the world. When I got totally into my murder project, he seemed supportive. In fact, when I picked the families I wanted to start interviewing, he came with me, joined in, was totally part of everything. And that . . . that's when . . . the monster emerged." She paused and took a sip of her coffee.

"As Robby got more involved, he started taking over. He wasn't helping me with *my* project anymore—it became *our* project, and then he started acting like it was *his* project. After we'd meet with one of the families, he'd give them *his* card with *his* contact information, tell them they could get in touch with *him* anytime. In fact, that's when this ridiculous Montague thing started, when he had those cards printed up: 'Robert Montague, Documentary Productions and Creative Consultancy.' "

Gurney looked skeptical. "He was trying to elbow you out, steal the project?"

"It was sicker than that. Robby Meese looks like a god, but he came from a screwed-up home where bad things happened, and he spent most of his childhood in equally messed-up foster homes. Deep down he's the most pathetically insecure person you'll ever meet. Some of the families we were talking to, trying to sign up for official interviews—Robby was desperate to impress them. I think he'd have done *anything* for their approval, anything to be accepted by them. To make them *like* him. It was kind of disgusting."

"What did you do about it?"

"Initially I didn't know what to do. Then it came to a head when I discovered he'd been having discussions on his own with one of the key family members, a guy I really wanted to get to. When I confronted Robby about it, the whole thing blew up into a screaming match. That's when I threw him out of our apartment—*my* apartment. And I got Connie's lawyer to draft a nice threatening letter to keep him away from the project—*my* project."

"How did he take it?"

"At first he got very nice, slimy-nice. I told him to fuck off. Then he started telling me that messing around with old murder cases could be risky and I should be careful—that maybe I didn't know what I was getting into. He'd call me late at night, leave messages on my phone about how he could protect me and how a lot of the people I was dealing with—including my thesis adviser—weren't what they seemed to be."

Gurney sat up a bit straighter in his chair. "What next?"

"Next? I told him if he didn't leave me alone, I'd get a restraining order and have him arrested as a stalker."

"That have any effect?"

"Depends what you mean. The calls stopped. But then the weird stuff started happening."

Madeleine stopped what she was doing at the sink and came to the table. "Sounds like this is getting intense. Mind if I join you?"

"No problem," said Kim. Madeleine sat down, and Kim continued. "Kitchen knives started disappearing. One day I got home from a class and I couldn't find my cat. Eventually I heard this little meow. The cat was in one of the closets with the door closed—a closet I never used. And there was one time I overslept because the time on my alarm clock had been changed."

"Aggravating, but fairly harmless," said Gurney. The look on Madeleine's face suggested strong disagreement, so he added, "I don't mean to downplay the emotional impact that nasty pranks can have. I'm just thinking about the legally actionable degrees of harassment."

Kim nodded. "Right. Well, the 'pranks' got nastier. One night I got home late and there was a drop of blood on the bathroom floor—like the size of a dime. And one of my missing kitchen knives was lying next to it."

"My God," said Madeleine.

"A few nights later, I started hearing these eerie sounds. Something would wake me up—I wasn't sure what—and then I'd hear a board creaking, then nothing, then something that sounded like breathing, then nothing."

Madeleine looked horrified.

"This is an apartment?" asked Gurney.

"It's a small house, divided into one upstairs and one downstairs apartment, plus a basement. There are a lot of crummy houses like it outside the campus, broken up into cheap apartments for students. Right now I'm the only tenant."

"You're *alone* there?" said Madeleine, wide-eyed. "You're a lot braver than I am. I'd get out of there so fast—"

There was a flash of anger in Kim's eyes. "I'm not running away from that little jerk!"

"You've reported these incidents to the police?"

She uttered a bitter little laugh. "Sure. The blood, the knife, the sounds in the night. The cops come to the house, they poke around, they check the windows, they look bored to death. When I call and give them my name and address, I can picture them rolling their eyes. It's pretty clear they think I'm a paranoid pain in the ass. An attention seeker. The crazy little bitch with the exaggerated boyfriend problems."

"I assume you've had the locks changed?" said Gurney mildly.

"Twice. It hasn't made any difference."

"You think Robby Meese is responsible for all this . . . intimidation?"

"I don't think it. I *know* it."

"What makes you so sure?"

"If you heard his voice—the calls he made to me after I threw him out? Or saw the looks on his face when we'd pass each other on campus? Then you'd know. It was the same *weirdness*. I don't know how to explain it, but the stuff that's been happening? It's creepy, the same way Robby is creepy."

In the ensuing silence, Kim wrapped her hands tightly around her coffee cup. It reminded Gurney of the way she was standing at the door earlier, her palms pressed against the glass. Emotion and control.

He thought about her program idea, her slant on the pain created by murder. There was truth in what she said. In some cases the wound inflicted by a killer tore a hole through a family—left spouse, children, parents desolate—filled their lives with sadness and rage.

In other cases, though, there was little grief, little emotion of any kind. Gurney had seen too many of those cases. Men who lived ugly lives and died ugly deaths. Drug dealers, pimps, career criminals, teenage gangbangers playing video games with real guns. The human devastation was breathtaking. Sometimes he had a dream, always the same, with an image from the concentration camps. A bulldozer pushing half-skeletonized bodies into a broad trench. Pushing them in like mannequins. Like rubble.

He sat gazing at the intense, dark-eyed young woman who was still grasping her lukewarm mug, leaning toward it, her shining hair hiding most of her face.

Then he glanced over at Madeleine with a question in his eyes.

She gave a tiny shrug, a hint of a smile. It felt like a nudge in the direction of action.

He looked back at Kim. "Okay. Let's return to the basic issue. How can I help you?"

## Chapter 4

# Like a Coffin

What she wanted was for Gurney to follow her back to her apartment in Syracuse, where she kept everything related to her project. That way he could see it all firsthand—her correspondence with potential interviewees, the two initial interviews she'd conducted and submitted as part of her proposal, her plans for the interviews yet to come, her contract with Rudy Getz at RAM-TV, the general positioning and promotional copy she was preparing for the series. He could see everything, get a feel for it, tell her what rang true, what didn't.

He had as little appetite for driving to Syracuse as he'd had for any activity in recent months, which was close to none. But it struck him as the quickest way to discharge whatever obligation he felt toward Connie Clarke. He'd go, he'd look, he'd comment. Duty discharged. "Huge favor" granted. Then back into his cave.

The Google directions to Kim's address that he'd printed out in the event they got separated estimated a journey of one hour and forty-nine minutes from Walnut Crossing, but there was almost no traffic on the two interstates that constituted most of the trip, and the little Miata ahead of him rarely descended to anywhere near the speed limit.

In a better mood, Gurney might have enjoyed the trip, passing through a rolling landscape of woods and meadows, wide rushing streams, farm fields with black earth newly plowed for spring planting, iconic silos and red barns. But in his state of mind, these bucolic views were reduced to a damp, muddy expanse—a wasteland of agricultural decline and bad weather.

His first sight of the environs of Syracuse reinforced his bleak thoughts. He recalled reading somewhere that the city sat at the foot of Onondaga Lake, whose fame arose from having been one of the most polluted lakes in America. It triggered a memory from his Bronx childhood—a memory of Eastchester Bay, whose murky navigation channel was constantly churned by barges and tugboats. The bay was an oily extension of Long Island Sound, in which nothing seemed to live except filthy seaweed and hideous brown crabs—armored, inedible, primeval, scuttling things—the thought of which could still raise gooseflesh on his arms.

He followed Kim's Miata off the interstate into a neighborhood that had a worn look and no obvious zoning restrictions. He drove past a haphazard sequence of small single-family houses, spacious older homes now fractured into multiple apartments, shabby convenience stores, dreary commercial buildings, and desolate open areas surrounded by chain-link fences.

At a corner take-out place—Onondaga Princes of Pizza—the Miata turned onto a smaller side street and came to a stop in front of an Archie Bunker house. It was separated by a narrow driveway from an identical house on each side. A patch of rough earth in front—not much larger than a double grave—was in desperate need of flowers or grass. Gurney parked behind Kim and watched as she emerged from the little car, locked and double-checked both doors. She looked up at the house and along the driveway—warily, it seemed to him. As he walked over to her, she gave him a nervous smile.

"Anything wrong?" he asked.

"No, everything . . . seems fine." She climbed the three steps to the front door, which was unlocked. That door, however, provided entry only to a tiny vestibule with two more doors. The one on the right had two serious-looking locks, which she opened with separate keys. Before turning the knob, she looked at it suspiciously and gave it a couple of sharp yanks.

That door opened into a hallway. She led him into the first room on the right—a small IKEA-furnished living room with the bare essentials: a futon couch, a coffee table, two low wooden armchairs with loose cushions, two minimalist floor lamps, a bookcase, a two-drawer metal file cabinet, and a table being used as a desk with a straight-backed chair behind it. The floor was covered by a worn-looking earth-tone rug.

He smiled curiously. "What was that yanking on the doorknob all about?"

"There were a couple of times it came off in my hand."

"You mean it was purposely loosened?"

"Oh, it was purposely loosened all right. Twice. The first time, the police took one look and dismissed it as a practical joke someone played on me. The second time, they didn't even bother to send someone out. Cop on the phone seemed to think it was funny."

"Doesn't sound funny to me."

"Thank you."

"I know I already asked you this, but . . ."

"The answer is yes, I'm sure it's Robby. And no, I don't have any proof. But who else could it be?"

As she finished speaking, the doorbell rang—a complex musical chime.

"Oh, God. My mother's idea. She gave me that when I moved in here. There used to be a buzzer, which she hated. Just a second." She headed out of the room for the front door.

She returned a minute later with a large pizza box and two cans of Diet Coke.

"Pretty good timing. I ordered this stuff on my cell on the way up here. I figured we'd need some lunch. Pizza okay with you?"

"Pizza's fine."

She laid the box on the coffee table, opened it, and dragged one of the light armchairs over to the table. Gurney sat on the couch.

After they'd each eaten a slice and washed it down with some soda, she said, "Okay. Where do you want to start?"

"You had this idea about talking to the families of murder victims. So I assume the first thing you had to do was figure out which murders to pick?"

"Right." She was watching him intently.

"There's no shortage of homicide cases. Even if you limited yourself to New York State, even to a single year, you'd have hundreds to choose from."

"Right."

He leaned forward. "So tell me how you made your choices. What were the criteria?"

"The criteria changed along the way. At first I wanted to include all kinds of victims, all kinds of homicides, all kinds of families, different racial and ethnic backgrounds, different lengths of time between the crime and now. Total variety! But Dr. Wilson kept telling me, 'Simplify, simplify.' Minimize the variables, he said. Look for a hook, make it easy for the viewer to understand. 'The narrower the focus, the sharper the point.' Like maybe the dozenth time he said that, I got it. Everything started connecting, falling into place. And after that I was like, '*Yes!* This is it! I know exactly what I'm going to do!' "

As Gurney listened to her, he felt strangely touched by her enthusiasm. "So what did the final criteria turn out to be?"

"Pretty much everything Dr. Wilson said: Minimize the variables. Narrow the focus. Find a hook. Once I started thinking that way, the answer just sort of materialized. I saw that I could zero the whole project in on the victims of the Good Shepherd."

"The guy who shot a bunch of Mercedes drivers eight or nine years ago?"

"Ten. *Exactly* ten years ago. His attacks all occurred in the spring of the year 2000."

Gurney sat back in his chair, nodding thoughtfully, recalling the infamous series of six shootings that had half the Northeast afraid to drive at night. "Interesting. So the nature of the initiating event is the same in all six instances, elapsed time from the crime to the present is the same, same shooter, same motive, same level of investigative attention."

"Right! And the same failure to bring the killer to justice— the same lack of closure, the same open wound. It makes the Good Shepherd case a perfect way to examine how different families react over time to the same catastrophe, how they live with the loss, how they deal with the injustice, what it does to them—especially what it does to the children. Different outcomes to the same tragedy."

She stood and went to the filing cabinet next to the table-desk. She removed a shiny blue folder and handed it to Gurney. On the cover

was a label with bold type that read, THE ORPHANS OF MURDER, A DOCU-
MENTARY PROPOSAL BY KIM CORAZON.

Perhaps because she noticed his gaze settle on "Corazon," she said,
"Did you think my name was Clarke?"

He thought back to the time when Connie had interviewed him
for the *New York* magazine profile. "I think Clarke was the only family name I heard mentioned."

"Clarke is Connie's maiden name. She went back to it when she
divorced my father, when I was a kid. His name was—*is*—Corazon.
And so is mine." Under the thin surface of this factual statement, there
was an obvious resentment. He wondered if that resentment was the
cause of her reluctance to refer to Connie as "Mom" or "Mother."

Gurney had no desire to probe that area. He opened the folder,
saw that it held a thick document, well over fifty pages. The cover
page repeated the title. The second page provided a table of contents:
"Concept," "Documentary Overview," "Style and Methodology,"
"Case-Selection Criteria," "The Good Shepherd Homicide Victims and
Circumstances," "Prospective Interviewees," "Contact Summaries and
Status," "Initial Interview Transcripts," "TGSMOI (Appendix)."

He went through the contents list again, more slowly. "You wrote
this? Organized it this way?"

"Yes. Is there a problem?"

"Not at all."

"What, then?"

"The way you spoke about this earlier showed a lot of passion. The
organization shows a lot of logic." What he was thinking was that her
passion reminded him of Madeleine and her logic reminded him of
himself. "This sounds like something I'd have written."

She gave him a sly look. "I guess that's a compliment, right?"

He laughed out loud for the first time that day, maybe the first
time that month. After a pause he glanced back at the last item of the
contents list. "I assume TGS stands for 'The Good Shepherd.' What
about the MOI?"

"Oh, that was his actual heading on the twenty-page explanation
he sent to the media and the police: 'Memorandum of Intent.' "

Gurney nodded. "Now I remember. The media started calling it a 'manifesto'—the same label they'd slapped on the Unabomber document five years earlier."

Now it was Kim's turn to nod. "Which kind of brings us to one of the questions I wanted to ask you—about the whole serial-killer thing. It seems kind of confusing. I mean, the Unabomber and the Good Shepherd don't seem to have much in common with Jeffrey Dahmer and Ted Bundy—or with those monsters you arrested yourself, like Peter Piggert or that Satanic Santa guy who was mailing pieces of his victims to the local cops. *Jeez!* That kind of behavior isn't even human!" A visible tremor passed through her body. She rubbed her upper arms energetically, as if to warm them.

Somewhere outside in the gray Syracuse sky, Gurney could hear the distinctive throbbing of a helicopter grow gradually louder, then fainter, then fade away into silence. "Some social scientists would be annoyed at me for this," he said, "but the whole 'serial killer' concept, like a lot of the terminology in the field, has fuzzy edges. Sometimes I think these 'scientists' are just a self-consecrated bunch of labelers who've managed to form a moneymaking club. They conduct questionable research, lump similar behaviors or characteristics together into a 'syndrome,' give it a scientific-sounding name, then offer degree courses that allow like-minded muddleheads to memorize the labels, pass a test, and join the club."

He noticed she was staring at him with some surprise.

Aware that he was sounding testy—and that the testiness probably had as much to do with his prevailing mood as with the state of criminology—he changed course. "The short answer to your question is that from the point of view of apparent motive there doesn't seem to be much common ground between a cannibal turned on by power and control and a guy who claims he's rectifying societal ills. But there may be more of a connection than you think."

Kim's eyes widened. "You mean, they're both killing people? And you think that's what it's all about, regardless of what the motive looks like on the surface?"

Gurney was struck by her energy, her intensity. It made him smile. "The Unabomber said he was trying to eliminate the destructive effects of technology on the world. The Good Shepherd, if I remember correctly, said he was trying to eliminate the destructive effects of greed. And yet despite the intelligence apparent in their written statements, they both chose a counterproductive route to their stated goals. Killing people could never achieve what they *said* they wanted to achieve. There's only one way that route makes any sense."

Her mind seemed to race almost visibly. "You mean, if the route was actually the goal."

"Right. We often get them reversed—the means and the end. The actions of the Unabomber and the Good Shepherd make perfect sense—if you base them on the assumption that the killing itself was the real goal—the emotional payoff—and the so-called manifestos were the enabling justifications."

She blinked, looked like she was trying to grasp the implications for her project. "But how much would that mean . . . from the point of view of the victim?"

"From the point of view of the victim, it wouldn't mean anything. For the victim, motive is irrelevant. Especially when there's no prior personal connection between victim and killer. On a dark road, from an anonymous passing car, a bullet in the head is a bullet in the head, regardless of the motive."

"And the families?"

"Ah, the families. Well . . ."

Gurney closed his eyes, thinking back slowly over his homicide career to one sad conversation after another. So many of them over the years. Over the decades. Parents. Wives. Lovers. Children. Stunned faces. Refusals to believe the dreadful news. Desperate questions. Screams. Groans. Wails. Rage. Accusations. Wild threats. Fists smashing into walls. Drunken stares. Empty stares. Old people whimpering like children. A man staggering backward as if punched. And worst of all, the ones with no reactions. Frozen faces, dead eyes. Uncomprehending, speechless, emotionless. Turning away, lighting a cigarette.

"Well . . ." he continued after a while, "I've always felt that the truth was the best thing. So I guess having a slightly better understanding of why someone they loved was killed might be a good thing for surviving family members. But remember, I'm not saying I know why the Unabomber and the Good Shepherd did what they did. They probably don't know the reason themselves. I just know it's not the reason they said it was."

She gazed across the coffee table at him and seemed about to ask another question—was starting to open her mouth—when a light thump somewhere in the upper wall of the house stopped her. She sat stiffly, listening. "What do you think that was?" she asked after several long seconds, pointing toward the source of the sound.

"No idea. Maybe a knock in a hot-water pipe?"

"That's what that would sound like?"

He shrugged. "What do *you* think it is?"

When she didn't answer, he asked, "Who lives upstairs?"

"No one. At least no one is *supposed* to be living there. They were evicted, then they came back, the cops raided the apartment, shithead drug dealers, so they were all arrested, but they're probably out by now anyway, so who the hell knows? This city is pretty sucky."

"So the upstairs is vacant?"

"Yeah. Supposedly." She looked at the coffee table, focusing on the open pizza box. "Jeez. That's looking nasty. Should I reheat it?"

"Not for me." He was about to say that it was time for him to get going, but he realized he hadn't been there very long at all. It was one of those constitutional tendencies of his that had gotten worse over the past six months—the desire to minimize the amount time he spent with other people.

Holding up the shiny blue folder, he said, "I'm not sure I can go through this whole thing right now. It looks pretty detailed."

Like a fast-moving cloud on a bright day, her look of disappointment came and went. "Maybe tonight? I mean, you can take that with you and look at it when you have time."

He was oddly affected by her reaction—"touched" was the only word for it, the same feeling he'd had earlier, when she was telling him how she'd narrowed her focus to the Good Shepherd murders. Now he thought he understood what the feeling was about.

It was her wholehearted commitment, her energy, her hopeful-ness—her bright, determined *youthfulness*. And the fact that she was doing this alone. Alone in an unsafe house, in a desolate neighbor-hood, pursued by a mean-spirited stalker. He suspected that it was this combination of determination and vulnerability that was stirring his atrophied parental instinct.

"I'll take a look at it tonight," he said.

"Thank you."

The throbbing sound of a helicopter again emerged faintly from the distance, grew louder, passed, faded away. She cleared her throat nervously, clasped her hands in her lap, spoke with evident difficulty. "There's something I wanted ask you. I don't know why this is so hard." She shook her head sharply, as if in disapproval of her own confusion.

"What is it?"

She swallowed. "Could I hire you? For maybe like just one day?"

"*Hire* me? To do what?"

"I'm not making any sense, I know. This is embarrassing, I know I shouldn't be pressuring you like this. But this is so important to me."

"What do you want me to do?"

"Tomorrow . . . could you maybe sort of come with me? You don't have to *do* anything. The thing is, I have two meetings tomorrow. One with a prospective interviewee, the other with Rudy Getz. All I would want you to do is *be* there—listen to me, listen to them—and afterward just give me your gut reaction, your advice, I don't know, just . . . I'm not making any sense at all, am I?"

"Where are these meetings tomorrow?" he asked.

"You'll do it? You'll come with me? Oh, God, thank you, thank you! Actually, they're not too far from you. I mean not really close, but not too far. One is in Turnwell—Jimi Brewster, son of one of the victims. And Rudy Getz's place is about ten miles from there, on the top of a mountain overlooking the Ashokan Reservoir. We'll be meeting with Brewster first, at ten, which means that I should pick you up around eight-thirty A.M. Is that okay?"

The reflexive response forming in his mind was to decline the ride and take his own car. But it made more sense to use the drive time with her to ask the questions that were sure to occur to him between now and then. To get a better sense of what he was walking into.

"Sure," he said. "That's fine." Already he was regretting his decision to get involved, even for one day, but he felt unable to refuse.

"There's a consultancy line item in the preliminary budget I worked out with RAM, so I can pay you seven hundred and fifty dollars for your day. I hope that's enough."

He was about to say that she didn't need to pay him, that wasn't why he was doing it. But something about her businesslike earnestness made it clear she wanted it this way.

"Sure," he said again. "That's fine."

A little while later, after some desultory conversation about her life at the university, and about Syracuse's all-too-typical drug problems, he got up from his chair and reiterated his commitment to see her the following morning.

She saw him to the door, shook his hand firmly, thanked him again. As he descended the steps to the cracked sidewalk, he heard the two heavy door locks clicking into place behind him. He glanced up and down the dismal street. It had a dirty, salty look—the dried residue, he assumed, of whatever had been sprayed on it to melt the last snow accumulation. There was a hint of something acrid in the air.

He got into his car, turned the key, and plugged in his portable GPS for directions home. It took a minute or so for it to acquire its satellite signals. As it was issuing its first instruction, he heard a door bang open. He looked up and saw Kim rushing out of the house. At the bottom of the steps, she fell, sprawling onto the sidewalk. She was pulling herself up with the help of a garbage can as Gurney reached her.

"You all right?"

"I don't know . . . My ankle . . ." She was breathing hard, looked frightened.

He was holding her by the arms, trying to support her. "What happened?"

"Blood . . . in the kitchen."

"What?"

"Blood. On the kitchen floor."

"Is anyone else inside?"

"No. I don't know. I didn't see anyone."

"How much blood?"

"I don't know. Drops on the floor. Like a trail. To the back hallway. I'm not sure."

"You didn't see anyone or hear anyone?"

"No. I don't think so."

"Okay. You're okay now. You're safe."

She started blinking. There were tears in her eyes.

"It's okay," he repeated softly. "You're okay. You're safe."

She wiped away the tears, tried to compose her expression. "Okay. I'm okay now."

When her breathing began to return to normal, he said, "I want you to sit in my car. You can lock the door. I'll take a look in the apartment."

"I'm coming with you."

"It would be better to stay in the car."

"No!" She looked at him pleadingly. "It's *my* apartment. He's not going to keep me out of *my* apartment!"

Although it was inconsistent with normal police procedure to allow a civilian to reenter the premises under these conditions before they'd been searched, Gurney was no longer a police officer and procedure was no longer the controlling issue. Given Kim's state of mind, he decided it would be better to keep her with him than to insist that she remain alone in his car—locked or not.

"Okay," he said, removing the Beretta from his ankle holster and slipping it into his jacket pocket. "Let's check it out."

He led the way the back inside, leaving both doors open behind him. He stopped outside the living room. The hallway continued straight ahead for another twenty feet or so, ending at an archway that opened into a kitchen. Between the living room and the kitchen were two open doorways on the right. "Where do those lead?"

"The first is my bedroom. The second is the bathroom."

"I'm going to take a look in each one. If you hear anything at all, or if you call my name and I don't answer immediately, get out through the front door as fast as you can, lock yourself in my car, and call 911. Got that?"

"Yes."

He moved down the hall, looked inside the first room, then stepped in and switched on the ceiling light. There wasn't much to see. A bed, a small table, a full-length mirror, a couple of folding chairs, a rickety armoire in place of a closet. He checked the armoire, checked under the bed. He stepped back out into the hall, gave Kim a thumbs-up sign, moved on to the bathroom, and repeated the process.

Next was the kitchen.

"Where did you see the drops of blood?" he asked.

"They start in front of the refrigerator and go into the back hall."

He entered the kitchen cautiously, glad for the first time in six months that he was armed. The kitchen was a wide room. On the far right was a dinette table and two chairs in front of a window that faced the driveway and the adjoining house. The window brought some light into the room, but not much.

In front of him was a countertop with cabinets under it, a sink, and a refrigerator. Between him and the refrigerator was a small butcher-block island. On the island he saw a meat cleaver. As he stepped around the island, he spotted the blood—a sequence of dark drops on the worn linoleum floor, each about the size of a dime, one every two or three feet, stretching from in front of the refrigerator door over to the rear doorway of the kitchen and out into a shadowy area beyond it.

Without warning he heard the sound of breathing behind him. He spun around in a crouch, pulling the Beretta from his pocket. It was Kim, standing just a few feet away, the cliché deer in the headlights, staring at the muzzle of the little .32, mouth half open.

"Jesus," he said, taking a breath, lowering the pistol.

"Sorry. I was trying to be quiet. You want me to turn on the light?"

He nodded. The switch was on the wall over the sink. It operated two long fluorescent bulbs mounted on the ceiling. In the brighter light, the blood drops on the floor looked redder. "Is there a light switch for that back hall?"

"On the wall to the right of the fridge."

He found it, turned it on, and the darkness beyond the doorway was replaced by the buzzing, flickering, cold light of a cheap fluorescent fixture at the end of its life. He moved slowly toward the doorway, the Beretta pointed downward.

Except for a green plastic garbage barrel, the short rear hallway was empty. At its far end, a solid-looking exterior door was secured by a substantial dead-bolt lock. There was a second door in the right wall of this cramped space. It was to this one that the trail of blood drops led.

Gurney glanced quickly at Kim. "What's behind that door?"

"Stairs. The stairs . . . to the basement." Fear was creeping back into her voice.

"When was the last time you were down there?"

"Down . . . oh, God, I don't know. Maybe . . . maybe a year ago? A circuit breaker cut out, and the landlord's maintenance guy was showing me how to reset it."

"Is there any other access?"

"No."

"Any windows?"

"Little ones at ground level, but they have bars on them."

"Where's the light switch?"

"Right inside the door, I think."

There was a drop of blood in front of the door. Gurney stepped over it. Standing flat against the wall, he turned the knob and pulled the door open quickly. The smell of dead, musty air filled the little hallway. He waited, listened, then looked down the stairs. They were dimly illuminated by the flickering fixture in the hall behind him. There was a switch on the wall. He flipped it, and a faint yellowish light came on somewhere in the basement.

He told Kim to turn off the hall fluorescent, to stop the buzzing noise.

When it was off, he listened again for at least a minute. Silence. He looked down the stairs. On every second or third step, he saw a dark spot.

"What is it? What do you see?" If Kim's voice got any more brittle, it was going to crack.

"A few more drops," he said evenly. "I'm going to take a closer look. Stay where you are. You hear anything at all, run like hell out the front door, go to my car——"

She cut him off. "No way! I'm staying with you!"

Gurney had a talent for projecting a calmness that increased in direct proportion to the agitation of those around him. "Okay. But here's the deal: You've got to stay at least six feet behind me." He tightened his grip on the Beretta. "If I have to move quickly, I'll need some room. Okay?"

She nodded.

He began to make his way slowly down the steps. The staircase was a creaky structure with no handrails. When he reached the bottom, he could see that the trail of dark spots continued across the dusty basement floor toward what appeared to be a long, low chest in the far corner. On one wall a furnace stood alongside two oil tanks. On the adjacent wall, there was an electrical-service breaker box, and above it, almost touching the exposed joists, there was a row of small horizontal windows. External bars on each were dimly visible through filthy glass. The low light was emanating from a single bare bulb as begrimed as the windows.

Gurney's attention returned to the chest.

"I have a flashlight." Kim's voice came from the stairs. "Do you want it?"

He looked up at her. She switched it on and handed it to him. It was a Mini Maglite. Its little batteries were about due for replacement, but it was better than nothing.

"What do you see?" she asked.

"I'm not sure. Last time you were down here, do you remember a box or a chest against the wall?"

"Oh, God, I have no idea. He was showing me the circuit things, the switches, I don't know what. What do you see?"

"I'll let you know in a minute." He moved forward uneasily, following the trail of blood to the long, low box.

On the one hand, it appeared to be nothing more than a very old blanket chest. On the other hand, he couldn't get the melodramatic notion out of his head that it was about the right size for a coffin.

"Oh, my God. What's that?" Kim had followed him and was now standing just a few feet behind him. Her voice had dropped to a whisper.

Gurney put the flashlight between his teeth, pointed down at the box. With the Beretta in his right hand, he lifted the lid gingerly with his left.

For a second he thought there was nothing there.

Then, gleaming softly in the flashlight's little pool of yellow light, he saw the knife.

A kitchen paring knife. Even in the weak, dirty light, he could see that the blade had been honed until it was unusually thin and sharp. On the point was a tiny drop of blood.

## Chapter 5

# Into a Tangle of Thorns

Despite Gurney's efforts to persuade her, Kim refused to call the police.

"I told you, I've called before. I'm not doing it again. Nothing happens. Worse than nothing. They come to the apartment, they poke around the doors and windows, and they tell me there's no sign of any forced entry. Then they ask if anyone was injured, if anything of value was stolen, if anything of value was broken. It's like if the problem doesn't fit one of those categories, then it's not a problem. Last time, when I called about finding the knife in my bathroom, they lost interest when they learned it was mine—even though I kept telling them that the knife had been missing for two weeks before that. They scraped up the little drop of blood that was next to it on the floor, took it with them, never said another word about it. If they're going to come here and give me this look like I'm some hysterical woman wasting their time, then the hell with them! You know what one of them did the last time? He yawned. He actually, unbelievably, yawned in my face!"

Gurney thought about this, thought about the instinctive triage process every busy urban cop goes through when a new incident is tossed on his plate. It's all relative—relative to whatever else is on his plate—relative to the other urgencies of that month, that week, that day. He remembered a partner he'd had many years ago in NYPD Homicide, a guy who lived in a sleepy little town in western New Jersey, on the far edge of commutability. One day the guy brought in his local newspaper. The big front-page story was about a bird bath that had gone missing from someone's backyard. This was at a time when there were an average of twenty murders a week in New York City—most of which barely rated a one-line mention in the city papers. The fact was that everything depended on context. And, although he didn't say it to Kim, Gurney understood how the discovery of her own knife on her own bathroom floor might not have seemed like the end of the world to a cop dealing with rapes and homicides.

But he also understood how disturbed she was. More than that, there was an obviously sinister quality to the intruder's actions that he himself found disturbing. He suggested that it might be a good idea for her to get out of Syracuse, maybe stay for a while at her mother's house.

The suggestion converted her fear into fury. "That fucking son of a bitch!" she hissed. "If he thinks he's going to win this battle, he doesn't know me very well."

Gurney waited until she was calmer, then asked if she remembered the names of the detectives who'd responded to her previous calls.

"I told you, I'm not calling them again."

"I understand. But I'd like to talk to them myself. See if they know anything they're not telling you."

"About what?"

"Maybe about Robby Meese? Who knows? I won't know till I talk to them."

Kim's dark eyes searched his, her lips tightening. "Elwood Gates and James Schiff. Gates is the short one, Schiff is the tall one. Same jerk, two bodies."

Detective James Schiff had taken Gurney into a spare interrogation room a couple of corridors away from the reception area. He'd left the door open, hadn't brought a chair, and hadn't offered Gurney one either. The man covered his face with his hands, struggled to stifle a yawn and lost the battle.

"Long day?"

"You could say that. Been on for eighteen hours straight, six more to go."

"Paperwork?"

"You got that right, times ten. You see, my friend, this department is exactly the wrong size. Just large enough to have all the bureaucratic bullshit of the big city and just small enough to have no place to hide. So we had this raid last night on a crack house that turned out to be surprisingly crowded. Result is I've got one holding pen full of mopes and another one full of crack whores, plus a mountain of evidence bags that I need to finish processing. So let's get to it. What exactly is the NYPD's interest in Kim Corazon?"

"Sorry . . . maybe I didn't make my position clear enough on the phone. I'm NYPD, retired. Got out two and half years ago."

"*Retired?* No, I kinda missed that. So you're what? A private investigator?"

"More like a friend of the family. Kim's mother is a journalist, writes a lot of stuff about cops. We crossed paths while I was still on the job."

"So how well do you know Kim?"

"Not well. I'm just trying to help her out with a journalism project, something about unsolved murders, but we ran into a bit of a complication today."

"Look, I don't have a lot of time here. Maybe you could be a little more specific?"

"The young lady has a stalker in her life, not a very nice one."

"That so?"

"You didn't know?"

Schiff's gaze darkened. "I'm getting lost. Why are we having this conversation?"

"Good question. Would you be surprised if I told you that right now in Kim Corazon's apartment there's fresh evidence of an unauthorized entry and some very freaky vandalism, with a clear intent to intimidate?"

"Surprised? I can't say that I would be. We've been up and down that road with Ms. Corazon quite a few times."

"And?"

"Lot of potholes."

"I'm not sure I understand."

Schiff picked some wax out of his ear and flicked it on the floor. "She tell you who she thinks is responsible?"

"Her ex-boyfriend, Robby Meese."

"You ever talk to Meese?"

"No. How about you?"

"Yeah, I talked to him." He checked his cell phone again. "Look, I can give you exactly three minutes. Professional courtesy. By the way, you got any ID on you?"

Gurney showed him his PBA card and his driver's license.

"Okay, Mr. NYPD, quick summary, off the record. Basically, Meese's story sounds as good as hers. Each one of them claims the other one is angry, unstable, reacting badly to their breakup. She says he got into her apartment three or four times. Bunch of silly crap—loosened doorknobs, moved things, hid things, took the knives, put back the knives—"

Gurney interrupted. "You mean, put a knife on her bathroom floor along with a drop of blood. I wouldn't call that 'putting back the knives.' I don't see how you could ignore—"

"Whoa! Nobody ignored anything. The initial stuff, doorknobs, crap like that—that was all responded to by uniformed patrol. Did we run out and dust the loose knobs for fingerprints? We'd have to be nuts to do that. We live in a real city here with real problems. But procedures were followed. I've got the incident reports in the case file. The later blood complaint was referred to us by patrol. My partner and I took a look, samples to the lab, knife to fingerprints, et cetera. Turned out the only fingerprints on the knife were Ms. Corazon's. Tiny drop of blood on the floor was beef blood. You know? Like steak."

"You questioned Meese?"

"Of course we questioned Meese."

"And?"

"He isn't admitting to anything, and there's zero evidence of his involvement. He's sticking to his story that Corazon's a vindictive bitch who's trying to get him in trouble."

"So what's the current theory here?" asked Gurney incredulously. "That Kim is crazy enough to be doing this stuff herself? So she can blame her ex-boyfriend for it?"

Schiff's stare seemed to communicate a willingness to believe exactly that. Then he shrugged. "Or some third party is doing it, for reasons yet to be discovered." He glanced at his cell phone for the third time. "Got to go. Time flies when you're having fun." He started moving toward the open interrogation-room door.

"How come no cameras?" asked Gurney.

"Say again?"

"The obvious response to repeated trespass and vandalism complaints would be to install hidden security cameras on the premises."

"I made that suggestion strongly to Ms. Corazon. She refused. Characterized it as an intolerable invasion of her privacy."

"I'm surprised she'd react that way."

"Unless her complaints are bullshit and a camera would prove it."

They walked in silence back to the reception area, past the desk sergeant, to the main door. As Gurney was about to exit, Schiff stopped him. "Didn't you say a few minutes ago that you'd discovered fresh evidence in her apartment that I ought to know about?"

"That's what I said."

"So? What was it?"

"You sure you want to know?"

There was a flash of anger in Schiff's eyes. "Yeah, I'd like to know."

"There are drops of blood leading from the kitchen to a chest in the basement. There's a sharp little knife in the chest. But maybe that's no big deal, right? Maybe Kim just squeezed the juice out of another steak, dripped it down the stairs. Maybe she's just getting crazier and more vindictive by the minute."

G urney's drive home was an uncomfortable one. He kept hearing the echo of his own sarcastic parting shot at Schiff. The more he turned it over in his mind, the more it appeared to fit a pattern—the pattern of petty combativeness that had dominated his thinking and behavior since his injuries.

He'd always had a habit of challenging the prevailing wisdom in any situation, as well as a talent for detecting discrepancies. But slowly he was becoming aware of something else going on inside him, something less objective. His intellectual bent for testing the logic of every opinion, every conclusion, had been infused with hostility—a hostility that ranged from a cranky contrariness to something verging on rage.

He'd become increasingly isolated, increasingly defensive, increasingly resistant to any idea not his own. And he was convinced it had all begun six months earlier with the three bullets that had nearly killed him. Objectivity, once an asset he took for granted, was now a quality he needed to strive for. But he knew it was worth the effort. Without objectivity he had nothing.

A therapist had told him long ago, "Whenever you're disturbed, try to identify the fear beneath the disturbance. The root is always fear, and unless we face it, we tend to act badly." Now, taking a cool step back, Gurney asked himself what he was afraid of. The question occupied him for most of the remaining trip home. The clearest answer he could come up with was also the most embarrassing.

He was afraid of being wrong.

He parked next to Madeleine's car by the side door of the farmhouse. The mountain air felt chilly. He went into the house, hung up his jacket in the mudroom, continued on into the kitchen, and called out, "I'm home." There was no response. The place had an indescribable deadness about it—a peculiar sort of emptiness it had only when Madeleine was out.

He had to go to the bathroom, started in that direction, then remembered that he'd forgotten to bring in Kim's blue folder from the car. He went back out for it, but before he got to the car, something bright and red to the right of the parking area caught his eye. It was in the middle of the raised garden bed where Madeleine had planted flowers the previous year—a fact that was responsible for his first impression: that it was some sort of red blossom atop a straight stem. A second later it occurred to him that the time of year would make any blossom unlikely. However, when he reached the bed and realized what he was actually looking at, the truth didn't make any more sense than a rose in full bloom would have.

The straight stem was the shaft of an arrow. The arrow was sticking point-down into the soft wet earth, and the "blossom" was the fletching on the notched end—three scarlet half feathers, shining brilliantly in the angled sun.

Gurney gazed at it wonderingly. Had Madeleine put it there? If so, where had she gotten it? Was she using it as some sort of marker? It looked new, unweathered, so it couldn't have been under the snow the whole winter. If Madeleine hadn't put it there, who could have? Was it possible it wasn't "put" there at all but shot there by someone with a bow? To have ended up embedded like this at a nearly vertical angle, though, it would have to have been shot nearly vertically into the air. When? Why? By whom? Standing where?

He stepped up onto the low bed, grasped the shaft close to the ground, and slowly extracted it. It was tipped with a four-pronged razor broadhead—making it the kind of arrow that a hunter with a serious bow can propel clear through a deer. As he studied the deadly projectile, he was struck by the improbable coincidence of coming upon two sharp weapons surrounded by troubling questions on the same day.

Of course, Madeleine might have a simple explanation for the arrow. He took it into the house, to the kitchen sink, and rinsed it clean under the running water. The broadhead appeared to be carbon steel, keen enough to shave with. Which brought his mind back to the knife in Kim's basement, which reminded him that her folder was still in the car. He laid the arrow gently on the pine sideboard and headed out through the little hallway past the mudroom.

As he opened the side door, he came face-to-face with Madeleine, dressed in one of her startling color combinations—rose sweatpants, a lavender fleece jacket, and an orange baseball cap. She had that pleasantly exercised, slightly-out-of-breath look she always had when she returned from a hill walk. He stepped back to let her in.

She smiled. "It's soooo beautiful! Did you see that amazing light on the hillside? With that blush in the buds—did you notice that?"

"What buds?"

"You didn't see it? Oh, come here, come." She led him outside by the arm, pointing happily to the trees beyond the upper pasture. "You only see it in the early spring—that hint of pink in the maples."

Gurney saw what she was talking about but failed to share her blissful reaction. Instead the faint wash of color over the brownish gray background of the landscape jogged loose an old memory—one that sickened him: brownish gray water in a ditch next to an abandoned service road behind La Guardia Airport, a faint reddish tint in the fetid water. The tint was oozing from a machine-gunned body just below the surface.

She looked at him with concern. "Are you okay?"

"Tired, that's all."

"You want some coffee?"

"No." He said it sharply, didn't know why.

"Come inside," she said, taking off her jacket and hat and hanging them in the mudroom. He followed her into the kitchen. She went to the sink and turned on the tap. "How did your trip to Syracuse work out?"

It occurred to him that the damn blue folder was still in his car. "I can't hear you with the water running," he said. That made . . . what? Three times he'd forgotten to bring it in? *Three times in the past ten minutes? Jesus.*

She filled a glass and turned off the water. "I asked about your trip to Syracuse."

He sighed. "The trip was peculiar. Syracuse is pretty bleak. Hold on . . . I'll tell you about it in a minute." He went out to the car and this time returned with the object in hand.

Madeleine looked perplexed. "I'd heard that there were some very nice old neighborhoods. Maybe not in the part of town you were in?"

"Yes and no. Nice old neighborhoods interspersed with neighborhoods from hell."

She glanced at the folder in his hand. "Is that Kim's project?"

"What? Oh. Yes." He looked around for a place to put it and noticed the arrow where he'd left it on the sideboard. He pointed to it. "What do you know about *that*?"

"That?" She stepped closer, examined it without touching it. "Is that the thing I saw outside?"

"When did you see it?"

"I don't know. When I went out. Maybe an hour ago?"

"You don't know anything about it?"

"Only that it was sticking in the flower bed. I thought you'd put it there." There was a long silence as he stared at the arrow and she stared at him. "You think someone is hunting up here?" she asked, her eyes narrowing.

"It's not hunting season."

"Maybe some drunk thinks it is."

"Pleasant thought."

She glared at the arrow, then shrugged. "You look exhausted. Come, sit down." She gestured toward the table by the French doors. "Tell me about your day."

When he had recounted everything he could remember, including Kim's request to hire him to accompany her to two meetings the following day, he searched Madeleine's face for a reaction. But instead of commenting on his narrative, she changed the subject.

"I had kind of a weighty day, too." She leaned forward as she spoke, her elbows on the table, and pressed her palms together in front of her face, resting her chin on her thumbs. She closed her eyes and, for what seemed like a very long time, said nothing.

Then she opened her eyes, put her hands in her lap, straightened her back. "Do you remember me mentioning the mathematician?"

"Vaguely."

"The math professor who was a client at the clinic?"

"Oh. Right."

"He was originally referred to us as the result of a second DWI. Had career problems leading to no career at all, nasty divorce, alienation from his children, problems with the neighbors. Dark outlook, trouble sleeping, obsessed with the negative aspects of every situation he was involved in. Brilliant mind, but trapped in a downward spiral of depression. He came to three group sessions a week, plus one individual session. He was generally willing to talk. Or maybe I should say he was willing to complain, willing to blame everyone for everything. But never willing to *do* anything. Not even willing to leave the house, unless it was court-mandated. Wouldn't take antidepressant medication, because that would mean accepting the fact that his own mental chemistry might be part of all his other problems. It's almost funny. He was determined to do everything his way, and his way was to do nothing." She smiled sadly and gazed out the window.

"What happened?"

"Last night he shot himself."

They sat quietly at the table for a long while, looking out over the hills from the crossed angles of their individual chairs. Gurney felt strangely unhooked from time and place.

"So," she said, turning back to him, "the little lady wants to hire you. And all you have to do is follow her around and tell her how you think she's handling herself?"

"That's what she says."

"You're wondering if there might be more to it?"

"If today was any indication, there might be a few hidden twists."

She gave him one of those long, thoughtful looks of hers that felt like explorations of his soul. Then, with evident effort, she constructed a bright smile. "With you on the job, I don't imagine they'll stay hidden long."

## Chapter 6

# Twists and Turns

As the sun set, they had a quiet dinner of sweet-potato soup and spinach salad. Afterward, Madeleine built a small fire in the old woodstove at the far end of the room and settled into her favorite armchair with a book—*War and Peace,* a tome she'd been plodding through, on and off, for nearly a year now.

He noted that she hadn't bothered to get her reading glasses and the book rested in her lap unopened. He felt the need to say something. "When did you find out about the . . . ?"

"The suicide? Late this morning."

"Someone called?"

"The director. She wanted everyone who'd had contact with him to come in for a meeting. Ostensibly to share information, absorb the shock together. Which, of course, was nonsense. It was all about ass covering, damage control, whatever you want to call it."

"How long did the meeting last?"

"I don't know. What difference does it make?"

He didn't answer, really had no answer, didn't even know why he'd asked. She opened her book, seemingly at random, stared down at it.

After a minute or two, Gurney got Kim's project folder from the sideboard and brought it back to the table. He flipped past the sections titled "Concept" and "Documentary Overview" and quickly scanned the "Style and Methodology" section, pausing only to read more carefully a sentence that Kim had emphasized by typing it with an underscore: <u>Interviews will examine the lasting effects of the original murders, exploring deeply all the ways in which the lives of the families were altered.</u>

He skimmed through several more sections, slowing down when he came to one titled "Contact Summaries and Status." It was organized in the sequence of the six Good Shepherd shootings. The information was laid out in the form of a spreadsheet, with columns under three headings: Attack Victims, Available Family Members, Current Attitude Toward Participation.

His eye ran down the victim list: Bruno and Carmella Mellani, Carl Rotker, Ian Sterne, Sharon Stone, Dr. James Brewster, Harold Blum. After Carmella Mellani's name, there was an asterisk with a corresponding footnote that read, "Survived massive cranial trauma during attack, remains in persistent vegetative coma."

He skipped over the second column, which provided a detailed list of family members (with their locations, life situations, ages, and personal descriptions), and glanced at the third-column summaries of their "current attitudes."

The widow of Harold Blum was said to be "totally cooperative, grateful for the interest being shown, deeply emotional, still cries during discussion of the subject."

The son of Dr. Brewster was described as "abusive toward the memory of his father, in open sympathy with the philosophy of TGS, obsessed with the evils of materialism."

The son of Ian Sterne, dental entrepreneur, was "low-key, resistant to participating, concerned about the project's disruptive emotional effects, skeptical of the intentions of RAM-TV, critical of the relentless sensationalism of their original coverage of the shootings."

The son of real-estate broker Sharon Stone "expressed great enthusiasm for the project, spoke eagerly about his mother's strengths, the horror of her death, the devastating effect on his own life, the intolerable injustice of the killer's escape."

There were more family members and more status descriptions, followed by the transcripts of two interviews—with Jimi Brewster and with Ruth Blum—and a twenty-page copy of the Good Shepherd's "Memorandum of Intent." As Gurney was about to put the folder aside, he noticed that there was a final page that had not been cataloged in the table of contents—a page headlined "Contacts for Background Information."

There were three names on it, with e-mail addresses and phone numbers for each: FBI Special Agent in Charge Matthew Trout, (Former) NYSP Senior Investigator Max Clinter, and NYSP Senior Investigator Jack Hardwick.

He stared with surprise at the third name. Jack Hardwick was a super-smart, super-abrasive detective with whom Dave had a complex relationship—having crossed Hardwick's path in bizarre and contentious circumstances.

Gurney headed for the phone to call Kim. He was interested in talking to Hardwick, but before he did, he wanted to find out why she'd listed the man as an information source.

She picked up immediately. "Dave?"

"Yes."

"I was just going to call you." Her voice sounded more strained than pleased. "Your conversation with Schiff got things pretty stirred up."

"How so?"

"He came here to my apartment, I guess right after you spoke to him. He wanted to see everything you'd told him about. He seemed really pissed off that I'd cleaned up the kitchen floor, but too bad, right? How was I supposed to know he was coming? He said an evidence guy would be back here tonight to check out the basement. I guess it's a good thing that I couldn't bring myself to go down there and clean the stairs. Jeez, I get the chills thinking about it! And he's insisting on sticking those creepy little spy cameras all around the apartment."

"Is it true that you previously refused them?"

"He said that?"

"He also said he ran lab tests on the bathroom bloodstain."

"So?"

"I'd gotten the impression from you that he hadn't done much of anything."

She paused before answering. "It wasn't so much what he did or didn't do. The problem was his *attitude*. It was really sucky. He couldn't have cared less."

Although this response didn't quite resolve the matter in Gurney's mind, he decided to let it drop—at least for now.

"Kim, I'm looking at the background sources listed on the final page of your document—in particular a detective by the name of Hardwick. How does he happen to be involved in this?"

"You know him?" Her voice sounded wary.

"Yes, I do."

"Well . . . when I started researching the Good Shepherd case a few months ago, I gathered the names of the law-enforcement people who were mentioned in news reports back when it happened. One of the earlier shootings took place in Hardwick's jurisdiction, and he was one of the state police investigators who was temporarily involved."

"Temporarily?"

"Everything changed after the third weekend, I think it was, when one of the shootings occurred over the state line in Massachusetts. At that point the FBI took over."

"Special Agent in Charge Matthew Trout?"

"Yeah, Trout. Control-freak asshole."

"You've spoken to him?"

"He told me to go back and read the press releases issued by the FBI at the time. Then he instructed me to submit my questions in writing. Then he refused to answer any of them. If you call that speaking to him, then I guess I did. Officious jerk!"

Gurney smiled to himself. *Welcome to the FBI.*

"But Hardwick was willing to talk to you?"

"Not so much at first—not until he discovered that Trout was trying to control the information flow. Then he seemed happy to do whatever would make Trout unhappy."

"That's Jack. Used to say that FBI stood for Fucking Blithering Idiots."

"He's still saying it."

"So why is Trout on your information list if he refuses to provide any?"

"That's more for the RAM people. Trout might not talk to me, but Rudy Getz is different. You'd be amazed at who returns his calls. And how fast."

"Interesting. And what about the third name—Max Clinter?"

"Max Clinter. Well. Where to start? Do you know anything about him at all?"

"The name rings a distant bell, that's about it."

"Clinter was the off-duty detective who got entangled in the final Good Shepherd attack."

The memory of the tabloid accounts came back. "Was he the guy with the art student in his car . . . drunk out of his mind . . . firing his gun out the window . . . sideswiped a guy on a motorcycle . . . got blamed for the Good Shepherd escaping?"

"Yep."

"He's one of your sources?"

Kim's voice was defensive. "I'm taking whatever and whoever I can get. The problem is that just about everyone involved in the case refers all questions to Trout—which is like dropping them into a black hole."

"So what have you managed to find out from Clinter?"

"That's not easy to answer. He's a strange man. With a lot on his mind. I'm not sure I understand all of it. Maybe we could talk about it tomorrow in the car? I didn't realize how late it was getting, and I need to take a shower."

Although Gurney didn't believe her, he didn't object. He was eager to talk to Jack Hardwick.

The call went into voice mail. He left a message.

Dusk was rapidly darkening into night. Rather than turn on the light in the den, he took Kim's project folder out to the kitchen table. Madeleine was still sitting in her armchair by the flickering woodstove at the far end of the room. *War and Peace* had moved from her lap to the coffee table in front of her, and she was knitting.

"So have you figured out where that arrow came from?" she asked, without looking up.

He glanced over at the sideboard, at the black graphite shaft and its red fletching. Something about it made him feel almost queasy.

Then, as though the feeling had been the herald of a rising memory, he recalled an incident in the apartment house of his Bronx childhood. He was thirteen. It was dark out. His father was either working late or out drinking. His mother was at one of her ballroom-dancing lessons at a studio in Manhattan—a consuming mania that had displaced her former obsession with finger painting. His grandmother was in her bedroom, muttering over her rosary beads. He was in his mother's bedroom—hers exclusively, ever since his father had begun sleeping on the living-room couch and keeping his clothes in a closet in the hallway.

He'd opened one of the two windows from the top. The air was cold and smelled of snow. He had a wooden bow—a real one, not a toy. He'd purchased it with money saved from two years of allowances. He dreamed one day of hunting with it in a forest far from the Bronx. He stood in front of the wide-open sash with the cold air flowing over him. He notched one scarlet-fletched arrow on his bowstring and, driven by a strange sense of excitement, raised the bow toward the black sky outside that sixth-floor bedroom window, drew back the bowstring, and let the arrow fly out into the night. With sudden fear gripping his heart, he listened for the sound of its impact—its thwack on the roof of one of the lower buildings in the neighborhood, or its metallic clunk on the roof of a parked car, or its sharp bang on a sidewalk—but he heard nothing. Nothing at all.

The unexpected silence began to terrify him.

He imagined how silent the impact of a sharp arrow on a person might be.

For the rest of the night, he considered the possible consequences. The possible consequences scared him to death. But the lasting disturbance, the piece of the experience that was indigestible, the piece that plagued him even now, thirty-five years later, was the question he was never able to answer: Why?

Why had he done it? What had possessed him to do something so patently reckless, so lacking in any rational reward, so full of pointless danger?

Gurney looked again at the sideboard and was struck by the bizarre symmetry between the two mysteries: the arrow he'd shot from his mother's window, with motive and landing place unknown, and the arrow that had landed in his wife's garden, with motive and starting place unknown. He shook his head, as if to clear it of some internal fog. It was time to move on to another subject.

Conveniently, his cell phone rang. It was Connie Clarke.

"There's something that I wanted to add—something I didn't mention this morning."

"Oh?"

"I didn't purposely leave it out. It's just one of those vague things that sometimes seems related to the situation and sometimes not."

"Yes?"

"I guess it's more like a coincidence than anything else. The Good Shepherd murders all happened exactly ten years ago, right? Well, that's also the same time that Kim's father dropped out of sight. We'd been divorced for two years at that point, and he'd been talking all that time about wanting to travel around the world. I never thought he'd actually do it—although he could be amazingly impulsive and irresponsible, which is part of the reason I divorced him—and then one day he left a phone message for us saying that the moment had come, it was now or never, and he was going. I mean, it was absurd. But that was it. The first week of spring, ten years ago. We never heard another word from him. Can you believe it? Selfish, thoughtless bastard! Kim was devastated. More so than she'd been by the divorce two years earlier. *Completely devastated.*"

"You see some significance in the timing?"

"No, no, I don't mean to suggest that there's any connection between the Good Shepherd case and Emilio's disappearance. How could there be? It's just that both events happened the same month—March of 2000. Maybe part of the reason Kim feels as strongly as she does about the pain of those families at losing someone is that she lost her own father at the same time."

Now Gurney understood. "And the shared lack of closure—"

"Yes. The Good Shepherd murders were never fully resolved, because the murderer was never caught. And Kim hasn't been able to close the door on her father's disappearance, because she could never find out what really happened to him. When she talks about the families of murder victims suffering from an ongoing misery, I think she's talking about herself."

After concluding his conversation with Connie, Gurney sat for a long while at the table, trying to digest the implications of Emilio Corazon's departure from Kim's life.

He gradually became aware of Madeleine's knitting needles clicking softly and steadily. She was sitting in a pool of yellow lamplight, a ball of sage-colored yarn at her side in the armchair, a sage-colored sweater taking shape in her lap.

He opened the blue folder to the section devoted to the Good Shepherd's "Memorandum of Intent." On a page of background information at the beginning of the section, someone, presumably Kim, had indicated that the original document had been delivered by express mail in a nine-by-twelve manila envelope, addressed to "The Director, New York State Police, Bureau of Criminal Investigation." The delivery date was March 22, 2000—the Wednesday following the weekend of the first two shootings.

Gurney turned the page and began to read the text of the memorandum itself. It began abruptly, with a summary statement consisting of numbered sentences:

> *1. If the love of money, which is greed, is the root of all evil, then it follows that the greatest good will be achieved by its eradication. 2. Since greed does not exist in a vacuum but exists in its human carriers, it follows that the way to eradicate greed is to eradicate its carriers. 3. The good shepherd culls the flock, removing the diseased sheep from the healthy sheep, because it is good to stop the spread of infection. It is good to protect the good animals from the bad. 4. Although patience is a virtue, it is no sin to lose patience with greed. It is no sin to take up arms against wolves who devour children. 5. This is our declaration of war on the vain carriers of greed, the pickpockets who call themselves bankers, the limousine lice, the Mercedes maggots. 6. We will free the earth of this ultimate contagion, carrier by carrier, replacing the silence of passivity with the shattering of skulls until the earth is clean, the shattering of skulls until the flock is culled, the shattering of skulls until the root of all evil is dead and gone from the earth.*

The next nineteen pages reiterated these sentiments at length, the manifesto drifting back and forth in its tone from prophetic to academic. The rational aspects of the argument were supported by extensive wealth-distribution data, purporting to demonstrate the unfairness of America's economic structure—complete with trend statistics showing the nation's drift toward a Third World economy of extremes, in which enormous wealth is concentrated at the very top, poverty is expanding, and the middle class is shrinking.

The main body of the document concluded:

> *This gross and growing injustice is driven by the greed of the powerful and the power of the greedy. Moreover, the control exerted by this vile and devouring class over the media—society's primary engine of influence—is virtually absolute. The channels of communication (channels which in free hands might be agents of change) are owned, directed, and infected by mega-corporations and by individual billionaires whose interests are motivated by the virulent quality of greed. This is the desperate condition which forces us to our inescapable conclusion, our clear resolve, and our direct actions.*

The document was signed, "The Good Shepherd."

In a separate note, clipped to the final page, the writer had included information on the precise times and locations of the two preceding attacks.

Since these facts had not yet been released to the public, they provided support for the writer's claim to be the killer. A postscript to the note indicated that copies of the entire document had been simultaneously delivered to a long list of national and local news organizations.

Gurney went through it all again. When he put the folder down half an hour later, he understood why the case had achieved its iconic status in criminology—and why it had replaced the earlier Unabomber case as the academic archetype for societal-mission-driven murders.

The document was clearer and less digressive than the Unabomber's manifesto. The logical nexus between the stated problem and the murderous solution was more direct than Ted Kaczynski's messy letter bombs to victims whose relevance to the issue was questionable at best.

The Good Shepherd had neatly summed up his approach in the first two numbered statements in his memorandum: "1. If the love of money, which is greed, is the root of all evil, then it follows that the greatest good will be achieved by its eradication. 2. Since greed does not exist in a vacuum but exists in its human carriers, it follows that the way to eradicate greed is to eradicate its carriers."

What could be more direct than that?

And the Good Shepherd murder spree was inherently memorable. It had the elements of riveting theater: a simple premise, a concentrated time frame, high suspense, a vivid threat, a dramatic assault on wealth and privilege, easily defined victims, horrific moments of confrontation. It was the stuff of legend, and it occupied a natural place in people's minds. In fact, it occupied at least two natural places: To those who felt threatened by an attack on wealth, the Good Shepherd was the incarnation of the bomb-throwing revolutionary, intent on bringing down the structure of history's greatest society. To those who viewed the rich as pigs, the Good Shepherd was an idealist, a Robin Hood, rectifying the worst injustice of an unjust world.

It made sense that the case had over the years become a favorite in psychology and criminology classes. Professors would enjoy presenting it, because it made the points they wanted to make about a certain kind of murderer and—a rare blessing in the soft sciences—it made those points unambiguously. Students would enjoy hearing about it, because, like many simple horrors, it was grotesquely entertaining. Even the killer's escape into the night became a plus—giving the affair an open-ended *currency* that had a tingly appeal.

As Gurney closed the folder, pondering the visceral power of the case narrative, he found himself with mixed feelings.

"Problem?"

He looked up, saw Madeleine gazing across the room at him, her knitting needles resting in her lap.

He shook his head. "Probably just my constitutional crankiness."

She was still looking at him. He knew she was waiting for a better answer.

"Kim's documentary is all about the Good Shepherd case."

Madeleine frowned. "Hasn't that been done to death? Back when it happened, it was pretty much the only thing on television."

"She has her own angle on it. Back then it was all about the manifesto and the hunt for the killer and theories about his hypothetical background, hypothetical education, where he might be hiding, violence in America, lax gun laws, blah, blah, blah. But Kim is ignoring all that and zeroing in on the permanent damage to the victims' families—how their lives were changed."

Madeleine looked interested, then frowned again. "So what's the problem?"

"Nothing I can put my finger on. Maybe it's just me. Like I said, I'm not in a great mood."

## Chapter 7

# Ahab the Whale Chaser

The next morning, typical of spring in the Catskills, was cold and overcast, with occasional snowflakes blowing sideways past the Gurneys' French doors.

At 8:00 A.M. Kim Corazon called with a revised plan. Instead of meeting with Jimi Brewster in Turnwell in the morning and then going on to a lunch meeting with Rudy Getz in Ashokan Heights, the first meeting was being scrapped in favor of an afternoon meeting with Larry Sterne at his Stone Ridge home, about twenty minutes south of the Ashokan Reservoir. The Getz lunch would remain in place.

"Any special reason for the change?" Gurney asked.

"Sort of. I set up the original schedule before I knew you'd be available. But Larry is more standoffish than Jimi, so I'd rather you were present for that. Jimi is a very opinionated leftist. So he'll definitely participate—gives him a soapbox to attack materialism. But Larry's not so easy. He seems disillusioned with media in general, because of the sensationalism surrounding a friend's death years ago."

"You understand I'm not helping you make a sales pitch, right?"

"Of course not! I just want you to listen, get a feel, tell me what you think. So I'll be picking you up at eleven-thirty this morning instead of eight-thirty. Okay?"

"Okay," he said, without enthusiasm. He had no specific objection to the new schedule, just a passing sense that something was off center.

As he was about to slip his cell phone into his pocket, it occurred to him that Jack Hardwick hadn't returned his call, so he tapped in the number.

After just one ring, a raspy voice said, "Patience, Gurney, patience. I was about to call you."

"Hello, Jack."

"My hand is just barely healed, ace. You setting up another opportunity to get me shot?"

It was a reminder that six months earlier, at the climax of the Perry case, one of the three bullets that had struck Gurney passed through his side and lodged in Hardwick's hand.

"Hello, Jack."

"Hello your fucking self."

Such was the routine of beginning any conversation with New York State Police Senior Investigator Hardwick. That combative man with pale blue malamute eyes, a razor-keen mind, and a sour wit seemed determined to make every communication with him an ordeal.

"I'm calling about Kim Corazon."

"Little Kimmy? The kid with the school project?"

"I guess you could call it that. She has your name listed as a background source for information on the Good Shepherd case."

"No shit. How'd you cross paths with her?"

"Long story. I thought maybe you could give me some information."

"What did you have in mind?"

"Anything I'm not likely to find on the Internet."

"Colorful case tidbits?"

"If you think they're significant."

There was a wheezing sound on the phone. "I haven't had my coffee yet."

Gurney said nothing, knowing what was coming.

"So here's the deal," growled Hardwick. "You deliver a nice big Sumatra from Abelard's and maybe I'll be motivated to deliver significant tidbits."

"Are there any?"

"Who knows? If I can't remember any, I'll make some up. Of course, one man's significance is another man's horseshit. I'll take my Sumatra black with three sugars."

• • •

Forty minutes later, with two large coffees in the car, Gurney was driving up the twisty dirt road that led from Abelard's General Store in Dillweed to an even twistier dirt road, hardly a road at all—more like an abandoned cattle path—at the end of which Jack Hardwick lived in a small rented farmhouse. Gurney parked next to Hardwick's attitude car—a partially restored red 1970 Pontiac GTO.

The sparse, intermittent snowflakes had been replaced by a pin-pricky mist. As Gurney stepped up onto the creaking porch, one coffee container in each hand, the door swung open to reveal Hardwick in a T-shirt and cutoff sweatpants, his shaggy gray crew cut uncombed. They'd seen each other face-to-face only once since Gurney's hospital-ization six months earlier, at a state-police inquiry into the shooting, but Hardwick's opening line was characteristic.

"So tell me—how the fuck do you know little Kimmy?"

Gurney extended one of the coffees. "Through her mother. You want this?"

Hardwick took it, opened the flap on the lid, tasted it. "Is the mom as hot as the kid?"

"For Christ's sake, Jack . . ."

"That a yes or a no?" Hardwick stepped back to let Gurney in.

The outer doorway led directly into a large front room that Gur-ney would have expected to be furnished as a living room, but it was hardly furnished at all. The pair of leather armchairs with a stack of books between them on a bare pine floor looked more like things about to be moved than a planned seating arrangement.

Hardwick was watching him. "Marcy and I broke up," he said, as if explaining the emptiness of the place.

"Sorry to hear that. Who's Marcy?"

"Good question. Thought I knew. Apparently not." He took a longer sip of his coffee. "I must have a big blind spot when it comes to evaluating loony women with nice tits." Another sip, even longer. "But so what? We've all got our blind spots, right, Davey?"

Gurney had figured out long ago that the part of Hardwick that went through him like a needle was the part that reminded him of his father—this despite the fact that Gurney was currently forty-eight and Hardwick, although gray-haired and roughly weathered, was not quite forty.

Every so often Hardwick would hit the precise note of cynicism, the perfect echo, that would transport Gurney back into the apartment from whose high window he'd shot that inexplicable arrow, the apartment from which his first marriage had provided an escape.

The image that came to him now: He was standing in their cramped apartment's living room, his father dispensing drunken wisdom, telling him his mother was loony, telling him all women were loony, couldn't be trusted. Best not to tell them anything. "You and I are men, Davey, we understand each other. Your mother's a little . . . a little *off*, you know what I mean? No need for her to know I was drinking today, right? Only cause trouble. We're men. We can talk to each other." Gurney was eight years old.

The forty-eight-year-old Gurney made an effort to return to Hardwick's living room, to the moment at hand.

"She helped herself to half the shit in the house," said Hardwick. He took another sip, sat in one of the armchairs, waved Gurney toward the other one. "What can I do for you?"

Gurney lowered himself into the chair. "Kim's mother is a journalist I know from years ago on the job. She asked me for a favor—'Look over Kim's shoulder' is the way she put it. Now I'm trying to find out what I'm involved in, thought maybe you could help. Like I said on the phone, Kim listed you as a source."

Hardwick stared at his coffee container as if it were a perplexing artifact. "Who else is on her list?"

"FBI guy by the name of Trout. And Max Clinter, the cop who fucked up the pursuit of the shooter."

Hardwick let out a harsh bray that turned into a fit of coughing. "Wow! The uptight prick of the century and a psycho drunk. I'm in hot-shit company."

Gurney took a long swallow from his coffee container. "When do we get to the colorful, significant tidbits?"

Hardwick extended his scarred, muscular legs and leaned far back in his chair. "Stuff the press never got hold of?"

"Right."

"I guess one thing would be the little animals. You didn't know about those, did you?"

"Little animals?"

"Little plastic replicas. Part of a set. An elephant. A lion. A giraffe. A zebra. A monkey. A sixth one I can't remember."

"And how were these——"

"One was found at the scene of each attack."

"Where?"

"In the general vicinity of the victim's car."

"General vicinity?"

"Yeah, like they'd been tossed there from the shooter's car."

"Lab work on these little animals lead anywhere?"

"No prints, nothing like that."

"But?"

"But they were part of a kid's play set. Something called Noah's World. Like one of those diorama things. The kid builds a model of Noah's Ark, then he puts the animals in it."

"Any distribution angle, stores, factory variables, ways of tracing that particular set?"

"Dead end. Very popular toy. A Walmart staple. They sold like seventy-eight thousand of them. All identical, all made in one factory in Hung Dick."

"Where?"

"China. Who the fuck knows? It doesn't matter. The sets are all the same."

"Any theories regarding the significance of those individual animals?"

"Lots of them. All bullshit."

Gurney made a mental note to readdress that issue later.

*When later?* What the hell was he thinking? The plan was to look over Kim's shoulder. Not volunteer for a job no one had asked him to do.

"Interesting," said Gurney. "Any other little oddities that weren't released for public consumption?"

"I suppose you could call the gun an oddity."

"My recollection is that the news reports just referred to a large-caliber handgun."

"It was a Desert Eagle."

"The .50-caliber monster?"

"The very one."

"The profilers must have zeroed in on that."

"Oh, yeah, big-time. But the oddity wasn't just the size of the weapon. Out of the six shootings, we retrieved two bullets in good enough shape for reliable ballistics and a third that would be marginal for courtroom use but definitely suggestive."

"Suggestive of what?"

"The three bullets came from three different Desert Eagles."

"What?"

"That was the reaction everyone had."

"Did that ever lead to a multiple-shooter hypothesis?"

"For about ten minutes. Arlo Blatt came up with one of his dumber-than-dumb ideas: that the shootings might be some kind of gang-initiation ritual and every gang member had his own Desert Eagle. Of course, that left the little problem of the manifesto, which read like it was written by a college professor, and your average gang member can barely spell the word 'gang.' Some other people had less stupid ideas, but ultimately the single-shooter concept won out. Especially after it was blessed by the Behavioral Unit geniuses at the FBI. The attack scenes were essentially identical. The approach, shooting, and escape reconstructions were identical. And after a little psychological tweaking of their model, it made as much sense to the profilers for this guy to be using six Desert Eagles as it made for him to be using one."

Gurney responded only with a pained expression. He'd had mixed experiences with profilers over the years and tended to regard their achievements as no more than the achievements of common sense and their failures as proof of the vacuity of their profession. The problem with most profilers, especially those with a streak of FBI arrogance in their DNA, was that they thought they actually *knew* something and that their speculations were *scientific*.

"In other words," said Gurney, "using six outrageous guns is no more outrageous than using one outrageous gun, because outrageous is outrageous."

Hardwick grinned. "There's one final oddity. All of the victims' cars were black."

"A popular Mercedes color, isn't it?"

"Basic black accounted for about thirty percent of the total production runs of the models involved, plus maybe another three percent for a metallic variant of black. So a third—thirty-three percent. The odds, then, would be that two of the six vehicles attacked would have been black—unless the color black were part of the shooter's selection criteria."

"Why would color be a factor?"

Hardwick shrugged, tilting his coffee container and draining the last of it into his mouth. "Another good question."

They sat quietly for a minute. Gurney was trying to connect the "oddities" in some way that might explain them all, then gave up, realizing he would need to know a lot more before such random details could be arranged into a pattern.

"Tell me what you know about Max Clinter."

"Maxie is a special kind of guy. A mixed blessing."

"How mixed?"

"He's got a history." Hardwick looked thoughtful, then let out a grating laugh. "I'd love to see you guys get together. Sherlock the Logical Genius meets Ahab the Whale Chaser."

"The whale in question being . . . ?"

"The whale being the Good Shepherd. Maxie always had a tendency to sink his teeth into something and not let go, but after the little mishap that ended his career, he became a walking definition of demented determination. Catching the Good Shepherd was not the *main* purpose of his life, it was the *only* purpose. Made a lot people back away." Hardwick gave Gurney a sideways look, accompanied by another rough laugh. "Be fun to see you and Ahab shoot the shit."

"Jack, anybody ever tell you your laugh sounds like someone flushing a toilet?"

"Not anybody who was asking me for a favor." Hardwick rose from his chair, brandishing his empty coffee container. "It's a miracle how fast the human body converts this stuff into piss." He headed out of the room.

He returned a couple of minutes later and perched on the arm of his chair, speaking as though there'd been no interruption. "If you want to know about Maxie, best place to start would be the famous Buffalo mob incident."

"Famous?"

"Famous in our little upstate world. Important Big Apple dicks like you probably never even heard about it."

"What happened?"

"There was a mob guy in Buffalo by the name of Frankie Benno, who had organized the resurgence of heroin in western New York. Everyone knew this, but Frankie was smart and careful and protected by a handful of scumbag politicians. The situation started to obsess Maxie. He was determined to bring Frankie in for questioning, even though he couldn't find anything specific to charge him with. He decided to bring things to a head by 'harassing the fucker into making a mistake'—that was the last thing Maxie said to his wife before he went to a restaurant that was a known hangout for Frankie's people, in a building that Frankie owned."

Gurney's first thought was that "harassing the fucker into making a mistake" was a tricky objective. His second thought was that he'd done it often enough himself, except he called it "putting the suspect under pressure to observe his reactions."

Hardwick went on. "Maxie goes into the restaurant dressed and acting like a thug. He goes straight into the back room where Frankie's crew hung out when they weren't busy cracking heads. There's two wiseguys in the room, sucking up linguine in clam sauce. Maxie walks over to them, pulls out a gun and a little disposable camera. He tells the wiseguys they have a choice: They can have their picture taken with their brains blown out or they can have it taken giving each other blow jobs. Up to them. Their choice. They have ten seconds to decide. They can grab each other's cocks or their brains are on the wall. Ten . . . nine . . . eight . . . seven . . . six . . ."

Hardwick leaned toward Gurney, eyes sparkling, seemingly enthralled by the events he was recounting. "But Maxie is standing kinda close to them—too close—and one of the wiseguys reaches out and grabs the gun away from him. Maxie backs away and falls on his ass. The wiseguys are about to stomp the shit out of him, but Maxie suddenly drops the thug routine and starts screaming that he's not what he was pretending to be, *he's really just an actor.* He says somebody put him up to it, and nobody would have gotten hurt anyway, because the gun isn't even real, it's a stage prop. He's practically crying. The wiseguys check the gun. Sure enough, it's a fake. So now they want to know what the fuck's going on, who put him up to it, et cetera. Maxie claims he doesn't know, but that he's supposed to meet the guy the next day to give him back the camera with the blow-job pictures and get five grand for his trouble. One of the wiseguys goes out to a pay phone on the street—this is before everybody had cell phones. When he comes back in, he tells Maxie they're going to take him upstairs because Mr. Benno is upset. Maxie looks like he's about to shit in his pants, begs them please just let him go. But they take him upstairs. Upstairs there's a fortified office. Steel doors, locks, cameras. Major security. Frankie Benno is up there with two other wiseguys. When they bring Maxie into the inner sanctum, Frankie gives him a long, hard look. Then a nasty smile—like a great idea has just dawned on him. He says, 'Take off your clothes.' Maxie starts to whine like a baby. Frankie says, 'Take off your fucking clothes and give me the fucking camera.' Maxie gives him the camera, backs up against the wall like he's trying to get as far away from these guys as he can. He takes off his jacket and shirt, then drops his pants. But his shoes are still on. So he sits down on the floor and starts pushing his pants down, but they're caught up in a bunch around his ankles. Frankie tells him to hurry up. Frankie's four wiseguys are grinning. Suddenly Maxie's hands come up from the pants around his ankles, and in each hand he's got a neat little SIG .38 pistol." Hardwick paused dramatically. "What do you think of that?"

The first thing he thought about was his own concealed Beretta.

Then he thought about Clinter. Although the man was definitely a gambler and probably a little nuts, he knew how to create a layered narrative and how to manage it under pressure. He knew how to manipulate vicious and impulsive people, how to make them reach the conclusions he wanted them to reach. For an undercover cop—or a magician—there was no set of skills more valuable than that. But Gurney could sense something lurking in the arc of the story—something that foretold an ugly ending.

Hardwick continued. "Exactly what happened next was the subject of an extensive Bureau investigation. But in the final analysis all they really had was Max's word for it. He said simply that he'd believed his life was in immediate danger and he'd acted accordingly, with force appropriate to the circumstances. Bottom line, he left five dead mobsters in that office and walked away without a scratch on him. From that day until the night five years later when he flushed it all down the toilet, Max Clinter had an aura of invincibility."

"Do you know what he's doing now, how he supports himself?"

Hardwick grinned. "Yeah. He's a gun dealer. Unusual guns. Collectibles. Crazy military shit. Maybe even Desert Eagles."

## Chapter 8

# Kim Corazon's
# Complicated Project

When Gurney arrived home from Hardwick's place in Dillweed at 11:15 A.M., Kim was parked by the side door in her red Miata. As he pulled in next to her, she put away her phone and rolled down her window. "I was just going to call you. I knocked on the door, and no one answered."

"You're early."

"I'm always early. I can't stand being late. It's like a phobia. We can head for Rudy Getz's right now unless there are things you need to do first."

"I'll just be a minute." He went into the house to use the bathroom. He checked for phone messages. There weren't any. Then he checked the laptop for e-mail. It was all for Madeleine.

When he went back outside, he was struck by the smell of wet earth in the air. The earthy scent in turn conjured up the image of the arrow in the flower bed—red feathers, black shaft, embedded in the dark brown soil. His gaze went to the spot, half expecting . . .

But there was nothing there.

*Of course not. Why would there be? What the hell is the matter with me?*

He walked over to the Miata and got into the low-slung passenger seat. Kim drove bumpily through the pasture, past the barn and the pond, to the dirt-and-gravel road that followed the stream down the mountain. Once they were heading east on the county route, Gurney asked, "Any new problems since yesterday?"

She made a face. "I think I'm getting too wound up. I think it's what psychiatrists call 'hypervigilance.' "

"You mean constantly checking for danger?"

"Constantly checking, and doing it so obsessively that *everything* looks like a threat. It's like having a smoke alarm that's so sensitive it goes off every time you use the toaster. It's like, Did I really leave my pen on that table? Didn't I already wash that fork? Wasn't that plant two inches farther to the left? Stuff like that. Like last night. I went out for an hour, and when I got home, the light was on in the bathroom."

"You're sure you turned it off before you left?"

"I always turn it off. But that's not all. I thought I could smell Robby's horrible cologne. Just the tiniest trace of it. So I start running around the apartment sniffing everywhere, and for a second I'd think maybe I could smell it again." She sighed in exasperation. "You see what I mean? I'm losing it. Some people start seeing things. I'm smelling things." She drove for several miles in silence. The mist had begun again, and she turned on her wipers. At the end of each arc, they made a sharp squeaking sound. She seemed oblivious to it.

Gurney was studying her. Her clothes were neat, subdued. Her features were regular, her eyes dark, her mouth quite lovely. Her hair was a lustrous brown. Her clear skin had a hint of Mediterranean tan. She was a beautiful young woman—full of ideas, full of ambition, without being full of herself. And she was smart. That was the part Gurney liked best. But he was curious how someone so smart had gotten tangled up with someone as troubled as Robby.

"Tell me a little more about this Meese guy."

He began to think she hadn't heard him, it took her so long to answer. "I told you he was removed from some kind of sick family situation and put in a series of foster homes. Maybe some people come out of that okay, but most don't. I never knew any of the details. I just knew he seemed different. *Deep.* Maybe even a little dangerous." She hesitated. "I think the other thing that made him attractive was that Connie hated him."

"That made you like him?"

"I think she hated him and I liked him for the same reason—he reminded us both of my dad. My dad was kind of erratic, and he had a crazy background."

*My dad.* From time to time, those words had the power to trigger a wave of sadness in Gurney. His feelings about his father were conflicted and largely repressed. So were his feelings about himself as a father—the father of two sons, one living and one dead. As the emotion began to subside, he tried to hasten its exit by pushing his attention toward some other aspect of Kim's project, some other point of interest.

"You started to tell me on the phone about your contact with Max Clinter, that you found him *strange*. I think that was the word you used."

"Very intense. Actually, beyond intense."

"How far beyond?"

"Pretty far. He sounded paranoid."

"What made you think that?"

"The look in his eyes. That I-know-terrible-secrets look. He kept saying that I didn't know what I was getting into, that I was risking my life, that the Good Shepherd was *pure evil*."

"He seems to have gotten under your skin."

"He did. 'Pure evil' sounds like such a cliché. But he made it sound real."

After another few miles, Kim's GPS directed them off Route 28 at the Boiceville exit. They drove alongside a cascading white-water stream, swollen from snowmelt, until they came to Mountainside Drive, an ascending switchback road through a steep evergreen forest. That brought them to Falcon's Nest Lane. The addresses on the lane were posted next to driveways that led back to homes shielded from view by thick evergreens or high stone walls. Each driveway occurred at an interval Gurney estimated to be no less than a quarter mile from its nearest neighbor. The final address on the lane was *Twelve*—etched in cursive script on a brass plaque affixed to one of the two fieldstone pillars that bracketed the entrance to the driveway. Atop each of the pillars was a round stone the size of a basketball, and atop each of these was perched a sculpted stone eagle with wings spread aggressively and talons extended.

Kim turned in to the elegant Belgian-block driveway and drove slowly ahead through a virtual tunnel of massive rhododendrons. Then the tunnel opened, the driveway widened, and they were in front of Rudy Getz's home—an angular glass-and-concrete affair, hardly homey.

"This is it," said Kim with nervous excitement as she came to a stop in front of cantilevered concrete steps leading up to a metal door.

They got out of the car, climbed the steps, and were about to knock when the door opened. The man who greeted them was short and stocky, with pale skin, thinning gray hair, and hooded eyes. He was dressed in black jeans, black T-shirt, and an off-white linen sport jacket. He held a colorless drink in a short, fat glass. He reminded Gurney of a porno-film producer.

"Hey, nice to see you," he said to Kim with the cordiality of a drowsy Gila monster. He eyed Gurney, his mouth stretching into an emotionless grin. "You must be her famous detective adviser. Pleasure. Come in." He stepped back, gesturing them into the house with his glass. He squinted at the gray sky. "Fucking inclement weather, you know?"

The interior of the house was as aggressively modern and angular as the outside—mostly leather, metal, glass, cold colors, white oak floors.

"What are you drinking, Detective?"

"Nothing."

"Nothing. Right. And for you, Ms. *Corazon*?" He gave the name an exaggerated Spanish inflection that, combined with his smile, was like a lewd caress.

"Maybe just some water?"

"Water." He nodded, repeating the word as though it were an interesting comment she'd made, rather than a request. "So. Come in, sit down." He gestured with his glass toward a seating area in front of a cathedral-size window. As he spoke, a young woman in a skintight black leotard flew across the expansive room on eerily silent Rollerblades and disappeared through a doorway in the far wall.

Getz led the way to a set of six brushed-aluminum chairs around an oval acrylic coffee table, his mouth widening into a smile-like expression, shocking in its lack of warmth.

After they'd seated themselves at the low table, the Rollerblader flew back across the room, disappearing into another doorway. "Claudia," Getz announced with a wink, as though revealing a secret. "She's cute, eh?"

"Who is she?" asked Kim, who seemed taken aback by the display.

"My niece. She's staying here for a while. She likes to skate." He paused. "But we're here for business, right?" The smile evaporated, as though the time for small talk had passed. "So I have some great news for you. *Orphans of Murder* got a top score in our audience polling."

Kim looked more confused than pleased. "Polling? But how did you—"

Getz interrupted her. "We have a proprietary system for evaluating program concepts. We create a representative slice of the show, expose it via podcast to a statistically representative audience sample, and get real-time online feedback. Turns out to be super predictive."

"But what material did you use? My interviews with Ruth and Jimi?"

"Slices. Representative slices. Plus a little surrounding info to set the scene."

"But those interviews were shot on my amateur cameras. They weren't intended—"

Getz leaned forward over the table toward Kim. "Fact is, the so-called amateur look in this case turns out to be perfect. Sometimes the zero-production-values look is exactly right. It says honesty. Just like your personality. Earnest. Open. Young. Innocent. See, that's another thing our test audience told us. I shouldn't tell you this, but I will. Because I want you to trust me. They love you. They absolutely love you! So I'm thinking we have a future in front of us. What do you think of that?"

Kim was wide-eyed, her mouth open. "I don't know. I mean . . . they just saw a slice of an interview?"

"Wrapped in a little blanket of explanation, perspective—like we'd do in the actual show. The testing vehicle on the restricted podcast is put together like a one-hour show, composed of four program concepts—thirteen minutes each. So in this case we included yours, plus three other programs we're considering. This testing vehicle is called *Run It or Dump It.* Some people think that sounds crude. But there's a good reason for it. It's *visceral.*" Getz intoned the word with a confidential, almost reverential intensity. "You want to know the real RAM News success secret? That's it. It's *visceral*. In the old days, the networks used to think that news was news and entertainment was entertainment. That's why their news operations lost money. They were sitting on a gold mine and didn't know it. They thought news was about pure facts, presented as boringly as possible." Getz shook his head indulgently at mankind's capacity for delusional thinking.

Gurney smiled. "Obviously they got it all wrong."

Getz pointed a finger at him, like a teacher drawing attention to a bright student. "Obviously! News is life, life is emotion, emotion is *visceral*. Drama, blood, triumph, tears. It's not about some starched asshole reading dry facts and figures. It's about conflict. It's about fuck you! . . . No, fuck *you*! . . . Who the fuck are you saying 'fuck you' to? . . . Bam! bam! bam! Forgive my language—but you get what I'm saying?"

"Clear as crystal," said Gurney mildly.

"So that's why we call the show where we test our ideas *Run It or Dump It*. Because that's what people like. Simple choices. Power. Like the emperor looking down on the gladiator. Thumbs-up, he lives. Thumbs-down, he dies. People love black and white. Gray gives them headaches. Nuance makes them nauseous."

Kim blinked, swallowed. "And . . . *Orphans of Murder* . . . got a thumbs-up?"

"Big thumb, way up!"

Kim started to ask another question, but Getz cut her off, continuing along his own train of thought. "Way up! Which I find personally gratifying. Karma, full circle! Because it was our original coverage of the Good Shepherd murder spree that catapulted RAM News to the top. Where we belong. The idea of coming back to it now, exactly ten years later—that has the perfect vibe. I feel it in my bones! Now, how about a fantastic lunch?"

On cue, Claudia reappeared, balancing a large tray, which she placed on the coffee table. Her gel-spiked hair, which Gurney had originally taken for black, he now noted was a deep blue—a blue just a bit darker than her eyes, which met his momentarily with a disturbing frankness. He doubted she was out of her teens. She pirouetted on the tip of one blade, then cruised languidly across the room, looking back once before gliding out of sight.

There were three plates on the tray. On each there was an elaborate, delicately arranged display of sushi. The colors were beautiful, the shapes intricate. None of the ingredients were familiar to Gurney—nor, apparently, to Kim, who was studying the display with alarm.

"Another Toshiro masterpiece," said Getz.

"Who's Toshiro?" asked Kim.

Getz's eyes glinted. "He's the prize I stole from a hot sushi restaurant in the city." He took one of the bright little chunks from the plate nearest him and popped it into his mouth.

Gurney followed suit. It was unidentifiable but surprisingly delicious.

Kim, who appeared to be calling on her reserves of courage, tried a piece and visibly relaxed after a few seconds of chewing. "Lovely," she said. "So now he's your personal chef?"

"One of the rewards."

"You must be very good at what you do," said Gurney.

"I'm very good at recognizing what people will connect with." Getz paused, then added as though the idea had just dawned on him, "My talent is the ability to recognize talent."

Gurney nodded blandly, intrigued by the man's shameless self-regard.

Kim seemed eager to move the conversation back to *Orphans.* "I was wondering . . . did you learn anything from your *Run It or Dump It* polling that I should take into account with my remaining interviews?"

He gave her a shrewd look. "Just keep doing what you're doing. You've got that natural innocent thing going for you. Don't overthink it. That's for now. Long-term I smell an extension opportunity and a spin-off opportunity. The *Orphans* concept has strong emotional appeal. It's got legs that take it way beyond the six Good Shepherd victim families. It extends easily to families of other murder victims. It's a natural franchise, so maybe we can run with it. But it also leads to a second concept—the *unsolved* angle. Right now we've got both those things wrapped up together. You got the pain of the families, right?

But you also have an escaped murderer, the lack-of-closure thing. So I'm thinking if *Orphans* runs out of juice, we could switch the emphasis. I'm thinking of a spin-off deal—*In the Absence of Justice*—new show, we just shift the slant to the injustice of unsolved crimes. The lingering injustice."

Getz sat back, watching her absorb this.

She looked uncertain. "That . . . could work . . . I guess."

Getz leaned forward. "Look, I understand where you're coming from—the emotional angle, the pain, the suffering, the loss. Just a matter of adjusting the balance. Series one, we have more pain-and-loss emphasis. Series two, we have more unsolved-crime emphasis. And now I just got a whole other idea. Came to me out of the blue, just looking at this guy here." He pointed at Gurney, with the glint of discovery in his hooded eyes.

"Listen to this. I'm just thinking out loud here, but . . . how would you two like to be America's hot new reality team?"

Kim blinked, looked simultaneously excited and baffled.

Getz elaborated. "I see some natural dramatic chemistry here. A juicy personality conflict. The emotional kid who cares only about the victims, the heartache—locked in a love-hate partnership with the steely-eyed cop who only cares about making the collar, closing the case. It's got life. It's *visceral!*"

## Chapter 9

# A Reticent Orphan

"W hat are you thinking?" asked Kim, glancing nervously over at Gurney as she made another adjustment in the speed of her wipers.

They'd just crossed the Ashokan Reservoir causeway and were heading south toward Stone Ridge. It was a little after two. The afternoon had remained gray and sporadically misty.

When he didn't answer, she added, "You look pretty grim."

"Listening to your business associate brought back some memories of how RAM handled the Good Shepherd case. I'm sure you don't remember. I doubt you were watching much TV news at the age of thirteen."

She blinked, stared ahead at the wet road. "How did they cover it?"

"Overheated fear pieces, twenty-four/seven. Kept putting different names on the shooter—Mercedes Madman, Midnight Madman, Midnight Murderer—until he sent his manifesto out to the media, signed 'The Good Shepherd.' After that, that's what they called him. RAM zeroed in on the anti-greed message in the manifesto and started whipping up a panic that the shootings were the start of some kind of revolution—a socialist guerrilla campaign against America, against capitalism. It was loony stuff. Twenty-four hours a day, they had their talking-head 'experts' ranting about the horrible possibilities, the things that might happen, the conspiracies that might be behind it all. They had 'security consultants' saying it was time for every American to be armed—a gun in your house, gun in your car, gun in your pocket. The time had come to stop coddling anti-American criminals. The time had come to put an end to 'criminal rights.' Even when the shootings stopped, RAM just kept going. Kept talking about class warfare—how it had gone underground, how it was sure to break out again in a more horrendous way. They beat that drum for another year and a half. The ultimate RAM mission was clear: generate maximum anger and maximum panic in the service of audience numbers and ad revenue. Sad thing is, it worked. RAM coverage of the Good Shepherd case created the ultimate trash model for cable news: mindless debates, amplification of conflict, ugly conspiracy theories, the glorification of outrage, blame-based explanations for everything. And Rudy Getz seems perfectly happy to take credit for it."

Kim's hands were tight on the steering wheel. "What you're saying is, this is not someone I should be dealing with?"

"I'm not saying anything about Getz that wasn't obvious in the meeting we just had."

"If you were in my position, would you deal with him?"

"You're smart enough to know that's a meaningless question."

"No it's not. Just imagine you were in the same situation I'm in."

"You're asking me what kind of decision I'd make if I weren't *me*—with my background, my feelings, my thoughts, my family, my priorities, my life. Don't you see? *My* life couldn't possibly put me in *your* position. It's a nonsensical statement."

She blinked, looked perplexed. "What are you so angry about?"

That question took him by surprise. She was right. He *was* angry. It would be easy to say that amoral reptiles like Getz made him angry, that the transformation of the news media from relatively harmless information sources into cynical engines of polarization made him angry, that turning murder into "reality" entertainment made him angry. But he knew enough about himself to know that external reasons for his anger were often excuses for internal ones.

A wise man had once told him, Anger is like a buoy on the surface of the water. What you think you're angry about is only the tip of the issue. You have to follow the chain all the way down in order to discover what it's attached to, what's holding it in place.

He decided to follow the chain. He turned to Kim. "Why did you bring me to that meeting?"

"I explained that to you."

"You mean I was there to look over your shoulder? To *observe*?"

"And to give me your perspective on what you saw, on how I handled things."

"I can't evaluate your performance if I don't know what your goal was."

"I didn't have a *goal*."

"Really?"

She turned toward him. "Are you calling me a liar?"

"Watch your driving." His voice was stern, parental.

When she looked back at the road, he continued. "How come Rudy Getz doesn't know you only hired me for one day? How come he thinks I'm more involved in this thing than I really am?"

"I don't know. It's not because of anything I said." Her lips tightened.

Gurney had the impression she was trying not to cry. He said calmly, "I want to know the whole story. I want to know why I'm here."

She nodded almost imperceptibly, but at least another minute elapsed before she replied. "After my thesis adviser submitted my proposal and initial interviews to Getz, things started moving very fast. I never thought he'd actually buy it, and when he did, I sort of panicked. This huge thing was being offered to me, and I didn't want it to be taken away. I thought, suppose the RAM people suddenly wake up and say to themselves, 'This is just a twenty-three-year-old kid. What does she know about murder cases? What does she know about anything?' Connie and I thought that if someone with real experience was involved, a real-life expert, it would make everything more solid. We both thought of you. Connie said that nobody knew more than you did about murder, and that the article she'd written about you had made you sort of famous. So you'd be perfect."

"Did you show the article to Getz?"

"When I called him yesterday to tell him about your agreeing to help me, I think I did mention it."

"And what about Robby Meese?"

"What about him?"

"Were you hoping I might help you deal with him, too?"

"Maybe. Maybe I'm more scared of him than I said."

Gurney's long experience as a cop had taught him that deception comes in various packages, some wrapped elaborately, some hastily; but there is a bareness and spareness about the truth. Regardless of the complexities of life, the truth is usually simple. He sensed that simplicity now in Kim's voice. It made him smile.

"So I'm supposed to be your expert murder consultant, a celebrity detective, a provider of credibility, a reality-show cohost, an anti-stalker bodyguard. Anything else?"

She hesitated. "As long as I'm being exposed as a manipulative idiot, I should confess to another crazy hope. I was thinking that your presence at the meeting we're on our way to now—with Larry Sterne—might convince him to participate after all."

"Why?"

"This is going to sound really underhanded. I was thinking, since you were a famous homicide detective, he might think the hunt for the killer was being revived—and having new hope of the killer's being caught might persuade him to take part."

"So in addition to everything else, I'm supposed to be your cold-case specialist on the trail of the Good Shepherd?"

She sighed. "Stupid, right?"

He didn't volunteer an answer, and she didn't press for one.

Somewhere high above them in the dense overcast, the heavy, thumping heartbeat of a helicopter grew stronger, then weaker, then dwindled away to nothing.

In contrast to Rudy Getz's dramatic eagles, Larry Sterne's driveway was marked by an ordinary mailbox next to an opening in a low fieldstone wall. The house, one of the eighteenth-century stone cottages typical of the area, was set back about two hundred feet behind a casual country lawn. Kim parked the Miata outside a detached garage.

The front door of the house was open when they got to it. The man standing just inside was of medium build and medium height, and appeared to be in his late thirties or early forties. He was dressed in a golf shirt, a rumpled cardigan, loose slacks, and expensive-looking loafers—all in shades of tan that blended seamlessly with his light brown hair.

According to Gurney's recollection of the information in Kim's blue folder, Larry Sterne was, like his murder-victim father whose practice he'd taken over, a top-shelf dentist.

"Kim," he said smilingly, "nice to see you again. This would be Detective Gurney?"

"*Retired,*" emphasized Gurney.

Sterne nodded pleasantly, as though happy with the distinction. "Come in, we'll use this room here." As he spoke, he led them into a bright sitting room with wide-board floors and tasteful antique furniture. "I don't mean to be rude, Kim, but I don't have much time today, so I hope we can get right to the point."

They sat in wing chairs arranged around a circular rug in front of a stone fireplace. The red-coal remnants of a fire made the room pleasantly warm.

"I know how you feel about RAM News," said Kim with great earnestness, "but I felt it was important to try one more time to address your objections."

Sterne smiled patiently. He spoke as one might to a child. "I'm always willing to listen to you. I hope you're equally willing to listen to me."

The man's gentle tone of voice reminded Gurney of someone he couldn't place.

"Of course," said Kim, unconvincingly.

Sterne leaned a little forward, the picture of polite attention. "You go first."

"Okay. Number one, I'll be the person responsible for shaping the format and style of the series. So it's not like you'd be dealing with some faceless media corporation. I'll be conducting the interviews, asking the questions. Number two, the children of the victims—people like you—will be providing ninety-five percent of the content. Your answers to my questions are what it's all about. The substance of the series will be made up almost entirely of your own words. Number three, I have no personal interest in anything but the truth—the true impact of murder on a family. Number four, RAM News may have its own corporate agenda, but in this case they are just the venue, just the communications channel. They are the medium. You are the message."

Sterne smiled patiently. "Very eloquent, Kim. However, my concerns haven't gone away. I'll borrow your numbering technique to make my own points. Number one, RAM is not a nice organization.

They're at the cutting edge of everything that's wrong with the media today. They've become a megaphone for the ugliest and most divisive sentiments in society. They glorify aggressiveness and make a virtue of ignorance. Your priority may be to convey the truth, but that's not their priority. Number two, they have more experience in manipulating people like you than you have in managing people like them. There's no realistic chance of your maintaining control over your series. I know you're asking your participants to sign exclusivity agreements with you, but don't be surprised if RAM finds some way around that. Number three, even if RAM didn't have a poisonous agenda, I'd still advise you to abort your project. You have an interesting premise, but you also have the potential for generating great pain. The price of your project outweighs its rewards. You have good intentions, but good intentions can create suffering—especially when you publicize private feelings. Number four, my personal experience still remains, after all these years, vivid proof of everything I'm saying. I've alluded to this before, Kim, but perhaps I should be more specific. Nineteen years ago, when I was in dental school, a close friend at another university was killed. I remember the media coverage as hysterical, shallow, cheap, utterly disgusting. And utterly typical. The sad fact is that the underlying imperatives of the media business favor the production of trash. The market for trash is larger than the market for sensitive, intelligent comment. That's simply the nature of the business, the nature of the audience. Media Economics 101."

They went back and forth a few more times, both restating the thoughts they'd already expressed, the edges of their disagreement muffled by cordiality. The exchange ended when Sterne checked the time and apologized for not being able to continue.

"Do you commute from here to your practice in the city?" asked Gurney.

"Only one or two days a week. I do very little hands-on work anymore. The practice in reality is a substantial dental-medical corporation, and I'm more like the chairman of the board than a working dentist. I'm blessed with good partners and efficient managers. So I spend most of my time involved with outside medical and dental organizations—charities and suchlike. In that respect I'm a very fortunate man."

"Larry, dear . . ."

In the doorway of the sitting room stood a tall, very shapely, almond-eyed woman, pointing at a delicate gold watch on her wrist.

"Yes, Lila, I know. My guests are just leaving."

She smiled and retreated.

As Sterne accompanied Kim and Gurney to the front door, he urged her to keep an open mind and invited her to stay in touch with him. Shaking hands with Gurney, smiling politely, he said, "I hope at some time in the future we have an opportunity to talk about your police career. The article by Kim's mother made it sound quite fascinating."

It was then that Gurney realized who the man reminded him of.

Mister Rogers.

Mister Rogers with a wife from a sultan's harem.

## Chapter 10

# A Dramatically
# Different Point of View

At the end of Sterne's driveway, even though there was no traffic, Kim stopped the car before turning out onto the road. "Before you ask," she announced confessionally, "the answer is yes. When I set up our appointment and told him you'd be coming with me, I gave him the website link to Connie's article."

Gurney said nothing.

"Are you annoyed at me for doing that?"

"I feel like I'm in the middle of an archaeological dig."

"What do you mean?"

"Little bits and pieces of the situation keep emerging. I'm wondering what's next."

"There's nothing 'next.' Nothing I can think of. Is that what your job was like?"

"Like what?"

"An archaeological dig."

"In some ways, yes."

In fact, it was an image that had occurred to him often: uncovering the puzzle pieces, laying them out, studying the shapes and textures, fitting them together tentatively, searching for patterns. Once in a while, you could take your time. More frequently you had to move swiftly—in an ongoing serial-murder case, for example, when delays in finding and interpreting the pieces could mean more murders, more horror.

Kim took out her cell phone, looked at it, looked at Gurney. "You know, I'm thinking, since it's not even three o'clock yet . . . Would you possibly be up for one more meeting before I drive you home?" Before he could answer, she added quickly, "It would be on the way, so it wouldn't take much extra time."

"I need to be home by six." This wasn't entirely true, but he wanted to create a boundary.

"I don't think that's a problem." She tapped in a number, then held the phone to her ear, waiting. "Roberta? It's Kim Corazon."

A minute later, after the briefest of conversations, Kim expressed her thanks, and they were on their way.

"That sounded easy," said Gurney.

"Roberta's been hot on the documentary idea ever since I first got in touch with her. She's not shy about her feelings—or her opinions. With the possible exception of Jimi Brewster, she's the most aggressive participant."

Roberta Rotker lived just outside the village of Peacock in a brick house that looked like a fortress. It was set squarely in the middle of a farm field. The field had been rough-mowed to resemble a lawn. There were no trees, no shrubs, no foundation plantings of any kind. The property was surrounded by a six-foot-high chain-link fence. Security cameras were mounted on posts at regular intervals inside the fence. The heavy-duty entrance gate was of the sliding variety on rollers, electrically operated from the house.

As they arrived in front of it, the gate opened. A straight macadam driveway led to a macadam parking area in front of a three-car brick garage. The place had an institutional aura, like some sort of safe house operated by a government agency. Gurney counted four additional security cameras: two on the front corners of the garage, two under the eaves of the house.

The woman who opened the front door looked as businesslike as the building. She wore a plaid work shirt and dark twill pants. The unflattering style of her short, sandy hair emphasized her apparent disinterest in her appearance. The gaze she fixed on Gurney was uninviting and unblinking. She reminded him of a cop—an impression reinforced by the nine-millimeter SIG Sauer pistol in a quick-draw holster affixed to her belt.

She shook hands with Kim in that determinedly firm way often adopted by women working in traditionally male professions. When Kim had introduced Gurney and explained his presence as an "adviser" on the project, Roberta Rotker gave him a short nod, stepped back, and waved them into the house.

Structurally, it was a traditional center-hall Colonial, but the center hall itself was completely bare—an empty passageway that led from the front door to the back door. On the left were two doors and a staircase; on the right were three doors, all closed. This was not a house that divulged information casually.

As Gurney and Kim were led through the first door on the right into a minimally furnished living room, he asked, "Are you in law enforcement?"

Roberta Rotker didn't answer until she'd closed the door firmly behind them. "Very definitely," she said.

It was an unusual response. "What I meant was, are you employed by a law-enforcement agency?"

"Why is my employment a matter of interest to you?"

Gurney smiled blandly. "Just curious whether the sidearm is a job requirement or a personal preference."

"That's a distinction without a difference. The answer is, all of the above. Make yourself comfortable." She pointed to a hard-cushioned couch that reminded Gurney of the one in the waiting room at the clinic where Madeleine worked three days a week. When he and Kim were seated, Rotker continued. "It's a personal preference because it makes me feel better. And it's also a requirement—required by the state of the world we live in. I believe it's the job of a responsible citizen to respond to reality. Does that satisfy your curiosity?"

"Some of it."

She stared at him. "We're at *war*, Detective. At war with creatures who lack our sense of right and wrong. If we don't get them, they get us. That's reality."

Gurney reflected, for maybe the hundredth time in his life, on how emotion created its own logic, how anger was invariably the mother of certainty. It was surely one of the great ironies of human nature that when our passions most severely disorient us, we are most positive that we see things clearly.

"You were a cop," Rotker went on. "So you know what I'm talking about. We live in a world where glitter is expensive and life is cheap."

This bleak summation led to a silence, broken by Kim with what sounded like diversionary cheeriness. "Oh, by the way, I meant to tell Dave about your private shooting range. Maybe you could show it to him? I bet he'd love to see it."

"Why not?" said Rotker with neither hesitation nor enthusiasm. "Come."

She brought them out through the hallway, through the back door, next to which a fenced kennel ran half the length of the house. Four heavily muscled Rottweilers erupted in a furious din that ceased the instant their master issued a command in German.

Past the kennel, in a field behind the house, a narrow, window-less building extended out toward the rear fence. Rotker unlocked its metal door and switched on the lights. Inside was a basic pistol range with a single firing position and a motorized target placer.

She walked to the waist-high table at the near end and held her finger against the wall switch beside it. A fresh paper target with a stylized man-size image on it, already suspended from the wire carrier, began moving down the range. It stopped at the twenty-five-foot mark. "Any interest, Detective?"

"I'd rather watch you," he said with a smile. "I have a feeling that you're good."

She returned the smile, coldly. "Good enough for most situations."

She put her finger back on the wall switch, and the target began to move farther away. It stopped at the range's fifty-foot end point. She took hearing protectors and safety glasses off a hook by the switch and put them on, glancing back at Gurney and Kim. "Sorry I don't have extras. I don't usually have an audience." She unholstered her SIG, checked the magazine, flipped off the safety, and for a moment stood perfectly still, her head bowed like an Olympic diver's before the crucial moment. Then she did something that Gurney knew would be with him for the rest of his life.

She screamed—an enraged, bestial sound that made the word that initiated it more like lightning tearing through the room than like anything verbal. What she screamed was "FUCK!"—and as she screamed it, she raised the pistol in a sudden movement and, without any visible act of aiming, fired off every round in the fifteen-round magazine in what Gurney guessed was less than four seconds.

Then she lowered the gun slowly and laid it on the table, removed her safety glasses and hearing protectors and hung them neatly on the wall. She raised her hand to the switch, and the target glided from the end of the range up to the table. She detached it carefully and turned around, smiling placidly, seemingly in full possession of herself.

She held the target up for Gurney's inspection. The normal aiming area—the center of the body mass—was untouched. In fact, there were no bullet holes anywhere in the human-shaped outline, except in one place.

The center of the forehead had been obliterated.

*Chapter 11*

# The Strange Aftermath

Kim and Gurney were in the Miata, passing through the almost nonexistent village of Peacock, heading for the county road that would eventually bring them, through a succession of hills and dales, to Walnut Crossing. It was just past five, the overcast was thinning, and the mist had finally ended.

"I was a hell of a lot more startled by that business than you were," said Gurney.

Kim shot him an appraising glance. "Making you conclude I'd seen it before? You're right."

"Which is why you suggested that she show me the shooting range? So I could see her little performance for myself?"

"Yep."

"Well, it made an impression."

"I want you to see everything. Or at least as much as you have time to see."

They both fell silent. It seemed to Gurney that he'd already seen a lot. It was hard to believe that he'd gotten the call from Connie Clarke only the previous morning. He closed his eyes and tried to arrange the flood of observations, conversations. It was dizzying. The project was bizarre. His involvement in it was bizarre.

He awoke as Kim was turning onto the narrow lane that wound its way up the mountain to his home. "Jesus. Didn't mean to fall asleep."

"Sleep is good," she said, looking tired and serious.

Three deer ran up an embankment just ahead of them.

"You ever hit one?" she asked.

"Yes."

Something about the way he said it made her look at him curiously.

It had happened six months earlier. A doe had crossed Route 10 from the woods on the left side of the road, well in front of him, to an open field on the right. Just as he was passing the place she'd crossed, her fawn dashed out in front of his car.

He winced now at the still-vivid memory of the thump.

Pulling over. Stopping. Walking back. The small, twisted body. The eyes open and lifeless. The doe standing in the field, looking back. Waiting. He was filled with sadness and horror, could feel it now.

Kim drove past a scruffy hill farm with a dozen scruffy cows and half a dozen rusted cars. "You friendly with your neighbors?" she asked.

Gurney made a sound halfway between a grunt and a laugh. "Some yes, some no."

Half a mile farther on, they came within sight of his red barn at the end of the lane, next to the pond. "Stop and let me out," he said. "I want to walk up through the pasture. It'll wake me up, clear my head."

She frowned. "The grass looks wet."

"Doesn't matter. I'll be taking my shoes off when I get to the house."

She pulled up in front of the barn door and turned off the engine, leaving her hand on the ignition key in an oddly preoccupied way.

Instead of getting out of the car, he sat and waited, sensing that she had something to say.

"So . . ." she began, stopped, and began again. "So . . . where do we go from here?"

Gurney shrugged. "You hired me for one day. The day is over."

"Any chance of one more?"

"To do what?"

"Talk to Max Clinter?"

"Why?"

"Because I can't figure him out. It's like he *knows* something about the Good Shepherd case. Something terrible. But I don't know whether he really knows something or if it's just some crazy thing in his mind, some kind of delusion. I thought maybe with your shared backgrounds as detectives, maybe he'd be more straight-up with you—especially if I wasn't there, if it was just the two of you, talking cop to cop."

"Where does he live?"

"You'll do it? You'll talk to him?"

"I didn't say that. I asked you where he lives."

"Not far from Cayuga Lake. Pretty close to his disastrous car chase. That's part of what makes me worry that he's a little off the wall."

"Because he wants to live there?"

"Because of *why* he wants to live there. He says that's the place he and the Good Shepherd crossed paths and that's where karma will bring them together again."

"And this is the guy you want me to talk to?"

"Nuts, right?"

He told her he'd think about it.

"I guarantee you'll find him . . . interesting."

"We'll see. I'll let you know." He got out of the little car, watched her turn around and head back down the narrow road.

His short walk up through the pasture provided a powerful break from the day, flooding his consciousness with the aromas of nature in early spring: the complex sweetness of the moist earth, air that smelled clean enough to purify one's soul—to wash away the obstructions that stood between one's mind and the truth of things.

Or so it seemed—until he was in the house five minutes, had gone to the bathroom, washed his face, and Madeleine had asked about his day.

He recounted as comprehensively as he could the details of the three peculiar meetings he'd had with Kim and the people with whom she was involved—Rudy Getz with his Rollerblader, Larry Sterne with his Mister Rogers cardigan, Roberta Rotker with her unhinged exhibition of marksmanship. And he told her everything he knew about Max Clinter—the peculiar, tragic character whose life was forever changed by the Good Shepherd.

He was sitting at the table by the French doors, and Madeleine was chopping vegetables on a cutting board by the sink.

"Kim wants me to stay involved in this thing for another day. I'll be damned if I know what to do."

Madeleine sliced the end off a large red onion. "How's your arm?"

"What?"

"Your arm. The numb spot. How is it?"

"I don't know. I mean, I haven't . . ." His voice trailed off as he rubbed his forearm and wrist. "Okay . . . the same, I guess. Why do you ask?"

She turned the onion around in her hand, peeling off a couple of layers of the tough outer skin.

"How about the pain in your side?"

"Fine, at the moment. It's an intermittent thing, comes and goes."

"Every ten minutes or so, I think you told me?"

"More or less."

"How often did you feel it today?"

"I'm not sure."

"Not sure if you felt it at all?"

"I couldn't say."

She nodded, sliced a large zucchini down the middle, laid the halves on the board, and began chopping them into bite-size half-moons.

He blinked, stared at her, cleared his throat. "So what you're saying is that I should let Kim hire me for another day?"

"Did I say that?"

"I think you did."

There was a long silence. Madeleine cut up an eggplant, a yellow squash, and a sweet red pepper, then put everything into a large bowl that she carried to the stove, tilting the contents into a sizzling wok. "She's an interesting young woman."

"In what way?"

"Smart, attractive, ambitious, subtle, energetic—don't you think?"

"Hmm. She definitely has some depth."

"Maybe you should introduce her to Kyle."

"My son?"

"I don't know any other Kyle."

"What is it about them that makes you think . . . ?"

"I can see them together, that's all. Different personalities, but on the same wavelength."

He tried to imagine the hypothetical relationship chemistry. In less than a minute, he gave up the effort. Too many possibilities, too little data. He envied the efficiency of Madeleine's intuition. It enabled her to leap over unknowns that stopped him dead.

## Chapter 12

# The Madness of
# Max Clinter

"Arriving at destination, on the right."

Gurney's GPS had just delivered him to an unmarked intersection at which a narrow dirt road teed into the paved road—a road he'd been following for two miles without seeing a single house that didn't look like it was falling down.

On one side of the dirt road was an open steel gate. On the other side was a dead oak tree, the scar of a lightning bolt etched in its bark. Nailed to the trunk was a human skeleton—or, Gurney assumed, a remarkably convincing replica. Hanging from the skeleton's neck was a hand-painted sign: THE LAST TRESPASSER.

Based on what Dave knew of Max Clinter so far, including the impression he'd gotten during a phone conversation with him that morning, the sign was not surprising.

Gurney made the turn onto the rutted lane, which soon traversed, like a primitive causeway, the center of a large beaver pond. Beyond the pond it continued through a thicket of swamp maples and, beyond that, arrived at a log cabin built on a raised patch of dry land, surrounded by an expanse of water and marsh grasses.

There was a peculiar border around the cabin: a moatlike swath of tangled weeds enclosed by a fine-mesh fence. The pathway to the cabin door passed through the weed swath, separated from it by a length of fencing on either side. As Gurney was taking this in, speculating on its purpose, the cabin door opened and a man emerged onto a small stone step. He was dressed in a military camouflage shirt and pants, jarringly offset by a pair of snakeskin boots. He had a hard look about him.

"Vipers," he said in a gravelly voice.

"Sorry?"

"In the weeds. That's what you were wondering about, wasn't it?" His speech was oddly accented, his eyes intent on Gurney's. "Small rattlesnakes. The small ones are the most dangerous. Word gets around. Excellent deterrent."

"I wouldn't think they'd be much use, hibernating in cold weather," said Gurney pleasantly. "I assume you're Mr. Clinter?"

"Maximilian Clinter. Weather is only an issue for *physical* snakes. It's the *idea* of the snakes that keeps the undesirables out. Weather has no effect on the snakes in their heads. You get my point, Mr. Gurney? I'd invite you in, but I never invite anyone in. Can't handle it. PTSD. If you went in, I'd have to stay out. Two's a crowd. Can't fuckin' breathe." He grinned, a little wildly. His accent, Gurney realized, was an antic brogue that came and went, like Marlon Brando's in *Missouri Breaks*. "I entertain all my guests in the open air. Hope you're not offended. Follow me."

He led Gurney around the outside of the fenced weeds to a weathered picnic table in back of the cabin. Beyond the table, parked just at the edge of the bog, was an original military Humvee, painted desert tan.

"You drive that thing?" asked Gurney.

"On special occasions." Clinter winked conspiratorially as he sat at the table. He picked up a pair of spring-loaded hand exercisers from the bench seat and began squeezing them. "Make yourself comfortable, Mr. Gurney, and tell me what your interest is in the Good Shepherd case."

"I told you on the phone. I was asked to—"

"Look over the lovely shoulder of the lovelorn Miss Heart?"

"Miss Heart?"

"*Corazón* means 'heart.' Basic Spanish. But I'm sure you knew that. Perfect name for her, don't you think? Affairs of the heart. Passions gone awry. Bleeding heart for the victims of crime. But how does this involve Maximilian Clinter?" In this last question, the transient brogue disappeared. The man's eyes settled into a sharp, steady gaze.

Gurney had to decide quickly how to proceed. He opted for brash openness. "Kim thinks you know stuff about the case, stuff you're not telling her. She can't figure you out. I think you scare the shit out of her." Gurney would swear that Clinter was pleased by this but didn't want to show it. Cards on the table seemed to be the way to go. "Incidentally, I was impressed with the story of your Buffalo performance. If half of what I heard is true, you're a talented man."

Clinter smiled. "Big Honey."

"Say again?"

"That was Frankie Benno's name in the mob."

"Because of what a sweet guy he was?"

Clinter's eyes glittered. "His hobby. He was a beekeeper."

Gurney laughed at the thought of it. "And what about you, Max? What sort of gentleman are you? I heard that you might be in the specialty-arms business."

Clinter gave him a shrewd look, his hands compressing the exercisers rapidly, almost effortlessly. "Deactivated collectibles."

"You mean guns that don't work?"

"The big military hardware has all been rendered more or less unfireable. I also have some interesting smaller pieces that do work. But I'm not a dealer. Dealers need federal licenses. So I'm not a dealer. I'm what the law calls a hobbyist. And sometimes I sell something in my personal collection to another hobbyist. You get my point?"

"I think so. What kind of guns do you sell?"

"Unusual guns. And I have to feel in each case that it's the right match for the particular individual. I make that perfectly clear. *If all you want's a fuckin' Glock, then go to fuckin' Walmart.* That's my firearms philosophy, and I'm not shy about it." The brogue was creeping back in. "On the other hand, if you want a Second World War Vickers machine gun, more or less deactivated, with a matching antiaircraft tripod, we might have reason to converse, assuming you were a hobbyist like myself."

Gurney pivoted lazily around on the bench so he could look out over the brown water of the marsh. He yawned and stretched, then smiled at Clinter. "So tell me, do you actually know anything about the Good Shepherd case, as Kim thinks you do? Or is that all just a bunch of bobbing and weaving and bullshit?"

The man stared at Gurney for a long time before he spoke. "Is it bullshit that all the cars were black? Is it bullshit that two of the victims went to the same high school in Brooklyn? Is it bullshit that the Good Shepherd murders tripled the ratings and profits of RAM News? Is it bullshit that the FBI erected a total wall of silence around the case?"

Gurney turned his hands up in bafflement. "What's that supposed to add up to?"

"Evil, Mr. Gurney. At the bottom of this case, there is an incredible evil." His hands were squeezing, releasing, squeezing, releasing the exercisers with movements so rapid they appeared convulsive. "By the way, did you know there are some fucked-up people in the world who have orgasms watching films of car crashes? Did you know that?"

"I think someone made a movie about it back in the nineties. But that isn't what you think the Good Shepherd case is about . . . is it?"

"I don't think anything. I just have questions. Lots of questions. Was the manifesto just the wrapping on a different sort of bomb—a Christmas present in an Easter box? Did our Clyde have a Bonnie in his car? Is the key to it all the set of six little animals from Noah's Ark? Are there secret links among the victims no one's looked at yet? Was it wealth itself that painted targets on their backs or was it how they got the wealth? Now, that's an interesting question, don't you think?" He winked at Gurney. It was clear he wasn't interested in an answer. He was on a rhetorical roll all his own. "So many questions. Might the shepherd be a shepherdess—a Bonnie by herself—a crazy bitch with a grudge against the rich?"

He fell silent. The sole sound in the eerie stillness was the repetitive squeaking of the springs in his exercisers.

"You must be developing very strong hands," said Gurney.

Clinter flashed a fierce grin. "The last time I met the Good Shepherd, I was terribly, shamefully, tragically underprepared. That won't be the case next time."

Gurney had a momentary vision of the climactic scene in *Moby-Dick*. Ahab with his hands gripping the harpoon, driving it into the back of the whale. Ahab and the whale, the entangled pair, disappearing into the depths of the sea forever.

## Chapter 13

# Serial Massacre

O nce Gurney had departed from Clinter's outlandish compound—from its real or imagined vipers, its swampy moat, its skeleton sentinel—and had put a few miles behind him, he pulled over into a roadside turnaround. It was near the top of a gentle rise that gave him a view of the northern end of Lake Cayuga, as brilliantly blue as the sky above it.

He took out his phone, entered Jack Hardwick's number, and got voice mail.

"Hey, Jack, I have questions. Just had a talk with Mr. Clinter. Need your perspective on a couple of things. Call me. Sooner the better. Thanks."

Then he called Kim.

"Dave?"

"Hi. I'm up in your general neighborhood, looking into a few things. Thought it might make sense to have a word with Robby Meese. You have an address and phone number for him?"

"What . . . Why do you want to talk to him?"

"Is there a reason you don't want me to?"

"No. It's just that . . . I don't know . . . Sure, okay, just a second." In less than a minute, she picked up again. "He has an apartment in the Tipperary Hill neighborhood, 3003 South Lowell." Then she read off a cell number, which Dave copied down. "Remember, he's using the name Montague, not Meese. But . . . what are you going to do?"

"Just ask questions, see if I can find out anything that makes sense."

"Sense?"

"The more I learn about this project of yours—or the case it's based on—the fuzzier it gets. I'm hungry for a little clarity."

"Clarity? You think you're going to get that from *him*?"

"Maybe not directly, but he seems to be a player in our little drama, and I don't really know who the hell he is. That makes me uncomfortable."

"I told you everything I know about him." She sounded hurt, defensive.

"I'm sure you did."

"Then why—"

"If you want my help, Kim, you need to give me some room."

She hesitated. "Okay . . . I guess. Be careful. He's . . . weird."

"Guys with more than one last name often are."

He ended the call. The phone rang as he was putting it in his pocket. The ID said it was J. Hardwick.

"Hello, Jack, thanks for getting back."

"I'm just a humble public servant, Sherlock. What can I do for the famous detective today?"

"I'm not sure. What kind of Good Shepherd file stuff can you lay your hands on?"

"Oh, I see." His voice had the arch tone Gurney hated.

"See what?"

"I sense that some of Sherlock's retired brain cells are coming back to life."

Gurney ignored this. "So what do you have access to?"

Hardwick cleared his throat with stomach-turning thoroughness. "Original incident reports, victim ID and background data, photographs of large-caliber bullet damage to faces and skulls—Speaking of which, a colorful anecdote comes to mind. One of the victims, a fancy real-estate lady, lost major portions of her jaw and head to that Desert Eagle cannonball. Young fella on the evidence team, combing the crime scene, made a discovery he'll never forget. A dime-size piece of the lady's earlobe was hanging on the branch of a roadside sumac bush, with her big diamond-stud earring still in it. Can you picture it, ace? That's the kind of thing tends to stick in the memory." He paused for a moment, as if to permit full appreciation of the image. "So anyway, we got lots of details like that, plus ME findings, evidence-team reports, lab reports up the ass, investigative reports, FBI Behavioral Unit's profile of the shooter, yadda, yadda, yadda, tons of other shit—some accessible, some not. What are you looking for?"

"How about whatever you can send me without too much trouble?"

Hardwick responded with his sandpaper laugh. "Everything the FBI is involved in is potential trouble. Pack of arrogant, political, control-freak assholes." He paused. "I'll see what I can do. I'll send you a couple of things right away, more later. Keep checking your e-mail." Hardwick was always most obliging when regulations were likely to be broken and sensitive toes stepped on.

"By the way," said Gurney, "I just came from a meeting with Mr. Clinter."

The Hardwick laugh erupted again, louder. "Maxie made an impression on you?"

"You ever seen that place of his?"

"Bones, snakes, Hummers, and horseshit. That the place you're talking about?"

"Sounds like you don't give Mr. Clinter's ramblings a lot of weight."

"You do?"

"I haven't decided yet what to make of him. There's a psycho component in the package, but there's also a performer-pretending-to-be-a-psycho component. It's hard to pin down the line between them. He said something about PTSD. You happen to know if that came from the drunken crash that got him fired?"

"No. The First Gulf War. Friendly fire from a helicopter blew up a guy next to him. Back then Maxie toughed it out, stuffed it, whatever. But it probably set him up for his big collapse after the Good Shepherd mess. Who knows? Maybe he thought he was shooting at a fucking helicopter that night."

"Anyone pay attention to his theories about the case?"

"He didn't have theories. He had wild-ass ideas, based on whatever shit popped into his head. You ever listen to a nutcase explain how the number of legs on a chair multiplied by the mystical number seven gives you the number of days in a lunar month? Maxie was loaded to the eyeballs with that kind of crap."

"So you don't think he has anything real to contribute?"

Hardwick grunted thoughtfully. "The only real things Maxie brings to the table are hatred, obsession, and a crazy kind of smarts."

It was a combination Gurney had run into before. It was a recipe for disaster.

A quarter of an hour later, just outside Auburn, having cruised through the pastoral hills that separated Cayuga Lake from Owasco Lake, Gurney pulled into a combination gas station/mini-mart to refill his tank with gas and recharge his brain with a large coffee. According to his dashboard clock, it was 1:05 P.M.

After getting his gas receipt, he pulled away from the pump to a corner of the parking area to sip his coffee and plan his interview with Meese-Montague.

His cell phone rang. It was a text message: CHECK YOUR E-MAIL.

When he did, he discovered one from Hardwick. The covering message said, "See attached documents: Incident Reports (6), Prior Movements Supplement, ViCAP Reports, Common Elements Summary, Pre-Autopsy Victim Pics."

The title of each of the incident documents was composed of a number between one and six, which apparently denoted its place in the series, plus the victim's surname. Gurney selected the document 1-MELLANI and began scrolling through its fifty-two pages.

Included were the responding officer's observations, crime-scene diagrams, photographs of the site, an evidence-based event reconstruction with hypothetical narrative, vehicle-damage report, evidence-collection report, list of units and officers responding, ME's preliminary report, and a list of lab tests.

If this first of six incident reports was representative of the others in length and detail, there would be over three hundred fifty pages to wade through. This was not a task Gurney intended to undertake on the three-inch screen of his cell phone.

He went back to the list of attachments and selected the Common Elements document—the factors linking the six homicides. He was pleased to see one page with thirteen concise points.

    1. Attacks occurred on consecutive weekends, between March 18 and April 1, 2000.

2. Attacks occurred within 2-hour window, 9:11 P.M. to 11:10 P.M.

3. Attacks occurred within a 200-mile-by-50-mile rectangle extending across central New York into Massachusetts.

4. Attacks occurred on leftward road curves with good forward visibility.

5. Moderate vehicle speeds (46–58 mph) at time of gunshot.

6. Little to no traffic, no known witnesses, no known surveillance cameras, no nearby commercial or residential structures.

7. Attacks occurred on secondary rural roads linking major highways with upscale communities.

8. Victims' vehicles: late-model black Mercedeses, super-luxury class (MSRP range $82,400 to $162,760).

9. Single shot to the driver's head, massive brain damage, relatively instant fatality.

10. Estimated shooter-to-victim distance in each instance: 6–12 feet.

11. All recovered rounds Action Express .50 caliber—unique to Desert Eagle handgun.

12. Plastic animals from popular child's play set deposited at crime scenes. Order of appearance: lion, giraffe, leopard, zebra, monkey, elephant.

13. Driver-victim male in 5 of 6 attacks.

Almost every item on the list raised a question or two in Gurney's mind. He closed Common Elements and opened Pre-Autopsy Vic Pics—grimacing at the thought of what he'd be looking at. There were twelve photographs, two of each victim: one taken in the vehicle at the crime scene and one taken full-face on the autopsy table.

Gurney gritted his teeth and proceeded through the horror gallery of photos. He was reminded again that cops and ER personnel share the dubious privilege of knowing something that 99 percent of the population never will: what a large hollow-point bullet can do to a human head. It can reduce it to something appallingly, nauseatingly ridiculous. It can reshape a skull into a shattered helmet, a scalp into a crazy hat askew on the forehead. It can rearrange a face into a mockery of humor or surprise. Bend it into a comic-book expression of idiocy or outrage. Or blast it away completely—leaving only a pulpy terrain of brains and holes and teeth.

Gurney closed the photo file, quit the e-mail program, and picked up his coffee. It was cold. He took a few sips anyway, then put it aside and called Hardwick.

"Fuck's up now, Sherlock?"

"Thanks for the data. That was quick."

"Right. What do you want now?"

"I called to thank you."

"Bullshit. What do you want?"

"I want whatever isn't written down."

"You seem to think I know more than I do."

"I've never met anyone who's got a better memory than you. Shit just seems to stick in your brain, Jack. It may be your greatest talent."

"Fuck you."

"You're welcome. Now, can you please paint me a quick picture of the victims, maybe where they were coming from when they were shot?"

"First attack, Bruno Mellani. Bruno and his wife, Carmella, were on their way from a christening on Long Island to their country estate in Chatham, New York. The christening was really about paying respects to business associates. Bruno was all about money and business. There were rumors that he may have been connected, but probably no more so than a lot of guys in the New York construction industry, and the rumors probably did him some good. Bullet came through the side window of his Mercedes, took away about a third of his head, hit Carmella, and put her in a coma. Son, Paul, and daughter, Paula, in their late twenties at the time, seemed legitimately broken up, so maybe Dad had some good qualities. This the kind of crap you're looking for?"

"Whatever comes to mind."

"Okay. Second attack. Carl Rotker was heading home to a gated community near Bolton Landing on the west shore of Lake George from his giant plumbing-supply outlet in Schenectady. As was often the case with Carl, his route had been lengthened by a detour to the condo of a Brazilian woman half his age. Carl had his Mercedes sound system cranked way up, playing a Sinatra CD. We know this because the fucking thing was still blasting 'I Did It My Way' when the trooper found the car flipped over next to the road, with most of Carl's blood pooling on the inside of the roof. You want more?"

"As much as you can give me."

"Third one. Ian Sterne was a *very* successful dentist—owner, operator, and chief promoter of a highly profitable practice employing over a dozen professionals on Manhattan's Upper East Side. Orthodontics, cosmetic prosthodontics, maxillofacial and plastic surgery—essentially, a factory that turned out perfect smiles and perfect cheekbones for people eager to trade the money they had for the beauty they lacked. The doctor himself, a wizened little creature, looked like a clever lizard. Had a nice artistic relationship going with a young Russian piano major at Juilliard. Rumors of marriage. Amusing finale—when the big bullet shattered Ian's cerebral cortex and the big black S-Class Mercedes ended up hubcap-deep in a nearby stream, the first thing the first responder saw clearly—just above the water, illuminated by the flashing hazard lights switched on by the impact—was Ian's license plate: A SMILE 4U. Had enough yet?"

"Far from it, Jack. You're a born storyteller."

"Number four. Sharon Stone, hotshot real-estate broker with a helluva name, was heading home to the chic little village of Barkham Dell from a big party with powerful friends in state government. Lived in a gorgeous antique Colonial with her gay twenty-seven-year-old son and a muscular gardener widely rumored to be involved with both mother and son. Ms. Stone was the owner of the misplaced earlobe I told you about before." Hardwick paused, as though waiting for a reaction.

"Onward," said Gurney.

"Five was James Brewster, a big cardiac surgeon. The man's skill, hot rep, and workaholic schedule made him rich, ended his first two marriages, and turned his son into a bitter, off-the-grid recluse who hadn't spoken to him for years and seemed happy that he was dead. On that final night, he was heading from the Albany Medical Center to his home in the gently rolling, genteelly moneyed hills outside Williamstown, Massachusetts. With the cruise control on his Mercedes

AMG coupe set precisely at the speed limit, the doctor was dictating his response to an invitation to keynote an Aspen meeting of cardiac surgeons. The shards of the recording device he was using were spattered with his brains all over the passenger seat of the car. The fact that it happened a couple of miles over the Massachusetts state line was what finally brought the FBI circus to town."

"BCI didn't see that as a big plus?"

This time the laugh sounded tubercular. "Which brings us to the grand finale. Number six. Harold Blum, Esquire, was far from the top of the law profession and, at the age of fifty-five, wasn't about to rise any higher. Harold was the kind of guy who strove to give the impression that all his striving was paying off. According to his wife, Ruthie, who had a lot to say, Harold was the perfect consumer, always making purchases beyond his means, as though those possessions might make a difference—or at least attract a better class of clients. She seemed pretty fond of him. He was on his way that night from his office in Horseheads to his home on Lake Cayuga, driving his gleaming new Mercedes sedan, whose lease payment, the wife said, was already choking him. According to the accident reconstruction, the Good Shepherd, true to form, came up on his left side and fired a single shot. Harold's visual cortex was probably blown to pieces before it could even register the muzzle flash."

"And that's when Max Clinter enters the picture?"

"Enters the picture with tires squealing. Maxie hears the shot that killed Blum loud and clear. He looks out the window of his parked car in time to glimpse Blum's Mercedes skidding onto the shoulder and the taillights of the second vehicle speeding away. So he jams his 320 HP Camaro SS into drive and swerves out from behind a rhododendron bush onto the state road in rubber-burning pursuit of the taillights. Problem is, Max isn't alone, and he isn't sober. Although he's married with three kids, in the passenger seat is a twenty-one-year-old he met an hour earlier in one of Ithaca's college bars and with whom he was having awkward, drunken sex in his car behind the rhododendron. He has the accelerator floored now, the Camaro's doing about a hundred and ten—but he has no plan, no cell phone, no rational idea of where this is going. This is pure, primitive, animal pursuit. The young woman starts to cry. He tells her to shut up. The guy ahead of him is getting away. Maxie's out of his mind now on alcohol, ego, and adrenaline. He reaches under his jacket, pulls out his .40-caliber Glock, lowers his window, and starts firing at the vehicle ahead of him. An insane thing to do. Insanely high-risk, insanely illegal. The girl is screaming, Maxie is losing it completely, the Camaro is fishtailing."

"You sound like you were in the backseat."

"He told the story to a lot of people. It got around. Hell of a story."

"A hell of a career ender, you mean."

"That's the way it turned out. But if Max had gotten lucky and one of those shots had brought the Shepherd down, if no innocent parties had been injured, or if the injuries had been less serious, if his blood-alcohol level hadn't been three times the legal limit . . . maybe the lunacy of firing fifteen shots in eight seconds from a moving vehicle at a poorly defined target on a dark road, occupant or occupants unknown, while proceeding at a recklessly endangering speed . . . maybe all that could have been softened or reexpressed in a way that wouldn't have completely fucked him. But that isn't what happened. What happened was that everything went south at once. As the Camaro fishtailed into the oncoming lane, a motorcyclist came over a blind rise with too little space to get out of the way. The bike went down, rider was thrown. Max's car did a one-eighty at ninety miles an hour, skidding backward on the tarmac and up an embankment into a jutting rock ledge. The impact fractured Max's back in two places, broke the young woman's neck and both her arms, and blasted the windshield into their faces. The Shepherd escaped. Maxie did not escape. That night cost him his career, his marriage, his home, his relationship with his children, his reputation, and, according to some people, his mental and emotional balance. But that's a whole other issue."

"That was a hell of a memory feat, Jack. You ought to donate your brain to science."

"Question is, what are you going to do with the information?"

"I don't know."

"So you called to waste my time?"

"Not exactly. I just have a funny feeling."

"About what?"

"The whole Good Shepherd thing. I feel like I'm missing something. On the one hand, it's all so simple. Shoot the rich guys, make the world a better place. Classic mission-driven nutcase. On the other hand . . ."

"On the other hand, what?"

"I don't know. Something's wrong. Can't put my finger on it."

"Davey boy, I am in awe of you, absolutely in awe." Hardwick was in his snide mode.

"Why is that, Jack?"

"You are aware, no doubt, that what you refer to as 'the whole Good Shepherd thing' has been pondered and repondered, analyzed and reanalyzed by the best and the brightest. Shit, even your hot little psychologist friend had her say."

"What?"

"You didn't know that?"

"Who are you talking about?"

"Shit, now I really am in awe. Exactly how many Ph.D. hotties are you involved with?"

"Jack, I don't know what the hell you're talking about."

"I think Dr. Holdenfield would be hurt by your attitude."

"Rebecca Holdenfield? Are you out of your mind?" Gurney knew he was overreacting—not because of any actual misbehavior on his part but perhaps because he had, during the two cases on which they'd worked together, paid a bit more attention than he should have to the forensic psychologist's undeniable attractiveness.

He also realized that his overreaction had been Hardwick's aim. The man had an exquisite sensitivity to other people's discomforts and a keen appetite for enhancing them.

"Her work is footnoted in the FBI profile of the Good Shepherd," said Hardwick.

"You have a copy of that?"

"Yes and no."

"Meaning?"

"No, because it's an FBI document that they've declared confidential, with controlled distribution on a need-to-know basis, which is a need I don't currently have and therefore I don't officially have access to the profile."

"Wasn't it published in all the big newspapers right after the six murders?"

"An abstract was released to the media, not the profile itself. Our big FBI brothers are touchy about who gets to see the unedited products of their special wisdom. They definitely see themselves as the Deciders, with a capital *D*."

"But would it be possible somehow . . . ?"

"Anything is possible somehow. Given enough time. And motivation. Isn't that like a law of logic?"

Gurney knew Hardwick well enough to know how to play this game. "I wouldn't want you to get in big trouble with the Fucking Blithering Idiots."

A thoughtful silence stretched out between them, pregnant with possibilities. It was finally broken by Hardwick.

"So, Davey boy, there anything else I can do for you today?"

"Sure, Jack. You can shove that 'Davey boy' stuff up your ass."

Hardwick laughed long and hard. Like a tiger with bronchitis.

The man's peculiar saving grace was that he was just as fond of receiving abuse as he was of dishing it out.

It seemed to be his idea of a healthy relationship.

## Chapter 14

# A Strange Visit to an
# Agitated Man

After ending his conversation with Hardwick, Gurney finished what was left of his cold coffee, entered the address Kim had given him for Robby Meese into his GPS, pulled out onto the county route, and headed for Syracuse. He used the drive time to consider ways of approaching the young man—the various interview personas he might adopt. In the end he settled on a semifactual way of presenting himself and the purpose of his visit. Once they were talking, he'd follow the lay of the land and maneuver however he needed to.

The western approach to the city, as much as he could see from the car, was depressing. The area was scarred by dead, dying, and generally ugly industrial and commercial enterprises. Zoning seemed an iffy matter, a patchwork quilt at best. The voice of his GPS directed him off the main route through a neighborhood of small, poorly tended houses that seemed to have had the color, life, and individuality drained out of them long ago. It reminded Gurney of the neighborhood he'd grown up in—a defensive place of narrow achievement, ignorance, racism, and an insular sort of pride. How small a place it had been, small in so many ways, sad in so many ways.

Another instruction from his GPS brought Gurney back to the task at hand. He made a left, went a block, crossed a major thoroughfare, went another block, and found himself in a different sort of neighborhood—one with more trees, bigger houses, neater lawns, cleaner sidewalks. Some of the houses had been divided into apartments, and even these had a well-kept appearance.

The GPS announced his "arrival at destination" as he drove past a large multicolored Victorian. He continued another hundred yards to the end of the block, turned around, and parked on the opposite side of the street in a position from which he could see the porch and the main door.

As he started to get out of the car, his phone emitted its text ring. He stopped and checked it, saw that it was from Kim: PROJECT IS A TOTAL GO!! NEED TO TALK ASAP!! PLEASE!!

Gurney considered "ASAP" a flexible concept, stretchable at least to sometime after his meeting with Meese. He got out of the car and walked down the block to the big Victorian.

The front door opened from the wide porch into a tiled foyer with two more doors. Two mailboxes were mounted on the wall between them. The box on the right was labeled *"R. Montague."* Gurney knocked on the door, waited, knocked again more firmly. There was no response. He took out his phone, found Meese's number, and called it—putting his ear to the door to see if he could hear a ring. There was no detectable sound. When the call went into voice mail, he broke the connection and returned to his car.

He reclined the seat a few inches and relaxed. Then he spent the next hour skimming through the lengthy incident reports and supplementary annexes describing the movements of the victims in the hours prior to the shootings. He was immersing himself in the details, instinctively scanning for anything striking, anything the original investigators might have missed in that mass of data.

Nothing jumped out. There were no conspicuous connections among the victims, nor any conspicuous similarities beyond a certain level of financial ability, a shared preference for the Mercedes brand, and a primary or secondary residence within a certain fifty-mile-by-two-hundred-mile rectangle. Beyond their occupational facts, next of kin, and movements the night of each shooting, not much background information had been gathered on the victims themselves—understandably, in a case in which the obvious victim-selection criterion turned out to be their vehicle. If the Mercedes badge was the shooter's target, it mattered little who wore it or where they'd gone to high school.

*But what did I expect to find? And what is it about the Good Shepherd murders that's making me so damn itchy?*

Not only was he itchy, he was thirsty. Gurney remembered seeing some kind of store a block or two back on the main drag. He locked the car and headed for it on foot. It turned out to be a shabby grocery store with high prices, no customers, dusty shelves, and an unpleasant odor. The drinks cooler smelled of sour milk, although there was no milk in it. Gurney bought a bottle of water, paid the bored counter girl, and got out of there as quickly as possible.

Back in the car, as he was opening the water, his phone rang. It was another text from Hardwick: CHECK YOUR E-MAIL. TGS PROFILE. NOTE REFERENCE TO THE BEAUTIFUL BECCA.

He retrieved the e-mail, opened the attachment, and read slowly.

The Federal Bureau of Investigation
Critical Incidents Response Group
National Center for the Analysis of Violent Crime
Behavioral Analysis Unit-2

## ACCESS: RESTRICTED, NCAVC, CODE B-7

Criminal Investigative Analysis Service Category: Offender Profile
Date: April 25, 2000
Subject: Unknown
Alias: "The Good Shepherd"

Conclusions based on inductive and deductive profiling methodologies, employing factual, physical, historical, linguistic, and psychological analyses of unsub's "Memorandum of Intent"; forensic study of crime-scene evidence, photographic documentation, timing, and organization; and victim-selection criteria.

## SUMMARY OPINION REGARDING UNKNOWN SUBJECT

Unsub is a white male, mid-twenties to late thirties, college graduate with possible postgraduate education, exceptional intelligence. Excellent cognitive functioning.

Unsub is polite, introverted, formal in his manner and social interactions. He is controlling in relationships, with a low capacity for intimacy. He is a compulsive perfectionist with no close friends.

He is well coordinated, with good reflexes. He may exercise regularly in a private setting. He would be seen as self-contained and methodical. He is skilled in the use of a handgun and may be a gun collector or target shooter.

His vocabulary is subtle and precise. Syntax and punctuation are flawless, with no ethnic or regional traits. This may be the result of a cosmopolitan education or broad cultural exposure, or the result of an effort to obliterate the evidence and memories of his upbringing.

Noteworthy are the employment of biblical cadences and avenging imagery in his condemnation of greed, his choice of "The Good Shepherd" as his form of identification, and the placement of the Noah's Ark animals at attack locations. The religious context—in which white (light) represents good and black (darkness) represents evil—may explain the targeting of black vehicles, underscoring the equivalence of wealth with evil.

His preparation and execution are highly organized. The attack locales indicate careful reconnaissance—all situated on roads commonly used as connecting arteries between main highways and upscale communities (i.e., promising areas for him to find his target victims). The roads are all unlit, thinly populated, with no tollgate or other surveillance-camera positions.

All attacks were carried out on leftward curves. All of the victim vehicles, subsequent to the shootings, exited the pavement on the right side. The evident reason being driver incapacitation resulting in the relaxation of purposeful leftward pressure on the steering wheel, resulting in the car's tendency to drift from the direction of the turn back to a straighter line of movement. The further consequence would be for the disabled (unsteered) vehicle to move *away* from the shooter's vehicle (which would be in the lane to the left of the target at the moment of the shot), thus minimizing the chance of a collision. The level of foresight and timing in this process would place our unsub among the most organized of killers.

MOTIVATION LEVEL-1: Unsub's stated rationale for attacks is the injustice inherent in the unequal distribution of wealth. He claims that the cause of this inequity is the vice of greed and that greed can be eliminated only by eliminating the greedy. He conflates greed with the ownership of a super-luxury vehicle and has chosen Mercedes as the archetype of that vehicle, making it the identifying characteristic of his target victims.

MOTIVATION LEVEL-2: The Good Shepherd case appears to be one in which a classic psychoanalytic formulation may apply: an underlying oedipal rage against a powerful and abusive father. Throughout his Memorandum of Intent, the unsub repeatedly conflates greed, wealth, and power. Also supporting the psychoanalytic interpretation, the unsub's choice of weapon (one of the world's largest handguns) has unavoidable phallic implications and is an obvious marker for this type of pathology.

NOTE: An objection might be raised to the father-hatred motivation, based on the inclusion of a woman among the victims. However, Sharon Stone was exceptionally tall for a woman, had her hair styled in a unisex crew cut, and was wearing a black leather jacket. Viewed at night through her vehicle's side window with only faint dashboard illumination outlining her face, she may have presented a visual impression that appeared more male than female. It may also be that the unsub's single criterion was the luxury vehicle itself, making the gender of the driver irrelevant.

The document concluded with a list of related journal articles in fields such as forensic linguistics, psychometrics, and psychopathology. That was followed by a list of professional books by heavily credentialed Ph.D. authors: *The Sublimation of Rage, Sexual Repression and Violence, Family Structure and Societal Attitudes, Pathologies Fostered by Abuse, Societal Crusades as Expressions of Early Trauma,* and, last on the list . . . *Mission-Driven Serial Murder* by Rebecca Holdenfield, Ph.D.

After staring for a long moment at that final familiar name, Gurney scrolled back to the beginning of the document and read the whole thing through one more time—doing his best to keep an open mind. It was difficult. The less-than-scientific conclusions wrapped in scientific language, and the overall academic smugness of the writing, triggered the same argumentative feelings in him that were triggered by every profile he read.

In his over two decades of homicide experience, he'd discovered that profiles were occasionally dead-on, occasionally dead wrong, but mostly a mixed bag. You never knew until the game was over whether you had a good one, and, of course, if the game never ended, you ended up never knowing.

But it wasn't just the fallibility of profiles that bothered him. It was the failure of many of their creators and users to recognize that fallibility.

He wondered why he'd been so eager to read this one, why it couldn't wait till later, seeing that he had so little faith in the art. Was it just the combative mood he was in? The desire to pick holes in something, to argue about something?

He shook his head, disgusted with himself. How many pointless questions could he come up with? How many angels could dance on the head of a pin?

He sat back and closed his eyes.

He opened them with a start.

The dashboard clock said it was 5:55 P.M. He looked down the street at the house where Meese lived. The sun was low in the sky, and the house was now in the shadow of the giant maple in front of it.

He got out of his car and walked the hundred yards or so to the house. He went to Meese's door and listened. Some kind of techno music was playing. He knocked. There was no response. Again he knocked, again no response.

He took out his phone, blocked the ID, and called Meese's number. To his surprise, it was picked up on the second ring.

"This is Robert." The voice was smooth, actorish.

"Hello, Robert. This is Dave."

"Dave?"

"We need to talk."

"Sorry? Do I know you?" The voice had tightened a bit.

"Hard to say, Robert. Maybe you know me, maybe you don't. Why don't you open your door and take a look at me?"

"I beg your pardon?"

"Your door, Robert. I'm outside your door. Waiting."

"I don't understand. Who are you? Where do I know you from?"

"We have friends in common. But don't you think it's kind of stupid to be talking on the phone when you're right there and I'm right here?"

"Wait a second." The voice was confused, anxious. The connection was broken. Then the music stopped. A minute later the door was opened tentatively, not quite halfway.

"What do you want?" The young man who asked the question was standing partly behind the door, using it as a kind of a shield or, Gurney thought, as a way of concealing whatever he was holding in his left hand. He was about the same height as Gurney, just under six feet.

He was slim, with finely cut features, tousled dark hair, and shockingly blue movie-star eyes. Only one thing marred the picture of perfection: a sour look around the mouth, a hint of something nasty, something spiteful.

"Hello, Mr. Montague. My name is Dave Gurney."

There was an infinitesimal tremor in the young man's eyelids.

"Is that a familiar name to you?" asked Gurney.

"Should it be?"

"You looked like you recognized it."

The tremor continued. "What do you want?"

Gurney decided to follow a low-risk strategy, one that he found particularly useful when he was uncertain how much a target subject knew about him. The strategy was to stick to the facts but play with the tone. Manipulate the undercurrents.

"What do I want? Good question, Robert." He smiled meaninglessly, speaking with the world-weariness of a hit man whose arthritis was acting up. "That depends on what the situation is. To start with, I need some advice. You see, I'm trying to decide whether to accept a job I've been offered, and if I do, what the terms ought to be. You familiar with a woman by the name of Connie Clarke?"

"I'm not sure. Why?"

"You're not sure? You think maybe you know her, but not definitely? I don't get that."

"The name is familiar, that's all."

"Ah. I see. Anything come to mind when I tell you her daughter's name is Kim Corazon?"

He blinked rapidly. "Who the hell are you? What's this about?"

"Can I come in, Mr. Montague? This is pretty personal stuff to be talking about in a doorway."

"No, you can't." He shifted his weight slightly, his left hand still out of view. "Please get to the point."

Gurney sighed, scratched his shoulder in a vaguely absent way, and fixed a dead stare on Robby Meese. "The thing is, I've been asked to provide personal security for Ms. Corazon, and I'm trying to decide how much to charge."

"Charge? I don't . . . I mean . . . I don't see . . . What?"

"The thing is, I want to be fair. If I don't really have to do anything—if I just have to hang around, keep my eyes open, be ready to handle what comes along—then that's one kind of fee schedule. But if the situation requires, shall we say, preemptive action, then that's another kind of fee schedule. You get my question here, Bobby?"

The eyelid tremor seemed to be getting worse. "Are you threatening me?"

"Am I *threatening* you? Why would I do that? Threatening you would be against the law. As a retired police officer, I have great respect for the law. Some of my best friends are police officers. Some of them are right here in Syracuse. Jimmy Schiff, for example. You might know him. Anyway, the thing is, I always like to do a fee analysis before I commit to a job. You can understand that, right? So let me ask you again: Do you know of any reason why my provision of personal security services to Ms. Corazon would require me to charge anything more than my normal fee?"

Meese started getting a shaky look in his eyes. "What the hell am I supposed to know about her *security* problems? What's this got to do with *me*?"

"You've got a good point there, Bobby. You look like a nice young man, very handsome young man, who would never want to cause anybody any trouble. Am I right?"

"I'm not the one causing trouble."

Gurney nodded slowly, waited, feeling the current shifting.

Meese bit his lower lip. "We had a great relationship. I didn't want it to end the way it did. These stupid accusations. False charges. Lies. Defamation of character. Bullshit complaints to the police. Now you. I don't even understand what you're here for."

"I told you what I'm here for."

"But it doesn't make any sense. You shouldn't be bothering me. You should be visiting the scumbags she brought into her life. If she has security problems, it's because of them."

"Who would these scumbags be?"

Meese laughed. It was a wild, caroming sound. A theatrical sound effect. "Did you know she's fucking her professor, her so-called academic adviser? Did you know she's fucking everybody who could possibly advance her trashy career? Did you know she's fucking Rudy Getz, the biggest scumbag in the whole fucking world? Did you know she's completely fucking crazy? Did you know that?" Meese seemed to be riding an emotional horse that was getting away from him.

Gurney wanted to keep it going, see where it would lead. "No, I didn't know any of that. But I'm grateful for the information, Robert. I didn't realize she was crazy. And that's the kind of thing that could affect my fee schedule, big-time. Providing security for a crazy woman can be a huge fucking pain in the ass. How crazy would you say she is?"

Meese shook his head. "You'll find out. I'm not saying another word. You'll find out. You know where I was this afternoon? At my attorney's office. We're taking legal action against that bitch. My advice to you is to stay away from her. Far away." He slammed the door.

The slam was followed by the sound of two locks snapping in place.

It might all be an act, thought Gurney, but it sure as hell was an interesting one.

## Chapter 15

# Escalation

As Gurney followed the directions of his GPS back toward the interstate, the murky reflection of a fuchsia sunset was spreading across Onondaga Lake. On just about any other upstate body of water, it might have been beautiful. What lurks in the backs of our minds, however, has a profound effect on the way we process the data our optic nerves transmit. Thus what Gurney saw was not a reflected sunset but the imagined hell of a chemical fire burning on the toxic lake bed fifty feet below the surface.

He was aware that remediation efforts were addressing the damage to the lake. But this movement in the right direction made little difference in how he saw the place. In an odd way, it made it worse. Like seeing a guy coming out of an AA meeting makes his problem look more serious than seeing him coming out of a bar.

A few minutes after he got on I-81, Gurney's phone rang. The ID was from his home landline. He glanced at the time. It was 6:58 P.M. Madeleine would have been home from her part-time job at the clinic for at least three-quarters of an hour. He felt a little stab of guilt.

"Hi, sorry, I should have called," he said quickly.

"Where are you?" She sounded more concerned than annoyed.

"Between Syracuse and Binghamton. I should be home a bit after eight."

"You were with that Clinter fellow that long?"

"With him, with Jack Hardwick on the phone, in my car with case documents Hardwick e-mailed me, with Kim Corazon's ex-boyfriend, et cetera, et cetera."

"The stalker?"

"I'm not sure what he is. For that matter I'm not sure what Clinter is either."

"What you told me last night made him sound dangerously unstable."

"Yeah, well, he might be. Then again . . ."

"You'd better pay attention to—"

Gurney had driven into a cell dead zone. The connection was broken. He decided to wait for her to call him back. He stood the phone upright in one of the drink holders in the console. Less than a minute later, it rang.

"The last thing I heard you say," he began, "was that I'd better pay attention to something."

"Hello?"

"I'm here. We were in a dead spot."

"I'm sorry—what did you say?" It was a female voice, but not Madeleine's.

"Oh, sorry, I thought it was someone else."

"Dave? This is Kim. Are you in the middle of something?"

"That's all right. By the way, sorry I didn't get back to you. What's happening?"

"You got my message? That RAM is going ahead with the first installment?"

"Something like that. 'Project is a total go,' I think is what you said."

"The first show will air this Sunday. I had no idea it would happen so fast. They're using the rough demo material I shot with Ruth Blum, just like Rudy Getz said. And they want me to proceed with as many more interviews as we can do with the other families. The series will run on consecutive Sundays."

"So things are moving ahead the way you were hoping?"

"Definitely."

"But?"

"Oh, I don't have any reservations about that. That's all great."

"But?"

"But . . . I have a . . . a silly little problem here."

"Yes?"

"The lights. They're out again."

"The lights in your apartment?"

"Yes. I told you about the time all the bulbs were loosened?"

"That's been done again?"

"No. I checked the lamp in the living room, and the bulb is tight. So I guess it must be the circuit breaker. But there's no way I'm going down in the basement to check it."

"Have you called anybody?"

"They don't consider this an emergency."

"Who doesn't?"

"The police. They *might* be able to ask somebody to drop by later. But I shouldn't count on it. Circuit breakers are not a police matter, they said. I should call the landlord, or a maintenance person, or an electrician, or a friendly neighbor, or, apparently, anybody but them."

"Did you?"

"Call my landlord? Sure. Got his voice mail. God only knows if or when he checks it. Maintenance guy? Sure. But he's down in Cortland working at another building owned by the same guy. Says it's ridiculous for him to drive clear up to Syracuse to flip a circuit breaker. No way he's going to do that. The electrician I called wants a hundred-fifty-dollar minimum to come to the house. And I don't have any *friendly* neighbors." She paused. "So that's . . . my silly little problem. Any advice?"

"Are you in your apartment now?"

"No. I came back out. I'm in my car. It's getting dark, and I don't want to be in there with no lights. I'd keep thinking about the basement and what could be down there."

"Any chance you could go back home, stay at your mother's until things get sorted out?"

"No!" Her response was as angry as the last time he'd raised the issue. "That's not my home anymore—*this* is my home. I'm not running off like a frightened little girl to my mommy, just because some asshole is playing games with me."

But a frightened little girl is exactly what she sounded like to

Gurney. A frightened little girl trying to act the way she thought a grown-up would act. The image filled him with an almost painful feeling of anxiety and responsibility.

"Okay," he said, impulsively moving into the right lane and onto an exit ramp at the last second. "Stay where you are. I can be there in twenty minutes."

After driving most of the way at eighty miles an hour, nineteen minutes later he was back in Syracuse on Kim Corazon's run-down block, parked across the street from her apartment. Dusk had slipped into night, and Gurney hardly recognized the place he'd seen in the daylight two days earlier. He reached into his glove box and took out a heavy black metal flashlight.

As he walked across the street, Kim got out of her car. She looked jittery and embarrassed.

"I feel so stupid." She crossed her arms tightly, as though she were trying not to shiver.

"Why?"

"Because it's like I'm afraid of the dark. Afraid of my own apartment. I feel terrible, making you turn around like that."

"Turning around was my idea. You want to wait out here while I take a look inside?"

"No! I'm not a complete infant. I'm coming in with you."

Gurney remembered having this conversation before and decided not to argue.

Both the front door of the house and Kim's apartment door were unlocked. They went inside, Gurney first, his flashlight illuminating the way. When he came to a set of switches on the hallway wall, he flipped them up and down with no effect. At the living-room door, he swept the flashlight around the space. He did the same at the doors to the bathroom and bedroom before moving on to the last room off the hall——the kitchen.

Moving the beam slowly around the room, he asked, "Did you check the place at all before you went back out to your car?"

"Really quick-like. I hardly looked into the kitchen at all. And I definitely didn't go near the basement door. I know that the switch for the ceiling light didn't work. The only other thing I noticed was that the time display on the microwave was off. Which means the problem must be the circuit breaker, right?"

"That would be my guess."

He stepped into the kitchen with Kim very close behind him, her hand on his back in the semidarkness. The only light came from the shifting reflections of the flashlight beam off the walls and appliances. He heard what sounded like a faint tap. He stopped and listened. He heard it again a few seconds later and realized it was nothing more than a slow drip in the metal sink.

He went forward quietly, in the direction of the rear hallway that led from the kitchen to the basement stairs and the rear door of the house. Kim's hand moved from his back to his arm, gripping it firmly. When he got to the hallway, he could see that the door to the basement was closed. The exterior door at the end of the hallway appeared secure, with the dead bolt's twist knob in its locked position. The sound of the water drip from the kitchen behind him seemed to be captured and amplified by the enclosed space.

When he reached the basement door and was about to open it, Kim's fingers dug into the back of his arm.

"Take it easy," he said softly.

"Sorry." She loosened her grip, but not much.

He opened the door, shining the light down the stairs, listening.

Drip . . . drip . . .

Nothing else.

He turned back toward Kim. "Stay right here at the door."

She looked terrified.

He searched for something to say—something pedestrian, maybe a distracting question—to calm her down. "The electrical service box . . . does it have one main circuit breaker in addition to the breakers for all the individual circuits?"

"What?"

"Just wondering what kind of box it is that I'll be dealing with."

"What kind? I have no idea. Is that a problem?"

"No, not at all. If I need a screwdriver, I'll call up to you, okay?" He knew that all this was irrelevant, no doubt confusing to her, but confusion was better at this point than a panic attack.

He descended the stairs carefully, sweeping the light back and forth.

Everything seemed perfectly still.

Then, just as the thought came to mind that a banister would be a wise addition to the rickety staircase structure—just as he was placing his weight on the third stair tread from the bottom—there was a sharp crack, the tread collapsed, and Gurney pitched forward.

It all happened in less than a second.

His right foot descended along with the broken tread into empty space as his body pivoted forward and downward, his arms rising instinctively to protect his face and head.

He crashed onto the concrete floor at the base of the stairs. The lens of the flashlight shattered, the light went out. A sharp pain shot like an electrical shock through the bone of his right forearm.

Kim was screaming. Hysterical. Asking if was he all right. Footsteps retreating, running, stumbling.

Gurney was stunned but conscious.

He was about to try some tentative movements, assess the physical damage.

But before his muscles could respond, he heard a sound that raised the hairs on his neck. It was a whisper, very close to his ear. A whisper harsh and sibilant. A whisper that hissed like the hiss of a furious cat:

"Let the devil sleep."

# Part Two

# In the Absence
## of Justice

# Chapter 16

# Doubts

When Gurney awoke the next morning at home, he was anxious and exhausted, with a deeply burning sensation in his right forearm and a painful stiffness through his whole body. The bedroom windows were open, and there was a damp chill in the air.

Madeleine was already up, as usual. She liked getting up with the birds. There seemed to be a secret ingredient in the first light of dawn that energized her.

His feet were cold and sweaty. The world outside the windows was gray. It was a long time since he'd had a hangover, but he felt like he had one now. He'd had a miserably restless night. Recollections of the events in Kim's basement, the discoveries he'd made after his fall, and the hypotheses they suggested kept racing around in his head without coherence or conclusion, twisted and derailed by his multiple aches. He'd finally fallen asleep just before dawn. Now, two hours later, he was awake again. His level of mental agitation told him that further sleep would be impossible.

The urgent imperative was to organize and understand what had happened. He went over it all one more time, reaching into his memory for as much detail as possible.

He recalled stepping cautiously down the stairs, using his flashlight to illuminate not only the staircase but the basement areas to the right and left of it. No hint of any sound or movement. When he was still several steps from the bottom, he'd swept the beam in a wide arc around the walls to locate the electrical panel. It was a gray metal box, mounted on a wall not far from the ominous chest where the bloodstains had led him two days earlier. The darkened stains were still clearly visible on the wooden steps and on the concrete floor.

He remembered stepping down onto the next stair tread, then hearing and feeling the startling snap of it giving way under his foot. The beam of his flashlight had swung in a wild arc as his hands flew out reflexively in front of his face. He knew he was falling, knew he couldn't stop it, knew it would be bad. Half a second later, his arms, right shoulder, chest, and the side of his head collided brutally with the basement floor.

There was a scream from the top of the stairs. First a pure scream, then two screamed questions: *"Are you all right? What happened?"*

For a moment he was dazed, unable to answer. Then, somewhere, he couldn't tell in what direction, he heard what sounded like the scramble of feet running, maybe bumping into a wall, maybe tripping, running again.

He had tried to move. But the whisper, so close by, had stopped him.

It was a feverish sound, more animal than human, the words hissing out under pressure, like steam escaping through clenched teeth.

He'd reached for his ankle holster, pulled out the Beretta, lay there in the silent darkness, listening. The situation was so deeply unnerving that he had little recollection of the time interval that elapsed—thirty seconds, a minute, two minutes or more—before Kim returned with her Mini Maglite, the beam much brighter than it had been when they'd used it to examine the chest at the end of the bloodstain trail.

She'd started down the stairs just as he was getting shakily to his feet, hot pain shooting from his wrist to his elbow, legs unsteady. He told her not to come any further, simply shine the light on the stairs. Then he climbed up to her as quickly as he was able to, almost losing his balance twice from dizziness. He took the flashlight from her, turned around, and covered as much of the basement floor as he could see from that position.

He'd moved down two more steps, gun in one hand, flashlight in the other, and repeated the back-and-forth searching movement with the narrow beam. Another two steps . . . and then he was able to sweep the beam around the entire basement space—floors, walls, steel support columns, ceiling beams. Still no sign of the whisperer. Nothing was upset, nothing in disarray, no movement other than the eerie shadows of the support columns moving across the cinder-block walls as he angled the little Maglite.

When he reached the basement floor, steadily sweeping the beam around him, he'd concluded—with as much bafflement as relief—that there were no nooks, no hiding places, no dark corners where a man could hide from the light. With the possible exception of the chest, the basement offered no apparent opportunities for concealment.

He'd asked Kim, hovering in nervous silence at the top of the stairs, if she'd heard anything after he fell.

"Like what?"

"A voice . . . a whisper . . . anything like that?"

"No. No, what do you mean?" she'd asked with rising alarm.

"Nothing, I just . . ." He shook his head. "I was probably just hearing my own breathing." Then he asked if the running footsteps had been hers.

She said yes, probably yes, she probably ran, at least she thought she had, maybe sort of stumbled, walked fast, maybe—couldn't actually remember, being in a panic—feeling her way to the bedroom, where she kept her flashlight on her night table. "Why do you ask?"

"Just checking my impressions," he said vaguely.

He didn't want to speculate aloud on the alternate possibility that the intruder had bounded up the staircase out of the basement as Kim was on her way to her bedroom, had made use of the dark to conceal himself, was perhaps at some point within inches of her, and when she came back had slipped past her out of the house.

But wherever he'd gone, however he'd gotten out—assuming he *had* gotten out and wasn't crouching in the chest—what sense did it make? Why was he in the basement to begin with? Could it conceivably have been Robby Meese? Logistically, it was possible. But what was the purpose?

All this had been going through Gurney's mind at the foot of the stairs, as he held the beam of the flashlight on the chest, trying to decide what to do next.

Rather than deal with whomever or whatever the chest might

contain with no light other than what was in his hand, he'd called up to Kim, telling her to flip the light switch at the top of the stairs to the ON position—even though he knew it would make no immediate difference. Shining his little beam alternately on the chest and on the main electrical panel, he made his way to the panel. Tucking the flashlight under his arm, he opened the metal door and saw that the main breaker at the top was in the OFF position. He flipped the stiff plastic switch in the opposite direction.

The bare bulb in the basement ceiling had come on immediately. What sounded like a refrigerator motor upstairs began to hum. He heard Kim say, "Thank God!"

He glanced quickly around the basement, confirming there was indeed nowhere anyone could hide but inside the chest.

He walked over to it, fear and gooseflesh dissipated now by anger and an appetite for confrontation. A touch of caution told him not to lift the lid but to roll the chest over. He stuffed the Maglite in his jacket pocket, gripped the corner of the chest, and yanked it over onto its side, discovering from the ease of doing so that it was empty—a fact he confirmed by kicking the top open.

Kim was halfway down the stairs now and peering around the basement like a scared cat. Her gaze stopped at the broken step. "You could have been killed," she said, wide-eyed, as though the implications of the accident had only then occurred to her. "It broke, just like that, when you stepped on it?"

"Just like that," he said.

As she examined with a kind of horror the place where he'd fallen, he was touched by something fundamentally naïve in her expression. This young woman who was putting together an ambitious documentary on the horrific impact of murder seemed startled by the notion that life could be perilous.

Following her gaze, he, too, looked down at the break in the wood—and quickly noticed what she had either failed to see or failed to grasp the meaning of. The stair tread, prior to breaking, had been sawed almost completely through on both ends.

When he pointed this out to her, she'd frowned in apparent confusion. "What do you mean? How could that be?"

All he'd said was, "One more mystery to add to the others."

• • •

Now, as he lay in his bed, gazing up at the ceiling, massaging his arm without much effect, reconstructing the previous night's chain of events, he thought that answer through in more detail.

The sabotage was likely the work of the whispering intruder, Kim was likely the intended victim, and perhaps he, Gurney, had simply gotten in the way.

Booby-trapping a staircase by partially sawing through one of the treads was a crime-movie cliché. One that would be hard to miss. The easily detectable saw marks would make it clear that the step hadn't broken by accident—meaning that the saw marks themselves were almost certainly intended to be discovered. In that sense they would be an integral part of the warning.

Perhaps the choice of a low step was part of the warning also—designed to cause a nasty fall but not as bad a fall, say, as one might have from a higher step. Not a fatal fall. Not yet.

The message might be as explicit as, If you ignore my warnings, they'll get more violent. More painful. More deadly.

But what, precisely, was Kim being warned away from? The obvious answer was her murder documentary, since it was the biggest thing going on in her life. Maybe the message was, *Back away, Kim, stop digging into the past, or the consequences will be terrible. There's a devil buried in the Good Shepherd case, and you'd better not wake him.*

Did that mean that the intruder was someone connected with that famous case? Someone with a serious vested interest in things staying as they were?

Or was it, as Kim had been insisting, only rotten little Robby Meese?

Was it credible that all the recent interferences in her life, the assaults on her peace of mind, had been orchestrated by a pathetic ex-boyfriend? Was he that morbidly bitter at Kim's ending their relationship? Could everything—the loosened bulbs, missing knives, bloodstains, sawed step, even the demonic whisper—have been motivated by pure jealousy, pure vindictiveness at being cast aside?

On the other hand, maybe the perpetrator was indeed Meese, but maybe the young man was driven by a motivation darker and sicker than spite. Maybe he was warning Kim that unless she took him back, his resentment would grow into something truly awful. Unless she took him back, he'd become a monster, a devil.

Maybe Meese's inner life was more pathological than Kim realized.

The intensity of that whisper seemed pathological beyond question.

But that raised yet another possibility. It was the possibility that scared Gurney most of all. A possibility he hardly dared consider.

The possibility that there was no whisper.

Suppose what he'd "heard" was the result of his fall, a kind of mini-hallucination? Suppose the "sound" was merely a by-product of the jarring of his barely healed head wound? After all, the low, whistling tinnitus in his ears was not a real whistle; as Dr. Huffbarger had explained, it was a cognitive misinterpretation of a misplaced neural agitation. Suppose the whispered threat—with all its seething fury—had no real-world substance? The idea that sights and sounds might be nothing more than the offspring of bruised tissues and disrupted synapses sent a shiver through him.

Perhaps it was an unconscious insecurity about the whisper that had kept him from mentioning it to the patrol officer who'd come to Kim's apartment in response to the 911 call he'd made after discovering the tread-sawing evidence. And perhaps that same insecurity had kept him from mentioning the whisper to Schiff when he'd arrived there half an hour later.

It was difficult at the time to decipher Schiff's expression. One thing was clear: There was no joy in it. He kept looking at Gurney as if he sensed that some part of the story was missing. Then the skeptical detective had turned his attention to Kim, asking her a string of questions designed to pin down a time window in which the vandalism could have occurred.

"That's what you're calling this?" Gurney had interjected the second time Schiff used the term. "Vandalism?"

"For now, yeah," said Schiff blandly. "You have a problem with that?"

"Painful form of vandalism," said Gurney, slowly rubbing his forearm.

"You want an ambulance?"

Before Gurney could answer, Kim said, "I'm going to drive him to the ER."

"That so?" asked Schiff, his eyes on Gurney.

"Sounds good to me."

Schiff stared at him for a moment, then said to the patrol officer who was standing in the background, "Make a note that Mr. Gurney declined ambulance transportation."

Gurney smiled. "So how are we doing on those cameras?"

Schiff gave the impression that he hadn't heard the question.

Gurney shrugged. "Yesterday would have been a good day to install them."

There was a flash of anger in Schiff's eyes. He took a final look around the basement, muttered something about lifting prints the following day from the circuit panel, asked about the chest turned on its side, peered into it.

Eventually he picked up the sawed step and took it upstairs with him, then spent the next ten minutes examining the apartment's windows and doors. He asked Kim whether she'd had any unusual communications in the past few days, or any communications at all from Meese. Finally he asked how he could gain access to the apartment the following day, if he needed to. Then he left, trailed by the patrol officer.

*Chapter 17*

# A Simple Initiative

The bedroom ceiling seemed a little brighter now, the sheet covering Gurney a little warmer. He felt satisfied that his sequential reconstruction of the previous evening's affair was reasonably complete and orderly. Its significance, causes, purposes, motivations were yet to be determined. But at least he was starting to feel that he was on a path.

He closed his eyes.

He was awakened minutes later by the phone, followed by footsteps. It was picked up at the end of the fourth ring. He heard Madeleine's voice, indistinctly, coming from the den. A few sentences, silence, then footsteps again. He thought she might be bringing the phone to him. Someone asking for him. Huffbarger, the neurologist? He thought back on the testy exchange with the doctor's office person. Christ, when was that? Two or three days ago? Seemed like forever.

The footsteps passed the bedroom door, went out to the kitchen.

Female voices.

Madeleine and Kim.

Kim had driven him to Walnut Crossing after taking him to the emergency room in Syracuse. He hadn't been able to grip the gearshift in his Outback without a red-hot stabbing sensation in his elbow—giving him the idea that his arm might be fractured and that trying to shift with it might not be smart—and Kim had seemed more than happy for an excuse to spend the night someplace other than in her apartment.

He recalled how she'd emphasized that it wouldn't be safe for him to drive himself—even after the X-rays had shown that there was no fracture.

There was something about Kim's attitude, her way of presenting herself to the world, that made him smile. She could gladly leave her apartment on a mission of mercy, but never because she'd been driven away by fear.

He forced himself out of bed—discovering new muscle aches as he did so. He took four ibuprofens and got into a hot shower.

The shower and pills performed, to some degree, their restorative magic. By the time he was dried off and dressed and out by the kitchen coffeemaker, pouring his vital first cup, he was feeling a bit better. He flexed the fingers of his right hand, found that the pain was tolerable. He squeezed the coffee cup. Despite the wince it produced, he concluded that he could manage his gearshift if he needed to drive. It wouldn't be comfortable, but he wasn't helpless.

There was no sign of either Madeleine or Kim in the house. He could hear a low murmur of voices through an open window by the sideboard. He took his cup to the breakfast table by the French doors. Then he saw them, out beyond the bluestone patio, beyond the overgrown apple tree, in the small mowed area of the field that he and Madeleine referred to as "the lawn."

They were sitting in a pair of matching Adirondack chairs. Madeleine was wearing one of her wildly colorful jackets, and Kim was wearing a similar one—no doubt provided by Madeleine. They were each cradling a coffee mug in a two-handed grip, as though warming their fingers around a pleasant flame. The lavenders and fuchsias and oranges and lime greens of their jackets were radiant in the pale morning sunlight beginning to filter through the overcast. Their expressions suggested that their conversation, like their clothing, was more animated than Gurney's mood.

He was tempted to open the French doors to see if the sun was taking any of the chill out of the atmosphere. But he knew that as soon as Madeleine saw him, she'd tell him he should come out, tell him what a lovely morning it was turning out to be after all, tell him how sweet everything smelled. And the more she'd rhapsodize about the glory of being out in the open air, the more he'd insist on staying in. It was a ritual battle they often fought, virtually reading their lines from a script. In the end, after making it clear he was too busy to come out, he'd inevitably reconsider, and, once out, inevitably he'd be pleased by the beauty of the day and embarrassed by his childish opposition.

At the moment, however, he had no desire to initiate the ritual. So he chose not to open the door. Instead he decided to get a second cup of coffee, print out a hard copy of the Good Shepherd profile, and try to approach it with an open mind: a mind open to the possible presence of truth, rather than a mind hypervigilant for the presence of bullshit.

He went into the den and opened the Hardwick e-mails on his desktop computer, a welcome improvement over the tiny screen of his cell phone. While the profile was printing out, he opened the first of the incident-report documents that he'd hurried through the previous afternoon.

He wasn't sure what he was looking for. He was still at the stage when the important thing was to look at everything, absorb as much data as he could. The decisions about what was significant, the search for patterns—that would come later.

He realized he'd been in too much of a rush the first time. He needed to slow down. He'd discovered over the years that one of the most destructive errors a detective can make is to leap to a possible pattern with too little data. Because once you think you see a pattern, there's an inclination to dismiss data that doesn't fit into it. The brain's natural affinity for pattern formation devalues dots that don't contribute to the picture. Add to that a detective's professional need to grasp the outline of a situation quickly, and the result is a tendency to jump to premature conclusions.

The period of simple *looking, listening, absorbing* had tremendous value. Giving that period its full due was always the best way to begin an investigation.

Begin an investigation?

Begin an investigation of what, exactly? At whose request? With what legal authorization? In potential collision with Schiff and who else?

He decided to simplify the matter—or at least detoxify the terminology—by thinking of it as nothing more than a private fact-finding initiative, a modest effort to answer a few questions. Questions such as:

Who was behind the original "pranks" that had disturbed Kim?

Which was closer to the truth—Kim's characterization of Meese or his characterization of her?

Who set the vicious little trap that had thrown him to the basement floor? Was he the intended victim or was Kim?

If the whisper had been real, who was the whisperer? Why was he lurking in the basement? How and when had he gotten into the house, and how had he gotten away?

What was the meaning of the warning "Let the devil sleep"?

And what, if anything, did these present events have to do with a ten-year-old series of roadway murders?

Gurney envisioned his fact-finding initiative beginning with a review of everything in the incident reports, the report annexes, the ViCAP reports, the FBI profile, the status reports in Kim's project folder, and the notes he'd taken while listening to Hardwick's acerbic summaries of the victims' personalities.

All of that he could address by himself. But he also felt a growing urge to sit down with Rebecca Holdenfield and delve more deeply into the Good Shepherd profile and the case hypothesis—how the primary data was gathered, analyzed, prioritized; how theoretical alternatives had been tested; how consensus had emerged; and whether any beliefs she had about the case had changed over the years. He was also curious to know whether she'd ever spoken to Max Clinter.

Gurney still had Holdenfield's number in his cell phone. (They'd collaborated briefly on the Mark Mellery and Jillian Perry cases, and he'd imagined they might cross paths again.) He brought the number up on the screen and placed the call. It went into her voice mail.

He listened to a lengthy introductory message regarding her office hours and location, website, and the e-mail address to which inquiries could be sent. The sound of her voice conjured up an image of the woman. Tough, brainy, athletic, and ambitious. Her facial features were perfect without being pretty. Her eyes were striking, intense, but lacked the warmth that might have made them beautiful. She was a driven professional whose therapy practice filled whatever time was left over from her primary career in forensic psychology.

He left a terse message that he hoped would intrigue her. "Hi, Rebecca. This is Dave Gurney. Hope all is well. I'm involved in an unusual situation that I'd like to discuss with you, get your insight and advice. It involves the Good Shepherd case. I know how incredibly busy you are. Get to me when you can." He ended the call with his cell number.

For anyone else he hadn't spoken to for six months, that message might have been too lean and impersonal, but for Holdenfield he knew there was no such thing as *too* lean or *too* impersonal. Which is not to say that he didn't like her. In fact, he could recall moments in the past when he'd found her sharp edges disturbingly attractive.

Making the call gave him a satisfying sense of having set something in motion. He went back to the open incident report on his desktop screen and started working through it. He was halfway through the fifth report an hour later when the phone rang. He glanced at the ID: ALBANY FORENSIC CONSULTANTS.

"Rebecca?"

"Hello, David. Just pulled over for gas. What can I do for you?" Her voice underscored her odd combination of brusqueness and availability.

"I understand you're a bit of an expert on the Good Shepherd case."

"A bit."

"Any chance we could get together for a quick chat?"

"Why?"

"Strange things have been happening that may be related to it, and I need some insight from someone who knows what she's talking about."

"There's a ton of stuff on the Internet."

"I need a point of view I can trust."

"When does this need to happen?"

"Sooner the better."

"I'm on my way to the Otesaga."

"Beg pardon?"

"The Otesaga Hotel in Cooperstown. If you can meet me there, I can set aside forty-five minutes—from one-fifteen to two."

"Perfect. Where shall I——"

"Come to the Fenimore Room. I'm presenting a paper there at twelve-thirty, followed by a brief question session, followed by schmoozing around the buffet. The schmoozing I can skip. Can you be there at one-fifteen?"

He opened and closed his right hand, convincing himself again that he could manage the shift knob. "Yes."

"See you then." She broke the connection.

Gurney smiled. He felt an affinity with anyone who was willing to skip the schmoozing. Maybe that's what he liked best about Holdenfield—the minimalism of her sociability. For a moment his mind wandered into musing about what form that characteristic might take in her sex life. Then he shook his head, banishing the thought.

He returned to the middle of the fifth incident report—the section consisting of captioned crime-scene and vehicle photographs—with renewed concentration. Dr. James Brewster's Mercedes was shown from multiple angles, compacted to half its length against a roadside tree trunk. Like most of the other target vehicles, the doctor's hundred-thousand-dollar prestige capsule had been shattered into something unrecognizable, nameless, worthless.

Gurney wondered if that was part of the Shepherd's goal, part of his thrill—not only to kill the presumably wealthy owners but to reduce the symbols of their wealth to meaningless piles of junk. The final humiliation of the high-and-mighty. Dust to dust.

"Are we interrupting something?" It was Madeleine's voice.

Gurney looked up, startled. She was standing in the den doorway with Kim behind her. He hadn't heard them come into the house. They were still wearing their explosively colorful jackets. "Interrupting?"

"You had a look of great concentration."

"Just trying to absorb some information. What are you two up to?"

"Sun's out. It's turning into a beautiful day. I'm taking Kim on the ridge hike."

"Won't it be muddy?" He could hear the crankiness in his own voice.

"She can borrow a pair of my boots."

"You're going *now*?"

"Is there a problem with that?"

"No, of course not. Matter of fact, I need to go out for a couple of hours myself."

She looked at him with alarm. "In the car? With your arm the way it is?"

"Ibuprofen is a great thing."

"Ibuprofen? Twelve hours ago you fell down a flight of stairs, ended up in an emergency room, had to be driven home. Now a couple of pills and you're good as new?"

"Not good as new. But not so crippled I can't function."

Her eyes widened in exasperation. "Where do you have to go that's so important?"

"You remember a Dr. Holdenfield?"

"I remember the name. Rebecca, wasn't it?"

"Right. Rebecca. A forensic psychologist."

"Where is she?"

"Her office is in Albany."

Madeleine raised an eyebrow. "Albany? That's where you're going?"

"No. She's going to be in Cooperstown today for some kind of professional symposium."

"At the Otesaga?"

"How did you know that?"

"Where else in Cooperstown could they hold a symposium?" She looked at him curiously. "Did something urgent come up?"

"No, nothing came up. But I have some questions about the Good Shepherd case. A book of hers on serial murder was footnoted in the FBI profile. And I think she may have written some articles about the case later on."

"You couldn't ask your questions on the phone?"

"Too many. Too complicated."

"What time will you be home?"

"She's giving me forty-five minutes, ending at two o'clock, so I should be home by three at the latest."

"Three at the latest. Remember that."

"Why?"

Her eyes narrowed. "Are you asking why you should remember it?"

"What I mean is, is something happening at precisely three o'clock that I don't know about?"

"When you tell me you're going to do something, I think it would be nice if you actually did it. If you tell me you're going to be home at three o'clock, then I'd like to be able to rely on the fact that you'll be home at three o'clock. That's all. Is that okay?"

"Definitely." If Kim weren't standing there, he might have been less immediately agreeable, more tenacious in asking why the issue was of particular importance that particular day. But he'd grown up in a home where even the slightest disagreement would never be aired in front of an outsider. That stiff Irish-English reticence was still in the marrow of his bones.

Kim looked worried. "Shouldn't I be coming with you?"

"It barely makes sense for *me* to go. There's certainly no need for two of us."

"Come on," said Madeleine, turning to Kim. "I'll get you some boots. While the sun is out, let's head for the ridge."

Two minutes later Gurney, still in the den, heard the side door being opened and then being shut firmly, and the house became very quiet. He turned to his computer screen, closed the document with the photos of Dr. Brewster's crushed Mercedes, and entered a Google search for the terms "Holdenfield" and "Shepherd."

The top result referring to Rebecca's work on the case was a journal article with a daunting academic title. "Pattern Resonance: inferences for personality formation, as applied to an unknown shooter (aka The Good Shepherd), employing bivalent inductive-deductive modeling protocols. R. Holdenfield et al."

Gurney scrolled down through the results—skipping over hits in which the search terms had brought up everything from a news article about a man in Holdenfield, Nebraska, who had been bitten by a German shepherd to an obituary for Shepherd Holdenfield, a black trombonist. In the end he counted a dozen relevant entries that linked Rebecca to the murder case, all citing professional articles.

He went through these but found in most instances that the articles could be accessed only by subscribing to the journals that published them. The subscription costs were greater than his curiosity, and if the language describing her article on pattern resonance was any indication, wading through the full texts would be migraine-inducing.

## Chapter 18

# Pattern Resonance

Cooperstown was situated around the southern end of a long, narrow lake in the rural hills of Otsego County. It was a town with a personality split between quiet money and baseball tourism, between a main street glutted with sports-memorabilia stores and sedate side streets where Greek Revival homes were shaded by century-old oaks. It was Middle America in the middle of town and Brooks Brothers under the tall trees.

The drive from Walnut Crossing took a little over an hour, longer than he'd expected, but it didn't matter, because he'd left early enough to get to the Otesaga well ahead of his appointment time. He had a notion in the back of his mind that he might like to hear Holdenfield's speech, or at least part of it.

Late March was not a popular upstate vacation season, especially not for lake resorts. The parking lot was barely a third full, and the estatelike grounds, though perfectly groomed, were deserted.

Gurney believed he could tell how expensive a hotel was by how quickly and smilingly the front door was opened for him. By that measure he concluded that a room at the Otesaga would be well beyond his means.

The elegance of the lobby confirmed his impression. Gurney was about to ask for the location of the Fenimore Room when he came upon a wooden easel supporting a sign with an arrow that answered his question. The arrow pointed down a broad hallway with classical panel moldings on the walls. The sign indicated that the room was reserved that day for a meeting of the American Philosophical Psychology Association.

A duplicate sign stood next to an open door at the end of the hall-way. As Gurney approached it, he heard a burst of applause. When he reached it, he could see that Rebecca Holdenfield had just been introduced and was taking her place behind a raised podium at the far end of the room—a high-ceilinged space in which a gathering of Roman senators would not have seemed out of place.

*Not bad*, thought Gurney.

His quick guesstimate put the number of chairs at about two hundred, of which most were taken. The vast majority of the attendees were male, and most seemed to be middle-aged or older. He stepped inside the room and took an end seat in the back row—an echo of his behavior at weddings and other events at which he felt out of place.

Holdenfield caught his eye but gave no sign of recognition. She smoothed out a few sheets of paper on the top of the podium and smiled at her audience. The expression conveyed confidence and intensity rather than warmth.

Nothing new in that, thought Gurney.

"Thank you, Mr. Chairman." The smile was switched off, the voice was clear and commanding. "I'm here today to bring you a simple idea. I don't ask you to agree with it or to disagree with it. I ask you to think about it. What I bring you is a new view of the role of *imitation* in our lives—and how it affects everything we think, feel, and do. I suggest to you that imitation is a survival instinct of the human species—as indispensable as sex. This simple idea is *revolutionary*. Imitation has never been classified as an instinct—a tendency to action, driven by the buildup and release of tension. But isn't that exactly what it is?"

She paused. Her audience was perfectly still.

"Perhaps the most revealing and overlooked fact about imitation is that . . . *it feels good.* The process of imitation provides the human organism with a form of pleasure—a release of tension. In everything we do, there is a bias in favor of repetition—because it feels good."

Holdenfield's eyes were shining, and her audience seemed entranced.

"We enjoy seeing what we have seen before and doing what we have done before. The brain seeks *pattern resonance* because resonance provides pleasure."

She stepped away from the podium, as though to connect more

directly with her listeners. "The survival of any species depends on each new generation's being able to replicate the behaviors of the previous generation. The replication may arise from genetic programming or from learning. Ants rely heavily on genetic programming for their behavior. We rely heavily on learning. Insect brains are born knowing virtually everything they need to know, while human brains are born knowing virtually nothing they need to know. *The survival imperative of the insect is to act. The survival imperative of the human is to learn.* The insect's instincts drive it through the *specific acts* of its life cycle, while our imitation instinct drives us through the process of learning *how to act*."

As far as Gurney could judge from the back of the room, everyone was hanging on her words. In this room she was a rock star.

"Within this instinct lie the roots of art, habit, the joy of creativity, the pain of frustration. Much human misery results from the imitation instinct's being directly opposed by external rewards and punishments. Consider the case of a parent who hits a child to punish him for hitting another child. Two lessons are being taught: that hitting is the *wrong* way to deal with behavior we find objectionable (since it is being punished) and that hitting is the *right* way to deal with behavior we find objectionable (since it is being modeled as the way to punish). The parent who hits a child to teach him not to hit is, in fact, teaching him to hit. The potential for psychic damage is enormous when the behavior being modeled is the behavior being punished."

For the next half hour, it seemed to Gurney that Holdenfield was just repeating in other words what she'd already said. But far from boring her audience, she seemed only to be enthralling them further. Pacing and gesturing dramatically in this grand meeting room, she looked like a woman in the heaven she'd always imagined.

Finally she returned to her position behind the podium with an expression that struck Gurney as nothing short of triumphant. "Therefore I ask you to consider the possibility that the drive to satisfy the imitation instinct may be the most important missing ingredient in our understanding of human nature itself. Thank you for your attention."

Strong applause spread through the room. A florid-faced, white-haired member of the audience rose in the front row and addressed his fellow attendees with the reassuring voice of an old-time radio

152  JOHN VERDON

announcer. "On behalf of the group, I'd like to thank Dr. Holdenfield for that remarkable presentation. She said she wanted to give us something to think about, and there's no doubt she did exactly that. A most intriguing concept. In about fifteen minutes, we'll have our open bar and a nice buffet. In the meantime you have an opportunity for questions and comments. Is that acceptable to you, Rebecca?"

"Of course."

The "questions" that followed were largely composed of praise for the originality of her thinking and expressions of gratitude for her presence. After twenty minutes of this, the white-haired man rose again, deferentially thanked Rebecca once more on behalf of the group, and announced that the bar was now open.

"Interesting," said Gurney with a wry smile.

Holdenfield gave him a look that was half assessing, half combative. They were sitting at a small patio table on a veranda overlooking a manicured lawn, dotted with boxwood shrubs. The sun was shining, and the lake beyond the lawn was as blue as the sky. She was wearing a beige silk suit and a white silk blouse. She had no makeup on, no jewelry—with the exception of a pricey-looking gold watch. Her auburn hair was loosely arranged, neither long nor short. Her dark brown eyes were studying him. "You showed up quite early," she said.

"Might as well learn as much as I can."

"About philosophical psychology?"

"About you and the way you think."

"The way I think?"

"I'm curious about how you reach your conclusions."

"In general? Or do you have a specific question you're not asking?"

He laughed. "How've you been?"

"What?"

"You look great. How have you been?"

"Okay, I guess. Busy. Very busy, in fact."

"Seems to be paying off."

"What do you mean?"

"Fame. Respect. Applause. Books. Articles. Speeches."

She nodded, cocked her head, watched him, waited. "So?"

He looked out over the lawn at the shimmering lake. "I'm just remarking on what a remarkable career you've put together. First a big name in forensic psychology, now a big name in philosophical psychology. The Holdenfield brand is growing and glowing. I'm impressed."

"No you're not. You're not that impressionable. What do you want?"

He shrugged. "I need some help understanding the Good Shepherd case."

"Why is that?"

"Long story."

"Give me the short version."

"The daughter of an old acquaintance is producing a TV documentary about the families of the Good Shepherd's victims. Wants me to look over her shoulder, act as sort of a police sounding board for her, et cetera." Even now, as Gurney was speaking, the ill-defined "et cetera" part was eating at him.

"What do you need to know?"

"A lot. Hard to decide where to start."

There was a restless twitch at the corner of her mouth. "Anywhere would be better than nowhere."

"Pattern resonance."

She blinked. "What?"

"It's a term you used in your presentation today. You also used it as the title of a journal article you wrote nine years ago. What does it mean?"

"You read that article?"

"I was intimidated by the long title and figured the rest of it would be over my head."

"God, you're such a bullshit artist." She made it sound like a compliment.

"So tell me about pattern resonance."

She glanced again at her watch. "I'm not sure I have enough time."

"Try."

"It refers to the transfer of energy between mental constructs."

"In the vocabulary of a humble retired detective, born in the Bronx, that would mean . . . ?"

There was a flash of amusement in her eyes. "It's a rethinking and revision of Freud's concept of sublimation—the forcible diversion of dangerous aggressive or sexual energy into safer alternative channels."

"Rebecca, humble retired detectives speak plain English."

"Christ, Gurney, you're so full of crap. But okay, we'll do it your way. Forget about Freud. There's a famous poem about a young girl by the name of Margaret who experiences grief at the falling leaves of autumn. But the last two lines are, 'It is the blight man was born for, / It is Margaret you mourn for.' That's pattern resonance. The intense emotion she feels at observing the death of the leaves is really coming from a deeper knowledge of her own inevitable fate."

"Your point being that the emotional energy in one experience can be transferred to another without—"

"Without our realizing that what we're feeling right now may not be coming from what's happening now. That's the point!" There was a proprietary pride in her voice.

"How does all this apply to the Good Shepherd?"

"*How?* In just about every way possible. His actions, his thinking, his language, his motivation—they fit the concept perfectly. That case is one of the clearest validations of the concept. This kind of mission-driven killing is never about what it seems to be about on the surface. Underneath the killer's conscious motive, there is always another source of energy, a traumatic experience or set of experiences that occurred much earlier in his life. He has a storehouse of repressed fear and rage generated by that experience. Through a process of association, he connects his past experience with something happening in the present, and the old feelings begin to animate his current thoughts. We're hardwired to believe that what we're feeling now is the result of what we're experiencing now. If I feel happy or sad, I assume it's because something in my current life is going well or badly—not because some bit of emotional energy has been transferred from a repressed memory into the present. Normally this is a harmless error. But it's not so harmless when the transferred emotion is a pathological rage. And that's exactly what happens with a certain kind of killer—the Good Shepherd being a perfect example."

"Any idea what kind of childhood experience provided all that transferred energy behind the murders?"

"My best guess would be traumatic terror of a violent, materialistic father."

"So why do you think he stopped after six?"

"Has it occurred to you that he might be dead?" Holdenfield looked at her watch with an alarmed frown. "Sorry, David, I really don't have any more time."

"I appreciate your fitting me into your hectic schedule. By the way, during your study of the case, did you ever speak to Max Clinter?"

"Hah! Clinter. Yes, of course. What about him?"

"That's my question to you."

Holdenfield sighed impatiently, then spoke very quickly. "Max Clinter is a furious narcissist who believes that the Good Shepherd case is all about him. He's full of conspiracy theories that make no sense. He's also a self-indulgent drunk who screwed up his own life and his family's life in the course of one calamitous evening—and ever since then he's been trying to connect the dots in any weird way he can to blame everybody but himself."

"Why do you think he's dead?"

"What?"

"You said the Good Shepherd might be dead."

"That's right. *Might* be."

"So why else would he have stopped?"

She uttered another impatient sigh, more theatrical than the last. "Maybe one of Clinter's wild bullets came too close for comfort or even hit him. Maybe he had a breakdown, a psychotic decompensation. He could be in a mental hospital or even prison, for events unrelated to the shootings. There could be any number of reasons he dropped out of sight. There's no point in speculating without additional evidence." Holdenfield stepped away from the table. "Sorry. Got to go." She gave Gurney a quick farewell nod and started to head for the door that separated the veranda from the hotel lobby.

Gurney spoke to her back. "Is there any reason someone would want to prevent a reexamination of the case?"

She turned and stared at him. "What are you talking about?"

"The young woman who's making the documentary I mentioned earlier? Strange things have been happening to her. Things that could be interpreted as threats. Or, at the very least, as hostile suggestions that she back away from the project."

Holdenfield looked perplexed. "Like what?"

"Unauthorized entries into her apartment, personal objects moved, kitchen knives missing and reappearing in places they shouldn't be, drops of blood, flipped circuit breakers cutting off the lights, a sawed step in the cellar stairs rigged to break . . ." He was about to mention the whispered warning, but his insecurity about it stopped him. "There's a chance she's being harassed for another reason, that the threats are not directly related to the case—but I think they are. Let me ask you something: In the event that the Good Shepherd is still out there somewhere, do you think he'd want to keep the case from being discussed on television?"

She shook her head definitively. "Just the opposite. He'd love it. You're talking about someone who wrote a twenty-page manifesto and then mailed it to every major media outlet in the country. These psychopaths with societal grudges want an audience. They *crave* it. They want the importance of their mission to be recognized. By everyone."

"Can you think of anyone else who might want to get in the way?"

"No, I can't."

"So I've got an odd little mystery on my hands. I don't suppose Agent in Charge Trout would be willing to talk to me?"

"Matt Trout? You must be joking."

"Yeah, that's me. Old laugh-a-minute Dave. Thanks for your time, Rebecca."

The perplexed look was still on her face as she turned and went into the lobby.

## Chapter 19

# Making Waves

hree young boys in red T-shirts and shorts were kicking a soccer ball back and forth on the perfect lawn at the edge of the lake. They seemed not to care that the sun had disappeared behind an advancing cloud bank, pushing early spring back into late winter.

Gurney stood up from the table, rubbing the chill out of his arms. Just about every part of his body was aching now from his fall the night before. The tinnitus, of which he had been aware only sporadically, now seemed more intrusive. As he moved a little unsteadily toward the door that led to the lobby, it was opened for him by a conservatively uniformed young man with an automatic smile and an indistinct voice that blurred his words.

"Excuse me?" said Gurney.

The young man spoke louder, like an attendant in a nursing home. "Just asking, sir, is everything all right?"

"Yes, fine, thank you."

Gurney made his way back to the parking area. A foursome of golfers in traditional plaid pants and V-neck sweaters were just getting out of an oversize white SUV that reminded him of an upscale kitchen appliance. Normally the thought that someone had paid seventy-five thousand dollars to ride around in a giant toaster would have made him smile. But now it struck him as just one more symptom of a degenerating world, a world in which acquisitive morons were conniving endlessly to amass the largest possible piles of crap.

Maybe the Good Shepherd had a point.

He got into his car, sat back, and closed his eyes.

He realized he was thirsty. He looked into the backseat, where he knew he had a couple of bottles of water, but they were nowhere in sight, which meant they'd rolled off the backseat and under the front seat. He got out, opened the rear door, and retrieved one of the bottles. He drank about half of it and got into the car again.

He closed his eyes once more, thinking he might clear his head with a five-minute nap. But one thing Holdenfield had said kept interrupting his desire for oblivion.

You must be joking.

He told himself it was just an offhand comment—that Holdenfield had been referring to Trout's self-important pretense of inaccessibility, not to his own insignificance in the world of active law enforcement—or that it was simply her brusque way of deflecting what she interpreted as a request for an introduction. In either case, brooding over it would be a childish waste of time.

But those were rational arguments, and there was little rationality in the anger he felt. Anger at the pompous control freak who purportedly would refuse to see him, at Holdenfield for being too wrapped up in her own priorities to intercede, at the whole arrogant FBI culture.

His mind was reeling with bits and pieces of Holdenfield's lecture, her pattern-resonance concept of serial murder, the Good Shepherd profile, the sawed stair tread, Robby Meese's insistence that Kim Corazon was dangerously unhinged, the bizarre Max Clinter, the repellent Rudy Getz, the goddamn red-feathered arrow in the garden. But amid all the confusion, his thoughts kept returning to that stinging jab: *You must be joking.*

What response would he have preferred? Of course he'll meet with you. With your amazing NYPD reputation, how could Agent Trout not want to meet with you?

Christ! Was he that pathetically dependent on his reputation? On having his star-detective position in the world of law enforcement acknowledged? Whenever it was publicly acknowledged, it had made him uncomfortable. But now having it ignored was worse. Which led to another disturbing question:

*Who was he* without that position, without that reputation?

Just another guy whose career had run its course? Just another guy who didn't know who the hell he was because the power structure that had given him his identity also had the power to ignore him? Just another sad ex-cop, sitting on the sidelines, dreaming of the days when his life had made sense, hoping to be called back into the game?

Good God, what self-pitying bullshit!

Enough!

I'm a detective. Perhaps I always was, and in one way or another I always will be. That's a fact of my life—independent of the details of my paycheck or chain of command. I have a set of talents that make me what I am. The exercise of those talents is what matters—not the opinion of Rebecca Holdenfield, or Agent Trout, or anyone else. My self-esteem—my grip on life—depends on my own behavior, not on the reactions of a psychobabbling profiler or some bureaucratic fed I've never met.

He grabbed hold of this assertion, using it to steady himself, even as he sensed something excessive in its tone. He felt sure, however, that any level of conviction was better than none. And he realized that if he were to maintain his balance, like a man on a bicycle, he needed momentum. He needed to *do* something.

He took out his cell phone, accessed his e-mail, and once again opened the series of incident reports Hardwick had sent him.

Scrolling through them, he recalled that the real-estate agent—the one with the movie-star name—had been only a few miles from her home in Barkham Dell when she became the Good Shepherd's fourth victim.

Barkham Dell was not far from Cooperstown. In the incident report, he found the exact location on Long Swamp Road, with annotated photographs of the point at which half of Sharon Stone's face had been blown away and her car had plunged off the tarmac into the mire.

He entered the location into his GPS and drove out through the gates of the Otesaga's parking lot—not with any major expectation of discovery but with a modest sense of getting back to the beginning, of finally getting his feet on the ground.

The first visit to a crime scene, even ten years after the fact, had an effect on Gurney he found hard to label. To call it stimulating sounded perverse, but it definitely intensified his senses. The chemical reactions it catalyzed in his brain had the result of making everything he saw there far more memorable than the sights and events of his ordinary life.

It wasn't the first time he'd visited the scene of a murder committed long ago. A confession he'd once elicited from a serial killer included the murder of a teenage girl in a wooded area near Orchard Beach in the Bronx—a murder that had occurred twelve years prior to the confession.

Now, as Gurney drove slowly through the gentle leftward curve where Long Swamp Road moved away from the state highway toward Dead Dog Lake, he went through the same process he'd gone through at Orchard Beach—in his mind subtracting years of growth from the trees, erasing saplings and smaller bushes.

He had the incident-report photos to guide his adjustments. There had been no additions or subtractions of man-made structures. No buildings, no billboards, no telephone poles. The road hadn't had a guardrail in 2000, and it didn't now. Three tall landmark trees appeared virtually unchanged. The time of year, early spring, was the same then and now, giving the old photos an illusion of currency.

The position of the tall trees, combined with the photo notations and accompanying angle-and-distance measurements, made it possible for Gurney to locate the approximate position of Sharon Stone's car when the bullet struck her.

He drove back along the road to the point where it was intersected by a road that connected with the state highway. Then he drove from that point to the point of the shot, and from there through two miles of bog and marshland, past Dead Dog Lake, through the Currier & Ives village of Barkham Dell, and another mile to the point where Long Swamp Road teed into a busy county route.

Then he went back to his starting point and did it all again—but this time he did it as he imagined the Good Shepherd might have. First he found an unobtrusive spot to park by the side of the road not far from the connector to the state highway—a reasonable place for someone to lie in wait for a passing Mercedes, a popular vehicle among Barkham Dell's weekenders.

Then he pulled out behind an imaginary black Mercedes, "followed" it to the beginning of the long curve, accelerated into the curve, swung out into the left lane, lowered his passenger window, and at the approximate point indicated in the accident reconstruction he raised his right arm and pointed it toward the imaginary driver.

"BAM!" shouted Gurney as loud as he could, knowing that no sound he could make could approach even 10 percent of the report of the .50-caliber monster used in the actual shooting. As he faked the shot, he jammed on his brakes, visualizing the victim's car drifting from the arc of the curve, careening into the swamp, perhaps a hundred yards ahead of him. He pretended to lay the gun down on the seat, to take a tiny toy animal from his shirt pocket, and to toss it onto the shoulder of the road not far from the spot where he pictured the Mercedes embedded in the mud, surrounded by the remnants of the previous season's brown marsh grass.

Having completed the fantasy attack, he drove on toward Barkham Dell. On the way he considered all the available options for disposing of a Desert Eagle pistol. Three cars passed him going in the opposite direction. One happened to be a black Mercedes—sending a chill up the back of his scalp.

At the traffic light in the village, he made a U-turn—in order to repeat the whole procedure. But just as he was approaching Dead Dog Lake, pondering its pluses and minuses as a pistol depository, his cell phone rang. The caller ID was his own home landline.

"Madeleine?"

"Where are you?"

"On a back road near Barkham Dell. Why?"

"Why?"

He hesitated. "Is there a problem?"

"What time is it?" she asked with disturbing calmness.

"What time? I don't . . . Oh, Jesus . . . Yes, I see. I forgot."

The clock on his dashboard read 3:15 P.M. He'd promised to be home by three. By three *at the latest.*

"You forgot?"

"I'm sorry."

"That's it? You forgot?" There was real anger in her controlled tone.

"I'm sorry. Forgetting is not something over which I have much control. I don't purposely choose to forget things."

"Yes you do."

"How the hell could I? Forgetting is forgetting. It's not an intentional thing."

"You remember what you care about. You forget what you don't care about."

"That's not—"

"Yes it is. You always blame it on your memory. It's got nothing to do with your memory. You never forgot a court appearance, did you? You never forgot a meeting with the DA. You don't have a *memory* problem, David, you have a *caring* problem."

"Look, I'm sorry."

"Right. So when will you be home?"

"I'm on my way. Thirty-five, forty minutes?"

"So you're saying you'll be here by four?"

"Definitely by four. Maybe sooner."

"Fine. Four o'clock. Just an hour late. See you then."

The connection was broken.

A t 3:52 P.M. he reached the quiet lane that wound its way up, streamside, through a rising declivity in the hills, to their farmhouse. A mile up the lane, he pulled onto a grassy area in front of a rarely used weekender's cabin.

He'd spent the first ten minutes of the trip from Barkham Dell wondering why Madeleine had sounded so irritated—more irritated than usual by his forgetfulness, his carelessness, his failure to write down things that might slip his mind. The rest of the trip he'd devoted to pondering the Good Shepherd murders.

He wondered if any progress had been made on the case, once it came under the control of the FBI field office in Albany, that hadn't been noted in the NYSP files available to Hardwick. He also wondered if there was a way of answering that question without going through Agent Trout. He couldn't think of any.

However . . . if Trout was indeed as rigid as everyone seemed to think, then he would also be brittle. Gurney had learned time and again that a man tends to marshal his strongest defenses at his weakest point.

Thus a mania for control often betrays a terror of chaos.

And that suggested a path into the fortress.

He took out his phone and tapped in Holdenfield's number. The call went into her voice mail.

"Hi, Rebecca. Sorry to bother you again on such a busy day. But there are some things about the Good Shepherd case that don't quite fit together. In fact, there may be a fatal flaw in the FBI construct. When you have a moment, give me a call."

He slipped the phone back into his pocket and drove the rest of the way up the hill.

## Chapter 20

# Surprise

As he passed between the pond and the barn, and the house came into view at the top end of the pasture, he saw, just visible above the bent and broken tops of the brown pasture grass, the handlebars and gas tank of a motorcycle next to Madeleine's car.

He reacted to the sight with a mixture of interest and suspicion. When he pulled in next to it, his interest grew. The motorcycle, in pristine condition, was a BSA Cyclone, an increasingly rare machine that hadn't been manufactured since the 1960s.

It was reminiscent of a bike he'd once owned himself. In 1979, when he was a freshman at Fordham, living in his parents' Bronx apartment, he commuted to the campus on a twenty-year-old Triumph Bonneville. When it was stolen during the summer between his freshman and sophomore years, he'd already been through enough stinging rainstorms and near accidents on the Cross Bronx Expressway to make the boredom of the bus acceptable.

He went into the house through the side door, which led via a short hallway to the big kitchen. He expected to hear voices, perhaps the voice of the visiting biker, but all he heard was something sizzling on the stove. When he entered the room, it was full of the aroma of the onions Madeleine was sautéing in a wok. She didn't look up.

"Whose motorcycle is that?" he asked.

"Was it in your way?"

"I didn't say it was in my way." He waited, staring at her back. "So?"

"So?"

"So whose is it?"

"I'm not supposed to say."

"What?"

She sighed. "I'm not supposed to say."

"Why the hell not?"

"Because . . . someone wants his visit to be a surprise."

"Who? Where is he?"

"It's a surprise." She sounded unhappy with the position she'd been put in.

"Someone is here to see me?"

"Right." She turned off the burner, picked up the wok, and scraped the onions out over a layer of rice in a baking dish next to the stove.

"Where's Kim?"

"She and your visitor went for a walk." She went to the refrigerator, took out a bowl of raw peeled shrimp, a second bowl of chopped peppers and celery, and a jar of minced garlic.

"You know," said Gurney, "I'm not very fond of surprises."

"Neither am I." She turned up the gas under the wok, dumped the vegetables into it, and began stirring vigorously with a spatula.

Neither one said anything for a long minute. Gurney found the silence uncomfortable. "I assume it's someone I know?" He immediately regretted the inanity of the question.

Madeleine looked directly at him for the first time since he came in. "I hope so."

He took a deep breath. "This is impossibly silly. Tell me who came on that motorcycle and why he's here."

Madeleine shrugged. "Kyle. To see you."

"What?"

"You heard me. Your tinnitus isn't that bad."

"My son, Kyle? Came from the city on a motorcycle? To see me?"

"To surprise you. He originally planned to be here at three. Because that's when you said you'd be back. *Three at the latest.* Then he decided to arrive at two. So in case you got home earlier than three, he'd have more time with you."

"You set this up?" It came out as half question, half accusation.

"No, I didn't 'set it up.' It was Kyle's idea to come up and see you. He hasn't seen you since you were in the hospital. All I did was tell him what time you'd be here—the time you *said* you'd be here. Why are you looking at me like that?"

"Seems like quite a coincidence that yesterday you were suggesting that Kyle and Kim would make an interesting couple and now here they are, out for a walk together."

"Coincidences do occur, David. That's why the word exists." She turned her attention back to the wok.

Gurney felt more disturbed than he wanted to admit. He decided it was a symptom of his deep dislike of having his plans changed, the challenge to his illusion of control. That and the fact that his relationship with Kyle, his twenty-six-year-old son from his first marriage, had long been fraught with conflicting emotions and rationalizations. And the ibuprofens he'd taken for the pinched nerve in his arm were wearing off, and the overall achiness from his fall in the basement was getting worse. And, and, and . . .

He tried to keep the hostility and self-pity out of his voice. "Do you know where they went on their walk?"

Madeleine took the wok from the burner and added its contents to the rice and onions in the baking dish. She didn't answer until she'd scraped the wok clean, returned it to the stove, and added more oil. "I suggested the ridge path around to the trail that leads down to the pond."

"When did they leave?"

"When they discovered you'd be an hour late."

"I wish you'd told me about this."

"Would it have made a difference?"

"Of course it would have made a difference."

"That's interesting."

The oil in the wok was beginning to smoke. Madeleine went to the spice cabinet, came back with powdered ginger, cardamom, coriander, and a bag of cashews. She turned the stove exhaust fan to high, put a handful of the nuts into the wok, a teaspoon of each of the spices, and began stirring it all together.

She nodded toward the window next to the stove. "They're coming up the hill."

He stepped over to it and looked out. Ambling up the grassy path through the pasture were Kim in Madeleine's wildly hued Windbreaker and Kyle in faded jeans and a black leather jacket. They appeared to be laughing.

As Gurney was watching them, Madeleine was watching him. "Before they get to the door," she said, "you might want to put a more welcoming expression on your face."

"I was just thinking about the motorcycle."

She tipped the nuts-and-spices mixture from the wok onto the other ingredients in the baking dish. "What about it?"

"A fifty-year-old classic restored to mint condition isn't cheap."

"Hah!" She put the wok in the sink and let the water run on it. "Since when has Kyle ever owned anything that was cheap?"

He nodded vaguely. "The only other time he came up to this house was two years ago to show off that goddamn yellow Porsche he'd gotten with his Wall Street bonus. Now it's a pricey BSA. Jesus."

"You're his father."

"Meaning what?"

Madeleine sighed, looking at him with an odd combination of exasperation and sympathy. "Isn't it obvious? He wants you to be proud of him. Granted, he goes about it in a way that doesn't work. You two don't know each other very well, do you?"

"I guess not." He watched her put the baking dish into the oven. "This glittery, luxury stuff . . . all this brand-name crap . . . it just brings back too many memories of that materialistic gene he inherited from his real-estate-broker mother. She was great at making money, even better at spending it. Kept telling me I was wasting my time as a cop, I should go to law school, because there was a lot more money in defending criminals than in catching them. So now Kyle's in law school. Ought to make her happy."

"Are you angry because you think he wants to defend criminals?"

"I'm not angry."

She shot him a disbelieving glance.

"Maybe I am angry. I don't know what I am. Seems like everything is getting on my nerves lately."

Madeleine shrugged. "Make sure you remember it's your son who came to see you today, not your ex-wife."

"Right. I just wish that——"

He was interrupted by the sound of the side door opening, followed by Kim's excited voice in the hallway. "No way, that's much too weird! I mean, that's like the single sickest thing I ever heard!"

Kyle came into the kitchen first, smiling broadly. "Hey, Dad! Good to see you!"

They greeted each other with awkward hugs.

"Good to see you, too, son. Kind of a long trip up here on that bike, wasn't it?"

"It was perfect, actually. Traffic was light on 17, and from 17 to here the roads are ideal for a bike. How do you like it?"

"I don't think I've ever seen one that looked that good."

"Me neither. I love it. You used to have a bike like that, right?"

"Not that sharp."

"I hope I can keep it like that. I just got it two weeks ago at the Atlantic City Classic Motorcycle Show. Hadn't planned on buying anything, but I couldn't resist. Never saw one that nice—not even the one my boss has."

"Your boss?"

"Yeah, I'm kind of half back on the Street, working part-time for some guys from the old firm that went under."

"But you're still at Columbia?"

"Sure, absolutely. First-year crunch. Tons of reading. Designed to weed out the unmotivated. I'm so busy I'm nuts, but what the hell."

Kim came through the doorway into the kitchen with a cheery smile for Madeleine. "Thanks again for the jacket. I hung it up in the mudroom. Is that okay?"

"Fine. But I'm dying of curiosity."

"About what?"

"I'm trying to imagine 'the single sickest thing' you ever heard."

"What? Oh! You heard me say that? Kyle was telling me something. Yuck." She looked at him. "You tell her. I don't even want to say it."

"It, uh . . . it's about a peculiar disorder some people have. This might not be the best time to go into it. It takes some explanation. Maybe later might be better?"

"Okay, I'll ask you again later. Now I'm *really* curious. In the meantime would you like a drink or a snack? Cheese, crackers, olives, fruit, anything?"

Kyle and Kim looked at each other, shook their heads.

"Not for me," said Kyle.

"No thanks," said Kim.

"Then just make yourselves comfortable." Madeleine gestured toward the armchairs around the stone fireplace at the far end of the room. "I have to finish up a few things. We'll be having dinner around six."

Kim asked if she could help with anything, and when Madeleine said no, she excused herself and headed for the bathroom. Gurney and Kyle settled into a pair of wing chairs that faced each other over a low cherry coffee table in front of the hearth.

"So . . ." they began simultaneously, then simultaneously laughed.

Gurney had a strange thought. Apart from the fact that Kyle had his mother's mouth and jet-black hair, looking at him was like looking in a magic mirror at a restored image of himself—with two decades of wear and tear sanded off.

"You first," said Gurney.

Kyle grinned. It was his mother's mouth but his father's teeth. "Kim was telling me about this TV thing you're involved in."

"I'm not involved directly in the TV aspect. In fact, I'd like to stay as far away from that part of it as possible."

"What other part is there?"

Such a simple question, thought Gurney, as he tried to think of a simple answer. "The case itself, I guess."

"The Shepherd murders?"

"The murders, the victims, the evidence, the MO, the rationale presented in the manifesto, the investigative premise."

Kyle looked surprised. "You have doubts about any of that?"

"Doubts? I don't know. Maybe just some curiosity."

"I thought all that Good Shepherd stuff was analyzed to death ten years ago."

"Maybe I just have doubts about the basis for nobody's having any doubts. Plus, some odd little things have been happening."

"Like her crazy ex sabotaging the stairs?"

"Is that the way she described what happened?"

Kyle frowned. "There's another way?"

"Who knows? Like I said, I just have some curiosity." He paused. "On the other hand, this so-called curiosity of mine may be nothing more than mental indigestion. We'll see. There's an FBI agent I'd like to talk to."

"How come?"

"I'm pretty confident that I know as much as the state police know, but our friends at the fed level have a habit of keeping the occasional tidbit to themselves—especially the individual who was running the case."

"And you think you can get whatever it is out of him?"

"Maybe not, but I'd like to give it a shot."

There was a sharp clatter of breaking glass.

"Damn!" cried Madeleine at the other end of the room, raising her hand from the sink and staring at it.

"You all right?" asked Gurney.

She tore a piece of paper towel off the roll that stood on the sink island. The roll toppled over and fell to the floor. She ignored it, along with the question, and began dabbing at the heel of her left hand.

"You need some help?" He got up and headed over to look at her hand. He picked up the towel roll and set it back on the countertop. "Let me see."

Kyle followed him over.

"Why don't you gentlemen return to your seats," she said, frowning uncomfortably at the attention. "I think I can handle this. Just a little blood, nothing serious. All it needs is peroxide and a Band-Aid." She flashed a chilly smile and walked out of the room.

The two men looked at each other, producing identical little shrugs.

"You want some coffee?" asked Gurney.

Kyle shook his head. "I was trying to remember . . . It became an FBI case because of the Massachusetts guy, right? The heart surgeon?"

Gurney blinked. "How the hell did you remember that?"

"It was a giant homicide case."

Something in Kyle's expression suddenly got through to Gurney: the implication that of course Kyle would pay attention to something like that, because that was the world in which his father was an expert.

"Right," said Gurney, feeling the small stab of an unfamiliar emotion. "You sure you don't want any coffee?"

"Maybe I will. I mean, if you're having some, too."

As the coffee was brewing, they stood looking out through the French doors. The yellow afternoon sun was slanting across the stubbly pasture.

After a long silence, Kyle said, "So what do you think about this thing she's involved in?"

"Kim?"

"Yeah."

"That's a big question. I guess everything depends on the final execution."

"The way she explained it to me, it sounds like she really wants it to be an honest portrayal of the people involved."

"What she wants it to be and what RAM turns it into may be two different things."

Kyle blinked, looked worried. "They sure as hell did a job on the original events. Twenty-four/seven bullshit, week after week."

"You remember that?"

"It was all that was on. The shootings happened right after I moved out of Mom's to live at Stacey Marx's house."

"When you were . . . fifteen?"

"Sixteen. When Mom started going with Tom Gerard, the big real-estate guy." A bright, brittle emotion flashed in his eyes as he added with antic emphasis, *"Mom 'n' Tom."*

"So," said Gurney quickly, "you remember the television coverage?"

"Stacey's parents had the TV on all the time. RAM News, *all the time.* God, I can still picture the reconstructions."

"Of the shootings?"

"Right. They had an ominous-sounding announcer delivering a dramatic voice-over narration, based very loosely on the facts—while some actor was shown driving a shiny black car on a lonely road. They'd go through the whole thing like that—right up to the gunshot and the car careening off the road—with a tiny one-word 'reenactment' disclaimer flashed on the screen for half a second. It was like reality TV without the reality. Day after day. They got so much mileage out of that crap they should've been paying the Shepherd."

"I remember now," said Gurney. "All part of the RAM carnival."

"Speaking of the carnival, you ever watch *Cops?* That was pretty big on TV around that same time."

"I saw part of one episode."

"I don't think I ever told you this, but there was an asshole in junior year of high school who knew you were with the NYPD, and he always used to ask me, 'Is that what your cop dad does for a living—busts down doors in trailer parks?' Complete asshole. I used to tell him, 'No, asshole, that's *not* what he does. And by the way, asshole, he's not just a cop, he's a homicide detective.' Detective first class, right, Dad?"

"Right." Kyle sounded so young to him right then, like such a kid, it brought a tightness to his chest. He looked away, down the hill at the barn.

"I wish that *New York* magazine article about you had come out back then. That would have shut him up fast. That article was fantastic!"

"I guess Kim told you that her mother wrote that article?"

"Yeah, she did—when I asked how she knew you. She really likes you."

"Who?"

"Kim. At least Kim, maybe her mother, too." Kyle grinned and looked sixteen again. "That gold detective shield dazzles them, right?"

Gurney managed a small laugh.

A cloud passed slowly in front of the sun, and the pasture faded from golden tan to grayish beige. For a wrenching second, something about it reminded Gurney of the skin of a corpse. A particular corpse. A Dominican hit man whose sunny complexion had drained away with his blood on a Harlem sidewalk. Gurney cleared his throat, as if to dispel the image.

Then he became aware of a low thumping in the air. It grew louder, soon becoming recognizable as a helicopter. Half a minute later, it passed, visible only partially and only briefly behind the treetops along the ridge. The distinct, heavy thudding of the rotor faded away, and all was silent again.

"You have a military base up here?" asked Kyle.

"No, just reservoirs for the city."

"Reservoirs?" He seemed to be considering this. "So you think the helicopter is some kind of Homeland Security thing?"

"Most likely."

## Chapter 21

# More Surprises

They were sitting at the Shaker-style cherry trestle table that separated the kitchen area of the long room from the sitting area by the fireplace. They'd started eating, and Kim and Kyle had complimented Madeleine enthusiastically on her spiced shrimp-and-rice dish. Gurney had offered a preoccupied echo of their comments, after which they ate for a while without speaking.

Kyle broke the silence. "These people you've been interviewing—do they have much in common?"

Kim chewed thoughtfully, swallowing before she spoke. "Anger."

"All of them? After all these years?"

"In some it's more obvious, because they express it more directly. But I think the anger is there in all of them, in some form or other. It would have to be, wouldn't it?"

Kyle frowned. "I thought anger was a stage of grief that eventually passed."

"Not if there's no emotional closure."

"Because the Good Shepherd was never caught?"

"Never caught, never identified. And after the crazy Max Clinter car chase, he just evaporated into the night. It's a story without an ending."

Gurney made a face. "I think the story may lack more than an ending."

There was a brief silence around the table as everyone looked at him expectantly.

Kyle finally prompted him. "You think the FBI got part of it wrong?"

"That's what I want to find out."

Kim looked baffled. "Got what wrong? What part of it?"

"I'm not saying for sure that they got *anything* wrong. I'm just saying it's a *possibility*."

Kyle's expression became more excited. "What part might they have gotten wrong?"

"From what little I know at the moment, it's just possible they got it *all* wrong." He glanced at Madeleine. There was a flicker of conflicting emotions on her face, too subtle for him to identify.

Kim looked alarmed. "I don't understand. What are you saying?"

"I hate using words like this, but the whole thing has kind of a *wobbly* look. Like a very big building on a very small foundation."

Kim was shaking her head rapidly in a kind of reflexive disagreement. "But when you say they may have gotten it all wrong, what on earth . . . ?"

Her voice trailed off as the phone in Gurney's pocket began ringing.

He took it out, glanced at the ID, and smiled. "I have a feeling I'm going to get asked that question again in about five seconds." He stood up from the table and put the phone to his ear. "Hello, Rebecca. Thanks for getting back to me."

" 'A fatal flaw in the FBI construct'?" There was a cutting edge of anger in her voice. "What was that message all about?"

Gurney stepped away from the table in the direction of the French doors. "Nothing conclusive. I just have questions. There may or may not be a problem, depending on what the answers are." He stood with his back to the others, looking out toward the western hills and the purple remnants of the sunset without really registering the beauty of what he was seeing. He was focused on one objective: getting invited to a meeting with Agent Trout.

"Questions? What questions?"

"Actually, I have quite a few. You have time to listen?"

"Not really. But I'm curious. Go ahead."

"The first is the biggest. Did you ever have any doubts about the case?"

"Doubts? Like what?"

"Like what it was really all about."

"You're not making sense. Be more specific."

"You, the FBI, the forensic-psych community, criminologists, sociologists—just about everyone but Max Clinter—all seem to agree on everything. I've never seen such a cozy level of consensus around what is essentially an unsolved series of crimes."

"*Cozy?*" There was acid in her voice.

"I'm not implying anything corrupt. It just seems as if everyone— with the conspicuous exception of Clinter—is perfectly happy with the existing narrative. All I'm asking is whether this agreement is as universal as it seems and how *certain* you are about it personally."

"Look, David, I don't have all evening for this conversation. Cut to the chase and tell me what's bothering you."

Gurney took a deep breath, trying to defuse his irritation at her irritation. "What's bothering me is that there are a lot of elements in the case and they all have to be interpreted in a particular way in order to support the overarching narrative. And I get the impression that it's the narrative that's driving the interpretation of its elements, rather than the other way around." *Rather than the way a sane, objective, reliable analysis should be conducted,* he was tempted to add but didn't.

Holdenfield hesitated. "Be more specific."

"There are obvious questions raised by each data point, each bit of evidence, each fact. The answers to all of them appear to be coming from the investigative premise instead of the investigative premise coming from the answers to the questions."

"You call that being more specific?"

"Okay. Questions. Why only Mercedeses? Why stop at six? Why a Desert Eagle? Why more than one Desert Eagle? Why the little plastic animals? Why the manifesto? Why the combination of cool rational argument with hot religious language? Why the rigid repetition of—"

Holdenfield broke in, sounding exasperated. "David, each of those issues has been examined and discussed in detail—every one of them. The answers are clear, they make perfect sense, they form a coherent picture. I really don't understand your point at all."

"So you're telling me that there was never a competing investigative premise?"

"There was never any basis for one. What the hell is your problem here?"

"Can you picture him?"

"Picture who?"

"The Good Shepherd."

"Can I *picture* him? I don't know. Is that a meaningful question?"

"I think so. What's your answer?"

"My answer is that I don't agree that it's meaningful."

"It sounds to me like you can't picture him. Neither can I. Which makes me think there may be contradictions in the profile that are screwing up the gut-level process of imagining a face. Of course, *he* might be a woman. A woman strong enough to handle a Desert Eagle. Or *he* might be more than one person. But we'll put that aside for now."

"A woman? That's absurd."

"No time to argue that right now. I have one last question for you. Amid all the professional consensus, did you or any of your forensic-psych colleagues or anyone at the Behavioral Analysis Unit ever disagree among yourselves about *anything* in the case hypothesis?"

"Of course we did. There are always diverse opinions, differences in emphasis."

"For example?"

"For example, the concept of pattern resonance emphasizes the transference of energy from an original trauma into a current situation—which makes the current manifestation essentially an inanimate vehicle that is given life by the past. The application of the imitation-instinct paradigm would give the current situation a greater validity of its own. It's a repetition of a past pattern, but it does have life and energy of its own. Another concept that might apply is the transgenerational transmission of violence theory, which is a traditional learned-behavior model. There was ample discussion of all those ideas."

Gurney laughed.

"What's funny?"

"I can picture you guys staring out at a palm tree on the horizon and debating the number of coconuts on it."

"Your point being?"

"What if the palm tree itself is a mirage? A group delusion?"

"David, if anyone in this conversation is delusional, it's not me. Is that it for the questions?"

"Who benefits from the existing hypothesis?"

"What?"

"Who benefits from the——"

"I heard you. What the hell do you mean?"

"I have this sense of a sticky synergy connecting the facts of the case with the weak points of FBI methodology and the career dynamics of the professional forensic community."

"I can't believe you said that. I really can't. It's so insulting. Look, I'm about to hang up on you. I'll give you one chance to explain yourself before I do. Speak to me. Quickly."

"Rebecca, we all fool ourselves from time to time. God knows I do. There's no insult intended in my observation about this. When *you* look at the Good Shepherd case, *you* see a simple story of a brilliant psycho whose buried rage has found tragic expression in his attacks on symbols of wealth and power. When I look at the same case, I'm not sure what I see—maybe a case that people shouldn't be as sure about as they seem to be. That's all. I just think too many conclusions have been reached—and embraced—too quickly."

"And where does that take you?"

"I don't know where it takes me. But it does make me curious."

"Curious like Max Clinter?"

"Is that a real question?"

"Oh, definitely a real question."

"At least Max understands that the case isn't nearly as sewn up as you and your FBI buddies think it is. At least he understands that there could be another connection among the victims beyond the fact of Mercedes ownership."

"David, what do you have against the FBI?"

"Sometimes they get carried away by their way of doing things, their way of making decisions, their obsession with control, their *process.*"

"The simple reality is, they're excellent at what they do. They're smart, objective, disciplined, receptive to good ideas."

"Does that mean they pay your consultancy fees on time without complaining?"

"Is that supposed to be just another observation with no insult intended?"

"It's an observation that we tend to see the good in people who see the good in us."

"You know, David, you're so full of shit you ought to be a lawyer."

He laughed. "That's funny. I like that. But I'll tell you something. If I were a lawyer, I'd like to have the Good Shepherd as a client. Because I have a feeling that the FBI concept of the case is about as solid as smoke in the wind. In fact, I'm getting kind of itchy to prove it."

"I see. Lots of luck with that."

The connection was broken.

Gurney slipped his phone back into his pocket, his unusually aggressive tone echoing in his head. Slowly his gaze moved to the far landscape. All that was left of the sunset was a purplish smudge across the gray sky, like a darkening bruise above the line of hills.

"Who was that?" The voice was Kim's.

He turned around. She, Madeleine, and Kyle were still sitting at the table, their eyes on him. They all looked concerned, Kim more than the others.

"A forensic psychologist who's written a lot about the Good Shepherd case and consulted with the FBI on other serial-killer issues."

"What are you . . . what are you doing?" There was a pressure in her lowered voice, as though she were furious and trying not to show it.

"I want to know everything there is to know about the case."

"What was all that stuff about everybody's understanding of it being wrong?"

"Not wrong necessarily, just poorly supported by the facts."

"I don't know what you're talking about. I already told you Rudy Getz is going ahead with my documentary, with the set of test interviews I did. Rudy wants to use the raw footage I shot with my own camera. He says it enhances the reality. I *told* you this—that he's *going ahead* with the program—nationally, on the RAM News Network. Now you're telling me it's all wrong, or it *might* all be wrong? I don't get where you're going with this. This isn't what I asked you to do. You're turning everything upside down. Why are you doing this?"

"Nothing has been turned upside down. I'm just trying to get a grip on what's going on. Some disturbing things have happened, to you and to me, and I don't want—"

"That's no reason to go charging headfirst into the project, ripping it up, trying to prove it's all wrong!"

"The only place I went headfirst was down your stairs. I don't want either of us to get blindsided like that again."

"Then just keep an eye on my idiot boyfriend!" She corrected herself. "My idiot *ex*-boyfriend."

"Suppose it wasn't him. Suppose—"

"Don't be silly! Who else could it be?"

"Someone who knows about the project and doesn't want you to complete it."

"Who? Why?"

"Two excellent questions. Let's start with the first. How many people know what you're working on?"

"Know about the documentary? Maybe a million?"

"What?"

"A million, at least. Maybe a lot more. The RAM website, Internet news releases, e-mail blasts that go out to all the local stations and local newspapers, RAM Facebook pages, my own Facebook page, Connie's Facebook page, my Twitter account—God, there's so much—all the prospective participants, all their contacts . . ."

"So just about anyone could have access to the information."

"Of course. Maximum exposure. That's the goal."

"Okay. That means we need to come at it from a different direction."

Kim stared at him with a pained expression. "We don't need to 'come at it' at all—not the way you're talking about it. God, Dave . . ." Tears were coming to her eyes. "This is a critical moment. Don't you see that? I can't believe this. My first episode is set to run in a couple of days, and you're on the phone telling people that the whole Good Shepherd case is . . . is . . . what? I can't even follow what you're telling them." She shook her head, pressing the tears away from her eyes with the tips of her fingers. "I'm sorry. I don't . . . I don't . . . Shit! Excuse me."

She hurried out of the room, and a few seconds later Gurney heard the bathroom door slam shut.

He looked at Kyle, who had pushed his chair a foot or so back from the table and seemed to be studying a spot on the floor. He looked at Madeleine, who was gazing at him with a concern that he found unsettling.

He turned up his palms in a questioning gesture. "What did I do?"

"Think about it," she said. "You'll figure it out."

"Kyle?"

The young man looked up, gave a small shrug. "I think you scared the shit out of her."

Gurney frowned. "By suggesting to someone on the phone that the FBI concept of the case might be flawed?"

When Kyle didn't answer, Madeleine said softly, "You did more than that."

"Like what?"

She ignored the question and began moving some of the dinner dishes from the table to the sink.

Gurney persisted, addressing his question to a midpoint in the space between her and Kyle. "What did I do that's so awful?"

This time Kyle answered. "You didn't do anything *awful*, not intentionally, but . . . I think Kim got the impression that you were bringing her project to a screeching halt."

"You didn't just say there might be a little flaw somewhere," added Madeleine. "You implied that the whole thing was completely wrong, and not only that, you were going the prove it. In other words, you planned to tear the whole case apart."

Gurney took a deep breath. "There was a reason for that."

"A reason?" Madeleine looked amused. "Of course. You always have a reason."

He closed his eyes for a moment as if patience were more easily found in darkness. "I wanted to upset Holdenfield enough that she'd get in touch with the FBI agent in charge, a cold fish by the name of Trout, and upset *him* enough that *he'd* want to get in touch with *me*."

"Why would he want to do that?"

"To find out if I really know something about the case that might embarrass him. And that would give me an opportunity to find out if he knows things about the case that haven't been made public."

"Well, if your strategy was to upset people, you can consider yourself a success." She pointed at his plate, still heaped with shrimp and rice. "Are you going to eat that?"

"No." He heard the abrupt defensiveness in his own tone and added, "Not right now. I think maybe I'll step outside for a bit, get some air, clear my head."

He left the table, went to the mudroom, and put on a light jacket. As he was going out the side door into the deepening dusk, he heard Kyle saying something to Madeleine, his voice low, the tone tentative, the words largely indistinguishable.

The only two he heard clearly were "Dad" and "angry."

As Gurney sat on the bench by the pond, the evening rapidly descended into darkness. A fragile moon sliver behind a heavy overcast offered only the dimmest, most uncertain sense of the world around him.

The pain in his forearm had returned. It was intermittent, having no apparent relationship with the arm's angle, position, or muscle tension. The feeling magnified the frustration he felt at Holdenfield's attitude on the phone, at his own combativeness, at Kim's severe reaction.

He knew two things—two facts in collision with each other. First, a cool and rigorous objectivity had always been at the root of his success as a detective. Second, his objectivity was now questionable. He suspected that the slowness of his recovery, the feeling of vulnerability, the impression of being sidelined—the fear of *irrelevance*—had filled him with an agitation and anger that could easily warp his judgment.

He rubbed his forearm with no noticeable effect on the ache. It was as though the source of it were elsewhere, perhaps in a pinched nerve in his spine, and his brain was misreporting the location of the inflammation. It was like the tinnitus situation, in which his brain was misinterpreting a neural disturbance as a tinny, echoey sound.

Still, despite these self-doubts, these termites of uncertainty, if he were forced to wager all he had one way or the other, he'd bet there was something screwy about the Good Shepherd case, something that didn't *fit*. His finely tuned sense of discrepancy had never let him down, and he didn't think . . .

His train of thought was interrupted by a sound like footsteps that seemed to come from somewhere in the general area of the barn. When he looked in that direction, he saw a small light moving in the pasture between the barn and the house. As he watched, he realized it was a flashlight being held by someone coming down the pasture path.

"Dad?" The voice was Kyle's.

"I'm over here," Gurney called back. "By the pond."

The flashlight beam moved toward him, found him. "Are there any animals out here at night?"

Gurney smiled. "None that would have any interest in meeting you."

A minute later Kyle arrived at the bench.

"Mind if I sit?"

"Course not." Gurney moved a bit to make more room.

"Man, this is really dark out here." There was the sound of something falling in the woods on the other side of the pond. "Oh, shit! What the hell was that?"

"No idea."

"You sure there are no animals in those woods?"

"The woods are full of animals. Deer, bears, foxes, coyotes, bobcats."

"Bears?"

"Black bears. Generally harmless. Unless they have cubs."

"And you really have bobcats?"

"One or two. Sometimes I'll see one in my headlights as I'm coming up the hill."

"Wow. That's pretty wild. I've never seen a bobcat, not a real one." He fell silent for a minute or so. Gurney was about to ask him what was on his mind when he continued. "You really think there's more to the Shepherd case than people realize?"

"Could be."

"You sounded pretty sure on the phone. I think that's why Kim got so bothered."

"Yeah, well . . ."

"So what do you think everybody's missing?"

"How much do you know about the case?"

"Like I told you before dinner—everything. At least everything that was on TV."

Gurney shook his head in the dark. "It's funny—I don't recall you as being that interested at the time."

"Well, I was. But there's no reason you'd remember that. I mean, you were never really there."

"I was around when you came on weekends. Sundays anyway."

"You were there physically, but you always seemed . . . I don't know, like, mentally you were always tied up in something important."

After a pause Gurney said, a little haltingly, "And . . . I guess . . . after you got involved with Stacey Marx . . . you weren't coming every weekend."

"No, I guess not."

"After you broke up, did you stay in touch with her?"

"Didn't I ever tell you about that?"

"I don't think so."

"Stacey got all fucked up. In and out of rehabs. Kinda fried, actually. Saw her at Eddie Burke's wedding. You remember Eddie Burke, right?"

"Sort of. Redheaded kid?"

"No, that was his brother Jimmy. Anyway, no matter. Basically, Stacey is fried."

A long silence fell between them. Gurney's mind felt empty, unfocused, uneasy.

"It's kind of chilly down here," said Kyle. "You want to come back up to the house?"

"Yeah. I'll be up in a minute."

Neither of them moved.

"So . . . you never finished saying what it is about the Good Shepherd case that's getting to you. You seem to be the only person who has a problem with it."

"Maybe that's the problem."

"That's way too Zen for me."

Gurney uttered a sharp, one-syllable laugh. "The problem is a gaping lack of critical thinking. The whole goddamn thing is too neatly packaged, too simple, and way too useful to too many people. It hasn't been challenged, argued, tested, ripped, and kicked, because too many experts in too many positions of power and influence like it the way it is—a textbook crime spree by a textbook psycho."

After a short silence, Kyle said, "You sound pissed off."

"You ever see what someone looks like who's taken a .50-caliber hollow-point round in the side of the head?"

"Pretty bad, I guess."

"It's the most dehumanizing thing imaginable. The so-called Good Shepherd did that to six people. He didn't just kill them. He mangled them, turned them into something pathetic and horrible." Gurney stared off into the darkness for a long minute before going on. "Those people deserve more than they've gotten. They deserve a more serious debate. They deserve *questions.*"

"So what's the plan? Find loose ends and yank on them?"

"If I can."

"Well, that's what you're good at, right?"

"I used to be. We'll see."

"You'll succeed. You've never failed at anything."

"Of course I have."

Again there was a brief silence, broken by Kyle. "What kinds of questions?"

"Hmm?" Gurney's mind had drifted into the depths of his short-comings.

"Just wondering—what kinds of questions do you have in mind?"

"Oh, I don't know. Some big amorphous questions about the sort of personality that could be behind the language in the manifesto, the attack logistics, the choice of weapon. And lots of smaller questions, like why all the cars were the same make—"

"Or why they all came from Sindelfingen?"

"Why they all . . . what?"

"All six cars were built in the Mercedes plant in Sindelfingen, just outside Stuttgart. Probably doesn't mean anything. Just an odd little factoid."

"How on earth would you know a thing like that?"

"I told you I paid a lot of attention."

"That Sindelfingen thing was in the news?"

"No. The years and models of the cars were in the news. I was . . . you know . . . trying to figure things out. I wondered what the cars might have in common beyond what was obvious. Mercedes has a lot of assembly plants, in a lot of countries. But those six cars all came from Sindelfingen. Just a coincidence, right?"

Even though it was too dark to make out his face, Gurney turned toward Kyle on the bench. "I still don't get why you . . ."

"Why I bothered to look into that? I don't know. I guess I . . . I mean, I looked into a lot of stuff like that . . . like crimes . . . murders . . . stuff like that."

Gurney was stunned into silence. Ten years ago his son had been playing detective. And how long before that? Or after that? And why the hell hadn't he known about it? How had it escaped his attention?

*Jesus Fucking Christ, was I that unapproachable? That lost in my career, my thoughts, my personal priorities?*

He felt tears coming, didn't know what to do.

He coughed, cleared his throat. "What do they make at Sindelfingen?"

"Their top-of-the-line stuff. Which would explain it as a common factor, I guess. I mean, if the Shepherd was targeting only the most expensive Mercedes models, then that's the plant they all would have been made in."

"Still, it's an interesting point. And you took the time to discover it."

"So you want to come up to the house?" said Kyle after a pause. "Feels like it might rain."

"In a minute. You go ahead."

"You want me to leave the flashlight with you?" Kyle switched it on, shining it up the slope toward the asparagus patch.

"No need. I know the obstructions between here and there pretty well."

"Okay." Kyle stood up slowly, testing the evenness of the ground in front of the bench. There was a small splash at the edge of the pond. "The hell was that?"

"Frog."

"You sure? Are there any snakes?"

"Hardly any. All small, all harmless."

Kyle seemed to think about this for a while. "Okay," he said. "See you up at the house."

Gurney watched him, or rather the beam of his flashlight, moving gradually up the pasture path. Then he leaned back on the bench and closed his eyes, inhaling the damp air, emotionally drained.

His eyes opened suddenly at the sound of a small branch breaking somewhere in the woods behind the barn. Perhaps ten seconds later, he heard the sound again. He got up from the bench and listened, straining his eyes into the depthless black masses and ill-defined spaces that represented the area around him.

Hearing nothing more for the next minute or two, stepping tentatively, he walked carefully from the bench to the barn, which was about a hundred yards away. Once he reached the near corner of the big wooden structure, he walked slowly around it on the grassy verge that bordered it, stopping every so often to listen. Each time he stopped, he considered withdrawing the Beretta from its holster. But each time the thought was followed by a sense of overreaction.

The silence of the night now seemed absolute. The condensation in the grass was beginning to penetrate the seams of his shoes and seep into his socks. He wondered what he'd expected to discover, why he'd even bothered to circle the barn. He glanced up the slope toward the house. The amber light in the windows looked inviting.

Taking a shortcut through the field, he stumbled over a groundhog burrow and fell, which brought back for a few seconds the electric pain between his elbow and wrist. When he entered the house, he realized from Madeleine's expression that he must look disheveled.

"I tripped," he explained, smoothing out his shirt. "Where is everyone?"

She seemed surprised. "You didn't see Kim outside?"

"Outside? Where?"

"She stepped out a few minutes ago. I thought maybe she wanted a private word with you."

"She's out there in the dark by herself?"

"Well, she's not in here."

"Where's Kyle?"

"He went upstairs for something."

Her tone sounded odd to him. "Upstairs?"

"Yes."

"He's staying overnight?"

"Apparently. I offered him the yellow bedroom."

"And Kim's taking the other one?"

It was a silly question. Of course she was taking the other one. But before Madeleine could answer, he heard the side door opening and shutting, followed by the soft rustling sound of a jacket being hung up. A moment later Kim entered the kitchen.

"Did you get lost out there?" asked Gurney.

"No. I was just looking around."

"In the dark?"

"Looking to see if I could see any stars. Breathing the country air." She sounded uneasy.

"Not a good night for stars."

"No, not very good. Actually, it was kind of spooky out there." She hesitated. "Look . . . I want to apologize for the way I spoke to you before."

"No need. In fact, I want to apologize for upsetting you. I understand how important this thing is to you."

"Still, I shouldn't have said what I said the way I said it." She gave her head an embarrassed little shake. "My timing is really lousy."

He didn't understand what the "timing" reference meant, but he didn't question it, lest it prolong the exchange of apologies, which he found awkward. "I'm going to have some coffee. How about you?"

"Sure." She seemed relieved. "Good idea."

"Why don't you both have a seat at the table," said Madeleine firmly. "I'll put on enough for all of us."

They took their seats. Madeleine plugged in the coffeemaker. Two seconds later the kitchen lights went out.

"The hell happened?" said Gurney.

Neither Madeleine nor Kim answered.

"Maybe that thing tripped a circuit breaker?" he suggested.

He started to get up, but Madeleine stopped him. "The circuit breaker's fine."

"Then what could . . . ?" A low, flickering light came from the hall that led to the stairway.

The flickering light grew stronger. Then he heard Kyle's voice, singing, and a moment later the young man came in through the

arched doorway, carrying a cake covered with lit candles, his voice
growing louder with each word.

"Happy birthday to you, happy birthday to you, happy birthday,
dear Daa-aad, happy birthday to you."

"My God . . ." muttered Gurney, blinking. "Is today . . . really . . . ?"

"Happy birthday," said Madeleine softly.

"Happy birthday!" cried Kim with nervous enthusiasm, adding,
"Now you know why I feel like such a total idiot for behaving the way
I did, tonight of all nights."

"Jesus," said Gurney, shaking his head. "Bit of a surprise."

With a broad grin, Kyle laid the blazing cake gingerly in the middle of the table. "I used to get pissed when he'd forget my birthday.
But then I realized he couldn't even remember his own, so it wasn't
so bad."

Kim laughed.

"Make a wish and blow them out," said Kyle.

"Okay," said Gurney. Then, silently, he made his wish: *God help
me say the right thing*. He paused, took the deepest breath he could,
and blew out about two-thirds of the candles. He took a second breath
and finished the job.

"You did it!" said Kyle. He went out to the hall, to the main switch
for the kitchen lights, and flipped it back on.

"I thought I was supposed to get them all with one blow," said
Gurney.

"Not when there are that many. Nobody could blow out forty-nine
candles with one breath. The rule says you get a second try for any
number over twenty-five."

Gurney looked at Kyle and at the smoldering candles with bewil-
derment and, once again, felt the threat of an oncoming tear. "Thank
you."

The coffee machine began making sputtering sounds. Madeleine
went over to tend to it.

"You know," said Kim, "you don't look anywhere near forty-nine.
If I had to guess, I would have said thirty-nine."

"That would make me thirteen when Kyle was born," said Gurney, "and eleven when I married his mother."

"Hey, I almost forgot," said Kyle abruptly. He reached down

under his chair and brought up a gift box of the size that might contain a shirt or a scarf. It was wrapped in shiny blue paper with a white ribbon. Stuck under the ribbon was a birthday-card-size envelope. He handed it across the table.

"Jesus," said Gurney, accepting it awkwardly. He and Kyle hadn't exchanged birthday gifts for . . . how many years?

Kyle looked anxiously excited. "Just something I came upon that I thought you should have."

Gurney undid the ribbon.

"Check out the card first," said Kyle.

Gurney opened the envelope and began to withdraw the card.

On the front in a happily cursive script, it said, *"A Birthday Melody Just for You."*

He could feel a hard lump in the center—no doubt one of those little scratchy singing things. He assumed that when he opened the card, he would be treated to another rendition of "Happy Birthday to You."

But he didn't have a chance to find out.

Kim, whose attention had evidently been drawn to something outside the house, stood up so suddenly from the table that her chair toppled over backward. Ignoring the crash, she rushed to the French doors.

"What's that?" she cried in a rising panic, staring wide-eyed down the pasture slope, her hands coming up to her face. "God, oh, my God, what *is* that?"

## Chapter 22

# The Morning After

I t had rained intermittently from midnight till dawn. Now a thin fog hung in the midmorning air.

"Are you planning to go out that way?" asked Madeleine with a sharp glance at Gurney. She looked chilled, sitting at the breakfast table with a light sweater over her nightgown and her hands wrapped around her coffee mug.

"No. Just looking."

"Every time you stand there, the smell of smoke comes in."

Gurney shut the French doors, which he had opened a minute earlier—for the dozenth time that morning—for a clearer view of the barn, or what was left of the barn.

Most of the wood siding and all of the roof sheathing had been lost in the terrific blaze the night before. A skeletal structure of posts and rafters remained standing, but in too weakened a condition to be of any future use. Everything still erect would have to be torn down.

The wispy, slowly drifting fog gave the scene a disorienting weirdness. Or maybe, thought Gurney, the disorientation was in himself—the natural effect of not having slept. The dead-fish personality of the Bureau of Criminal Investigation arson specialist wasn't helping either. The man had arrived at 8:00 A.M. to take over from the local fire department and the uniformed troopers. He'd been poking through the ashes and debris for nearly two hours now.

"Is that guy still down there?" asked Kyle. He was sitting at the far end of the room in one of the armchairs by the fireplace. Kim was sitting in the other one.

"He's taking his time," said Gurney.

"Think he'll discover anything useful?"

"Depends on how good he is and how careless the arsonist was."

In the gray haze, the BCI investigator was walking once again with painstaking slowness around the perimeter of the ruined structure. He was accompanied by a large dog on a long lead. It looked like it might be either a black or a brown Lab—no doubt as thoroughly trained in accelerant detection as its master was in evidence collection.

"I still smell smoke," said Madeleine. "It's probably on your clothes. Maybe you should take a shower."

"In a while," said Gurney. "Too much to think about at the moment."

"At least you could change your shirt."

"I will. Just not this second, okay?"

"So," said Kyle after an awkward silence, "do you have any suspicions about who might have done it?"

"I have suspicions, like I have suspicions about all kinds of things. But that's a hell of a lot different from accusing anyone."

Kyle shifted forward to the edge of his chair. "I was thinking about it most of the night. Even after the fire trucks left, I couldn't sleep."

"I don't think any of us slept. I know I didn't."

"He'll probably give himself away."

Gurney looked from the door toward Kyle. "The arsonist? Why do you think so?"

"Don't these idiots always end up bragging to someone in a bar?"

"Sometimes."

"You don't think this one will?"

"Depends on why he started the fire to begin with."

Kyle appeared surprised by his father's response. "How about because he's a drunken lunatic hunter and was pissed off at your No Hunting signs?"

"I guess that's a possibility."

Madeleine frowned into her coffee mug. "Considering that he ripped down half a dozen of our signs and set fire to them in front of our barn door—wouldn't that make it more than 'a possibility'?"

Gurney glanced back down the hill. "Let's wait and see what the man with the dog has to say."

Kyle looked intrigued. "When he ripped down the signs to burn them, he probably left footprints in the dirt, maybe even fingerprints on the fence posts. Maybe he dropped something. Should we mention that to the arson guy?"

Gurney smiled. "If he knows his job, we don't need to tell him. And if he doesn't, telling him won't help."

Kim made an odd little shivering sound and sank farther down into her armchair. "It gives me the chills—knowing he was out there the same time I was, creeping around in the dark like that."

"The same time you were *all* out there," said Madeleine.

"That's right," said Kyle. "Down on the bench. Jeez. He could have been within a few yards of us. Damn!"

*Or within a few feet*, thought Gurney. Or even inches, recalling with an unpleasant twinge his blind circumnavigation of the barn.

"Something just occurred to me," said Kyle. "In the couple of years you've been here, have any guys approached you, wanting to hunt on your property?"

"Quite a few, when we first moved here," Madeleine answered. "We always said no."

"Well, maybe this guy is one of the ones who got refused. Did any of them seem particularly pissed off? Or claim that he had a right to hunt here?"

"Some were friendlier than others. I don't recall anyone claiming special rights."

"Any threats?" asked Kyle.

"No."

"Or vandalism?"

"No." She watched as Gurney's eyes went to the red-feathered arrow on the sideboard. "I think your father is trying to decide whether that counts as vandalism."

"Whether what counts?" asked Kyle, his eyes widening.

Madeleine just kept watching Gurney.

"A razor-tipped arrow," said Gurney, pointing at it. "Found it sticking in one of the garden beds the other day."

Kyle went over and picked it up, frowning. "That's weird. Any other weird shit been happening?"

Gurney shrugged. "Not unless you count an oddly jammed tractor brake that wasn't jammed the last time I used it, or a porcupine in the garage . . ."

"Or a dead raccoon in the chimney, or a snake in the mailbox," added Madeleine.

"A *snake*? In your *mailbox*?" Kim looked horrified.

"A tiny one, over a year ago," said Gurney.

"It scared me to death," said Madeleine.

Kyle looked back and forth between them. "If all that happened *after* you put up your No Hunting signs, doesn't that start to tell you something?"

"As I'm sure they point out in your law classes," said Gurney, more stiffly than he intended, "sequence doesn't prove causality."

"But if he tore down your No Hunting signs . . . I mean . . . If the arsonist wasn't some batshit hunter who thought you were taking away his God-given right to blow holes in deer, then who was it? Who else would do such a thing?"

While they were standing and talking by the French doors, Kim had quietly come over from the fireplace and joined them. She spoke in a small, uncertain voice. "Do you think it could have been the same person who sawed through the step in my basement?"

Gurney and his son both seemed about to respond to this when a metallic clang from somewhere outside the house diverted everyone's attention.

Gurney looked through the glass door down toward the remains of the barn. There was another clang. He could just make out the kneeling form of the investigator, wielding what appeared to be a small sledgehammer against the barn's concrete floor.

Kyle came over to his father's side. "The hell is he doing?"

"Probably widening a crack in the floor with a hammer and chisel to get a sample of the earth underneath it."

"What for?"

"When a liquid accelerant gets on the floor, it tends to seep into any available cracks, then down into the soil. If you can get an unburned sample, it makes precise identification easier."

Madeleine's eyes grew angry at this new aspect of the violation. "Our barn was doused with gasoline before it was set on fire?"

"Gasoline or something similar."

"How do you know that?" asked Kim.

When Gurney didn't answer immediately, Kyle explained, "Because of how fast it went up. A normal fire couldn't spread through a building that quickly." He glanced at his father. "Right?"

"Right," muttered Gurney vaguely. His attention had moved back to Kim's suggestion that the staircase saboteur and the barn burner might be the same individual. He turned to her. "Why did you say that?"

"Say what?"

"That it might be the same intruder—here and in your basement."

"It just popped into my head."

He thought about it. It brought to mind a question he hadn't wanted to ask her the night before. "Tell me something," he said softly. "Does the phrase 'Let the devil sleep' mean anything to you?"

Her response was immediate and startling.

Her eyes widened with fear, and she took a small step backward. "Oh, my God! How did you know about that?"

## Chapter 23

# Suspicion

Surprised by her reaction, Gurney hesitated.

"Robby!" she cried. "Damn it, Robby told you, didn't he? But if he told you, why are you asking if it means anything to me?"

"I'd like to hear about it from you."

"This isn't making any sense."

"Two nights ago in your basement, I heard something."

Kim's expression froze. "What?"

"A voice. A whisper, actually."

The color drained from her skin. "What kind of whisper?"

"Not a very pleasant one."

"Oh, my God!" She swallowed. "There was someone in the basement? Oh, my God! Was it a man or a woman?"

"Hard to tell. But a man, I think. It was dark. I couldn't see."

"Oh, my God! What did he say?"

" 'Let the devil sleep.' "

"Oh, my God!" Her frightened eyes seemed to be roving over some perilous terrain.

"What does that mean to you?"

"It's . . . the end of a story my father told me when I was little. The most frightening story I ever heard."

Gurney noticed that she was digging the fingernail of her middle finger into the cuticle of her thumb as she spoke, trying to gouge away bits of skin. "Sit down," he said. "Relax. You're going to be okay."

"*Relax?*"

He smiled, spoke gently. "Can you tell us the story?"

She steadied herself by holding on to the back of the nearest chair at the table. Then she closed her eyes and took a series of deep breaths.

After a minute or so, she opened her eyes and began in a shaky voice. "The story . . . was actually pretty short and simple, but when I was little, it seemed so . . . big. So scary. A world I got pulled into. Like a nightmare. My father called it a fairy tale. But he told it like it was real." She swallowed. "There was a king, and he made a law that once a year all the bad children in the kingdom had to be brought to his castle—all the children who'd gotten in trouble, who'd lied or been disobedient. Children who were so bad that their parents didn't want them anymore. The king kept them in the castle for a whole year. They had good food and clothes and comfortable beds, and they were free to do whatever they wanted to do. With one exception. There was a room in the deepest, darkest part of the castle basement that they were warned to stay away from. It was a small, cold room, and there was only one thing in it. A long, moldy wooden chest. The chest was actually an old, rotting coffin. The king told the children that it held a sleeping devil—the most evil devil in all the world. Each night after the children got into their beds, the king would walk from bed to bed, whispering in the ear of each child: '*Never go down to the darkest room. Stay far away from the rotting coffin. If you want to live through the night, let the devil sleep.*' But not all the children were wise enough to obey the king. Some of them suspected he made up the story about the devil in the chest because the chest was where he hid his jewels, and once in a while a child would get up in the night and sneak down into that dark room and open the rotting chest that looked like a coffin. Then a piercing shriek would rise through the castle, like the scream of an animal caught in the jaws of a wolf. And the child would never be seen again."

There was a stunned silence around the table.

Kyle was the first to speak. "Holy shit! That was the bedtime story your father told you when you were a little kid?"

"He didn't tell it that often, but every time he did, it terrified me." She looked at Gurney. "When you said 'Let the devil sleep' just now, that cold feeling came rushing back to me. But . . . I don't understand how someone could have been waiting for you in the basement. Or why whoever it was would have whispered that in your ear. What sense does it make?"

Madeleine plainly had a question that was troubling her as well. But before she could ask it, there was a firm knock at the side door.

When Gurney went and opened it, the arson investigator was standing there. The man was older, heavier, grayer-haired, and considerably less athletic-looking than most BCI detectives. The outside corners of his unsympathetic eyes seemed permanently drawn down by a lifetime of disappointment in human beings.

"I've completed my initial inspection of the site." His weary voice complemented his expression. "Now I need to get some information from you."

"Come in," said Gurney.

The man wiped his feet carefully, almost obsessively, on the doormat, then followed Gurney past the little mudroom into the kitchen. He glanced around with an air of disinterest that Gurney was sure veiled a habit of suspicious scrutiny. The arson investigators he'd known in the city were all keenly observant.

"As I just informed Mr. Gurney, I need to get some information from each of you."

"What's your name again?" asked Kyle. "I missed it when you arrived this morning."

The man looked at him blankly—no doubt, thought Gurney, assessing the aggressive edge in the young man's tone. After a moment he said, "Investigator Kramden."

"Really? Like Ralph?"

Another blank look.

"Ralph? In *The Honeymooners*?"

The man shook his head in a way that seemed more a dismissal of the question than an answer. He turned to Gurney. "I can conduct these interviews in my van or here in the house, if there's an appropriate area."

"Right here at the table would be good."

"I have to conduct them individually, without everyone present, to avoid one witness's recollections being influenced by another's."

"That's fine with me. Whether my wife and son and Ms. Corazon agree is up to them."

"It's fine with me, too," said Madeleine, although her tone was not very agreeable.

"I have . . . no objection," said Kim uncertainly.

"Sounds like Investigator Kramden is thinking we might turn out to be suspects," said Kyle, sounding eager for an argument.

The man withdrew a small iPod-like recording device from his pocket and studied it as though it were far more interesting than Kyle's comment.

Gurney smiled. "I wouldn't blame him. In arson, owners *are* usually prime suspects."

"Not always," said Kramden mildly.

"Did you get a good soil sample?" asked Gurney.

"Why do you ask?"

"Why do I ask? Because someone set fire to my barn last night, and I'd like to know whether the two hours you spent down there were productive."

"I'd say so." He paused. "What we need to do right now is complete these interviews."

"In what sequence?"

Kramden blinked again. "You first."

"I guess the rest of us should go into the den," said Madeleine coolly, "and wait for our turns?"

"If you don't mind."

As Kyle and Kim were leaving the room with her, she turned in the doorway. "I assume, Investigator Kramden, that you'll share with us at some point what, if anything, you've discovered about *our* barn?"

"We'll share whatever we can."

It was an answer so devoid of meaning that Gurney nearly laughed out loud. It was an answer he'd given countless times himself over the years.

"I'm delighted to hear that," said Madeleine with a blatant lack of delight. Then she followed Kim and Kyle down the hall to the den.

Gurney stepped over to the breakfast table, sat in one of the chairs, and motioned Kramden toward one across from it.

The man laid the recorder on the table, pushed a button, sat down, and began to speak in a flat, bureaucratic voice. "Investigator Everett Kramden, Albany Regional Headquarters, BCI . . . Recorded interview initiated ten-seventeen A.M., March twenty-fourth, 2010 . . . Interview subject is David Gurney . . . Interview location is the subject's house in

Walnut Crossing. Interview purpose is to gather information regarding a suspicious fire in a secondary structure on the Gurney property, designated as a barn, approximately two hundred yards southeast of the main house. Transcript and affidavits to follow."

He regarded Gurney with a gaze as colorless as his tone. "At what time did you first become aware of the fire?"

"I didn't look at the clock. I'd guess it was between eight-twenty and eight-forty."

"Who was the first to notice it?"

"Ms. Corazon."

"What drew her attention to it?"

"I don't know. She looked out through these glass doors for some reason and saw the flames."

"Do you know why she looked out to begin with?"

"No."

"What did she do when she saw the flames?"

"Shouted something."

"What did she shout?"

"I think 'My God, what's that?' or something similar."

"What did you do?"

"I came over from the dining table where I'd been sitting, saw the fire, rushed to the phone, called 911."

"Did you make any other calls?"

"No."

"Did anyone else in the house make any calls?"

"Not that I observed."

"Then what did you do?"

"Put on my shoes, ran down to the barn."

"In the dark?"

"Yes."

"Alone?"

"With my son. He was right behind me."

"The one named Kyle, who was just here?"

"Yes, my . . . only son."

"What was the color of the fire?"

"Predominantly orange. Fast-burning, very hot, loud."

"Burning mainly in one place or more than one?"

"Burning almost everywhere."

"Did you notice if the barn windows were open or shut?"

"Open."

"All of them?"

"I believe so."

"Is that the way you'd left them?"

"No."

"Are you sure?"

"Yes."

"Any unusual odors?"

"A petroleum distillate. Almost certainly gasoline."

"You have personal experience with accelerants?"

"Prior to my NYPD Homicide assignment, I cross-trained briefly with a fire-department arson unit."

Nearly invisible tremors in Kramden's bleak expression seemed to register a rapid succession of unspoken thoughts.

"I assume," Gurney went on, "that you and your sniffer dog found accelerant evidence along the inside base of the walls—as well as in your soil sample?"

"We made a thorough examination of the site."

Gurney smiled at the nonanswer. "And you're running your soil sample through a portable GLC in your van right now. Am I right?"

Kramden's only reaction to this speculation was a transient bulge in his jaw muscle, followed by a short pause before his next question. "Did you make any effort to put out the fire or enter the building before the arrival of the first responders?"

"No."

"You made no effort to remove anything of value from the building?"

"No. The fire was too intense."

"What would you have removed if you could have?"

"Tools . . . an electric wood splitter . . . our kayaks . . . my wife's bicycle . . . some spare furniture."

"Was anything of value removed from the building during the month preceding the fire?"

"No."

"Were the building and its contents insured?"

"Yes."

"What kind of policy?"

"Homeowners."

"I'll need an inventory of the building's contents, plus your policy number, broker's name, and the insurance company's name. Were there any recent increases in coverage?"

"No. Not unless there was an automatic inflationary adjustment that I'm not aware of."

"Wouldn't they notify you if there was one?"

"I don't know."

"Do you have more than one policy covering fire damage?"

"No."

"Have you had any previous insured losses of any kind?"

Gurney thought for a moment. "A theft-insurance payment. I had a motorcycle that was stolen in the city about thirty years ago."

"That's it?"

"That's it."

"Are you involved in any conflicts with neighbors, relatives, business associates, anyone at all?"

"It seems that we may have a conflict that we weren't aware of—with the firebug who tore down our No Hunting signs."

"When were they put up?"

"My wife put them up a couple of years ago, shortly after we moved here."

"Any other conflicts?"

It occurred to Gurney that having a step sawed out from under him and a bizarre warning whispered in his ear might be construed as evidence of a conflict. On the other hand, there was no proof that either the sabotage or the warning was meant for him personally. He cleared his throat. "No other conflicts I know of."

"Did you leave the house at any time during the two hours preceding the discovery of the fire?"

"Yes. I went down and sat on the bench by the pond after dinner."

"When was that?"

"I was down there right after dark, so . . . maybe around eight?"

"Why did you go there?"

"To sit on the bench, as I said. Relax. Unwind."

"In the dark?"

"Yes."

"You were upset?"

"Tired, impatient."

"About what?"

"A private business matter."

"Involving money?"

"Not really."

Kramden leaned back in his chair, his eyes fixed on a small spot on the table. He touched it curiously with his finger. "And while you were sitting there in the dark, relaxing, did you see or hear anything?"

"I heard a couple of sounds in the woods behind the barn."

"What kind of sounds?"

"Maybe small branches breaking? I couldn't say for sure."

"Was anyone else out of the house during the two hours preceding the fire?"

"My son came down to the bench for a while. And Ms. Corazon also stepped out for a while, I'm not sure for how long."

"Where did she go?"

"I don't know."

He raised an eyebrow. "You didn't ask?"

"No."

"How about your son? Do you know if he went anywhere other than back and forth between the house and the bench?"

"Just to the bench and back to the house."

"How can you be sure?"

"He had a lit flashlight in his hand."

"How about your wife?"

"What about her?"

"Did she leave the house at all?"

"Not that I know of."

"But you're not sure?"

"Not absolutely sure."

Kramden nodded slowly, as though these facts were forming some kind of coherent pattern. He ran his fingernail over the tiny black imperfection in the tabletop.

"Did you set the fire?" he asked, still staring at the spot.

Gurney knew that this was one of several standard arson-investigation questions that had to be asked.

"No."

"Did you cause it to be set by someone else?"

"No."

"Do you know who did set it?"

"No."

"Do you know anyone who might have had a reason to set it?"

"No."

"Do you have any other information at all that might help in the investigation?"

"Not right now."

Kramden stared at him. "What does that mean?"

"It means that *right now* I don't have any other information that could help in the investigation."

There was the tiniest flash of anger in the man's suspicious eyes. "Meaning you plan to have some relevant information in the future?"

"Oh, yes, Everett, I will definitely have some relevant information in the future. You can count on it."

## Chapter 24

# Raising the Stakes

Kramden devoted only about twenty minutes each to his interviews with Madeleine and Kyle but then spent over an hour with Kim.

At that point it was nearly noon. Madeleine offered the man lunch, but he declined with a look that was more sour than gracious. Without explanation he left the house, walked down the pasture slope, and got into his van, which was parked halfway between the pond and the wreckage of the barn.

The morning fog had dissipated, and the day had brightened somewhat under a high overcast. Gurney and Kim were sitting at the table, while Madeleine was washing mushrooms for omelets. Kyle was looking out the kitchen window. "What the hell's he up to now?"

"Probably checking on the progress of his gas-liquid chromatograph," said Gurney.

"Or eating his own private sandwich," said Madeleine with a touch of resentment.

"Once you get a GLC set up," Gurney continued, "it takes about an hour for it to run an analysis."

"How much can it tell him?"

"A lot. A GLC can break any accelerant down into its components—the precise amounts of each—which essentially produces a fingerprint of the chemical by type, sometimes even by brand if it's a distinctive formula. It can be pretty specific."

"Too bad it can't be specific about the son of a bitch who set the fire," said Madeleine, chopping a large mushroom with considerable force, the knife banging against the cutting board.

"Well," said Kyle, "Investigator Kramden may have a smart machine, but he's an asshole. Kept asking me about my flashlight, exactly what path I took to and from the house, how long I was down by the pond with Dad. He seemed to be suggesting that maybe I was lying about not knowing who started the fire. Jerk." He looked over at Kim. "He kept you the longest. What was that all about?"

"He seemed to want to know all about *The Orphans of Murder*."

"Your TV thing? Why would he want to know about that?"

She shrugged. "Maybe he thinks the two things are connected?"

"Did he already know about *Orphans*?" asked Gurney. "Or did you tell him about it?"

"I told him about it—when he asked how I was connected to you, how I happened to be here."

"What did you tell him about my role in the project?"

"That you were acting as a technical adviser on issues related to the Good Shepherd case."

"That's all?"

"Pretty much."

"Did you tell him about Robby Meese?"

"Yes, he asked about that."

"About what?"

"About whether I had any conflicts with anyone."

"So you told him about the . . . the peculiar things that have been happening?"

"He was very persistent."

"And about the staircase? And the whisper?"

"The stairs, yes. The whisper, no. I didn't personally hear it, so I figured that was up to you."

"What else?"

"That's about it. Oh, he wanted to know exactly where I was when I stepped out of the house last night. Did I hear anything, did I see you, see Kyle, see anyone else, stuff like that."

Gurney felt a slow wave of uneasiness rising in his chest. There was in any crime interview or interrogation a wide spectrum of data that might or might not be disclosed. At one end of the spectrum were irrelevant personal details that no reasonable officer would expect someone to volunteer. At the other end were major facts crucial to understanding the crime, facts whose concealment would constitute obstruction of justice.

In the middle was a gray area subject to debate and rationalization.

The question here was whether the personal conflict in Kim's life could be viewed, because of the basement incident, as a conflict in Gurney's life as well. If she reported a potential connection between her sawed step and his burned barn, shouldn't he have reported it as well?

More to the point, why hadn't he? Was it simply his ingrained cop inclination to control situations by controlling information?

Or was it the elephant in the room? His too-slow recovery from his injury. His fear that his abilities had been diminished—that he wasn't as strong, as sharp, as quick as he had once been—that there was a time when he wouldn't have fallen on his face, wouldn't have let the whisperer escape.

"You'll figure it out," said Madeleine, sliding a cutting board's worth of chopped mushrooms and onions into a large skillet on the stove.

He realized she'd been watching him and was demonstrating yet again her uncanny ability to read his mind—to see his thoughts and feelings in his eyes as clearly as if he'd spoken them. Earlier in their marriage, he'd found this faculty of hers almost frightening. Now he had come to regard it as one of the most benign and precious realities of their life together.

The skillet began to sizzle, and a pleasant aroma drifted across the room.

"Hey, that reminds me," said Kyle, looking around. "Dad's birthday present—he never finished opening it at dinner last night."

Madeleine pointed to the sideboard. The box, still in its light blue wrapping, lay next to the arrow. Kyle, grinning, retrieved it and placed it on the table in front of his father.

"Well . . ." said Gurney, vaguely embarrassed. He began removing the paper.

"David, for Godsake," said Madeleine, "you look like you're defusing a bomb."

He laughed nervously, pulled off the remaining paper, and opened the box, which was a matching blue. After unfolding several layers of crinkly white tissue paper, he found a handsome eight-by-ten sterling-silver frame. In the frame was a newspaper clipping, beginning to yellow with age. He stared at it, blinking.

"Read it out loud," said Kyle.

"I . . . uh . . . I don't have my reading glasses."

Madeleine regarded him with a combination of curiosity and concern. She turned down the gas under the skillet, came across the room, and took the framed clipping from him. She glanced through it quickly.

"It's an article from the *New York Daily News*. The headline reads, 'Serial Monster Nabbed by Newly Promoted Detective.' The article goes on: 'David Gurney, one of the city's youngest homicide detectives, put an end last night to the horrifying murder career of Charles Lermer, aka "The Slicer." Gurney's superiors give him the lion's share of the credit for the clever pursuit, identification, and final takedown of the monster said to be responsible for at least seventeen murders involving cannibalism and dismemberment over the past twelve years. "He came up with a radical new approach to the case that led to the breakthrough," explained Lieutenant Scott Barry, an NYPD spokesperson. "We can all sleep easier tonight," said Barry, declining to comment further, indicating that the pending legal process made it impossible to release full details at this time. Gurney himself was unreachable for comment. The hero detective is "allergic to publicity," according to a department colleague.' It's dated June first,1987."

Madeleine handed the framed article back to Gurney.

He held it carefully, with what he hoped was an appearance of suitable appreciation. The problem was, he didn't enjoy receiving gifts—especially expensive gifts. He also disliked being the center of attention, was ambivalent about praise, and lacked any sense of nostalgia.

"Thank you," he said. "What a thoughtful gift." He frowned at the blue box. "Is this silver frame from where I think it's from?"

Kyle smiled proudly. "Tiffany has great stuff."

"Jesus. Well. I don't know what to say. Thank you. How on earth did you get that old article?"

"I've had it pretty much all my life. I'm amazed it didn't fall apart years ago. I used to show it to all my friends."

Gurney was blindsided by a surge of emotion. He cleared his throat loudly.

"Here, let me have that," said Madeleine, taking it from him. "We'll have to find a nice prominent place for it."

Kim was watching with fascination. "You don't like being a hero, do you?"

Gurney's emotion burst out in the form of rough laughter. "I'm no hero."

"A lot of people see you that way."

He shook his head. "Heroes are fictional. They're invented to serve a purpose in stories. Media storytellers create heroes. And once they create them, they destroy them."

The observation created an awkward silence.

"Sometimes heroes are real," said Kyle.

Madeleine had taken the framed article to the far end of the room and was propping it up on the fireplace mantel. "By the way," she said, "there's a handwritten inscription on the matte border that I didn't read out loud before: 'Happy birthday to the world's greatest detective.' "

There was a sharp knock at the side door, which brought Gurney immediately to his feet. "I'll get it," he announced—he hoped not too eagerly. Exchanges of sentiment were not his strong suit, but neither did he want to appear to be in full flight from the generous emotions of others.

The stony pessimism etched into Everett Kramden's face was, perversely, less upsetting to him than was Kyle's filial enthusiasm. The man was standing several feet back from the door when Gurney opened it, almost as if some reverse magnetic force had repelled him.

"Sir, may I ask you to step outside for a moment?" It wasn't really a question.

Gurney complied—surprised by the man's tone but offering no visible reaction.

"Sir, do you own a five-gallon polyethylene gasoline container?"

"Yes. Two, in fact."

"I see. And where do you keep them?"

"One over there, for the tractor." Gurney pointed toward a weathered shed on the far side of the asparagus patch. "And one in the open lean-to structure at the back of the—" He stopped for a second. "I mean, where the back of the barn used to be."

"I see. Would you please come over to the van now and tell me if this gas container is one of yours?"

Kramden had parked his arson-unit vehicle in back of Gurney's car. He opened the rear door, and Gurney immediately identified the container inside.

"Are you sure?"

"Absolutely. There's a visible nick in the handle. No doubt about it."

Kramden nodded. "When did you last use it?"

"I don't use it that often. It's mainly for the weed whacker I keep down there. So . . . not since last fall."

"How much gas did you have in it?"

"I have no idea."

"Where did you last see it?"

"Probably in back of the barn."

"When did you last touch it?"

"Again, I have no idea. Possibly not since last fall. Possibly more recently, if I had to move it to get to something else. I have no specific recollection."

"Do you use a two-cycle oil additive in the gas?"

"Yes."

"What brand?"

"Brand? Homelite, I think."

"Do you have any idea why the gas container was concealed in a culvert?"

"Concealed? What culvert?"

"Let me rephrase the question. Do you have any idea why this gas container would be anywhere other than at the location where you said you left it?"

"No, I don't. Where exactly did you find it? What culvert are you talking about?"

"Unfortunately, I can't share any more detail on that. Is there anything you haven't told me, relative to the fire or to this investigation, that you wish to tell me at this time?"

"No, there isn't."

"Then we're finished for now. Do you have any other questions, sir?"

"None you'd be willing to answer."

Two minutes later Investigator Everett Kramden's van was heading slowly down the town road, out of sight.

The air was perfectly still. There was no hint of movement in the tall, brown grass, nor even in the smallest branches at the tops of the trees. The only sound was that faint, continuous ringing in Gurney's ears—the sound the neurologist had explained wasn't really a "sound" at all.

As he turned to go back into the house, the side door opened and Kyle and Kim emerged. "Is the asshole gone?" asked Kyle.

"Appears to be."

"While Madeleine has the omelets baking, I'm giving Kim a two-minute ride on the bike." He sounded excited. She looked pleased.

By the time Gurney reached the kitchen, the throaty twin-carbureted engine was in full, minimally muffled roar.

Madeleine was setting the timer on the oven. She looked over at him. "Did you ever see the French movie *The Man with the Black Umbrella*?"

"I don't think so."

"There's a clever scene in it. A man, dressed in a black raincoat and carrying a folded-up black umbrella, is being followed by a team of assassins with sniper rifles. They're following him through the winding cobblestone streets of an old town. It's a misty Sunday morning, and church bells are ringing in the background. Every time the two assassins try to line up the man with the umbrella in the sights of their rifles, he disappears around another corner. Then they come to an open plaza with a big stone church. Just as the assassins are aiming their rifles, the man hurries up the steps and slips into the church. So the assassins decide to take up positions on both sides of the plaza, where they can watch the church doors and wait for him to come out. Some time passes, it starts to rain, the church doors open. The assassins get ready to shoot. But instead of just the man who went in, two men come out, both dressed in black raincoats, and they both open up black umbrellas, so the assassins can't see their faces clearly. After a couple of seconds of confusion, the assassins decide to shoot both of them. But then another man comes out in a black raincoat with a black umbrella, and then another, and then ten or twenty more, and eventually the whole plaza is full of people under black umbrellas. It becomes rather surreal—the expanding pattern of umbrellas in the plaza. And the assassins are just standing there in the rain, getting soaked, with no idea what to do."

"How does it end?"

"I don't remember—I saw it so long ago. All I remember clearly are the umbrellas." She wiped the countertop with a sponge, then took it to the sink and rinsed it out. "What did he want?"

It took Gurney a second to realize what she was asking. "He found the gas container that I usually keep by the barn. The odd thing is, he found it hidden by the road somewhere."

"Hidden?"

"That's what he said. Wanted me to identify it. Doesn't make a lot of sense."

"Why would it be hidden? Did someone use it to start the fire?"

"Maybe. I don't really know. Investigator Kramden wasn't very communicative."

She cocked her head curiously. "The fire obviously was started on purpose. That was no secret, with the pile of No Hunting signs in front of the door, so what would be the point of hiding—"

"I have no idea. Unless, of course, the arsonist was so drunk that hiding the gas can made some kind of sense to him."

"You really think that's the explanation?"

He sighed. "Probably not."

She gave him one of those probing looks that made him feel transparent. "So," she said lightly, "what's the next step?"

"I can't speak for Kramden. Personally, I have to stare at the available facts for a while, figure out what's connected to what. There are some basic questions I need to get past."

"Like deciding whether you're dealing with one adversary or two?"

"Exactly. In some ways I'd prefer it to be two."

"Why?"

"Because if the same person is behind the intrusions into Kim's home and this attack on us, then we're facing something—and someone—a lot more serious than a resentful hunter."

The oven timer produced three loud dings. Madeleine ignored the summons. "Someone connected with the Good Shepherd case?"

"Or with Robby Meese—whom I may have underestimated."

The timer rang again.

Madeleine inclined her head toward the window. "I can hear them coming up the road."

"What?" The word was less a question than an expression of his irritation at the abrupt change of subject. She didn't bother to respond. He waited, and after a few seconds he, too, could make out the vintage growl of the BSA.

orty-five minutes later, after the omelets had been consumed and the table cleared, Gurney was in his den, again reviewing the e-mail documents he'd received from Hardwick—hoping he'd find something significant that he'd missed before.

He postponed looking again at the autopsy photos until he'd gone through everything else. He came close to bypassing what he told himself would be a useless, unpleasant experience—especially since the dreadful images were still so vivid in his mind from his first viewing. But he was finally pushed into it by that obsessive-compulsive gene that had been a plus in his career and a wrecking ball in his personal life.

Perhaps it was because he went through the photos in a different order, or perhaps because his mind at that instant was more receptive . . . but whatever the reason, he noticed something now he hadn't noticed the first time. The entry wounds in two of the heads appeared to be in exactly the same place.

He rooted through his desk drawer for an erasable marker, couldn't find one, went out to the kitchen, finally found one in the sideboard drawer.

"You look like you're hot on the trail of something," remarked Kyle. He and Kim were sitting by the fireplace, in armchairs that Gurney noted had been pulled a bit closer together.

He nodded without replying.

Back in the den, on his computer screen, using a credit card as a straightedge, he drew a tight rectangle around one of the two heads that had matching wounds. Then he drew intersecting lines through the middle of the rectangle, connecting its diagonally opposite corners, in order to establish its center point and confirm what he suspected would be the case: The lines crossed over the middle of the entry wound. He hurriedly wiped the screen clean with the sleeve of his shirt and repeated the exercise on the other photo—with the same result.

He called Hardwick and left a message: "Gurney here. Need to ask you a fast question about the autopsy photos. Thanks."

Then, one by one, he carefully examined the other four photos. When he was on the fourth, Hardwick called back.

"Hey, ace, what's up?"

"Just wondering about something. In at least two cases that I can verify, the entry wound is dead center on the profile. I can't tell about the other four, because it appears that those heads might have been in the process of turning toward the side window at the instant of impact. The entry wounds in those may be dead center also, relative to the direction of the shot. But since they aren't aligned to the autopsy camera at the same angle they were aligned to the gun barrel, I can't be positive."

"Not sure I'm getting your point here."

"I'm wondering if the various MEs took more wound-position and angle measurements than are included in the summaries you sent me. Because if—"

Hardwick interrupted. "Hold it! Hold it right there. Please remember, my boy, whatever data you have in your possession came into your possession some other way. It would be an actionable violation for me to have sent you any official material from the Good Shepherd files. That's clear, right?"

"Absolutely. Now let me finish. What I'm looking for is a set of numbers that will locate the entry-wound position on each face relative to the position of that face to the side window at the moment of the bullet's impact."

"Why?"

"Because two of the photos show shots that struck the precise center of the profile as presented to the shooter. If the victim's head had been a paper target, the shot in each of those two cases would have been a perfect bull's-eye. I mean *perfect*. In lousy conditions, in moving vehicles, with virtually zero visibility."

"And this means what to you?"

"I'd rather wait until I know about the other four. I'm hoping you might have access to the complete original autopsy notes, or access to someone who does, or that you might know one of the MEs well enough to pose the question."

"You'd rather wait until I creep around researching the other four for you before you tell me what the point is? I suggest you get to the fucking point now, or the answer I'm seriously contemplating is 'Fuck you.' "

Gurney was accustomed to Hardwick's manner and never let it get in the way of anything important. "The point," he replied calmly, "is that accuracy of that degree, firing through the window of a moving vehicle with nothing to illuminate the victim except minimal dashboard light—especially if the shooter managed it in all six instances—means that he has a decent set of night-vision goggles, a very steady hand, and ice water in his veins."

"So what? Night-vision equipment is available to anyone who wants it. There are a hundred sites on the Internet."

"That's not what I'm getting at. My problem is that the more pieces of data I have on the Good Shepherd, the less clear the picture gets. Who the hell is this guy? He's a super marksman—but he uses a comic-book cannon of a handgun. His manifesto is full of fiery little outbursts of biblical ranting—but his planning is as cool, consistent, and reasonable as it gets. He embarks on an all-consuming mission to kill every greedy person in the world—but he stops at six. His stated objective is insane—but he seems highly intelligent, logical, and risk-averse."

"*Risk-averse?*" Hardwick's rasping voice was even more skeptical than usual. "Racing around unlit roads at night shooting at people doesn't strike me as risk-averse."

"But what about the fact that he made every shot on the kind of curve that would minimize the chance of a collision, that he intercepted each victim's car at the same approximate midpoint of each curve, that he apparently discarded each gun after it was used, that he managed never to be caught on any surveillance camera and never to be seen by any witness? That way of doing things requires thought, time, and money. Jesus, Jack, discarding a pricey Desert Eagle after a single use? That alone looks to me like a very serious investment in risk control."

Hardwick grunted. "So you're saying on the one hand we have a Bible-waving drive-by lunatic boiling over with hate for the rich guys who are fucking up the world . . ."

". . . and on the other," said Gurney, completing the thought, "we have a stone-cold hit man who's apparently rich enough to toss fifteen-hundred-dollar handguns out the window."

A prolonged silence suggested that Hardwick was mulling this over. "And you want the autopsy data . . . to prove what?"

"Not to *prove* anything. Just to give me some idea of whether I'm on the right track with my sense of contradictions in this case."

"That's the whole reason? You know, ace, I'm thinking there might be something else."

Gurney couldn't help smiling at Hardwick's acuity. The man could be—and frequently was—a smirky, abrasive, boorish pain in the ass. But he was far from stupid.

"Yeah, there might be something else. I've been poking a sharp little stick at the accepted theory of the Good Shepherd murders. I intend to keep doing that. In the event that some FBI hornets come swarming out at me, I'd like to surround myself with as much data as I can."

Hardwick's interest rose a noticeable notch. He had an allergic reaction to authority, to bureaucracy, to *procedure,* to men in suits and ties—in other words, to organizations like the FBI. Poking a sharp stick in that direction was an activity he would naturally approve of. "You've stirred up a little conflict with our fed brothers, have you?" he asked, almost hopefully.

"Not yet," said Gurney. "But I may be about to."

"I'll see what I can do." Hardwick disconnected without saying good-bye, which was not unusual.

## Chapter 25

# Love and Hate

Gurney was slipping his phone back into his pocket when there was a light knock at the open den door behind him. He turned and saw Kim standing there.

"Could I interrupt you for just a minute?"

"Come in. You're not interrupting anything."

"I wanted to apologize."

"For what?

"For taking that ride on the back of Kyle's motorcycle."

"Apologize?"

"It wasn't the right thing to do. I mean, my timing was really thoughtless—going out for a silly motorcycle ride—when there's all this serious stuff going on. You must think I'm a selfish airhead."

"Taking a little break in the middle of a big mess seems pretty reasonable to me."

She shook her head. "I don't think it was appropriate for me to be out there acting like nothing happened, especially if there's a chance that your barn was destroyed because of me."

"Do you think Robby Meese is capable of that?"

"There was a time when I would have said, 'Not in a million years.' Now I'm not sure." She looked confused and helpless. "Do you think it was him?"

Kyle appeared in the doorway behind her, listening but saying nothing.

"Yes and no," said Gurney.

Kim nodded, as though his answer meant more than it did. "There's one more thing I need to say. I hope you realize that I had no idea a week ago what I was dragging you into. At this point I would totally understand and accept your decision if you wanted out."

"Because of the fire?"

"The fire, plus the booby trap in the basement."

Gurney smiled.

She frowned. "What's so funny?"

"Those are the reasons I *don't* want out."

"I don't understand."

Kyle spoke up. "The harder it gets, the more determined he gets."

She turned, startled.

He went on. "For my dad, difficulty is a magnet. Impossibility is irresistible."

She looked from Kyle back to Gurney. "Does that mean you're willing to stay involved in my project?"

"At least until we get things sorted out. What's next on your agenda?"

"More meetings. With Sharon Stone's son, Eric. And with Bruno Mellani's son, Paul."

"When are they supposed to happen?"

"Saturday."

"Tomorrow?"

"No, Sat—Oh, my God, tomorrow *is* Saturday. I lost a day. Do you think you'll be available?"

"As long as there are no new surprises."

"Okay. Great. I'd better get going. Time is disappearing. As soon as I get home, I'll confirm the appointments and call you with the addresses. Tomorrow we'll meet at the first interview location. That okay with you?"

"You're going back to your apartment in Syracuse?"

"I need clothes, other things." She appeared uncomfortable. "I probably won't stay there overnight."

"How are you getting there?"

She looked at Kyle. "You didn't tell them?"

"I guess I forgot." He grinned, blushed. "I'm giving Kim a ride home."

"On the back of the bike?"

"The sun's coming out. It'll be fine."

Gurney glanced out the window. The trees at the edge of the field were casting weak shadows over the dead grass.

Kyle added, "Madeleine's going to lend her a jacket and gloves."

"What about a helmet?"

"We can pick one up for her right down in the village at the Harley dealer. Maybe a big black Darth Vader thing with a skull and crossbones."

"Oh, *thanks*," said Kim with a cute imitation of sarcasm, poking his arm with her finger.

There were a number of things Gurney wanted to say. On second thought, none seemed as advisable as silence.

"Come on," said Kyle.

Kim smiled nervously at Gurney. "I'll call you with the interview schedule."

After they left, Gurney leaned back in his chair and stared out at the hillside, which was as motionless and muted as a sepia photograph. The landline phone on the far side of the desk rang, but he made no move to answer it. It rang a second time. And a third. The fourth ring was interrupted halfway through, evidently by Madeleine's picking up the handset in the kitchen. He heard her voice, but the words were indistinct.

A few moments later, she entered the den. "Man by the name of Trout," she whispered, handing Gurney the phone. "Like the fish."

He'd half expected the call but was surprised at how quickly it had come.

"Gurney here." It was the way he'd answered his phone on the job. In retirement he'd found it a hard habit to break.

"Good afternoon, Mr. Gurney. I'm Matthew Trout, special supervisory agent, Federal Bureau of Investigation." The words rolled out of the man like artillery fire.

"Yes?"

"I'm agent in charge on the Good Shepherd multiple-murder investigation. I believe you're already aware of that?" When Gurney didn't answer, he went on. "I've been informed by Dr. Holdenfield that you and a client of yours are involving yourselves in that investigation."

Gurney said nothing.

"Would you agree that's an accurate statement?"

"No."

"Excuse me?"

"You asked if your statement was accurate. I said it wasn't."

"In what way wasn't it?"

"You implied that a journalist I'm advising on matters of police procedure is trying to step into *your* investigation and that I myself am trying to do the same thing. Both those assertions are false."

"Perhaps I was misinformed. I was told you'd expressed a strong interest in the case."

"That's true. The case fascinates me. I'd like to understand it better. I'd also like to understand why you're calling me."

There was a pause, as though the man had been jarred by Gurney's brusque tone. "Dr. Holdenfield told me that you wanted to see me."

"That's also true. Is there a time that would be convenient for you?"

"Not really. But convenience is an irrelevant issue. I happen to be on a working vacation at our family lodge in the Adirondacks. Do you know where Lake Sorrow is?"

"Yes."

"That's surprising." There was something snobbish and disbelieving in his tone. "Very few people have ever heard of it."

"My brain is full of useless facts."

Trout did not respond to the not-so-subtle insult. "Can you be here at nine tomorrow morning?"

"No. How about Sunday?"

There was another pause. When Trout finally spoke, it was in a tightly controlled way, as though he were forcing his mouth into a smile to keep the sound of anger out of his voice. "What time Sunday can you be here?"

"Anytime you want. Earlier the better."

"Fine. Be here at nine."

"Be where at nine?"

"There's no posted address. Hold on and my assistant will provide directions. I advise you to write them down carefully, word for word. The roads up here are tricky, and the lakes are deep. And very cold. You wouldn't want to get lost."

The warning was almost comical.

Almost.

By the time he'd copied down the Lake Sorrow directions and returned to the kitchen, Kim and Kyle were on their way down through the low pasture on the BSA. A pale sun was breaking through the thinning overcast, and the bike's chrome was glittering.

Gurney's mind shot off into a branching pattern of anxious what-ifs—interrupted by the sound of a hanger dropping on the floor in the mudroom.

"Maddie?"

"Yes?" A moment later she appeared at the mudroom door, dressed more conservatively than usual—which is to say, less like a rainbow.

"Where are you off to?"

"Where do you think I might be off to?"

"If I knew, I wouldn't have asked."

"What day is today?"

"Friday?"

"And?"

"And? Ah. Right. One of your group things at the clinic."

She stood there looking at him with one of her complex expressions that seemed to contain elements of amusement, exasperation, love, concern.

"Do you need me to do anything regarding the insurance?" she asked. "Or do you want to take care of it? I assume we have to call someone?"

"Right. I guess our broker in town. I'll find out." It was a simple chore that had come and gone from his mind several times since the previous evening. "In fact, I'll do it now before I forget."

She smiled. "Whatever is happening, we'll get through it. You know that, don't you?"

He laid the directions to Lake Sorrow on the table, went over and hugged her, kissed her cheek and neck, then just held her tightly. She returned the hug, pressing her body against him in a way that made him wish she weren't leaving for work.

She stepped back, looked in his eyes, and laughed—just a small laugh, an affectionate murmur of a laugh. Then she turned and went through the short hallway to the side door and out to her car.

He stared out the window until her car was well out of sight.

It was then that his gaze fell on a piece of notepaper that had been Scotch-taped to the wall above the sideboard. There was a short sentence written on it in pencil. He leaned closer and recognized Kyle's handwriting.

It said, *"Don't forget your birthday card."* Under this was a little arrow pointing downward. On the sideboard directly below it was the blue envelope that had been attached to Gurney's gift. The distinctive Tiffany blue brought back his uncomfortable feeling about Kyle's need to spend that kind of money.

He withdrew the card from the envelope and once again read the words on the front: *"A Birthday Melody Just for You."*

He opened the card, still expecting that its embedded device would produce an irritating rendition of "Happy Birthday." But for three or four seconds there was no sound at all—perhaps to allow time for reading a second message on the inside: *"Peace and Joy on Your Special Day."*

And then the music began—nearly a full minute of a remarkable melodic passage from the "Spring" segment of Vivaldi's *Four Seasons.*

Considering the size of the sound device, smaller than a poker chip, the tonal quality was wonderful. But it wasn't the quality of it that stunned Gurney—it was the vividness of the memories it brought to life.

Kyle was eleven or twelve and still coming every weekend from his mother's house on Long Island to Dave and Madeleine's apartment in the city. He was starting to show an interest in the kind of music that to a parental ear sounded criminal, crude, and downright stupid. So Gurney made a rule: Kyle could listen to whatever music he chose, so long as he gave equal time to a classical composer. This had the dual effect of limiting his exposure to the dreadful music his junior-high ears seemed drawn to and exposing him to masterpieces he would never otherwise have listened to.

The arrangement was not without tension and disputes. But it also produced a happy surprise. Kyle discovered that he liked one of the classical composers whose works Gurney made available. He liked Vivaldi. He especially liked *The Four Seasons*. And of the four, he liked "Spring" best. Listening to it became the price he willingly paid for listening to the cacophonous garbage he claimed to prefer.

And then something happened—so gradually that Gurney hardly noticed. Kyle began listening, on and off, not only to Vivaldi but also to Haydn, Handel, Mozart, Bach—not as the price he had to pay for listening to junk but because he wanted to.

Years later he mentioned casually, not to Gurney but to Madeleine, that "Spring" had opened a magic door for him and that exposing him to it was one of the best things his father had ever done for him.

Gurney remembered Madeleine passing the comment along to him. He remembered how odd it had made him feel. Glad, of course, that he'd done something that had generated such a positive reaction. But also sad that it was such a small thing—a thing that required so little of himself. He wondered if the reason for its high ranking in his son's mind was that there were so few paternal gestures competing with it.

That same collision of emotions filled him now, as he held the open card in his hand, as the lovely baroque melody faded. His vision blurred, and he realized with some alarm that once again tears were about to flow.

*What the hell is the matter with me? Christ, Gurney, get a grip!*

He went to the kitchen sink and wiped his eyes roughly with a paper towel. He'd come close to crying more often in the past couple of months, he thought, than in all the years of his adult life put together.

*I need to do something—anything. Movement. Accomplishment.*

The first action that came to mind was to take inventory of the main items lost in the fire. The insurance company was sure to ask for that.

He didn't feel like doing it, but he pushed himself. He got a yellow pad and a pen from the desk in the den, got into his car, and drove down to the charred ruins of the barn.

As he got out of the car, he grimaced at the acrid odor of wet ashes. From somewhere far down the road came the intermittent whine of a chain saw.

Reluctantly, he stepped closer to the heaps of burned boards that lay within the warped but still-standing framework of the barn. In the area where their bright yellow kayaks had once rested atop a pair of sawhorses, there was now an unidentifiable brownish, bubbled, hardened mass of whatever the kayaks had been made of. He'd never been especially fond of them, but he knew that Madeleine was and that being out on the river, paddling along under a summer sky, was one of her special delights. Seeing the little boats destroyed—reduced to a solidified petrochemical glop—saddened and angered him. The sight of her bicycle was worse. The tires, seat, and cables had melted. The wheel rims were warped.

He forced himself to move slowly through the ugly scene with his pad and pen, making notes of the major tool and equipment casualties. When he finished, he turned away in disgust and got back into his car.

His mind was full of questions. Most of them were reducible to one word: *Why?*

None of the obvious hypotheses was persuasive.

Especially not the enraged-hunter theory. The local countryside was full of No Hunting signs, but it wasn't full of burned barns.

So what else could it be?

A mistake by an arsonist who'd gotten his target address wrong? A pyromaniac, hot to convert something big into flames? Mindless teenage vandals? An enemy from Gurney's law-enforcement past, acting out a revenge fantasy?

Or did it have something to do with Kim and Robby Meese and *The Orphans of Murder?* Was the arsonist the basement whisperer?

*Let the devil sleep.* If that quote was taken from a story Kim's father had told her in her childhood, as she claimed, then the admonition must have been meant for her. It would have special meaning only for her. Why whisper it to Gurney?

Could the intruder have believed that it was Kim who had fallen down the stairs?

Such an error seemed nearly impossible. When Dave fell, the first thing he heard was Kim's voice in the little passageway at the top of the stairs—screaming, calling to him frantically—then the sound of her footsteps running for the flashlight. It was only after that, lying on the basement floor, that he heard, quite close to him, the ominously hushed voice—the voice of someone who at that point must have known he wasn't talking to Kim.

But if he knew the person on the floor wasn't Kim, then why . . . ?

The answer struck Gurney like a slap in the face.

More accurately, it struck him like a crystal-clear melody from a Vivaldi violin concerto.

He drove back up to the house in such a hurry that he bottomed out the frame of the car twice on groundhog holes.

He went straight to his musical birthday card, looked at the back, and saw what he hoped to see—a company name and website: KustomKardz.com.

A minute later he was looking at the website on his laptop. Kustom Kardz was in the business of providing just that—individualized greeting cards bearing an embedded battery-driven digital playback device "with your choice of over a hundred different melodies from the world's best-loved classical compositions and traditional folk tunes."

In addition to the e-mail link on the "Contact Us" site page, there was an 800 number, which Gurney called. To start with, he had one key question for the customer-service representative. Rather than customizing the playback chip with a piece of music, could it be customized with spoken words?

The answer was yes, certainly. It would just be a matter of recording the message—which could be done over the phone—putting it in the proper audio format, and downloading it to the device.

He had two more questions, if she didn't mind. What were the options for triggering the playback if such a device were used in something other than a greeting card? And how much of a delay between the triggering and the playback could be built into the device?

She explained that triggering could be done in a number of ways—by pressure, by release of pressure, even by sound, like those light switches that respond to clapped hands. Other possibilities could be explored with Mr. Emtar Gumadin, their tech guru.

One final question. Someone he knew had received an interesting talking card that said, "Let the devil sleep." Had Kustom Kardz by any chance processed that particular message onto one of their sound chips?

She didn't think so, but if Gurney would hold on, she'd check with Emtar.

After a minute or two, she reported back that no one there could remember anything like that—unless perhaps Gurney was referring to the lullaby that began, "Go to sleep, dear one, rest . . ."

Did their company have a lot of competition?

Unfortunately, yes. The cost of the technology was dropping and its use was exploding.

As soon as Gurney ended his Kustom Kardz call, he placed a call to Kyle. He had no expectation of reaching anything other than voice mail, since he assumed that the BSA by now would be buzzing along I-88 and not even an impatient twenty-six-year-old would be likely to pull his phone out of his pocket on a speeding motorcycle.

But, as if to prove the futility of expectations, Kyle answered immediately. "Hey, Dad, what's up?"

"Where are you?"

"In a gas station by the interstate. I think the town is called Afton."

"Glad you could pick up. I'd like you to do something for me when you get to Kim's place in Syracuse. That voice I heard in her basement? I think it was a recording—probably on a miniature playback device, something like the one in the card you gave me."

"Jeez. How'd you figure that out?"

"The card gave me the idea. Here's what I want you to do. When you get to the apartment, go down in the basement—assuming the lights are working and there are no new signs of intrusions. Look around in the vicinity of the staircase for places where something the size of a fifty-cent piece could be concealed. Somewhere near the bottom of the stairs. The voice I heard was definitely within a few feet of where I fell."

"How concealed could it be? I mean, for the sound to be clear . . ."

"You're right—it couldn't be completely buried in the wall, but it could be in a shallow recess of some kind, maybe covered with paper or a painted fabric to blend in with the wall—something like that."

"Not in the floor, though, right?"

"No, the voice came from somewhere above me—as though someone were bending over me."

"Could it be in the staircase itself?"

"Could be, yes."

"Okay. Wow. We'll get going. I'll call you as soon as we get there."

"Don't speed. Half an hour one way or the other won't make any difference."

"Right." There was a pause. "So . . . did you like the card?"

"What? Oh, yes. Yes, absolutely. Thank you."

"You recognized the 'Spring' thing?"

"Of course I did."

"Okay. Great. Call you in a little while."

To prevent "the 'Spring' thing" and its memories from pulling him into an emotional morass, Gurney searched for something to do until he heard back from Kyle.

He went to the file cabinet in the den, got the phone number of their local insurance broker, and made the call. After several branching options, the automated answering system gave him another number to call "to report an accident, fire, or other loss covered by your homeowners policy."

As he was about the enter the new number, the phone rang in his hand. He glanced at the ID screen, saw that it was Hardwick. He debated the choice for about three seconds and decided the insurance call could wait.

The instant he pressed TALK, Hardwick started speaking.

"Shit, Gurney, everything you ask for is a pain in the ass, you realize that?"

"I figure your lazy ass needs the exercise."

"I need this like I need a vegan diet."

"What do you have for me, besides bullshit?"

Hardwick cleared his throat with his customary thoroughness. "Most of the original autopsy notes are buried deeper than I can get to today. Like I said, this is a giant—"

"I know what you said, Jack. The question is what do you *have*?"

"You remember Wally Thrasher?"

"The ME on the Mellery case?"

"The very one. Arrogant, wise-ass bastard."

"Like someone I know."

"Fuck you. Among his other fine qualities, Wally is obsessively-compulsively organized. And it just so happens that he did the autopsy on the big, flashy real-estate lady."

"Sharon Stone?"

"The very one."

"And?"

"Bull's-eye."

"You mean—"

"Entry wound was dead center in the side of her head. I mean, dead fucking center. Course, the exit wound was a whole other thing. Hard to find the center of something when there's nothing left to find the center of."

"It's the entry wound that matters."

"Right. So now you have the two bull's-eyes you already knew about, plus one more. You think that's good enough to prove whatever brilliant point you want to prove?"

"It just might be. I appreciate the input."

"I exist only to serve."

The connection was broken.

## Chapter 26

# An Explosion of Threats

Gurney was energized by the wound data, even though he wasn't sure yet what its full implications might be or how he might use it in his Sunday meeting with Trout. But his thoughts seemed to be moving faster now, as though he'd had a double espresso, and he turned quickly to a new question.

He placed another call to Kyle, but this time got his voice mail. Apparently the motorcycle was back on the road.

"As soon as you get this message, I want you to find out from Kim how many people are aware of the bedtime story. Not people who just know about it in a general way but who know the details, especially the line 'Let the devil sleep.' If there are more than two or three, ask her to make a list of the names, any addresses she might have, and the nature of her relationships with them. Thanks. Be careful. Talk to you soon."

As soon as he ended the call, a whole new issue came to mind. He reentered the number and left a second message: "Sorry for the multiple requests, but something else just occurred to me. After you check for that mini–playback thing in the basement, do a quick look-around for listening devices—electronic bugs. Check the most likely places—smoke alarms, surge protectors, night-lights. What you're looking for is anything in the innards of those items that seems like it might not belong there. If you find something, don't remove it. Leave it where it is. That's it for now. Call me as soon as you can."

The idea that Kim's apartment might be bugged—might have been bugged for God knows how long—raised a whole chain of perplexing questions with potentially disturbing answers. He got his copy of Kim's project folder out of the desk drawer and settled down on the den couch to go through it one more time.

Halfway through it, his energy spike began to decline as rapidly as it had risen. He told himself he'd close his eyes for five minutes. Ten at the most. He leaned back into the soft couch pillows. It had been a uniquely stressful and draining couple of days, with hardly any sleep at all.

A short nap . . .

He awoke with a start. Something was ringing, but for a moment he didn't know what. As he started to get up, he discovered a stabbing pain in his neck, stiff from the sideways position of his head.

The ringing stopped, and he heard Madeleine's voice.

"He's asleep." And then, "When I got home half an hour ago, he was totally unconscious." And then, "Let me go in and see."

She came into the den. Gurney was sitting up now, his feet on the floor, rubbing the blurriness out of his eyes.

"You're awake?"

"Sort of."

"Can you talk to Kyle?"

"Where is he?"

"At Kim's apartment. He says he's been trying to get you on your cell."

"What time is it?"

"Close to seven."

"Seven? Jesus!"

"He seems very eager to tell you something."

Gurney opened his eyes wider, stood up from the couch.

She pointed to the landline phone on the desk. "You can take the call there. I'll hang up the extension in the kitchen."

Gurney picked up the handset. "I'm here."

"Hey, Dad! Been trying to get you for the past two hours. You okay?"

"Fine, just exhausted."

"Yeah, I forgot, it's been like days since you got any sleep."

"You discover anything interesting?"

"More like weird. Where do you want me to start?"

"In the basement."

"Okay. In the basement. You know the long boards on each side of the staircase that the steps are set into? Well, I found a narrow slot cut into the bottom of one of them about two feet above the step that's missing, and there's this thing in the slot about half the size of one of those USB thumb drives for your computer."

"You removed it?"

"You said to leave it. I just kind of edged it out with the tip of a knife to see how big it was. But here's the weird part. When I pushed it back into the slot, I must have reset something, because about ten seconds later this really spooky whisper came out of it. Like some maniac in a horror movie hissing the words through his teeth. *'Let the devil sleep.'* I swear I almost pissed in my pants. I think I actually *did* piss in my pants."

"How obvious was this slot in the board?"

"Not obvious at all. It was like the guy had taken a plane and made a tiny wood shaving to cover the hole."

"So how did you——"

"You said it would be within a few feet of where you fell. Not a big area. I just kept looking till I found it."

"Did you ask Kim who else knows about the bedtime story?"

"She insists the only person *she* ever told was her crazy ex. Of course, the crazy ex could have told other people."

There was a silence, during which Gurney tried once again to draw together the disparate pieces of the case, which kept flying off in as many directions as there were pieces. And what case was he talking about anyway? The cold case of the six roadway murders, tied together by the manifesto of the Good Shepherd? The case of Kim Corazon's alleged harassment by Robby Meese, escalating into vandalism and reckless endangerment? The arson case? Or some hypothetical master case in which all these events were intertwined—perhaps even connected to the falling arrow in the garden?

"Dad, you still there?"

"Sure."

"There's more. I haven't told you the nastiest news," said Kyle.

"Jesus. What is it?"

"Every room in Kim's apartment is bugged, even the bathroom."

Gurney felt a small frisson rise up the back of his neck. "What did you find?"

"In your phone message you mentioned the obvious places to look? The first place I checked was the smoke alarm in the living room, because I know what the inside of a smoke alarm is supposed to look like. And I found something that clearly doesn't belong there. Not much bigger than a pack of matches with a fine wire sticking out of the end. Figured it was some kind of aerial."

"Was there anything resembling a lens?"

"No."

"It could be as small as half a grain of——"

"No, believe me, no lens. I thought about that, and I checked."

"Okay," said Gurney, absorbing the significance of this. The absence of video capability meant that the device wasn't part of the police's promised surveillance equipment. To identify an intruder, you planted a camera, not an audio bug. "Then you checked the other smoke alarms?"

"One in every room, and every one of them has one of those things in it."

"Where are you calling from?"

"Outside. On the sidewalk."

"Good thinking. Am I getting the impression you have more to tell me?"

"Did you know there's an access panel that leads to the apartment upstairs?"

"No. But I'm not surprised. Where is it?"

"In the laundry alcove off the kitchen."

Gurney recalled the kitchen and the laundry area as both having a ceiling pattern of large squares formed by intersecting strips of decorative molding—ideal for concealing a movable panel.

"What on earth prompted you to——"

"Check the ceilings? Kim told me sometimes she hears noises at night, creaking, other creepy little sounds. And she told me about all that other odd shit——things being moved, things missing and reappearing, the bloodstains——even though she'd had her locks changed. Plus the fact that the apartment upstairs is supposed to be vacant. So when you put all that together . . ."

"Very good," said Gurney, impressed. "You figured the most likely access to her apartment would be through the ceiling?"

"And the most likely ceiling would be the one with the panel moldings."

"Then what?"

"Then I got a ladder from the basement and started pressing on each square until I found one that felt a little different, had a different kind of give. I got a knife and loosened the molding around it, enough to see that there were cut lines underneath. I didn't go any further. If you didn't want me to move the bugs, I didn't think you'd want me to move the panel. Besides, it was secured from the other side, and I'd have to break it to get through it, which I didn't want to do, not knowing what might be up there."

Gurney noted the eagerness of the chase in his son's voice, tempered with barely enough caution. "You've had a busy afternoon."

"Got to catch the bad guys. What's the next step?"

"*Your* next step should be to get the hell out of there and come back here—both of you. *My* next step is to let these new facts sink in for a while. Sometimes when I go to bed with questions, I wake up with answers."

"Is that true?"

"No, but it sounds good."

Kyle laughed. "What questions are you going to bed with tonight?"

"Let me ask you the same thing. After all, you're the one who made the discoveries. Being on-site creates a better perspective. What do *you* think the big questions are?"

Even in Kyle's hesitation, Gurney could sense a palpable excitement. "As far as I can see, there's one really big one."

"Namely?"

"Are we dealing with an obsessed stalker or with something a whole lot nastier?" He paused. "What do you think?"

"I'm thinking that we might be dealing with both."

## Chapter 27

# Conflicting Reactions

Gurney stayed up that night until Kim and Kyle arrived from Syracuse—Kyle on his BSA and Kim in her Miata.

After they'd reviewed everything they'd discussed on the phone, Gurney had two more questions. The first was for Kyle, and he got only half of it out before it was answered. "When you took off the covers of the smoke alarms—"

"I took them off very quietly, very slowly. All the while Kim and I kept talking about something completely different—about one of her courses at school—so no one listening would realize what I was doing."

"I'm impressed."

"Don't be. I saw it in a spy movie."

Gurney's second question was for Kim. "Did you see anything in the apartment that wasn't familiar—any kind of small appliance, clock radio, iPod, stuffed animal, anything at all you hadn't seen before?"

"No, why?"

"Just wondering if Schiff ever got around to bringing in the promised video-surveillance equipment. In situations where the apartment renter is aware of the plan, it's easier to bring in a video transmitter that's prewired inside its cover object rather than concealing it in a ceiling fixture or something else on site."

"There wasn't anything like that."

The next morning at the breakfast table, Gurney noticed that Madeleine had skipped her usual bowl of oatmeal and had hardly touched her coffee. Her gaze out through the glass doors seemed focused on dark thoughts rather than on the sunny landscape.

"You thinking about the fire?"

It took her so long to answer that he began to think she hadn't heard him. "Yes, I suppose you could say I'm thinking about the fire. When I woke up this morning, you know what came into my mind, for maybe three seconds? I had the idea of enjoying this lovely morning by taking a ride on my bicycle along the back road by the river. But then, of course, I realized I don't have a bicycle. That charred, twisted thing on the barn floor isn't really a bicycle anymore, is it?"

Gurney didn't know what to say.

She sat silently for a while, her eyes narrowed in anger. Then she said, more to her coffee cup than to him, "This person who's been bugging Kim's apartment—how much do you think he's learned about us?"

"Us?"

"You, then. How much do you think he's found out about you?"

Gurney took a deep breath. "Good question." It was, in fact, a question that had been gnawing at him since his phone conversation with Kyle the previous evening. "Presumably the bugs are transmitting to a voice-activated recording device—giving him access to the conversations I had with Kim on my visits there, plus her side of all her cell-phone conversations."

"Conversations she had with you, with her mother, with Rudy Getz . . ."

"Yes."

Madeleine's eyes narrowed. "So he knows a lot."

"He knows a lot."

"Should we be afraid?"

"We need to be vigilant. And I need to figure out what the hell is going on."

"Ah. I see. I keep my eyes open for a potential maniac while you play with the puzzle pieces? Is that the plan?"

"Am I interrupting something?" Kim was standing at the kitchen door.

Madeleine looked like she was about to say, Yes, you are definitely interrupting something.

Instead Gurney asked, "You want some coffee?"

"No, thanks. I ... I just wanted to remind you ... we need to leave in about an hour for our first appointment. It's with Eric Stone in Barkham Dell. He still lives in his mother's house. You'll love meeting this one. Eric is ... unique."

Before they left, Gurney made his planned call to Detective James Schiff at Syracuse PD to ask about the surveillance equipment for Kim's apartment. Schiff was out on a call, and Gurney was transferred to Schiff's partner, Elwood Gates, who seemed familiar with the situation. Gates was, however, neither very interested in the problem nor apologetic for the delay in installing the promised cameras.

"If Schiff said we'll get to it, then we'll get to it."

"Any idea when?"

"Maybe when we're done with a few higher-priority things, okay?"

"Higher priority than a dangerous nutcase making repeated intrusions into a young woman's apartment, with the intention of inflicting serious bodily harm?"

"You talking about the broken step?"

"I'm talking about a booby-trapped staircase over a concrete floor, designed to create a potentially fatal injury."

"Well, Mr. Gurney, let me tell you something. Right now there's nothing 'potential' about the fatal injuries we're dealing with. I guess you didn't hear about the little crack-dealer turf war that erupted here yesterday? No, I didn't think so. But your giant trespassing problem is right up there at the top of our list—just as soon as we shut down about a dozen crazy scumbags with AK-47s. Okay? We'll be sure to keep you informed. You have a nice day."

Kim was watching Gurney's face as he slipped his phone back into his pocket. "What did he say?"

"He said maybe the day after tomorrow."

At Gurney's insistence they took separate cars on their trip to Barkham Dell. In the event something unexpected arose, he wanted the flexibility to separate himself from Kim's series of interviews.

She drove faster than he did, and they were out of sight of each other before they reached the interstate. It was a beautiful day—the only one so far that captured the concept of the season. The sky was a piercing blue. The widely scattered little clouds were radiant puffy things. Patches of tiny snowdrop flowers were blossoming in shaded areas along the highway. When the time-to-destination on his GPS told him he was halfway there, Gurney stopped for gas. After he filled his tank, he went into the station's convenience store for a container of coffee. Minutes later, sitting in the car with the windows open, sipping his French roast, he decided to call Jack Hardwick and ask for two more favors. He was concerned that the quid pro quo, whenever it might come, would be substantial. But he wanted information, and this was the most efficient way to get it. He placed the call, half hoping for voice mail. Instead he got the sarcastic sandpaper voice of the man himself.

"Davey boy! Bloodhound on the trail of evil incarnate! What the fuck do you want from me now?"

"Actually, quite a lot."

"You don't say! What a goddamn shock!"

"I'll be seriously indebted to you."

"You already are, ace."

"True."

"Just so long as you know it. Speak."

"First, I'd like to know everything there is to know about a Syracuse University student by the name of Robert Meese, aka Robert Montague. Second, I'd like to know everything there is to know about Emilio Corazon, father of Kim Corazon, former husband of New York City journalist Connie Clarke. Emilio dropped out of sight and out of communication ten years ago this week. Family efforts to locate him have failed."

"When you say 'everything there is to know,' what exactly—"

"What I mean is, everything that can be dug up within the next two or three days."

"That's it?"

"You'll do it?"

"Just don't forget all that indebtedness."

"I won't. Jack, I really appreciate—" Gurney began. Then he noticed that the connection had already been broken.

After he resumed his journey, he followed the instructions of his GPS off the interstate and onto a series of increasingly rural byways until he came to the turn for Foxledge Lane. There, parked at the side of the road, he saw the red Miata. Kim waved, pulled out onto the pavement in front of him, and drove slowly up the lane.

They didn't have far to go. The first driveway, flanked by impressive drystone walls, belonged to something called the Whittingham Hunt Club. The second driveway, a few hundred yards farther on, bore no identification or visible address, but Kim turned in and Gurney followed her.

Eric Stone's home was at the end of a quarter-mile driveway. It was a very large New England Colonial. Everywhere bits of paint were beginning to peel. The gutters needed tightening and straightening. There were frost-heave cracks in the driveway. Debris from the recent winter littered the lawn areas and flower beds.

There was an uneven brick walk connecting the driveway with the three steps leading up to the front door. The walk and the steps were covered with rotting leaves and twigs. When Gurney and Kim were halfway along this path, the door opened and a man emerged onto the broad top step. It occurred to Gurney that the man was shaped like an egg. His narrow-shouldered, large-bellied physique was wrapped from neck to knees in a spotless white apron.

"Do be careful. Please. It's a veritable jungle out there." His theatrical delivery was accompanied by a toothy smile and anxious eyes that fastened on Gurney. His short hair, prematurely gray, was neatly parted. His small pink face was freshly shaved.

"Gingersnaps!" he announced cheerily as he moved aside to let them into the big house.

As Gurney stepped past him, the scent of talcum powder gave way to the distinctive, spicy-sweet aroma of the only kind of cookie he thoroughly disliked.

"Just follow the hall all the way to the back. The kitchen is the coziest spot in the house."

In addition to the staircase to the second floor, the wide traditional center hall included several doors, but the patina of dust on the knobs suggested that they were rarely opened.

The kitchen at the back of the house was cozy only in the sense of being warm and full of oven aromas. It was huge and high-ceilinged and contained all the professional-commercial appliances that a decade or two earlier had become de rigueur in the homes of the well-to-do. The stove's ten-foot-tall exhaust hood brought to Gurney's mind a sacrificial altar in an Indiana Jones movie.

"My mother was a devotee of quality," said the egg-shaped man. Then he added, with a startling echo of Gurney's passing thought, "She was an acolyte at the altar of perfection."

"How long have you lived here?" asked Kim.

Instead of answering the question, he turned to Gurney. "I definitely know who you are, and I suspect you know who I am, but I still think it would be appropriate to be introduced."

"Oh, stupid me!" said Kim. "I'm so sorry. Dave Gurney, Eric Stone."

"Delighted," said Stone, extending his hand with an ingratiating smile. His large, even teeth were nearly as white as his apron. "Your very impressive reputation precedes you."

"Nice to meet you," said Gurney. Stone's hand was warm, soft, and unpleasantly moist.

"I told Eric about the article my mother wrote about you," said Kim.

After an awkward silence, Stone pointed to a fashionably distressed pine table at the end of the kitchen farthest from the grand stove. "Shall we?"

When Gurney and Kim had taken their seats, Stone asked if either one wanted anything to drink. "I have various coffees in various strengths, as well as teas in countless herbal varieties. I also have some peculiar pomegranate soda. Any takers?"

They both declined, and Stone, making an exaggerated show of disappointment, sat down in the third chair at the table. Kim took three small cameras and two mini-tripods out of her shoulder bag. She set up two of the cameras on the tripods, one facing Stone, one facing herself.

She then explained the production philosophy at length—how "the folks at RAM" were intent on ensuring that the look and feeling of the interview was as simple and low-tech as possible, keeping it within the same visual and audio framework that was familiar to all those viewers who were accustomed to recording family moments on their iPhones. The goal was to keep it real. Keep it simple. An unpredictable conversation, not a scripted scene. With room lighting, not stage lighting. Nonprofessional. Human beings being human. Et cetera.

Whether Stone had any reaction to this declaration of authenticity was unclear. His mind seemed to wander somewhere else, refocusing only when Kim wrapped up her comments by asking, "Do you have any questions?"

"Only one," he said, turning to Gurney. "Do you think they'll ever get him?"

"The Good Shepherd? I'd like to think so."

Stone rolled his eyes. "In your profession I bet you give a lot of answers like that—answers that aren't really answers at all." His tone was more depressed than challenging.

Gurney shrugged. "I don't know enough yet to tell you anything more."

Kim made some final framing adjustments in the viewfinders of her tripod cameras and put them both in HD-movie mode. She did the same with the third camera, which she kept in her hand. Then she ran her fingers back through her hair, sat up straighter in her chair, smoothed a few wrinkles out of her blazer, smiled, and began speaking.

"Eric, I want to thank you again for your willingness to participate in *The Orphans of Murder.* Our goal is an honest, unrehearsed presentation of your thoughts and feelings. Nothing is off-limits, nothing is out of bounds. We're in your home, not on a studio set. The story is yours, the emotions are yours. Begin wherever you wish."

He took a long, shaky breath. "I'll begin by answering the question you asked me when you walked into the kitchen a few minutes ago. You asked me how long I've lived here. The answer is twenty years. Half of those years in heaven, half in hell." He paused. "The first ten years, I lived in a world of sunlight cast by a remarkable woman, the last ten years in shadowland."

Kim let a long silence pass before responding in a soft, sad voice. "Sometimes it's the depth of the pain that tells us how much we've lost."

Stone nodded. "Mother was a rock. A rocket. A volcano. She was a force of nature. Let me repeat that—*a force of nature.* It's a cliché, but a good one. Losing her was like having the law of gravity repealed. *The law of gravity—repealed!* Imagine that. A world without gravity. A world with nothing to hold it together."

The man's eyes were glistening with incipient tears.

Kim's next words were a surprise. She asked Stone if she could have a cookie.

He burst out laughing—a giddy, hysterical outpouring that sent the tears down his cheeks. "Yes, yes, of course you can! My gingersnaps just came out of the oven, but there are also pecan chocolate chips, buttery-buttery shortbreads, and oatmeal raisin. All baked today."

"I think oatmeal raisin," she said.

"An excellent choice, madam." He sounded like he was, through his tears, attempting to mimic a smarmy sommelier. He went to the far end of the kitchen and retrieved a plate heaped with large brown cookies from the top of the oven. Kim held up her third camera, keeping him in the frame all the while.

As he was about to lay the plate on the table, a thought seemed to stop him. He turned to Gurney. "Ten years," he said, as if some new significance in the number had taken him by surprise. "Exactly ten years. A full decade." The pitch of his voice rose dramatically. "Ten years, and I'm still a basket case. What do you make of that, Detective? Does my pathetic condition motivate you to find, arrest, and execute the evil fucker who murdered the most incredible woman in the world? Or am I so ridiculous you just want to laugh?"

Gurney tended to ice over at displays of emotion. Now was no exception. He answered with a matter-of-fact blandness. "I'll do everything I can."

Stone gave him an archly skeptical look but didn't pursue the issue.

He offered them coffee again, and again they both declined.

After that, Kim spent some time eliciting descriptions of the man's life before and after his mother's murder. In Stone's detailed narrative, life before was better in every way. Sharon Stone had been an increasingly successful player at the top end of the second-home real-estate market. And she lived her personal life at the top end in every way, sharing that luxury freely with her son. Shortly before the brutal intervention of the Good Shepherd, she'd agreed to cosign a $3 million financing agreement to set Eric up as owner of the premier inn and restaurant in the Finger Lakes wine country.

Without her supportive signature, however, the deal collapsed. Instead of enjoying the life of an elite restaurateur and hotelier, he was at thirty-nine living in a house whose estate grounds he couldn't begin to maintain and trying to make a living baking cookies in his late mother's dream kitchen for local gourmet shops and B&Bs.

After an hour or so, Kim finally closed the small notebook she'd been consulting and surprised Gurney by asking if he had any questions of his own.

"Maybe a couple, if Mr. Stone doesn't mind."

"*Mr. Stone?* Please, call me Eric."

"All right, Eric. Do you know if your mother ever had any prior business or personal contact with any of the other victims?"

He winced. "Not that I know of."

"Any enemies you knew of?"

"Mother did not suffer fools gladly."

"Meaning?"

"Meaning she ruffled feathers, stepped on toes. Real estate, particularly at the level at which Mother operated, is a *very* competitive business, and she didn't like to have her time wasted by idiots."

"Do you remember why she bought a Mercedes?"

"Of course." Stone grinned. "Classy. Stylish. Powerful. Agile. A major cut above the others. Just like Mother."

"Over the past ten years, have you had any contact with anyone connected with the other victims?"

He winced again. "That word. I don't like it."

"What word?"

" 'Victim.' I don't think of her that way. It sounds so horribly passive, helpless, all the things that Mother *wasn't.*"

"I'll put it another way. Regarding any contact with the families—"

Stone interrupted. "The answer is yes, there was some contact at first—a kind of support group that came together after the shootings."

"Were all the families involved?"

"Not really. The surgeon who lived in Williamstown had a son who joined us once or twice, then announced he had no interest in a grief group because he had no grief. He said he was glad his father was dead. He was quite awful. Totally hostile. Very hurtful."

Gurney glanced at Kim.

"Jimi Brewster," she said.

"Is that all?" asked Stone.

"Just two more quick ones. Did your mother ever mention anyone she was afraid of?"

"Never. She was the most fearless human being who ever walked the earth."

"Was 'Sharon Stone' her real name?"

"Yes and no. Mostly yes. Her name was officially Mary Sharon Stone. After the huge success of *Basic Instinct,* she had a makeover— changed her hair from brown to blond, dropped the 'Mary,' and promoted the remarkable new persona. Mother was a promotional genius. She even got the idea of running photos of herself on billboards, sitting with her legs crossed in a short skirt, à la the famous scene in the film."

Gurney indicated to Kim that he had no more questions.

Stone added with an unsettling smile, "Mother had legs to die for."

An hour later Gurney pulled in next to Kim's Miata in front of the bleak strip-mall office of an accounting firm: Bickers, Mellani, and Flemm. It was situated between a yoga studio and a travel agency on the outskirts of Middletown.

Kim was on her cell phone. Gurney sat back and mused on what he would do if his name were Flemm. Would he change it, or would he wear it as a badge of defiance? Was the refusal to change one's name, when the name was as patently absurd as a donkey tattoo on one's forehead, laudably honest or stupidly stubborn? At what point did pride become dysfunctional?

*Christ, why am I occupying my brain with this nonsense?*

A sharp little rap and Kim's purposeful face at his side window brought him back to the moment. He got out of his car and followed her into the office.

The front door opened into an unimpressive waiting area with a few unmatched chairs against one wall. Worn copies of *SmartMoney* were fanned out on a small Danish Modern coffee table. A waist-high

LET THE DEVIL SLEEP

243

barrier separated this area from a smaller area that contained two bare
desks in front of a wall with a single door, which was closed. Atop
the barrier was an old-fashioned bell—a little silver dome that had a
raised plunger on the top.

Kim tapped firmly on the plunger, producing a surprisingly loud
*ding*. She repeated this half a minute later, with no response. As she
was reaching for her phone, the door in the rear wall opened. The man
in the doorway was thin, pale, tired-looking. He gazed at them without
curiosity.

"Mr. Mellani?" said Kim.

"Yes." His voice was dry and colorless.

"I'm Kim Corazon."

"Yes."

"We spoke on the phone? About my coming here to prepare for our
interview?"

"Yes, I remember."

"Well . . ." She looked around in mild confusion. "Where would
you like to . . . ?"

"Oh. Yes. You can come into my office." He stepped back inside.

Gurney opened a swinging panel in the low barrier and held it
for Kim. It was dusty, like the two unoccupied desks behind it. He
followed her into the back office—a windowless room with a large
mahogany table, four straight-backed chairs, and bookcases on three of
the four walls. The bookcases were filled with fat volumes on accounting rules and tax laws. The pervasive dust had settled on the books as
well. The air smelled stale.

The only illumination came from a desk lamp at the far end of the
table. There was a fluorescent fixture on the ceiling, but it was turned
off. As Kim surveyed the room for places to set up her cameras, she
asked if it could be turned on.

Mellani shrugged and flipped the switch. After a series of hesi-
tant flashes, the light stabilized, producing a low buzz. The fluorescent
glow emphasized the paleness of his skin and the shadows below his
eyes. There was something distinctly cadaverous about him.

As she had done in Stone's kitchen, she went through the process of
arranging the cameras. When she was finished, she and Gurney sat on
one side of the mahogany table, Mellani on the other. At that point she

gave, almost word for word, the same speech she'd given Stone about the production goals of informality, simplicity, naturalness—keeping the interview as close as possible to the kind of conversation two friends might have in their home, loose and candid.

Mellani didn't reply.

She told him that he should feel free to say anything he wished.

He said nothing, just sat and stared at her.

She looked around the claustrophobic space, whose inhospitable drabness the ceiling light had only managed to enhance. "So," she said awkwardly, seeming to realize that she would have to be the motivator of whatever conversation they were going to have, "this is your main office?"

Mellani seemed to consider this. "Only office."

"And your partners? They . . . they're here?"

"No. No partners."

"I thought . . . the names . . . Bickers . . . and . . . ?"

"That was the name of the firm. Formed as a partnership. I was the senior partner. Then we . . . we parted ways. The name of the firm was a legal thing . . . legally independent of who actually worked here. I never had the energy to change it." He spoke slowly, as though struggling with the unwieldiness of his own words. "Like some divorced women keep their married names. I don't know why I don't change it. I should, right?" He didn't sound as if he wanted an answer.

Kim's smile became more strained. She shifted in her seat. "Quick question before we go any further. Shall I call you Paul, or would you prefer that I call you Mr. Mellani?"

After several seconds of dead silence, he answered almost inaudibly, "Paul's okay."

"Okay, Paul, we'll get started. As we discussed on the phone, we're just going to have a simple conversation about your life after the death of your father. Is that all right with you?"

Another pause, and then he said, "Sure."

"Great. So. How long have you been an accountant?"

"Forever."

"I mean, specifically, in years?"

"Years? Since college. I'm . . . forty-five now. Twenty-two when I graduated. So forty-five minus twenty-two equals twenty-three years as an accountant." He closed his eyes.

"Paul?"

"Yes?"

"Are you all right?"

He opened one eye, then the other. "I agreed to do this, so I'll do it, but I'd like to get it over with. I've been through all this in therapy. I can give you the answers. I just . . . don't like listening to the questions." He sighed. "I read your letter . . . We talked on the phone . . . I know what you want. You want before and after, right? Okay. I'll give you before and after. I'll give you the gist of the then and the now." He uttered another small sigh.

Gurney had the momentary impression that they were miners trapped in an underground cave-in, their oxygen supply fading—a scrap of memory from a movie he saw as a child.

Kim frowned. "I'm not sure I understand."

Mellani repeated, the words heavier the second time around, "I've been through all this in therapy."

"Okay . . . and . . . therefore . . . you . . . ?"

"Therefore I can give you the answers without your having to ask the questions. Better for everyone. Right?"

"Sounds great, Paul. Please, go right ahead."

He pointed at one of her cameras. "Is that running?"

"Yes."

Mellani shut his eyes again. By the time he began his narrative, whatever Kim was feeling about the situation was breaking out in tics at the corners of her mouth.

"It's not like I was a happy person before the . . . event. I was never a happy person. But there was a time when I had hope. I think I had hope. Something like hope. A sense that the future could be brighter. But after the . . . event . . . that feeling was gone forever. The color in the picture got switched off, everything was gray. You understand that? No color. I once had the energy to build a professional practice, to *grow* something." He articulated the word as though it were a strange concept. "Clients . . . partners . . . momentum. More, better, bigger. Until it happened." He fell silent.

"It?" prompted Kim.

"The event." He opened his eyes. "It was like being pushed over the edge of something. Not a cliff, just ..." He raised his hand, miming the movement of a car reaching the apex of a hill, then tilting slightly downward. "Things started going south. Falling apart. Bit by bit. The engine wasn't running anymore."

"What was your family situation?" asked Kim.

"Situation? Apart from the fact that my father was dead and my mother was in an irreversible coma?"

"I'm sorry, I should have been clearer. What I meant was, were you married, did you have any other family?"

"I had a wife. Until she got tired of everything going downhill."

"Any children?"

"No. That was a good thing. Or maybe not. All my father's money went to his grandchildren—my sister's children." Mellani produced a smile, but there was bitterness in it. "You know why? This is funny. My sister was a very screwed-up person, very anxious. Both her kids are bipolar, ADHD, OCD, you name it. So my father ... he decides that *I'm* fine, *I'm* the healthy one in the family, but *they* need all the help they can get."

"Are you in contact with your sister?"

"My sister is dead."

"I'm sorry, Paul."

"Years ago. Five? Six? Cancer. Maybe dead isn't so bad."

"What makes you say that?"

Again the bitter smile, drifting into sadness. "See? Questions. Questions." He stared down at the tabletop as though he were trying to discern the outlines of something in murky water. "The thing is, money meant a lot to my father. It was the most important thing. You understand?"

His sadness was reflected in Kim's eyes. "Yes."

"My therapist told me that my father's obsession with money was the reason I became an accountant. After all, what do accountants count? They count money."

"And when he left everything to your sister's family ... ?"

Mellani raised his hand again. This time he mimed the slow descent of a car into a deep valley. "Therapy gives you all this insight, all this clarity, but that's not always a good thing, is it." It wasn't a question.

...

E merging from Paul Mellani's dreary office half an hour later into the sunny parking lot gave Gurney the jarring feeling he got coming out of a dark movie theater into daylight—a shift from one world to another.

Kim took a deep breath. "Wow. That was . . ."

"Dismal? Desolate? Morose?"

"Just sad." She looked shaken.

"Did you notice the dates on the magazines in the reception area?"

"No, why?"

"They were all from years ago, nothing current. And speaking of dates, you realize what time of year this is?"

"What do you mean?"

"It's the last week of March. Less than three weeks to April fifteenth. These are the weeks every accountant should be crazy busy."

"Oh, jeez, you're right. Meaning he has no clients left. Or not very many. So what's he doing in there?"

"Good question."

The drive back to Walnut Crossing in their separate cars took nearly two hours. Toward the end the sun was low enough in the sky to produce a hazy glare on Gurney's dirty windshield—reminding him for the third or fourth time that week that he was out of wiper fluid. What irritated him more than the absence of the fluid was his increasing dependence on notes. If he didn't write something down . . .

The ring of his phone interrupted his brooding over the state of his mind. He was surprised to see Hardwick's name on the screen.

"Yes, Jack?"

"The first one was easy. But don't think that reduces your debt."

Gurney thought back to the request he'd made that morning. "The first one being the history of Mr. Meese-Montague?"

"Actually, Mr. Montague-Meese, but more about that anon."

"Anon?"

"Yeah, anon. It means 'soon.' One of William Shakespeare's favorite words. Whenever he meant 'soon,' he said 'anon.' I'm expanding my vocabulary so I can speak with greater confidence to intellectual dicks like you."

"That's good, Jack. I'm proud of you."

"Okay, this is a first take. Maybe we'll have more later. The individual of whom we speak was born March twenty-eighth, 1989, at St. Luke's Hospital in New York City."

"Huh."

"What's the 'huh' about?"

"That means he's about to turn twenty-one."

"So fucking what?"

"Just an interesting fact. Proceed."

"There is no father's name indicated on the birth certificate. Little Robert was surrendered for adoption by his mother, whose name, incidentally, was Marie Montague."

"So little Robert was actually a Montague before he was a Meese. Very interesting."

"It gets more interesting. He was adopted almost immediately by a prominent Pittsburgh couple, Gordon and Celia Meese. Gordon, it so happens, was filthy rich. Heir to an Appalachian coal-mining fortune. Guess what comes next."

"The excitement in your voice tells me it's something horrible."

"At the age of twelve, Robert was removed from the Meese home by Child Protective Services."

"Were you able to find out why?"

"No. Believe me, that is one seriously sealed case file."

"Why am I not surprised? What happened to Robert after that?"

"Ugly story. One foster home after another. No one willing to keep him for more than six months. Difficult young man. Has been prescribed various drugs for a generalized anxiety disorder, borderline-personality disorder, intermittent-explosive disorder—gotta love that one."

"I guess I shouldn't ask how you got access to—"

"Right. So don't. Bottom line, it adds up to a very insecure kid with a shaky grip on reality and a major anger problem."

"Then how did this paragon of stability—"

"End up at the university? Simple. Right in the center of that screwed-up mind there lurks a sky-high IQ. And a sky-high IQ, combined with a troubled background, combined with zero financial resources, is the magic formula for a full college scholarship. Since entering the university, Robert has excelled in drama and has earned fair to lousy marks in everything else. He is said to be a natural-born actor. Movie-star handsome, fantastic onstage, able to turn on the charm, but basically secretive. He recently changed his name back from Meese to Montague. For a few months, he cohabited, as you may know, with little Kimmy. Apparently that ended badly. Currently lives alone in a three-room rental in a subdivided Victorian house on a nice street in Syracuse. Sources of income for rent, car, and other nonuniversity expenses are unknown."

"Any employment?"

"Nothing obvious. That's the story for now. If more shit turns up, I'll drop it on you."

"I owe you."

"You got that right."

Gurney's mind was swimming with so many free-floating facts that when Madeleine commented that evening over coffee on the spectacular sunset that had occurred an hour earlier, he had no recollection of having seen it. In its place was a mass of disquieting images, personalities, details.

The Humpty-Dumpty cookie baker, not wanting to think of his all-powerful mother as a "victim." The mother who "ruffled feathers, stepped on toes." Gurney wondered if the man was ever told about her earlobe on the sumac bush, the earlobe with the diamond stud in it.

Paul Mellani, a man whose rich father gave all his money, therefore all his love, to someone else. A man whose career had lost its meaning, whose life had turned gray, whose thoughts were grim and sour—and whose language, demeanor, and lifeless office were the equivalent of a suicide note.

Jesus . . . suppose . . .

Madeleine was watching him across the table. "What's the matter?"

"I was just thinking about one of the people Kim and I visited today."

"Go on."

"I'm trying to go back over what he said. He sounded . . . pretty depressed."

Madeleine's gaze grew more intense. "What did he say?"

"That's what I'm trying to remember. The thing that comes to mind was a comment he made. He'd just told us his sister was dead. Then he said, 'Dead isn't so bad.' Something like that."

"Nothing more direct? No expression of any intention to do anything?"

"No. Just . . . a heaviness, a . . . lack of . . . I don't know."

Madeleine looked anguished.

"The guy at your clinic, the patient who killed himself? Was he specific about . . . ?"

"No, of course not, or he would have been taken to a psych ward. But he definitely had that . . . *heaviness.* A darkness, a hopelessness."

Gurney sighed. "Unfortunately, it doesn't matter what we think someone *may* do. It only matters what people *say* they're going to do." He frowned. "But there's something I'd like to find out. Just for my own peace of mind." He got his cell phone from the sideboard and entered Hardwick's number. The call went to voice mail.

"Jack, I want to increase my enormous indebtedness to you by asking for one more tiny favor. There's an accountant down in Orange County by the name of Paul Mellani. Happens to be the son of Bruno Mellani, the first Good Shepherd victim. I'd like to know if he has any guns registered. I have a concern about him, and I'd like to know how much I should worry. Thanks."

He sat back down at the table and absently put a third spoon of sugar in his coffee.

"The sweeter the better?" asked Madeleine with a small smile.

He shrugged, stirring the coffee slowly.

She cocked her head a little to one side and studied him in a way that had once made him uneasy but in recent years he'd come to welcome—not because he understood what she was thinking, or what conclusions her "study" produced, but because he saw it as an expression of affection. To ask her what was on her mind would be like demanding that she define their relationship. But the part of any relationship that made it precious was not something that could be defined on demand.

She raised her cup to her lips with two hands, sipped from it, and put it down gently. "So . . . do you want to tell me a bit more about what's going on?"

For some reason the question took him by surprise. "You really want to know?"

"Of course."

"There's a lot."

"I'm listening."

"Okay. Remember, you asked for it." He leaned back in his chair and spoke with hardly a pause for twenty-five minutes, recounting everything that came to mind—from Roberta Rotker's firing range to the skeleton at Max Clinter's gate—with no effort to organize, prioritize, or edit the data. As he went on, he himself was struck by the sheer number of intense people, weird tangents, and sinister complexities in the affair. "And finally," he concluded, "there's the matter of the barn."

"Yes, the barn," said Madeleine, her expression hardening. "You believe it's connected with everything else?"

"I think it is."

"So what's the plan?"

It was an unwelcome question, because it forced him to face the fact that his intentions didn't add up to anything remotely like a *plan.* "Poke around in the shadows with a cattle prod, see if anyone yells," he said. "Maybe light a fire under the sacred cow."

"Can any of that be expressed in English?"

"I want to find out if anyone in official law enforcement actually has any solid facts, or if the sanctified theory of the Good Shepherd case is as fragile as I think it is."

"That's what you're doing tomorrow with the fish guy?"

"Yes. Agent Trout. At his cabin in the Adirondacks. On Lake Sorrow."

Just then Kyle and Kim came in the side door, accompanied by a rush of chilly air.

## Chapter 28

# Darker, Colder, Deeper

A t dawn the next morning, Gurney was back at the table with his first coffee of the day. Sitting by the French doors, he was watching a daddy longlegs dragging a captured earwig along the edge of the stone patio. The earwig was still putting up a fight.

For a moment Gurney was tempted to intervene—until he realized that his impulse was neither kind nor empathetic. It was nothing more than a desire to brush the struggle out of sight.

"What's the matter?" It was Madeleine's voice.

He looked up with a start to find her in a pink T-shirt and green madras shorts, fresh from her shower, standing next to him.

"Just observing the horrors of nature," he said.

She looked out through the glass doors at the eastern sky. "It's going to be a nice day."

He nodded without really hearing her. Another thought had absorbed his attention. "Before I went to bed last night, Kyle said something about going back to Manhattan this morning. Do you recall if he mentioned what time he was planning to leave?"

"They left an hour ago."

"What?"

"They left an hour ago. You were sound asleep. They didn't want to wake you."

"They?"

Madeleine gave him a look that seemed to convey her surprise at his surprise. "Kim has to be in the city this afternoon to record something for *The Orphans of Murder*. Kyle persuaded her to go down early with him, so they could spend the day doing things together. She didn't appear to need much persuading. In fact, I think the plan is for her to stay over at his apartment tonight. I can't believe you didn't see this coming."

"Maybe I did, but not so fast."

Madeleine went to the coffeemaker on the sink island and poured herself a cup. "Does it worry you?"

"Unknowns worry me. Surprises worry me."

She took a sip and returned to the table. "Unfortunately, life is full of them."

"So I've discovered."

She stood by the table, gazing through the far window toward the widening swath of light above the ridge. "Does Kim worry you?"

"To some extent. I wonder about the Robby Meese thing. I mean, that guy is pretty warped, and she let him move in with her. There's something wrong with that picture."

"I agree, but maybe not the way you mean it. A lot of people, mostly women, are attracted to damaged individuals. The more damage, the better. They get involved with criminals, drug addicts. They want to *fix* somebody. It's a horrible basis for a relationship, but not that unusual. I see it every day at the clinic. Maybe that's what was going on with Kim and Robby Meese—until she found the strength and sanity to get him out of her life."


With his detailed route directions in hand, Gurney left shortly after sunrise for Lake Sorrow. The drive through the Catskill foothills and rolling Schoharie farmlands up into the Adirondacks was a journey into discomfiting memories. Memories of preteen vacations at Brant Lake with his mother at the height of her emotional estrangement from his father. An estrangement that left her needy, anxious, and physically clingy. Even now, close to forty years later, the memories cast an unsettling pall.

As he drove farther north, the pitch of the mountain slopes increased, the valleys narrowed, and the shadows deepened. According to the instructions he'd been given by Trout's assistant, the last road he'd be taking with any posted identification would be Shutter Spur. From that point on, he'd have to rely on precise odometer readings to make the proper turns in a maze of old logging roads. The forest was part of a vast private landholding in which there were only a few seasonal cabins, no stores, no gas stations, no people, and major gaps in cell service.

The AWD system on Gurney's Outback was barely adequate to negotiate the terrain. After the fifth turn, which his instructions indicated would take him directly to Trout's cabin, he found himself instead in a small clearing.

He got out of the car and walked around the perimeter. There were four rough trails leading from the clearing into the forest in various directions, but no way of telling which one he was supposed to take. It was 8:58 A.M.—just two minutes shy of his projected arrival time.

He was sure he'd followed all the instructions accurately and reasonably sure that the punctilious-sounding man on the phone was not likely to have made a mistake. That left a couple of possible explanations, but only one he considered probable.

He returned to his car, got in, opened the side window for a bit of fresh air, reclined the seat as far as it would go, lay back, and closed his eyes. Every so often he checked the time. At nine-fifteen he heard the engine of an approaching vehicle. It stopped not far away.

When the expected knock came, he opened his eyes, yawned, raised his seat, and lowered the window. The man standing there had a lean, hard appearance, with sharp brown eyes and close-cropped black hair.

"You David Gurney?"

"You expecting anyone else?"

"You need to leave your car here and come up in the ATV." He gestured toward a camouflage-painted Kawasaki Mule.

"You didn't mention this to me on the phone."

The man's eyelids twitched. Maybe he didn't expect his voice to be so easily recognized. "The direct route isn't passable at the current time."

Gurney smiled. He followed the man to the ATV and got into the passenger seat. "You know what I'd be tempted to do if I had a place up here? Every once in a while, I might be tempted to play a little game with one of my guests. Make him think he was lost, maybe missed a turn, see if he'd panic—you know, out in the middle of nowhere with no cell coverage. Because if he screwed up on his way in, he wouldn't be able to find his way out, would he? Always fun to see who panics and who doesn't in a situation like that. Know what I mean?"

The man's jaw tightened. "Can't say that I do."

"Of course not. How could you? For someone to appreciate what I'm talking about, he'd have to be a real control freak."

Three minutes later—a jouncy half mile up and down a rocky trail, during which the man's angry gaze never left the treacherous terrain—they arrived at a chain-link fence with a sliding gate that opened as they approached it.

Inside the fence the trail faded into a broad bed of pine needles. Then, quite suddenly through the trees, the "cabin" appeared in front of them. It was a two-story structure in the modified Swiss-chalet style of some traditional Adirondack camps—rustic log construction with recessed porches, green doors and window trim, and a green shingle roof. The façade was so dark, and the porch in so much shadow, that it wasn't until the ATV pulled up to the front steps that Gurney saw Agent Trout—or the man he presumed to be Agent Trout—standing proprietarily in the center of the dismal porch, feet planted wide apart. He held a large Doberman on a short black leash. Accidentally or purposely, the arrogant pose and the imposing guard dog made Gurney think of a prison-camp commandant.

"Welcome to Lake Sorrow." The voice, emotionless and bureaucratic, conveyed *no* hint of welcome. "I'm Matthew Trout."

The few rays of sunlight that penetrated the huge pines were far apart and thin as icicles. The evergreen scent in the air was powerful. The low, persistent sound of an internal-combustion engine, most likely a generator, came from the direction of an outbuilding off to the right of the main house.

"Nice spot you have here."

"Yes. Please come inside." Trout issued a sharp command, the Doberman turned around, and together they preceded Gurney into the house.

The front door led directly into a spacious sitting room dominated by a stone fireplace. In the center of the rough-hewn mantel was a stuffed bird of prey with furious yellow eyes and extended talons, flanked by twin wildcats poised to leap.

"They're coming back," said Trout significantly. "New sightings in these mountains every week."

Gurney followed the man's gaze. "Wildcats?"

"Remarkable animals. Ninety pounds of muscle. Claws like steel razors." There was a definite excitement in his eyes as he looked up at the stuffed monsters on the mantel.

He was a small man, Gurney noted, perhaps five-five at the most, but with the well-developed shoulders of a bodybuilder.

He bent over and unclasped the Doberman's leash. A guttural command sent the dog trotting silently out of sight behind a leather couch, where he offered Gurney a seat.

Gurney sat without hesitation. Trout's transparent efforts at intimidation struck him as silly but also made him wonder what was coming next.

"I hope you understand how unofficial all this is," said Trout, still standing.

"How artificial . . . ?" said Gurney, pretending to have misunderstood.

"No. Unofficial."

"Sorry. Touch of tinnitus. Stopped a bullet with my head."

"So I heard." He paused, regarding Gurney's head with the sort of concern one might exhibit in the selection of a questionable melon. "How's the recovery going?"

"Who told you?"

"Told me what?"

"My head wound. You said you'd heard about it."

The low ring of a cell phone came from Trout's shirt pocket. He took it out and checked the screen. He frowned, presumably at the ID. For a moment he looked indecisive; then he pressed the TALK button.

"Trout here. Where are you?" As he held the phone to his ear for the next minute, his jaw muscles tensed several times. "Then we'll see you very soon." He pressed another button and slipped the phone back into his pocket.

"That was the answer to your question."

"The person who told you I'd been shot is coming here now?"

"Exactly."

Gurney smiled. "That's impressive. I didn't think she worked on Sundays."

The comment produced a surprised blink and pause. Trout cleared his throat. "As I was saying a moment ago, our little get-together is completely unofficial. I decided to meet with you for three reasons. First, because you asked Dr. Holdenfield if a meeting could be arranged. Second, because I felt that it was appropriate to extend a simple courtesy to someone formerly in law enforcement. Third, because I hope that our informal discussion will avert any confusion regarding the authority and responsibility for the investigation of the Good Shepherd murders. Good intentions can sometimes end up impeding an official process. You'd be amazed at what DOJ lawyers can construe as obstructions of justice."

Trout shook his head, as if in despair at those overscrupulous government attorneys who might come down on Gurney like the proverbial ton of bricks.

Gurney flashed a big, earnest smile. "Matt, believe me, I'm with you on that issue one hundred percent. Crossed wires are nothing but trouble. I'm a fan of full disclosure. Cards on the table. Open kimono. No secrets, no lies, no bullshit."

"Good." Trout's chilly tone drained any sense of agreement out of the word. "If you'll excuse me, there's something I need to take care of. I won't be long." He exited the room through a door to the left of the fireplace.

The Doberman emitted a low, rumbling growl.

Gurney leaned back on the couch, closed his eyes, and contemplated his game plan, such as it was.

When Trout returned fifteen minutes later, he was accompanied by Rebecca Holdenfield. Instead of looking harried or resentful at having her weekend interrupted, she looked energized and very intense.

Trout smiled with the closest thing to cordiality he'd shown so far. "I asked Dr. Holdenfield to join us here today. I believe together we can address the strange concerns you seem to have and put them to rest. I want you to understand, Mr. Gurney, that this is a highly unusual accommodation. I've also asked Daker to sit in. An extra pair of ears, an extra perspective."

On cue, Trout's assistant appeared in the doorway by the fireplace—where he remained as Trout and Holdenfield took seats in leather armchairs facing Gurney.

"Well now," said Trout. "Let's get right to these peculiar problems you have with the Good Shepherd case. The sooner we dispose of them, the sooner we go home." He gestured for Gurney to begin.

"I'd like to start with a question. During the course of your investigation, did you uncover any facts that struck you as inconsistent with your basic hypothesis? Little questions that weren't answerable?"

"Care to be more specific?"

"Was there any debate about the necessity for sniper goggles?"

Trout frowned. "What are you talking about?"

"Or the absurd choice of weapon? Or how many weapons there actually were? Or where he disposed of them?"

Despite a conspicuous effort at impassivity, Trout's eyes filled with a succession of concerns and calculations.

Gurney went on. "And then there's the fascinating conflict between the shooter's proven risk aversion and his stated fanaticism. As well as the conflict between his perfectly logical planning and completely illogical goals."

"Suicide bombings are full of similar contradictions," said Trout with a dismissive wave of his hand.

"The bombings may be, but the individuals involved in them aren't. The guy at the top with a political objective, the strategic thinker who chooses the target and lays out the plan, the recruiter, the trainer, the hands-on supervisor in the field, the martyr who volunteers to be blown up—they may function as a team, but each one is who he is. The net result may be crazy and counterproductive, but each component is internally consistent and understandable."

Trout shook his head. "I don't see the relevance."

In the doorway Daker yawned.

"The relevance is obvious," said Gurney. "The Osama bin Ladens of the world do not become pilots and fly planes into skyscrapers. The psychological components that create one do not create the other. Either the so-called Good Shepherd is more than one person or the unifying inferences you've made about his motives and personality structure are wrong."

Trout exhaled a loud sigh. "Very interesting. But you know what I find *most* interesting? Your comment about the gun—or guns. It reveals access to restricted information." He sat back in his chair, steepling his fingers thoughtfully under his chin. "That's a problem. A problem for you, being in possession of it, and a problem—perhaps a career-ending one—for whoever leaked it to you. Let me ask you a straightforward question: Do you have any other information from restricted federal law-enforcement files, pertaining to this case or to any other case?"

"Good Lord, Trout, don't be absurd."

The sinews in the man's neck tightened, but he said nothing.

Gurney went on. "I came here to talk about a potentially huge misunderstanding of a huge murder case. Do you really want to reduce this to a pissing contest over a hypothetical bureaucratic violation?"

Holdenfield raised her right hand in the traditional traffic-cop "Stop" gesture. "Could I make a suggestion here? Could we take this down a notch? We're here to discuss facts, evidence, reasonable interpretations. The emotional component is getting in the way. Maybe we could just—"

"You're absolutely right," said Trout with a tight smile. "I think we should let Mr. Gurney—Dave—have his say, put everything on the table. If there's a problem with our interpretation of the evidence, let's get to the bottom of it. Dave? I'm sure you have more to tell us. Please go ahead."

Trout's eagerness to get him to incriminate himself with a prosecutable admission of receiving stolen files was so transparent that Gurney came close to laughing in the man's face.

Trout added, "Maybe for the past ten years I've been too close to all of this. You're coming at it with fresh eyes. Tell me, what am I missing?"

"How about the fact that you've built a very big hypothesis on very few data points?"

"That's what the art of constructing an investigative premise is all about."

"It's also what schizophrenic delusions are all about."

"Dave . . ." Holdenfield's cautionary hand rose from her lap.

"Sorry. My concern is that the case study that's become enshrined in the annals of contemporary psych is just a giant circle dance. The manifesto, the details of the shootings, the offender profile, media mythmaking, popular imagination, and academic theorizing have all been contributing to the story—shaping it, polishing it, turning it into unassailable truth. Problem is, there's nothing solid to support this unassailable truth."

"Except, of course," said Holdenfield sharply, "the first two items you mentioned, which are very solid indeed—the manifesto and the details of the shootings."

"But suppose the details and the manifesto were specifically designed to reflect and reinforce each other? Suppose the killer is twice as smart as anyone thinks he is? Suppose he's been laughing his ass off at Agent Trout's team for the past ten years?"

Trout's eyes hardened. "You mentioned that you'd read the profile?"

Gurney grinned. "Which sounds to you like more proof of illegal access to precious files? Actually, that's not what I said. I *referred* to the profile, but I didn't say I'd *read* it. Let me just speculate for a minute. I bet the profile tries to explain how the killer is both efficient and inefficient, stable and crazy, atheistic and biblical. How am I doing?"

Trout sighed impatiently. "No comment."

"The problem is, you accepted the killer's manifesto as a legitimate expression of his thinking—because it confirmed your own thinking. It validated the ideas you were already forming about the case. It never occurred to you that the manifesto was a charade, that you were being played for fools. The Good Shepherd was telling you your conclusions were right. So of course you believed him."

Trout shook his head in a bad imitation of sad resignation. "I'm afraid we're on different planets here. I'd have thought from your background that we'd be on the same side."

"Nice thought. Bit out of touch with reality."

The head shaking continued. "The FBI goal with the Good Shepherd case—as it is with every case, and as it should be with every honest law-enforcement officer on every case—is to discover the truth. If we shared the integrity of our profession, then we'd be on the same side."

"You believe that?"

"It's the foundation of everything we do."

"Look, Trout, I've been around as long as you have, maybe longer. You're talking to a cop, not the goddamn Rotary Club. Sure, the goal is to discover the truth—except when another goal gets in the way. In most cases we don't get to the truth. What we get to, if we're lucky, is a satisfactory conclusion. We get to a credible way of characterizing something. We get to a way of convicting someone. You know damn well that the real-world structure of police agencies doesn't reward the pursuit of truth and justice. It rewards satisfactory conclusions. The goal in the heart of an individual cop may be to get to the truth. But the goal he's rewarded for is clearing the case. Hand the DA's office a perp to prosecute, preferably with a coherent narrative of fact and motive, best of all with a signed confession—that's the real game."

Trout rolled his eyes and looked at his watch.

"The point is," said Gurney, leaning forward, "you had a coherent narrative. In a way you had a signed confession—the manifesto. Of course, the fly in the ointment was the elusiveness of the perp. But what the hell. You came up with your offender profile. You had his detailed statement of intent. You had six murders that were consistent with what you and your Behavioral Analysis Unit *knew* about the Good Shepherd. Solid work, logical conclusions. Coherent, professional, defensible."

"What, precisely, is your problem with that?"

"Unless you have evidence you haven't revealed, everything you think you know is based on fiction. I'm hoping, by the way, that I'm wrong. Tell me you've got stuff in your files that nobody knows about."

"You're not making sense, Gurney. And I'm out of time. So if you don't mind—"

"Ask yourself two questions, Trout. First, what other theory of the case might you have developed if you'd never received the manifesto? Second, what if every word of that precious document is bullshit?"

"Interesting questions, I'm sure. Let me ask you one before you leave." The steepled hands returned to his chin. It was a professorial pose. "Considering your lack of any official standing or any basis for being involved in this in any way . . . where does all this hostile theorizing take you, other than into a world of trouble?"

Perhaps it was the threat in Trout's gaze. Or the smirk on Daker's lips as he leaned against the doorpost. Or the nettling reminder of his own lack of a badge. Whatever the root of the impulse, it pushed Gurney to say something he hadn't planned to say.

"It may force me to accept an offer I hadn't considered seriously until now. An opportunity at RAM News. They want to build a program segment around me."

"Around *you*?"

"Yes. Or my image. Using my arrest statistics."

Trout glanced curiously at Daker, who shrugged but said nothing.

"They seem to be overly impressed by the fact that I had the highest homicide-clearing rate in the history of the department."

Trout's mouth opened, but he closed it again without speaking.

"They want me to review famous unsolved cases and offer my opinion on where I think the investigations went off the tracks. Starting with the Good Shepherd case. They plan to call the series *In the Absence of Justice*. Catchy, eh?"

Trout examined his steepled fingers for a long minute, concluding with another sad shake of his head. "Everything keeps bringing me back to the problem of leaked documents, unauthorized access, transmission of confidential information, violations of regulations, violations of federal and state laws. Endless unpleasant complications."

"Small price to pay. After all, as you said before, the main thing is justice. Or was it truth? Something like that, right?"

Trout gave him a cold stare and repeated with slow emphasis, "Endless . . . unpleasant . . . complications." His gaze traveled to the mounted wildcats on the mantel. "Not such a small price. Not something I'd want to be in your shoes for. Especially not right now. Not on top of having to deal with that arson business."

"Excuse me?"

"I heard about your barn."

"How does that relate to what we're talking about?"

"Just another kind of pressure in your life, that's all. Another complication." He made a show of consulting his watch again. "We're definitely out of time." He stood up.

So did Gurney. So did Holdenfield.

Trout's mouth widened into an empty smile. "Thank you for sharing your concerns with us, Mr. Gurney. Daker will get you back to your car." He turned to Holdenfield. "Can you stay for a few minutes? I have a few items I need to discuss with you."

"Certainly." She stepped between Trout and Gurney and extended her hand. "Nice to see you again. Someday you'll have to tell me more about your barn problem. First I've heard of it."

When he took her hand, he felt a folded piece of paper being pressed against his palm. He accepted it, keeping it out of sight.

Daker was watching him but showed no sign of noticing the transfer. He pointed at the front door. "Time to go."

Gurney didn't take the paper out of his pocket until he was in his car, the engine was running, and Daker had disappeared back up the trail in the Kawasaki.

Unfolded, it was barely two inches across. There was one sentence on it: *"Wait for me in Branville at the Eagle's Nest."*

He'd never been to the Eagle's Nest. He'd heard it was a new restaurant, part of Branville's struggling renaissance from rural slum to quaint hamlet. It was convenient enough, located on a route he'd be taking anyway.

The main street of Branville was at the bottom of a valley next to a picturesque stream that provided the place with its sole source of charm, as well as occasional ruinous floods. The county road that connected Branville with the interstate made a long, winding descent from a line of hills and teed into the main street just a block from the Eagle's Nest. Although it was close to noon when Gurney walked in, only one of its dozen tables was occupied. He sat at a table for two by a bay window looking out on the street and ordered—a rarity for him—a Bloody Mary. He was still surprised by his choice when the server delivered it a few minutes later.

It was a generous drink, in a tall glass. It tasted exactly the way he expected it would. It brought a pleasant smile to his lips—another rarity in recent months. He savored it slowly, finishing it at 12:15.

At 12:16 Rebecca walked in. She sat down immediately. "Hope you weren't waiting too long." The way she smiled emphasized the taut contours of her mouth. Everything about her was controlled and alert.

"Just got here a few minutes ago."

She glanced around the room with that cool assessment with which she always greeted her surroundings. "What are you drinking?"

"Bloody Mary."

"Perfect." She turned and waved to the young female server.

When the girl arrived with a pair of menus, Holdenfield gave her a skeptical look. "Are you old enough to be serving drinks?"

"I'm twenty-three," she announced, sounding baffled by the question and depressed by the number.

"That old?" said Holdenfield with unappreciated irony. "I'll have a Bloody Mary." She pointed at Gurney's glass with a question mark in her eyes.

"No more for me."

The server departed.

Holdenfield, as usual, didn't waste any time getting to the point. "How come you were so aggressive with our FBI friends? And what was all that stuff about sniper goggles, the disposing of the guns, problems with the profile?"

"Just trying to nudge him off balance."

"Nudge? More like an elbow in the face."

"I'm a little frustrated."

"And where do you think your frustration is coming from?"

"I'm getting sick of explaining it."

"Humor me."

"You're all treating the manifesto like holy writ. It's not. It's a pose. Actions speak louder than words. The actions of this killer were super-rational, steady as a rock. The planning was patient and pragmatic. The manifesto is another matter altogether. It's a work of fiction, an effort to create a persona and a set of motivations that you and your buddies in the Behavioral Analysis Unit could analyze and regurgitate into that sophomoric profile."

"Look, David—"

"Just a second, I'm still 'humoring' you. The fiction took on a life of its own. There was something in it for everyone. Endless articles in the *American Journal of Theoretical Bullshit*. And now no one can back down. You're all desperate to shore up the house of cards. If it collapses, careers collapse with it."

"Finished?"

"You asked me to explain my frustration."

She leaned toward him and spoke softly. "David, I don't think I'm the one who's 'desperate' here." She paused and sat back up straight as the server arrived with her Bloody Mary. When the young woman retreated to the back of the room, she continued. "I've worked with you before. You were always the calmest, most reasonable person in the room. The Dave Gurney I remember wouldn't have threatened a senior FBI agent this morning. He wouldn't be claiming that my professional opinions are bullshit. Accusing me of dishonesty and stupidity. It makes me wonder what's *really* going on in your head. To be perfectly honest with you, this new Dave Gurney worries me."

"Is that so? You think the bullet that creased my brain knocked out a few logic circuits?"

"All I'm saying is that your thought process is being driven by a bigger emotional component than it used to be. Do you disagree with that?"

"What I disagree with is your effort to make my thought process the issue when the real problem is that you and your colleagues attached your names and reputations to a crock of shit that allowed a mass murderer to escape."

"That's colorful, David. You know who else speaks about the case in colorful terms? Max Clinter."

"Is that supposed to be a devastating criticism?"

She sipped her drink. "Just popped into my mind. Free association. So many similarities. Both of you seriously injured, both incapacitated for at least a month, both intensely distrustful of others, both with your official police days behind you, both obsessed with proving that the accepted view of the Good Shepherd case is wrong, both natural-born hunters who hate being marginalized." She took another sip. "Have you ever been evaluated for PTSD?"

He stared at her. The question took him by surprise, although it shouldn't have, not after her comparing him to Clinter. "Is that what you're doing here? Checking off diagnostic boxes? Did you and Trout discuss my emotional stability?"

She returned the stare. "I've never felt this kind of hostility from you before."

"Let me ask you something. Why did you want to meet me here?"

She blinked, looked down at the table, took a deep breath, let it out slowly. "Our phone conversation the other day? It was very disturbing. Frankly, I'm concerned about you." She picked up her Bloody Mary and drank down more than half of it.

When their eyes met again, she spoke in a softened voice. "Being shot is a shock. Our minds keep reliving that moment, the threat, the impact. Our natural reactions are fear and anger. Most men would rather be angry than afraid. They find it easier to express anger. I think the discovery of your own vulnerability, the fact that you're not perfect, not superman . . . has made you absolutely furious. And the slowness of your recovery is stoking that fury."

Was this earnest psychologist as authentic as she sounded at that moment? Was she offering him her honest and caring opinion? Did she actually give a damn? Or was this another step in an increasingly ugly effort to make him question himself rather than the case theory?

Searching for the answer, he looked into her eyes.

Her intelligent gaze was steady, unblinking.

He started to feel the fury she had mentioned. It was time to get the hell out of there before he said something he'd regret.

# Part Three

# At Any
# Cost

# Prologue

I t had taken time to get the wording right, more time than he'd expected. There had been so much going on, so much to manage. But he was finally satisfied. The message finally said everything it needed to say:

*Greed spreads in a family like septic blood in bathwater. It infects everyone it touches. Therefore the wives and children you hold up as objects of sorrow and pity shall also be cut down. The children of greed are evil, and evil are those whom they embrace. Therefore they, too, shall be cut down. Whomsoever you hold up for the fools of the world to console, they all shall be cut down, whether related by blood or by marriage to the children of greed.*

*To consume the product of greed is to consume its stain. The fruit leaves its mark. The beneficiaries of greed bear the guilt of greed, and they must bear its punishment. They will die in the spotlight of your praise. Your praise shall be their undoing. Your pity is a poison. Your sympathy condemns them to death.*

*Can you not see the truth? Have you gone blind?*

*The world has gone mad. Greed masquerades as laudable ambition. Wealth pretends to be proof of talent and worth. The channels of communication have fallen into the hands of monsters. The worst of the worst are exalted.*

*With devils in pulpits and angels ignored, it falls to the honest to punish what the mad world rewards.*

*These are the true and final words of the Good Shepherd.*

He printed two copies to be sent by overnight mail. One to Cora-zon, one to Gurney. Then he carried the printer out in back of the house and smashed it with a brick. He gathered the pieces, even shards of plastic as small as fingernail clippings, and put them in a garbage bag, along with the remaining printer paper, to be buried in the woods.

An investment in caution was always wise.

## Chapter 29

# Too Damn Many
# Bits and Pieces

s he drove out of Branville into the rolling hills and scrubby pastures of northeastern Delaware County, Gurney's mind was swirling. His natural facility for organizing data into meaningful patterns was stymied by the volume of it all.

It was like trying to make sense out of a heap of tiny puzzle pieces without knowing whether every piece was present—or even how many puzzles the pieces were part of. One minute he would be certain that all the debris was the result of a single central storm; the next minute he would be certain of nothing. Maybe he was too damn eager to come up with one explanation, one elegant equation.

Passing a roadside sign welcoming him to Dillweed suggested a modest next step. He pulled over and called the one Dillweed resident he knew personally. An undiluted face-to-face dose of Jack Hardwick could be a good antidote to fanciful thinking.

Ten minutes later, four miles up a succession of twisty dirt roads, he arrived at the unimposing rented farmhouse, much in need of paint, that Hardwick called home. The man answered the door dressed as usual in a T-shirt and cutoff sweatpants.

"You want one?" he asked, holding up an empty Grolsch beer bottle.

First Gurney said no, then he said yes. He knew he'd have alcohol on his breath when he got home, and he'd be more comfortable attributing it to a beer with Jack than to a Bloody Mary with Rebecca.

After getting Gurney a Grolsch and himself another, Hardwick sank down into one of two overstuffed leather chairs, motioning

Gurney toward the other. "So, my son," he said in a harsh whisper that pretended a level of inebriation that was belied by his sharp gaze, "how long has it been since your last confession?"

"Thirty-five years, more or less," said Gurney, humoring the man from whom he wanted help. He sampled the beer. It wasn't bad. He looked around the little living room. Like Jack's attire, the painfully bare space was the same as it had been on Gurney's last visit. Not even the dust had moved.

Hardwick scratched his nose. "You must be in a great deal of trouble to be seeking the solace of Mother Church after such a long time. Speak freely, my son, of all your blasphemies, lies, thievings, and adulteries. I'd be most interested in the details of the adulteries." He produced an absurdly salacious wink.

Gurney leaned back in the wide soft chair and took another swallow of beer. "The Good Shepherd case is getting complicated."

"Always was."

"The problem is, I'm not sure how many cases I'm dealing with."

"Too much shit for one latrine?"

"Like I said, I'm not sure." He recounted, in as much detail as he could, the long litany of facts, events, oddities, suspicions, and questions on his mind.

Hardwick took a rumpled tissue out of his sweatpants pocket and blew his nose in it. "So what are you asking me?"

"Just for your gut sense of how much of that stuff fits into one big picture and how much is likely to be something else entirely."

Hardwick made a clucking sound with his tongue. "I don't know about the arrow. Maybe if someone shot an arrow up your ass, but . . . stuck in the ground out there with the turnips? That doesn't mean much to me."

"And the other stuff?"

"The other stuff would get my attention. Apartment bugging, barn burning, booby-trapping the staircase, the trapdoor in the young lady's ceiling—that kind of shit requires an investment of time and energy, plus legal risks. So it's serious. Meaning there's something serious at stake. I'm not giving you any news here, right?"

"Not really."

"You're asking me, do I think it's all tied together in a grand conspiracy?" He screwed his face up into an exaggerated mask of inde-cision. "Best answer is something you said to me a long time ago when we were working on the Mellery job. 'It's safer to assume there's a connection that turns out to be false than to ignore one that turns out to be true.' But there's a bigger question." He paused to belch. "If the Good Shepherd case wasn't about the righteous slaughter of the evil rich, then what the fuck *was* it about? Answer that, Mr. Holmes, and you'll have the answers to all your other questions. You want another Grolsch?"

Gurney shook his head.

"By the way, if you really try to demolish the case premise, you'll be in the middle of a once-in-a-lifetime shit storm. Galileo at the Vati-can. You understand that, right?"

"I started getting the message today." Gurney pictured Agent Trout, baleful Doberman at his side, on his cheerless Adirondack porch. His references to "complications." His allusion to the arson situ-ation. And Daker, the assassin in a hundred films.

"Okay, my boy, just so you know. Because——" The ring of Jack's cell phone interrupted him. He pulled it out of his pocket. "Hardwick." He was quiet at first, his expression growing more interested, more per-plexed. "Right . . . Right . . . What? . . . Holy shit! . . . Yeah . . . That was the only one? . . . You have the original application date? . . . Okay . . . Right . . . Thanks . . . Yeah . . . Bye." When he ended the call, he con-tinued to stare at the phone as though some additional clarification might emerge from it.

"The hell was that about?" asked Gurney.

"Answer to your question."

"Which one?"

"You asked me to find out if Paul Mellani had any registered guns."

"And?"

"He has one handgun. A Desert Eagle."

F or most of Gurney's half-hour homeward drive from Dillweed to Walnut Crossing, he could think of little else. But as startling as the discovery was, it was more troubling than actionable. Rather like discovering that an ax murderer and his victim, previously believed to be unconnected, had shared a desk in kindergarten. Attention-getting, but what the hell did it mean?

It would be important to know how long Mellani had owned the gun. However, the record accessed by Hardwick's colleague, showing a currently valid concealed-carry permit, did not indicate the original application date. Calls to Mellani's office number and cell number had both gone into voice mail. Even if the man chose to return the calls, he was under no obligation to explain his unusual choice of sidearm.

Obviously this curious new fact exacerbated Gurney's original concern: that depression and easy access to a firearm could be a high-risk combination. But "concern" was all it was. There was no hard evidence that Paul Mellani was a credible danger to himself or others. He had said nothing—uttered none of the key phrases, none of the psychiatric alarm words—that would justify notifying the Middletown police, nothing that would justify any intervention beyond the personal calls that had been made.

But Gurney kept thinking about it—imagining the probable content of Kim's contacts with the man prior to their Saturday meeting, her letter and phone call explaining her project. These reminders of his father's death—reminders of his father's apparent lack of concern for him—may have focused him on the emptiness of his life, the sinking ship of his career.

Lost in the miasma of depression, might he be planning to end it all? Or, God forbid, perhaps he already had? Perhaps that's why the calls went into voice mail?

Or what if Gurney had it all backward? What if the purpose of the Desert Eagle wasn't suicidal but homicidal?

What if it had always *been* homicidal? What if . . .

*Jesus Christ! What if. What if. What if. Enough!* The man had a legal permit to possess a legal handgun. There were millions of depressed people in the world who never came close to harming themselves or anyone else. Yes, the brand name of the handgun raised obvious questions, but these questions could be asked and answered when Mellani called back, which he surely would. Strange coincidences usually had pedestrian explanations.

## Chapter 30

# Showtime

When Gurney arrived home at 2:02 P.M., Madeleine was out. Her car was still parked by the side door, which meant she was probably hiking one of the forest trails that radiated out from the high pasture.

During the final few miles of the drive, his obsession with Paul Mellani's gun had subsided—only to be replaced by the echo of Hardwick's Big Question: If the Good Shepherd murder spree wasn't the psycho mission described in the manifesto, *then what was it?*

Gurney got a pad and pen and sat down at the breakfast table. Putting things on paper was the best way he knew to minimize mental overload. The next hour produced the beginning of an investigatory premise and a short list of "starter" questions that might open up avenues worth exploring.

PREMISE: *There are irreconcilable differences in thought processes and style between the efficient, machinelike planning and execution of the murders and the sententious, fake-biblical pronouncements of the manifesto. True personality is revealed by behavior. Brilliance and efficiency can't be faked. The disconnect between the killer's way of acting and his emotional psycho-mission-based explanation of that action suggests that the explanation may be false and designed to distract attention from a more pragmatic motive.*

QUESTIONS:
*If not because of their "greed," why were these victims chosen?*

*What is the significance of the similar vehicles?*
*Why did the murders occur when they did, in the spring of
   the year 2000?*
*Was the sequence in which they occurred significant?*
*Were they all equally important?*
*Were any of the six necessitated by any of the others?*
*Why such a dramatic weapon?*
*Why the little plastic animals at the shooting sites?*
*What lines of inquiry did the arrival of the manifesto cut off?*

Gurney looked over what he had written, knowing that it was
the barest beginning and not expecting an immediate breakthrough
insight. He knew that "Aha!" moments never occurred on demand.

He decided to share his list with Hardwick to see what kind of
response it would provoke. And with Holdenfield, for the same reason.
He wondered about giving a copy to Kim and decided not to. Her goals
were different from his, and his questions would only upset her again.

He went to his computer in the den, wrote separate introductions
on e-mails to Hardwick and to Holdenfield, and sent them. After he
printed a copy to show to Madeleine, he stretched out on the den couch
and fell asleep.

"Dinner."

"Hmm?"

"Dinnertime." Madeleine's voice. Somewhere.

He blinked, gazed blearily up at the ceiling, thought he saw a pair
of spiders gliding across the white surface. He blinked again, rubbed
his eyes, and the spiders disappeared. His neck hurt. "What time is it?"

"Nearly six." She was standing in the den doorway.

"Jesus." He sat up slowly on the couch, rubbing his neck. "Dozed
off."

"You certainly did. Anyway, dinner's ready."

She returned to the kitchen. He stretched, went to the bathroom,
splashed cold water on his face. When he joined her at the table, she'd
already laid out two large bowls of steaming fish chowder, two green
salads, and a plate of buttery garlic bread.

"Smells good," he said.

"Have you reported the bugs to the police?"

"What?"

"The listening devices, the trapdoor in the ceiling—has anyone notified the police?"

"Why are you asking about that now?"

"Just wondering. That stuff is against the law, right? Bugging someone's apartment? If it's a crime, shouldn't it be reported?"

"Yes and no. Should be, maybe. But in most cases there's no legal requirement to report a criminal act, unless the failure could be interpreted as impeding an ongoing investigation."

She stared at him, waiting.

"In this situation, if I were the investigating officer, I'd want everything left as is."

"Why?"

"It's a potential asset. A working bug that the bugger doesn't know has been blown can give you a resource later for trapping him."

"How?"

"By letting him listen to a setup conversation that would then make him do something that would identify or incriminate himself. So it could be useful. But that might not be the way Schiff or other detectives in the Syracuse PD would see it. They might just stomp in and blow the whole thing. Once I tell Schiff, it's out of my control, and right now I'd like to hang on to every little plus I can."

She nodded and sampled her chowder. "It's good. Try it before it gets cold."

He took his first spoonful and agreed it was very good indeed.

She broke off a chunk of garlic bread. "While you were napping, I read that thing you left on the coffee table by the couch, with your questions about the case."

"I wanted you to."

"You're sure that the murders aren't about what everyone thinks they're about?"

"Sure enough."

"You're coming at the case like it was brand-new?"

"A brand-new case that just happens to be ten years old."

She studied her spoon. "If you're starting back at square one, I guess the most basic question would be, why do people murder other people?"

"Apart from sacred-mission delusions, the main motives are sex, money, power, and revenge."

"Which do you think it is?"

"Given the range of victims, it's hard to imagine it being sex."

"I bet it's about money," said Madeleine. "A lot of money."

"Why?"

She gave a little shrug. "Luxury cars, expensive guns, rich victims—just seems like that's what it's all about."

"But not about hating it? Hating the power of money? Or eliminating greed?"

"Oh, gosh, no. Probably just the opposite."

Gurney smiled. He had the feeling that Madeleine might be onto something.

"Finish your chowder," she said. "You don't want to miss the first episode of *The Orphans of Murder*."

They didn't have a television, but they did have a computer, and RAM News, in addition to putting the program on its cable channels, had advertised a simultaneous webcast.

As they sat in front of the iMac in the den, Gurney navigated through the RAM website. He was always appalled by new evidence of how trashy the media world had become. And it kept getting worse. Moronic sensationalism was like a ratchet that turned in only one direction. And RAM's toxic programming was leading the descent into the pit.

A home page consisting mainly of a huge red, white, and blue logo—"RAM NEWS NETWORK: THE WORLD WITHOUT THE SPIN"—was followed by a page that featured their most popular offerings. He scrolled quickly through the listings in his search for *Orphans*.

SECRETS AND LIES: What the Mainstream Media Won't
   Tell You
SECOND OPINION: *Questioning Conventional Wisdom*
APOCALYPSE NOW: *The Battle for America's Soul*

Gurney pressed on grimly to the next page of the website, where, at the top of a list of news specials, he found *The Orphans of Murder*.

Under the title was a short promotional teaser: "What happens to the survivors when a killer tears out the heart of a family? Shocking true stories of grief and rage. Premier Episode Tonight at 7:00 P.M. EDT."

Ten minutes later, at 7:00 P.M. precisely, the first episode began.

The screen was almost completely dark. The eerie cry of an owl suggested that the viewer was looking at a country road at night. A man walked out of the darkness into a narrow area of illumination cast by the headlights of a car parked on the grassy shoulder. The bone structure of the man's face in the angled headlights created the sharp shadows of a face in a thriller film.

He started to speak in a slow, portentous voice. "Exactly ten years ago, in the spring of the year 2000, in the rural hills of upstate New York, on a lonely road like this one, on a moonless night, with the chill of winter still in the air, the horror began. Bruno and Carmella Mellani were returning to their country home from a christening party in the city, perhaps discussing the happy events of the day, the dear friends and relatives they hadn't seen for so long, when another car came rapidly up behind them, then began to pass them on a long, dark curve. But when that strange, speeding car came abreast of Bruno and Carmella Mellani . . ."

The scene on the screen changed to the dimly lit interior of a moving vehicle at night, a driver and a passenger in the front seat, unrecognizable in the darkness. They were speaking, laughing softly. A few seconds later, the headlights of a vehicle behind them were visible. The approaching headlights grew brighter, moving to the left side of their car, suggesting that the pursuing vehicle was about to pass. Then there was a sudden flash of white light on the screen, with the simultaneous explosive sound effect of a gunshot, followed by the tire screech of a vehicle out of control, prolonged metallic crashing sounds, and the shattering of glass.

The narrator returned to the screen. He bent over and picked up a piece of twisted debris from the ground, brandishing it as though it were a significant piece of evidence from the crime he was describing. "The Mellani car flew off the road. It was so badly mangled that the first responders had trouble identifying the make and model. A third of Bruno Mellani's head was blown away by the impact of a bullet from a huge handgun. Carmella Mellani's injuries put her into a coma that she remains in to this day."

Staring at the computer screen, Madeleine screwed up her face in disgust. She seemed to be finding the RAM approach more disturbing than the event it was depicting.

The narrator went on to give super-dramatic descriptions of the five other Good Shepherd shootings, culminating in a long description of the Harold Blum fiasco that led to the unraveling of Max Clinter's career and life.

"God," said Madeleine, "this stuff is way over the top."

Gurney nodded.

The camera zoomed in to a medium shot of the narrator-turned-host, sitting in an interview environment with two men. "Ten years," he said. "Ten years, and yet to some of us it seems so recent. You may be asking, why revisit that horror now? The answer is simple: because a ten-year anniversary is a natural stopping point, a point at which we often find it appropriate to pause and look back on triumphs and tragedies alike."

The host addressed a dark-complected man in one of the chairs across from him. "Dr. Mirkilee, your specialty is forensic psycholinguistics. Could you explain that term to our audience?"

"Of course. It's finding the thinking in the words." His voice was small, quick, precise, very Indian. A subtitle appeared on the bottom of the screen: DR. SAMMARKAN MIRKILEE, PH.D.

"The thinking?"

"The person, the emotion, the background. The way the mind works."

"So you're an expert at the way words, grammar, style all come together to reveal the inner man?"

"This is true, yes."

"All right, Dr. Mirkilee, I'm going to read you some excerpts from a document sent by the Good Shepherd to the media ten years ago, and I'm going to ask you for your insights into the author's mind. Ready?"

"Of course."

As the host read a long screed about the way to "eradicate greed" and "exterminate human carriers," thereby freeing the earth of "this ultimate contagion," Gurney recognized the words as the introduction to the Good Shepherd's Memorandum of Intent—otherwise known as the "manifesto."

The host put the paper down on the table. "Okay, Dr. Mirkilee— what kind of individual are we dealing with here?"

"In layman terms? Very logical, yet very emotional."

"Expand on that. Please."

"Many tensions in the writing, many styles, attitudes."

"Are you saying he has multiple personalities?"

"No, that is a silly thing—no such disorder. It is for stories, movies."

"Ah. But I thought you said—"

"There are many *tones*. First one, then another, another. Very unstable man."

"And I take it you would characterize such a man as dangerous?"

"Yes, of course. He killed six people, no?"

"Good point. One last question. Do you think he's still out there, lurking in the shadows?"

Dr. Mirkilee hesitated. "Well, I'll say this: If he *is* out there, I would make a large bet that he is watching this program right now. Watching and considering."

"Considering?" The host paused, as if grappling with the significance of that statement. "Well, that's a chilling thought. A murderer walking our streets. A murderer who at this very moment may be *considering what to do next.*"

He took a deep breath, as if to settle his nerves before announcing, as the camera zoomed in on him, "It's time now for some important messages . . ."

Gurney grabbed the computer mouse and slid the volume icon to zero, a reflexive response to commercials.

Madeleine looked at him sideways. "We haven't even seen *Kim* come on yet, and I'm already losing my patience with this."

"Me, too," said Gurney, "but I need to at least watch Kim's interview with Ruth Blum."

"I know," said Madeleine. She gave a small smile.

"What is it?"

"There's a silly irony in this whole situation. When you were injured, when the aftereffects didn't disappear as quickly as you might have liked, you sank into a hole. The deeper you sank, the less you did. The less you did, the deeper you sank. It was painful to see you like that. Doing nothing was killing you. Now all the craziness that's going on, all the danger, is bringing you back to life. You used to sit at the breakfast table on a gorgeous morning, running your finger up and down your arm, checking the numb spot, checking to see if it had changed, if it had gotten worse. You know what? You haven't done that all week."

He didn't know what to say, so he said nothing.

On the screen the last in the series of commercials faded to black and the scene switched back to the interview table.

Gurney slid the volume icon up in time to hear the host ask a question of the other guest at the interview table.

"Dr. Monty Cockrell, so good to have you with us as well. America knows you as an expert on rage. Tell us, Doctor, what was the Good Shepherd murder spree really about?"

Cockrell paused dramatically before answering. "Quite simply—war. The shootings and the manifesto explaining them were an attempt to initiate class warfare. It was a delusional attempt to punish the successful for the failings of the unsuccessful."

With that the host and his two guests launched into a free-wheeling discussion that lasted for five full minutes—a lifetime in television—and left all three men agreeing that the right to bear arms was, at times, the only defense against such poisonous thinking.

Gurney lowered the volume again and turned to Madeleine.

"What?" she asked. "I can see your wheels turning."

"I was thinking about what the little Indian guy said."

"That your killer would be watching this moronic program?"

"Yes."

"Why would he bother?"

It was a rhetorical question, to which Gurney didn't respond.

It took several more minutes of painful viewing before Kim's interview with Ruth Blum finally came on. The two women were sitting across from each other at an outdoor table on the rear deck of a house. It was a sunny day. They were both wearing lightweight zippered jackets.

Ruth Blum was a plump, middle-aged woman whose facial features appeared weighed down by sadness. Her hairdo struck Gurney as touchingly silly—a tousled little pile of golden-brown curls that resembled a Yorkshire terrier perched on her head.

"He was the best man in all the world." Ruth Blum paused, as if to give Kim time to appreciate this great truth before continuing. "Warmhearted, kind, and . . . always trying to do better, always trying to improve himself. Did you ever notice how the best people in the world always try to do better? That was Harold."

Kim's voice was shaky. "Losing him must have been the worst thing that ever happened to you."

"My doctor told me I should take an antidepressant. *An antidepressant*," she repeated, as though it had been the single most inconsiderate piece of advice she'd ever received.

"Has anything changed with the passing of time?"

"Yes and no. I still cry."

"But you continue to live."

"Yes."

"Do you know anything about life now that you didn't know before your husband was killed?"

"I know how temporary everything is. I used to think that I'd always have what I had, that I'd always have Harold, that I'd never lose anything that mattered. Stupid to think that, but I did. The truth is, if we live long enough, we lose everything, everybody."

Kim took a handkerchief out of her jacket pocket and wiped her eyes. "How did you two meet?"

"We met at a school dance." During the next few minutes, Ruth Blum recounted the emotional highlights of her relationship with Harold, eventually circling back to her theme of a gift given and a gift taken away. "We thought it would last forever. But nothing does, does it?"

"How did you get through it?"

"The main thing was the others."

"The others?"

"The support we were able to give each other. We'd each lost a loved one the same way. We had that in common."

"You formed a support group?"

"For a while we were like family. Closer than some families. Everybody was different, but we had that one strong bond. I remember Paul, the accountant, so quiet, hardly ever said anything. Roberta, the tough one, tougher than any man. Dr. Sterne, he was the voice of reason, the one who had a way of calming people down. There was the young man who wanted to open a fancy restaurant. And who else? Oh, Lord, Jimi. How could I ever forget Jimi? Jimi Brewster hated everyone and everything. I often wonder what happened to him."

"I found him," said Kim, "and he agreed to speak to me. He's going to be part of this."

"Good for him. Poor Jimi. So much *anger.* You know what they say about people who are that angry?"

"What?"

"That they're angry at themselves."

Kim let a long silence pass before asking, "How about you, Ruth? Aren't you angry about what happened?"

"Sometimes. Mostly I'm sad. Mostly..." Tears started coming down her cheeks.

The video interview segment faded to black, and then the scene cut back to the studio, to a shot of the host at the table with Kim. Gurney assumed that this was the interview segment she'd gone to the city that day to record.

"I don't know what to say," said the host. "I'm speechless, Kim. That was so powerful."

She looked down at the table with an embarrassed smile.

"So powerful," he repeated. "I want to talk more about that in just a minute, Kim, but first I want to ask you something."

He leaned in her direction, lowering his voice in an imitation of confidentiality. "Is it true that you've gotten a highly decorated homicide detective involved in this documentary project? Dave Gurney. The man *New York* magazine once called 'Supercop'?"

A gunshot couldn't have grabbed Gurney's attention more completely. He studied Kim's face on the screen. She looked startled.

"Sort of," she said after a pause. "I mean, he's been advising me on some issues surrounding the case."

"*Issues?* Can you give us any details?"

Kim's hesitation convinced Gurney that she'd truly been caught off guard. "Odd things have been happening, things I'd rather not reveal yet. But it looks as if someone might be trying to stop *The Orphans of Murder* from being shown."

The host affected intense concern. "Go on . . ."

"Well . . . things have happened to us, things that could be inter-preted as warnings to back off, to stay away from the Good Shepherd case."

"And does your detective adviser have any theories?"

"He seems to have a view of the case that's different from every-one else's."

The host seemed riveted. "Are you saying that your police expert thinks the FBI has been on the wrong track all these years?"

"You'll have to ask him that yourself. I've already said too much."

*Goddamn right,* thought Gurney.

"If it's the truth, Kim, it's never too much! Maybe I'll follow up with Detective Gurney himself—in time for next week's installment of *The Orphans of Murder.* In the meantime I invite our viewers to speak out. React! Share your thoughts with us. Go to our website and speak your mind."

The Web address—RAM4NEWS.COM—appeared at the bottom of the screen in flashing red and blue letters.

The host leaned toward Kim. "We have one minute left. Can you sum up the essence of the Good Shepherd case in a few words?"

"In a few words?"

"Right. The essence of it."

She closed her eyes. "Love. Loss. Pain."

The camera zoomed in to a close-up of the host. "All right, folks. There you have it. Love, loss, and terrible pain. Next week we'll take a close look at the shattered family of another Good Shepherd victim. And remember, as far as we know, the Good Shepherd is still out there, still walking among us. *A man . . . to whom . . . human life . . . means noth-ing.* Stay tuned to RAM News for everything you need to know. Stay alert, my friends. It's a dangerous world."

The screen faded to black.

Gurney closed the browser, put the computer to sleep, and sat back in his chair.

Madeleine gave him a gently appraising look. "What's worrying you?"

"Right this minute? I don't know." He shifted in his chair, closed his eyes, and waited for the first troubling object to surface. Surprisingly, it wasn't the show they'd just watched—as disturbing as it was. "What do you think about this thing with Kim and Kyle?" he said.

"They seem to be attracted to each other. What's there to think about?"

He shook his head. "I don't know."

"What Kim said about you at the end of that RAM thing—your doubts about the FBI approach—will that make trouble for you?"

"It could ratchet up the unpleasantness with Agent Trout. Possibly tweak his control-freak nerves to the point of wanting to create some legal inconvenience for me."

"Is there anything you can do about that? Any way to head it off?"

"Sure. All I have to do is prove that his case is total nonsense. At which point he'll have bigger problems to worry about than me."

## Chapter 31

# The Return
# of the Shepherd

When Gurney awoke the following morning at seven-thirty, it was raining. It was the kind of light but steady rain that can go on for hours.

As usual, both windows were open a few inches from the top. The air in the bedroom was chilly and damp. Although it was officially almost an hour past sunrise, the skewed rectangle of sky visible from the position of his head on the pillow was the unpromising gray of a wet flagstone.

Madeleine was up before him. He stretched and rubbed his eyes. He had no desire to go back to sleep. His last dream, an uneasy one, had involved a black umbrella. As the umbrella opened, seemingly of its own volition, its unfolding fabric became the wings of an enormous bat. The bat shape-shifted into a black vulture, the curved umbrella handle sharpening into a hooked beak. And then, through the exotic sensory logic of dreams, the vulture was transformed into the cool draft from the open windows—the unpleasant touch of which had been the cause of his awakening.

He pushed himself out of bed, as a way of putting distance between himself and the dream. Then he took a hot shower for its mind-clearing and reality-simplifying benefits, shaved, brushed his teeth, dressed, and went out to the kitchen for coffee.

"Call Jack Hardwick," said Madeleine from the stove, without looking up, as she added a handful of raisins to something she was simmering in a small pot.

"Why?"

"Because he called here about fifteen minutes ago and wanted to talk to you."

"Did he say what he wanted?"

"Said he had a question about your e-mail."

"Hmm." He went to the coffeemaker and poured himself a cup. "I was dreaming about a black umbrella."

"He seemed very eager to talk to you."

"I'll call him. But . . . tell me, how did that movie end?"

Madeleine emptied the little pot into her bowl and brought it to the breakfast table. "I don't remember."

"You described that scene in great detail—the guy the snipers were following, how he went into the church, and later, when he came out, they couldn't tell who he was because everyone else coming out of the church with him was dressed in black and had a black umbrella. What happened after that?"

"I guess he got away. Because the snipers couldn't shoot everybody."

"Hmm."

"What's wrong?"

"Suppose they *did* shoot everybody."

"They didn't."

"But suppose they did. Suppose they shot everybody, because that was the only way they could make sure they got the one they were after. And suppose the police arrived later and found all those bodies, all those people who'd been shot dead in the street. What would they think?"

"What would the police think? I have no idea. Maybe that some maniac wanted to kill churchgoers?"

Gurney nodded. "Exactly—especially if they got a letter the same day from someone claiming that religious people were the scum of the earth and he was planning to kill them all."

"But . . . wait a minute." Madeleine looked incredulous. "Are you suggesting that the Good Shepherd killed all those people because he couldn't tell who his real target was? And that he just kept shooting people in a certain kind of car, until he was sure he got the person he was after?"

"I don't know. But I intend to figure it out."

Madeleine shook her head. "I just don't see how—" She was interrupted by the ring of the landline phone on the countertop next to the refrigerator. "You'd better get that. It's probably you-know-who."

He did. And it was.

"You out of that fucking shower yet?"

"Good morning, Jack."

"Got your e-mail—your investigatory premise, along with your list of questions."

"And?"

"You're making the point that there's a style conflict between the manifesto's words and the shooter's deeds?"

"You could put it that way."

"You're saying that the shooter's MO proves he's way too practical, way too cool, calm, and collected to think the thoughts presented in the manifesto. My little brain got that right?"

"What I'm saying is, there's a disconnect."

"Okay. That's interesting. But it creates a bigger problem than it solves."

"How?"

"You're saying the motive for the murders is something other than what's spelled out in the manifesto."

"Right."

"Therefore the victims were chosen for another reason—not because they were conspicuous displayers of luxury goods, greedy bastards who deserved to die?"

"Right."

"So this super-practical, super-cool genius had an undisclosed pragmatic reason for killing those people?"

"Right."

"You see the problem?"

"Tell me."

"If the shooter's real motive for choosing each victim was something other than the fact that he—or she—was driving a hundred-thousand-dollar Mercedes, then we have to believe that driving a hundred-thousand-dollar Mercedes was irrelevant. A fucking

JOHN VERDON

coincidence. You ever run into anything like that, Davey boy? It would be like discovering that every victim of Bernie Madoff just happened to have a leprechaun tattooed on his ass. You get my point here?"

"I get it, Jack. Anything else in my e-mail bothering you?"

"Matter of fact, yes—another one of your questions. Actually, three questions that all kind of circle around the same issue: Were all the murders equally important? Was the sequence important? Were any of them necessitated by any of the others? You want to tell me, what is it about the case that brings up that issue?"

"Sometimes it's what's missing that gets my attention. And because of the nature of the reigning hypothesis in this particular case, there's a hell of a lot missing—unexplored avenues, unasked questions. The basic assumption from the beginning was that these murders were identical components of a philosophical statement the killer was making. As soon as everyone accepted that, no one looked at them as individual events that could have different purposes. But it's possible the murders were not all equally important, or even all done for the same reason. You with me, Jack?"

"Hard to say. You got any specifics?"

"You ever see a movie called *The Man with the Black Umbrella*?"

He'd never seen it, never even heard of it. So Gurney told him the story, ending with the "what if the snipers shot them all?" speculation he'd raised with Madeleine.

After a long silence, Hardwick asked a variant of one of Madeleine's questions. "You're saying that the first five attacks were *mistakes*? And the shooter finally got lucky with the sixth? Help me understand this. I mean, if he was a professional, like the guys in your movie, what target ID was he given? Just that the target drove a top-of-the-line Mercedes? So he ought to drive around at night, shoot through a few Mercedes windows with the biggest fucking gun on earth, and see who he hits? I'm having trouble with this."

"Me, too. But you know what? I'm starting to get the feeling that I might be in the right ballpark, even though I'm not sure yet what the game is."

"Not *sure*? How about not having a fucking *clue* what it is?"

"You need to think more positively."

"You have any more words of wisdom, Sherlock, before I puke?"

"Just one thing. Special Agent Trout is fixated on the fact that I might have access to privileged information I'm not legally entitled to. Watch your back, Jack."

"Fuck Trout. Is there any other secret shit you want me to shovel your way?"

"Long as you're asking, do you have any tracer progress on Emilio Corazon?"

"Not yet. He's managed to become a surprisingly invisible man."

At eight forty-five, Madeleine left for her part-time job at the clinic. It was still raining.

Gurney went to his computer, brought up a copy of his e-mail to Hardwick, and went over the list of questions he'd included—stopping at the one that read, "Why did the murders occur when they did, in the spring of the year 2000?" The more certain he was that the murders were essentially pragmatic, the more significant the timing element became.

Psycho-mission killings usually took one of two forms: There's the Big Bang approach, where the shooter walks into the midst of multiple targets in the post office or the mosque and starts shooting, with no plan of escape. Ninety-nine times out of a hundred, those guys (and they're always guys) end up shooting themselves when there's no one else left to shoot. Then there's the other type—the guys who dribble out their bile for ten or twenty years. The guys who like to blow off somebody's head or hand with a letter bomb every year or two but aren't so eager to kill themselves.

The Good Shepherd murders didn't seem to fit either category. There was a palpable coolness, a lack of emotion, in their crisp planning and execution. In any event that's what Gurney was telling himself when the phone rang at nine-fifteen.

Once again it was Hardwick, but his tone was heavier than before.

"Whatever game is being played in whatever ballpark, it just got nastier. Ruthie Blum has turned up dead."

Gurney's first thought, one that made him instantly nauseous, was that she'd been shot in the head like her husband ten years earlier. The sickening image that leaped into his mind was of her perky Yorkshire-terrier hairdo blasted into a bloody, brainy mess.

"Oh, God, no. Where? How?"

"In her house. Ice pick to the heart."

"What?"

"You expressing surprise or bad hearing?"

"An ice pick?"

"Single thrust, upward, under the sternum."

"Jesus Christ. When?"

"Sometime after eleven last night."

"How do they know that?"

"She posted a Facebook message at ten fifty-eight. Body was found at three-forty this morning."

"This is the same house where she lived ten years ago when——"

"Right. Same house. Also the same house where little Kimmy interviewed her for that thing on RAM-TV."

Gurney's mind was racing. "Who found her?"

"Troopers out of the Auburn station in Zone E. Long story. Friend of Ruth's from Ithaca, up late, read her Facebook message. Found it disturbing. Responded to it on Facebook, asking Ruthie if she was all right. Got no answer back. E-mailed her, got no answer to that either. Started phoning her, no answer, only voice mail. So the friend gets panicky, calls the local cops, gets passed on to the sheriff's office, eventually gets passed on to Auburn. Auburn contacts a cruiser in the vicinity. Trooper comes by the house, everything looks peaceful, no problem, no signs of any disturbance, no——"

"Wait a second. You have any idea what Ruth Blum's original message said that started all this?"

"I just e-mailed it to you."

"How'd you manage that?"

"Andy Clegg."

"Who the hell is Andy Clegg?"

"Young guy up in E Zone. You don't remember him?"

"Should I?"

"The Piggert case."

"Okay. Now the name rings a bell. But I can't picture a face."

"His first assignment out of the academy—in fact, the first job he caught on his first day on the job—was to respond to my call for support when I found my half of Mrs. Piggert's body. That turned out to be Andy's first official vomit opportunity. And he took full advantage of it."

The infamous Peter Piggert incest-murder case was the beginning of the edgy but productive relationship between Hardwick and Gurney. Gurney was at the NYPD then, and Hardwick was with the NYSP. They were each investigating aspects of the Piggert case that fell within their separate jurisdictions, when a grotesque bit of serendipity brought them together. Over a hundred miles apart, on the same day, they each discovered half of the same body.

"Young Andy Clegg met us both at a joint get-together after you nailed the elusive Mr. Piggert, the mother-fucking mother killer. Andy was mightily impressed with your skills and, to a lesser extent, with my own. We stayed in touch."

"All this adds up to what?"

"When the basic facts on the Blum ice-pick homicide came in through CJIS this morning, I gave Detective Clegg a friendly call and got the whole story. I figured it was now or never. As soon as Trout gets hold of this and figures out the implications, he'll move in and declare the homicide to be part of his ongoing Good Shepherd investigation and slam the door."

"Which brings us back to my question. What did Ruth's—"

"Check your e-mail."

"Right."

Gurney laid down the phone and opened his e-mail. There it was.

Posted by Ruth J. Blum:

What a day! I spent so much time wondering what the first episode of The Orphans of Murder would be like. I kept trying to remember the things Kim had asked me when she came here. And my answers. I couldn't remember them all. I was hoping that I had managed to express what I really felt. I believe, like Kim says, that TV sometimes misses the point. They pay attention to sensational things too much, not the real things that matter. I was hoping that The Orphans of Murder might be different, because Kim seemed different. But now I don't know. I was a little disappointed. I think they must have cut out a lot of our interview to make room

for their "experts" and the commercials and all the other stuff. I'm going to
call Kim in the morning and ask about it.

    Sorry. I have to stop now. Someone just pulled into my driveway. Can
you imagine, it's almost eleven o'clock. Who could it be? One of those big
military-looking trucky kind of cars. More later.

Gurney read it again before picking up the phone. "You still there,
Jack?"

"Yeah. So her friend in Ithaca is going through her e-mail, around
midnight, and discovers that she has a Facebook notification, which
she clicks on, and she finds the message that Ruth posted at ten fifty-
eight—apparently before she went downstairs to see who was coming
to see her in that big military-looking whatever. Could be a Hummer,
what do you think?"

"Could be." Gurney pictured Max Clinter's combat-ready,
camouflage-painted Humvee.

"Well, if it wasn't a Hummer, what the fuck was it? Anyway, the
friend makes all these efforts to get through to Ruth, and, like I said,
eventually a trooper comes, checks things out, decides everything
looks fine, and he's about to leave—when the anxious friend shows
up in her car, having driven the twenty-five miles up from Ithaca, and
insists they break into the house—because she's afraid something bad
has happened. She says if he doesn't break into the house, she will.
Big argument, young trooper almost arrests her, then another trooper
comes by, older and wiser, calms everybody down. They start looking
around the outside of the house. Eventually they find an open window, more discussion, more debate, et cetera, et cetera. Bottom line,
the troopers finally go in and find Ruth Blum's body."

"Where?"

"In the entry hall, just inside the front door. Like she opened the
door and wham!"

"ME is sure the weapon was an ice pick?"

"Wasn't much doubt. According to Clegg, fucking thing was still
stuck in her."

"You don't suppose he could get me into the house, do you?"

"No way. By now it's been sealed off with a mile of yellow tape by
guys for whom you could only be a problem. Their one job right now is

to keep the scene pristine till the evidence techs go home and the BCI team hands the whole deal off to the FBI. They're not about to hang their asses out the window so some retired hotshot from the city can have a walk-through."

Gurney was itching to see it all for himself. Having a scene described to you was worth maybe 10 percent of being there. But he suspected that Hardwick was right. He couldn't think of any upside for anyone in BCI, much less the FBI, to get him involved. Which made him wonder again what the upside was for Hardwick. Every time the man passed along information from a confidential file or an internal source, he was putting himself at risk. And he was doing it a lot.

Was he such a pure seeker after truth that its pursuit trumped any concern for rules or his own career? Was he driven by an obsessive desire to embarrass the powerful? Or did the risk itself, the giddy edge of the cliff, attract him with the same power with which it repelled saner men? Gurney had asked himself these questions about the man before. Once again he concluded that the answer was probably yes to all of them.

"So, Davey boy . . ." Hardwick's voice jarred him back to the issue at hand. "The plot thickens. Or maybe this makes everything clearer to you. Which is it?"

"I don't know, Jack. A little of both. It depends on what happens next. In the meantime, is that everything Clegg told you?"

"Almost everything." Hardwick hesitated. His appetite for dramatic pauses irritated Gurney intensely, but it was a tolerable price to pay for what often followed. "Remember the little plastic animals the Good Shepherd left at the roadside shootings?"

"Yes." In fact, he'd been thinking about them that morning, wondering about their purpose.

"Well, they found a little plastic animal at the scene—balanced delicately on Ruth Blum's lips."

"On her lips?"

"On her lips."

"What kind of animal?"

"Clegg thinks it was a lion."

"Wasn't a lion the first animal in the original sequence of six?"

"Good memory, ace. So what are the odds we can expect five more?"

Gurney had no answer for that.

As soon as he got off the phone with Hardwick, he called Kim. He wondered if she was still at Kyle's apartment, wondered if they were in bed together, wondered what their plans were for the day, wondered if they knew . . .

The call went into her voice mail. He left a blunt message. "Hi. I don't know if it's on the news yet, but Ruth Blum is dead. She was murdered in her home in Aurora late last night. It's possible that the Good Shepherd is back, or someone wants us to think so. Call me as soon as you can."

He tried Kyle's number, got his voice mail, and left the same message.

He stood staring out the north window of the den at the wet, gray hillside. The rain had stopped, but the eaves continued to drip. The new information from Hardwick was scattering rather than organizing his thoughts. So damn many bits and pieces. It was impossible to see the path through the maze. To take a step forward, one had to know where forward *was*. He was overcome by a sick feeling that time was running out, that the endgame was rapidly approaching, without even knowing what that might mean.

He had to do *something*.

For want of a better idea, he found himself in his car, setting out for Aurora.

Two hours later he was turning onto the state road that ran alongside Lake Cayuga, his GPS indicating he was just three miles from Ruth Blum's address. The lake and its lakefront homes were visible through a border of bare trees on his left. On his right, separated from the road by a deep, grassy drainage swale, a pastoral mix of meadows and thickets sloped gradually up toward a high horizon of stubbled cornfields. Three commercial establishments on the upland side of the road were spaced out among a scattering of well-kept older homes. There was a gas station, a veterinary clinic, and an auto-body shop whose parking area held half a dozen cars in various stages of repair.

Not far past the body shop, Gurney rounded a long bend and saw ahead of him on the left side of the road the first indications of a major crime scene: an assortment of local, county, and state police cruisers. There were also four vans—two, presumably from regional media outlets, with satellite dishes on their roofs; one with the NYSP emblem, which Gurney assumed would contain the evidence team's equipment; and one that was unmarked, probably the forensic photographer's. There was no sign of a morgue vehicle, meaning someone from the ME's office had already come and gone and the body had been transported from the scene.

As he drew closer, Gurney counted six uniformed officers with various jurisdictional insignias, a woman and a man in the conservative business attire favored by detective units, an evidence specialist in the white coveralls and latex gloves required by his occupation, and a fashionably dressed female TV type huddled with two ponytailed male technicians.

A uniformed trooper was standing in the middle of the road, aggressively waving along any car that seemed to be passing too slowly. As Gurney was coming abreast of the trooper and the Blum house behind him, he could see that POLICE LINE—DO NOT CROSS tape had been wrapped around the entire property from the edge of the lake up to the edge of the road. He reached into his glove box and pulled out a thin leather wallet, flipping it open to reveal a gold NYPD detective's shield that bore in small letters at the bottom the word "Retired."

Before the frowning trooper could examine it thoroughly, Gurney tossed it back in his glove box and asked if Senior Investigator Jack Hardwick was on the scene.

The trooper's hat was tilted forward, its stiff brim shadowing his eyes. "Hardwick, BCI?"

"That's right."

"There some reason he should be here?"

Gurney sighed wearily. "I'm working on an investigation that could involve Ruth Blum. Hardwick's aware of it."

The trooper looked like he was having trouble deciphering that answer. "What's your name?"

"Dave Gurney."

The man eyed him with the combination of surface politeness and instinctive distrust with which most cops regard strangers. "Pull in right there." He pointed to a space on the shoulder between the evidence van and one of the TV vans. "Stay in your car." He turned away crisply and approached three figures engaged in an intense discussion next to the driveway. The individual to whom he spoke was a heavyset woman with short brown hair. She was wearing a navy blue jacket and matching pants. The gray-haired man on her right was in white coveralls. The younger man on her left wore a dark suit, white shirt, dark tie—the standard outfit shared by detectives, funeral directors, and Mormons. His heavily muscled shoulders, wide neck, and buzz cut made it clear which of those groups he belonged to.

As the traffic trooper was talking to them, the three looked over at Gurney in unison. The young man began grinning and speaking rapidly to the woman while gesturing in Gurney's direction.

The grin rang a distant bell.

"Detective!" the woman called out, raising her hand to get his attention. "Detective Gurney."

He got out of his car. As he did, he was greeted by the loud throb of a helicopter overhead. He looked up and through the treetops caught glimpses of the slowly circling craft. Giant white letters, RAM, painted on the bottom of the cabin caught his eye and provoked an involuntary grimace.

"Lieutenant Bullard wants to talk to you." The trooper had come back over to Gurney and was lifting the police tape for him to enter the enclosed area. His tone made the tape gesture seem more proprietary than courteous.

Gurney bent forward to pass under the tape. As he did so, he couldn't help noticing a deposit of roadway dirt that had settled into a long expansion crack separating the tarred driveway from the rougher composite pavement of the road shoulder. As he paused for a moment to take a closer look, the trooper let the tape drop on him and returned to his traffic duty.

When Gurney straightened up, the slightly familiar young man in the dark suit was walking toward him.

"Sir, you probably don't remember me. I'm Andrew Clegg. We met during your investigation of——"

Gurney broke in warmly, "I remember you, Andy. Looks like you've been promoted."

Again the grin. It turned him into a teenager. "Last month. Finally made it into BCI. You were one of my inspirations." As he spoke, he was leading Gurney to the solidly built woman, who was talking to the departing tech in the white suit.

"If you want to bag the rug and bring it in, that's fine, too. It's up to you." She turned toward Gurney. Her expression was alert and pleasantly businesslike. "Andy tells me that you and Jack Hardwick worked together on Piggert. Is that a fact?"

"That's a fact."

"Congrats. Big victory for the good guys."

"Thank you."

"His Satanic Santa case was even bigger," said Clegg.

"Satanic . . . ?" Now it was her turn to look as if a distant memory bell was ringing. "Was that the psycho who was cutting people up and mailing the pieces to the local cops?"

"In gift wrapping! As Christmas presents!" cried Clegg, clearly more captivated than horrified.

She stared at Gurney in amazement. "And you . . . ?"

"Just happened to be in the right place at the right time."

"That's remarkable." She extended her hand. "I'm Lieutenant Bullard. And you're obviously a man who needs no further introduction. To what do we owe the pleasure?"

"This situation with Ruth Blum."

"How so?"

"Did you see the program with her last night on RAM?"

"I'm aware of it. Why do you ask?"

"It might help you to understand what happened here."

"How?"

"The program was the first of a series, dealing with the aftereffects of the six murders committed by the Good Shepherd back in 2000. What happened here was almost certainly the seventh Good Shepherd murder. And there may be more coming."

Whatever cordiality had been in her expression had given way to cool assessment. "What exactly are you doing here?"

He began to consider his words carefully—but then thought to hell with that. "I'm here because I believe the FBI got the case backwards from day one, and what happened here may prove it."

Her expression was hard to read. "Have you told them what you think?"

He gave her a quick smile. "It didn't go over very well."

She shook her head. "I'm not quite getting what you're telling me. I don't know on whose behalf or on whose authority you've come here." She glanced at Clegg, who shifted uneasily from foot to foot. "Andy told me you were retired. We're in the crucial first hours of a murder investigation. Unless you can make your presence and purpose plain to me, you're going to have to leave. I hope I'm being clear without being rude."

"I understand." He took a deep breath. "I was hired as a consultant to the woman who interviewed Ruth Blum, and I've been taking a close look at the Good Shepherd case. I've come to the conclusion that there's a major flaw in the prevailing view. I'm hoping the investigation of this murder won't get screwed up like the first six. But, unfortunately, there already seems to be a problem."

"I beg your pardon?"

"He didn't park in the driveway."

"What are you talking about?"

"The man who killed Ruth Blum didn't park in this driveway. If you believe he did, you'll never understand what happened here."

She shot a glance in Clegg's direction, perhaps to see if he knew more about this unexpected challenge than she did, but his eyes showed only surprise and confusion. She looked back at Gurney, then at her watch. "Come inside. I'll give you exactly five minutes to make some sense. Meanwhile, Andy, you stay here and keep an eye on the TV vultures. They are not to put one toe on our side of the tape."

"Yes, ma'am."

She led Gurney down a sloping lawn by the side of the house and up the steps of the rear deck—which he recognized as the location of Kim's outdoor interview with Ruth Blum. He followed her through a back door that connected the deck with a large eat-in kitchen. A photographer was sitting at a table in a breakfast nook, downloading pictures from a digital SLR onto a laptop.

She looked around the kitchen, but it didn't offer much opportunity for privacy. "Excuse me, Chuck, can you give us a few minutes here?"

"No problem, Lieutenant. I can finish this in the van." He picked up his equipment and a moment later was gone.

The lieutenant sat in one of the chairs at the vacated table and motioned Gurney to the one directly opposite. "Okay," she said evenly. "I've had a long day so far, and it's nowhere near over. I have no time to waste. I'd appreciate some clarity and brevity. Speak."

"What makes you think he parked in the driveway?"

Her eyes narrowed. "What makes you think I do?"

"The way the three of you were standing carefully to the side of it when I arrived. The way everybody avoided walking on it, even though your tech crew must have already gone over it. So I figure it's being saved for a more thorough microscopic analysis. How come you're convinced he parked there?"

She studied him for a while before a cynical little smile appeared on her lips. "You already know something, don't you? Where's the leak?"

"No point in going down that path. That's the FBI path. Confrontational waste of time."

She continued to study him, not so long this time, then seemed to arrive at a decision. "The victim posted message on her Facebook page late last night. After some comments about the RAM program, she described a car that was pulling into her driveway as she was sitting there at her computer. Why do I have a feeling that you already know all this?"

Gurney ignored her question. "What kind of car?"

"Big. Military-looking. No make or model mentioned."

"Jeep? Land Rover? Hummer? Something like that?"

She nodded.

"So the theory is that he parks out in the driveway, walks up to the front door, knocks . . . and then what? He kills her in the doorway? She lets him in? She knows him? She doesn't know him?"

"Slow down. You asked me why we believe that the killer—or someone who coincidentally visited her at approximately the time she was killed—parked in the driveway. And I gave you the answer. We believe it because the victim herself told us that's what happened. It's the victim's eyewitness account, posted on her Facebook page, before she was killed." Lieutenant Bullard's expression of triumph was diluted with a pinch of worry. "So now you owe me a brief, clear explanation of why you think Ruth Blum would say those things if they weren't true."

"She didn't."

"Beg pardon?"

"None of it happened that way. The scenario you're presenting doesn't make any sense. First of all, before we get into the logical problem, you've got a physical-evidence problem at the end of the driveway."

"What physical-evidence problem?"

"The ground is fairly dry. How long has it been since the last rain?" He knew when it had rained in Walnut Crossing, but the weather system around the Finger Lakes was often quite different.

She thought for a moment. "It rained yesterday morning. It was over by noon. Why?"

"There's a strip of dirt in a crevice out there at the edge of the road, maybe an inch wide. Anyone coming into the driveway would have to cross it, unless they drove through the woods and across the lawn. But that little strip of dirt doesn't seem to have been disturbed, at least not since the last rain."

"An inch is not necessarily enough to register—"

"Maybe not, but it's suggestive. Plus, there's the psychological factor. If the Good Shepherd is back, if this is his seventh victim, then what we already know about him has to figure into it."

"Like what?"

"One thing we know is that he is extremely cautious, extremely risk-averse. And that short driveway is too exposed. Any vehicle sitting out there—especially anything the size of a Hummer—would have its rear bumper practically on the road. Way too eye-catching, way too identifiable. A local cop cruising by might zero in on a strange car like that, might stop to check it out, might run the plate number."

Bullard frowned. "But the fact is, Ruth Blum was killed, and if the killer came in a vehicle, he had to park it somewhere. So what are you saying? Where did he park it? On the shoulder of the road? That would be even more exposed."

"My guess would be at the body shop."

"The what?"

"Half mile down the state route, back in the direction of Ithaca, there's an auto-body shop. There are some cars and trucks in a scruffy little parking area beside it, either waiting to be worked on or waiting to be picked up. It's the one place in the neighborhood where a strange vehicle wouldn't raise a question—wouldn't even be noticed. If I were going to kill someone in this house in the middle of the night, I'd park there, and then I'd walk the rest of the way here in that deep swale by the side of the road to avoid being seen by passing drivers."

She stared down at the tabletop, as though trying to see the possibilities in an imaginary set of scrabble letters. She made a face. "*Theoretically,* that might make sense. Problem is, her Facebook posting specifically refers to a vehicle pulling in—"

"You mean *the* Facebook posting."

"I don't get what—"

"You're assuming it was *her* posting."

"It was her account, her page, her computer, her password."

"Couldn't her murderer have extracted the password from her before he killed her, opened the page, and composed the message himself?"

Bullard redoubled her scrutiny of the tabletop. She shook her head uncertainly. "That's *conceivable*. But like your body-shop theory, there's no evidence to support it."

Gurney smiled at the opening. "After your boys in the white suits confirm that the dirt in the crack at the end of the driveway hasn't been disturbed, ask them to pay a visit to the body shop. It would be interesting to see if they can find a relatively fresh set of tire tracks that don't match up with any of the vehicles there."

"But . . . why would the killer take the time and trouble to leave a message like that on Facebook?"

"Sand in our eyes. A twist in the maze. He's very good at that."

Something in her expression told him she was open to every speck of information she could lay her hands on.

"How much do you know about the original case?" he asked.

"Not as much as I need to," she admitted. "Someone from the FBI field office is on his way here to give me a briefing. Speaking of which, I'll need your address, e-mail, phone numbers where you can be reached twenty-four hours a day. You have any problem with that?"

"No problem at all."

"I'll give you my e-mail and cell number. I assume you'll pass along any relevant facts that come your way?"

"Be happy to."

"Okay. I'm totally out of time here. We'll talk again."

As Gurney left the house, the RAM helicopter was still circling noisily, its thumping rotor wash loosening the few dead leaves that were still clinging to the topmost branches of the trees, sending them swirling downward. Before he could reach his car, he was intercepted by the fluffy-coiffed, brightly made-up reporter with a mike in her hand and a video man behind her. "I'm Jill McCoy, Eye on the News, Syracuse!" she cried, her face showing the expression of alarmed curiosity that was a standard feature of her breed. "I've been told that you're Detective Dave Gurney, the man *New York* magazine called the Supercop. Dave, is it true that the Good Shepherd, the infamous mass murderer, has struck again?"

"Excuse me," said Gurney, forcing his way by her.

She extended the mike toward him, shouting a string of questions at his back as he opened his car door, got in, closed it, turned on the ignition. "Was she killed because of her TV appearance? Something she said? Is this horrible case too big for our local police? Is that why they brought you in? How are you involved? Is it true you have a problem with the FBI? What's that problem all about, Detective Gurney?"

As he edged out of his parking spot, the video camera was just inches from his side window. The traffic trooper was doing nothing to alleviate the problem. In fact, he was totally absorbed in a conversation with a new arrival on the scene. Pulling out onto the state road, Gurney caught a glimpse of the man—compact, dark-haired, unsmiling. It was just enough of a glimpse for Gurney to recognize him.

It was Daker.

## Chapter 32

# The Multiplier

As Gurney rounded the first bend in the road, the body shop came into view. He slowed as he passed it, noting the sign on the concrete-block building: LAKESIDE COLLISION. He was still convinced it was the perfect place to park a car inconspicuously.

Halfway to Walnut Crossing, he passed a billboard for Verizon Cellular, and it reminded him that he'd switched off his phone when he sat down at the kitchen table with Bullard. He switched it back on to check for messages. The screen said there were seven. Before he had a chance to listen to any of them, a new call came in.

Gurney pressed TALK.

The caller was Kyle, and he sounded agitated. "We've been trying to reach you for over an hour."

"What's the matter?"

"Kim is really freaked out. She's been trying to get you. She's already left three messages for you."

"Is it about Ruth Blum?"

"Mainly that. But also *The Orphans of Murder* thing last night on TV. She hated how they put it together, what they cut and what they added, especially those two jerks. She's really upset."

"Where is she?"

"In the bathroom, crying. Again. Wait, no. I hear the door opening. Hold on."

Gurney heard Kim asking Kyle who he was talking to, Kyle's voice saying, "My dad." Kim sniffling in the background, blowing her nose. The sound of the phone being handed from one to the other. Muffled voices. More nose blowing, throat clearing.

Finally she was speaking to him. "Dave?"

"I'm here."

"This is a nightmare. I can't believe it's happening. I want to go to sleep and wake up again and discover that none of it is real."

"I hope you're not blaming yourself for what happened to Ruth."

"Of course I am!"

"You're not responsible for——"

Kim interrupted, her voice rising. "She wouldn't be dead if I hadn't talked her into doing this stupid program!"

"You're not responsible for her death, and you're not responsible for what RAM News did with your interview, or what they put in, or how they——"

"They cut my interview in half and surrounded it with all that pompous nonsense from their so-called *experts*." She made the word sound like someone spitting. "Oh, God, I just want to disappear. I want to erase everything. Erase everything that killed Ruthie."

"A murderer killed her."

"But it wouldn't have happened if——"

"Listen to me, Kim. A murderer killed Ruth Blum. A murderer with his own agenda. Probably the same murderer who killed her husband ten years ago."

She didn't say anything. He could hear her breathing. Slow, shaky breaths. When she finally spoke, her near hysteria had declined into plain misery. "It's what Larry Sterne kept telling me—it all turned out to be true. He said RAM would twist everything and make it cheap and ugly and awful. He said they'd be better at using me than I'd be at using them, that all they cared about was getting the largest possible audience, that the price of my project would outweigh its rewards. And he was right. Totally right."

"What do you want to do?"

"Do? I want to get as far away from RAM as I can. I want out."

"Have you told Rudy Getz?"

"Yes." There was something uncertain in her voice.

"Yes . . . but?"

"I called him this morning—before I got your message about Ruth. I told him how disappointed I was, that the program was nothing like what we'd talked about."

"And?"

"I told him if that's the way it was going to be, then I didn't want to do it."

"And?"

"He said that he wanted me to meet with him, it wasn't something we could resolve on the phone, we had to talk about it face-to-face."

"You agreed to meet with him?"

"Yes."

"Did you speak to him again, after you found out about Ruth's murder?"

"Yes. He said that made it even more important for us to get together. He said the murder was a multiplier."

"A what?"

"*A multiplier.* He said that it raised the stakes, that we had to talk about it."

"It raised the stakes?"

"That's what he said."

"When are you getting together?"

"At noon on Wednesday. At his place in Ashokan Heights."

Gurney had the impression she was leaving something out. "And?"

There was a pause. "Oh, God . . . I hate to ask you this. I feel like such a naïve, helpless little idiot."

Gurney waited, pretty sure he knew what was coming.

"My vision of what this was going to be like . . . my assumptions . . . the way I thought . . . What I'm trying to say is . . . my thinking about all of this is obviously not very sound. I need . . . I need the support, the input of a clearer mind. I have no right to ask you this, but . . . please . . . ?"

"You want me to come to your Wednesday meeting with Getz?"

"Very much so. Would you? Could you?"

## Chapter 33

# Getting the Message

A t the sign on Franklin Mountain welcoming him back into Delaware County, Gurney left the afternoon sun behind him and descended into a clouded valley. Weather in the mountains seemed to change hourly.

During the remainder of his drive home, he had to keep switching his wipers on and off. He hated driving in the rain—heavy rain, light rain, drizzle, anything gray and wet. Grayness and wetness tended to fertilize his worries.

He became aware of a soreness in his jaw muscles. He'd been clenching his teeth—a side effect of the tension and anger propelling his thoughts.

PTSD. Post-traumatic stress disorder. Three unnerving words. If Holdenfield was right, if his thinking was damaged . . .

What was it Kim said she needed from him? The input of a clearer mind than hers? He let out a sharp little laugh. Clarity was not currently his strong point.

The thought of their phone conversation reminded him of the seven messages in his voice mail he hadn't listened to. He was just turning up the mountain lane to his farmhouse, telling himself he'd listen to the messages as soon as he got there. But, afraid of forgetting again, he decided to pull over and go through them.

The first three were from Kim—increasingly stressed requests for him to call her.

The fourth was from Kim's mother, Connie Clarke.

"David! What on earth is going on? All this crazy stuff on the news today? About Ruth what's-her-name getting killed after Kim's interview? And the talking heads all screaming that the Good Shepherd is back? Jeez! Give me a call, let me know what's going on. I just got a totally hysterical message from Kim—that she wants to quit, back out of the show, throw it all away. Completely out of control. I don't understand any of this. I called her back, couldn't get through, left a message, but I haven't heard back. I assume that you're in touch with her? That you know what the hell is happening? I mean, that was the whole idea, right? For Christ's sake, call me!"

Maybe he would, maybe he wouldn't. He definitely didn't feel like spending half an hour on the phone with her, filling her in on all the chaos, all the unanswered questions, just because her daughter wasn't returning her calls.

The fifth message had no ID beyond WIRELESS CALLER. But there was no mistaking the manic intensity of Max Clinter's voice.

"Mr. Gurney, so sorry you couldn't pick up. I was looking forward to some give-and-take. So much has happened since last we talked. The Shepherd would appear to be among us once again. Little Corazon brought him back to life. Heard your name invoked on that vile Orphans thing on TV. Ram-shit. But from what was said, it sounded like you had ideas. Ideas of your own. Maybe not unlike mine. Want to share and share alike? Win or lose, time to choose. The finale isn't far off now. This time I'll be ready. Final question: Is David Gurney friend or foe?"

Dave listened to that one three times. He still wasn't sure whether Clinter was a nutcase or just found it a comfortable role to play. Holdenfield had insisted that he was a mentally disturbed pain in the ass. But Gurney wasn't quite ready to discount the man who had talked himself into that little room in Buffalo and left five armed mobsters dead on the floor.

He looked at his dashboard clock. It was a minute past four. The mist had stopped, at least temporarily. He pulled back onto the gravel-and-dirt lane and headed up the mountain.

When he got to the little parking area by their side door, he saw that the light was on in the upstairs room that Madeleine sometimes used for her knitting and crocheting. She'd gone back to using it only in the last month or two. It had been the site of a threatening intrusion into the house during the course of the Perry investigation the previous September—the investigation that ended with Gurney being shot.

The thought of it brought his hand to the numb spot on his fore-arm, checking automatically for any change in feeling—a habit that the busyness of the past week had derailed. It would be nice to keep it derailed. He got out of the car and went into the house.

Madeleine wasn't knitting after all. He could hear her playing her guitar.

"I'm home!" he called out.

"I'll be down soon," came the voice from the second floor.

He listened as she played through a few more bars of something pleasantly melodic, ending in a loud resolving chord.

After a few seconds of silence she called down to him, "Listen to number three on the machine."

Jesus. Not another disturbing message. He'd had more than his fill for the day. He hoped this one would be innocuous. He went into the den to the old landline phone, pressed the button to get to number three, and listened.

"I hope I'm reaching the right Detective Gurney. I'm really sorry if I've got the wrong one. The Detective Gurney I'm looking for has been fucking a whore by the name of Kim Corazon. He's a pathetic, disgusting old fool who's at least twice the whore's age. If you're the wrong Detective Gurney, maybe you could pass along a question to the right one. Ask him if he knows that his son is fucking the same whore. Like father, like son. Maybe Rudy Getz could turn it into a RAM real-ity show—Gurney Family Gang Bang. Have a nice day, Detective."

It was the voice of Robby Meese, all pretense of smoothness stripped away, the vocal equivalent of a serrated knife.

As he was replaying the message, Madeleine appeared at the den door, her expression unreadable. "Do you know who that is?" she asked.

"Kim's ex."

She nodded grimly, as though the idea had already occurred to her. "He seems to know there's some sort of relationship between Kim and Kyle. How would he know that?"

"Maybe he saw them together."

"Where?"

"Maybe in Syracuse?"

"How would he know Kyle was your son?"

"If he's the one who bugged her apartment, he'd know a lot."

She folded her arms tightly. "Do you think he might have followed them back here?"

"Possibly."

"So he could also have followed them yesterday to Kyle's apartment?"

"Tailing someone in city traffic isn't as simple as it sounds, especially for someone not used to driving in Manhattan. It's too easy to get separated with all the stoplights."

"He sounds motivated."

"What do you mean?"

"I mean, he sounds like he really hates you."

## Chapter 34

# Allies and Enemies

They were finishing an early dinner of salmon, peas, and rice, with a sweet-pepper sauce. They'd been discussing the meeting that Madeleine would be attending that evening at the clinic for further exploration of the recent suicide and the procedures in place for identifying danger signals in the clients. She was noticeably edgy and preoccupied.

"With that horrible phone message and everything else going on today, I forgot to tell you that the insurance adjuster was here."

"He was here to examine the barn?"

"And ask questions."

"Like Kramden?"

"He covered the same ground. List of contents, who did what when, details of any other insurance policies we have, et cetera."

"I assume you gave him copies of the same stuff we gave Kramden?"

"Her."

"Sorry?"

"It was a woman. She wanted sales receipts for the bicycle and the kayaks." In Madeleine's voice there was sadness and anger. "You have any idea where they are?"

He shook his head.

She paused. "I asked her how soon we could demolish it."

"The part of the barn that's still standing?"

"She said the company would let us know."

"No hint of when?"

"No. They need written permission from the arson squad before they can okay anything." Her hands had closed into fists. "I can't stand looking at it."

He gave her a long look. "Are you mad at me?"

"I'm mad at the evil bastard who destroyed our barn. I'm mad at the creep who left that disgusting message on our phone."

Her anger created a silence between them, which lasted until she left for the clinic. In the interim he thought of things he might say, then reasons not to say them.

After watching her car head down the pasture path, Gurney carried their used dishes to the sink, squirted a bit of detergent on them, and turned on the hot water.

The cell phone in his pocket rang.

ID said G. B. BULLARD.

"Mr. Gurney?"

"I'm here."

"I wanted to fill you in on something, since it concerns a point you raised earlier today."

"Yes?"

"The matter of the tire tracks . . . ?"

"Yes?"

"I wanted you to know that we did find a set of tread marks, where you suggested they might be, at the auto-body shop."

"Indicating a car was parked in a space that the shop owner says was unoccupied?"

"Essentially that's correct—although he isn't absolutely sure about it."

"And the dirt strip at the end of Ruth Blum's driveway?"

"Inconclusive."

"Meaning not enough soil surface to be certain one way or the other, but no positive evidence of any vehicle entering or leaving?"

"Correct."

Gurney was getting curious about the purpose of her call. It was not common practice for an investigating officer to give a progress report outside the immediate chain of command, much less to someone outside the department.

"But there's a little twist," she went on. "I'd like your opinion. Our door-to-doors turned up two eyewitness reports of a Humvee in the area late yesterday afternoon. One witness insisted it was the original military model, not the later GM version. They both saw it passing back and forth two or three times along the stretch of road that includes the Blum residence."

"You're thinking someone was scouting out the area?"

"Possibly, but like I said, there's a twist. According to the tire tracks, the vehicle that was parked last night at the body shop was not a Humvee." She paused. "Any thoughts on that?"

Two scenarios came to mind. "The killer might have a helper. Or . . ." Gurney hesitated, working his way through his second option, weighing its plausibility.

"Or what?" prompted Bullard.

"Well, let's say I'm right about the Facebook message—that it was posted by the killer, not the victim. The message refers to some kind of military vehicle. So maybe the purpose of the message was to plant the Humvee idea. And maybe driving one up and down that road was designed to get it noticed, get it reported, make us sure it was the killer's vehicle."

"Why go to all that trouble if he was going to park a different car where it wouldn't be noticed anyway?"

"Maybe the Humvee idea is supposed to lead us somewhere."

*Maybe it's supposed to lead us to Max Clinter? But why?*

Bullard remained silent so long that Gurney was about to ask if she was still there.

"You have a serious interest in this, don't you?" she said finally.

"I tried to make that clear earlier today."

"Okay. Let me get to the point. I have a meeting tomorrow morning with Matt Trout to discuss the case and the jurisdictional issues. How would you like to come along?"

Gurney was momentarily speechless. The invitation made no sense. Or maybe it did. "How well do you know Agent Daker?" he asked.

"I met him for the first time today." There was a chill in her voice. "Why do you ask?"

Her reaction encouraged him to take a chance. "Because I think he and his boss are arrogant, controlling little bastards."

"My impression is that they hold you in equally high regard."

"I wouldn't have it any other way. Did Daker fill you in on the original case?"

"Filling me in was the stated purpose of the visit. The reality was a disorganized data dump."

"They probably want to overwhelm you, make you see the case as an impossible tangle of complications—so you fade away quietly and cede jurisdiction without an argument."

"The thing is," said Bullard, "I have this contrary streak in me. I have a hard time walking away from a potential fight. I especially don't like being underestimated by . . . what did you call them? 'Arrogant, controlling little bastards'? I don't know why I'm telling you this. I don't really know you or your allegiances. I must be a little bit nuts, talking like this."

Gurney figured she knew exactly what she was doing. "You know that Trout and Daker can't stand me," he said. "Isn't that enough reassurance?"

"I suppose it'll have to be. You know where our zone headquarters is in Sasparilla?"

"I do."

"Can you make it at nine forty-five tomorrow morning?"

"I can."

"Good. I'll meet you in the parking lot. One last thing: Our lab people took a close look at the victim's computer keyboard. They discovered something. Her fingerprints—"

Gurney broke in. "Let me guess. Her fingerprints on the specific keys necessary to compose the Facebook message were slightly smudged in a way that her fingerprints on the other keys weren't. And your lab techs consider the smudging consistent with someone tapping those keys with his fingers in latex gloves."

There was a second of silence. "Not necessarily latex, but how—"

"It's the most likely scenario. Because the only other way for the killer to have gone about it would have been to force Ruth to type the message herself as he dictated it. But she'd have been so terrified it would have created difficulties. He'd have felt exposed enough just extracting the password from her. The longer she was alive, the more risk he would have faced. She might have a breakdown and start screaming. Not a prospect he'd be comfortable with. This guy would want her dead as soon as possible. Less chance of uncontrollable outcomes."

"You're not shy about your opinions, are you, Mr. Gurney? Anything else you'd care to share?"

He thought of his summary sheet of comments and questions, the one he'd sent to Hardwick and Holdenfield. "I have some unpopular thoughts about the original case that you might find helpful."

"I'm getting the impression you consider unpopularity a virtue."

"Not a virtue. Just irrelevant."

"Really? I thought I might have detected an appetite for debate. Sleep well. Tomorrow morning should be interesting."

He hardly slept at all.

His attempt to get to bed early was disrupted by Madeleine's return from her clinic meeting—eager to voice the perennial complaint of social workers: "If the energy devoted to ass covering and bureaucratic baloney were devoted to helping people, it could change the world in a week!"

Three cups of herbal tea later, they finally made their way into the bedroom. Madeleine settled down on her side of the bed with *War and Peace*, the soporific masterpiece that she seemed determined to conquer by persistently biting off small chunks.

After setting his alarm, Gurney lay there pondering Bullard's motives and how they might play out in the Sasparilla meeting. She seemed to view him as an ally, or at least a useful tool, in her anticipated conflict with Trout and company. He didn't mind being used, so long as it didn't obstruct his own purposes. He knew that his alliance with her was very ad hoc, with no roots, so he'd need to be sensitive to any shifting winds at the meeting. Hardly a new experience. At the NYPD the winds were always shifting.

An hour later, as his mind was drifting into a state of pleasantly numb emptiness, Madeleine put her book aside and asked, "Were you ever able to get back in contact with that depressed accountant you were worried about—the one with the big gun?"

"Not yet."

The question refilled his mind with a tangle of questions and anxieties, and all hope of a restful night vanished. His thoughts and fitful dreams were infested with repetitive images of guns, ice picks, burning buildings, black umbrellas, smashed heads.

At sunrise he fell into a deep sleep, from which the sharp trill of his alarm roused him an hour later.

By the time he'd showered, dressed, and had his wake-up coffee in hand, Madeleine was already outside, loosening the soil in one of the garden beds.

He recalled she'd said something recently about getting the sugar-snap peas planted.

How bland the morning felt—in the way that mornings often felt bland, unthreatening, uncomplicated. Each morning—assuming that some minimal intervention of sleep had demarcated it from the day before—created the illusion of a new beginning, a kind of freedom from the past. Humans, it seemed, were truly diurnal creatures, not simply in the sense of being non-nocturnal but in the sense of being designed for living one day at a time—one *separated* day at a time. Uninterrupted consciousness could tear a man to pieces. No wonder the CIA used sleep deprivation as a torture. A mere seventy-two hours of uninterrupted *living*—seeing, hearing, feeling, thinking—could make a man wish he were dead.

The sun sets and we sleep. The sun rises and we wake. We wake and, ever so briefly, ever so blindly, we enjoy the fantasy of beginning anew. Then, without fail, reality reasserts its presence.

That morning, as he stood at the kitchen window with his coffee, gazing contemplatively down over the stubbly pasture, reality reasserted itself in the form of a dark figure astride a dark motorcycle, motionless, between the pond and the burned timbers of the barn.

Gurney put down his coffee, slipped on a jacket and a pair of low boots, and stepped outside. The figure on the motorcycle remained still. The air smelled more like winter than like spring. Four days after the fire, it still carried a hint of ashiness.

Gurney began walking slowly down the pasture path. The rider kick-started his machine—a big, muddy motocross bike—and began creeping erratically up the path from the low end, moving no faster than Gurney was walking. The result was that they met approximately in the middle of the field. It wasn't until the man flipped up his visor that Gurney recognized the intense eyes of Max Clinter.

"You should have told me you were coming," said Gurney in his unruffled way. "I have a meeting this morning. You might have missed me."

"Didn't know I was coming till I was coming," said Clinter—as edgy as Gurney was calm. "Awful lot of items on my list, hard to decide on the right order. Right order is the key. You understand that things are coming to a head?" His engine was still running.

"I understand the Good Shepherd is back, or someone wants us to think so."

"Oh, he's back. I feel it in my bones—the bones that got broken ten years ago. The evil fucker is definitely back."

"What can I do for you, Max?"

"I came to ask you a question." His eyes sparkled.

"If you'd left a number when you called me, I'd have called you back."

"When you didn't pick up, I took it as a sign."

"A sign of what?"

"That it's always better to ask a question face-to-face. Better to see a man's eyes, not just hear the voice. So here's my question: Where do you stand on this Ram-shit business?"

"Say that again?"

"World is full of evil, Mr. Gurney. Evil and its mirror. Murder and the media. Need to know where you stand on that."

"You're asking how I feel about news coverage of violence? How do *you* feel about it?"

A rough laugh burst from Clinter's throat. "Drama for idiots! Orchestrated by maggots! Exaggeration, garbage, and lies! That's what 'news coverage' is, Mr. Gurney. The glorification of ignorance! The manufacture of conflict for profit! The sale of anger and resentment as entertainment! RAM News, the vilest of all. Spewing bile and shit for the profit of pigs!"

Patches of white spittle had accumulated at the corners of Clinter's mouth.

"You seem pretty full of anger yourself," said Gurney placidly.

"Full of anger? Oh, yes! Full of it, you might even say consumed by it, driven by it. But I'm not *selling* it. I'm not a fat mouth selling anger on RAM News. My anger is not for sale."

Clinter's engine was still idling, more roughly now. He gave the throttle a twist, revving it up to a screaming roar.

"So you're not a salesman," said Gurney when the roar subsided. "But what are you, Max? I can't quite figure you out."

"I'm what that evil fucker made me. I'm the wrath of God."

"Where's the Humvee?"

"Funny you should ask."

"Any chance you were in the vicinity of Cayuga Lake the day before yesterday?"

Clinter stared at him long and hard. "There's a chance, yes."

"Mind if I ask why?"

Another appraising stare. "I was there by special invitation."

"Sorry?"

"His opening move."

"I'm not following you."

"Got a text message from the Shepherd—an invitation to meet him on the road, finish what we left unfinished. Foolish of me to take his words at face value. I wondered why he didn't show, couldn't figure it out, till I heard the morning news. The Blum murder. He set me up, don't you see? Had me driving by her house, back and forth, full of hate and hunger. Hunger to get even. He knew I'd show up. Okay, then. One point for him. Next one's for me."

"I don't suppose the source of the message could be traced?"

"To a prepaid anonymous cell phone? Not worth the effort. But tell me something. How'd you know I was out by the lake?"

"Door-to-door interviews the day after the murder. Apparently a couple of people remembered the vehicle. They told the cops, and a cop told me."

Clinter's eyes flashed with vindication. "See? A fucking setup! Designed to produce the result it produced."

"So you decided to get out of your house and hide the Humvee?"

"Until it's needed." He paused, licked his lips, wiped his mouth with the back of a black-gloved hand. "Thing of it is, I don't know how deep the setup goes, and if they were to pull me in for questioning or hold me on suspicion, I'd be in no position to deal with the enemy. You understand my difficulty?"

"I think so."

"Could you be clearer whose side you stand on?"

"I stand where I am, Max. I'm on no one's side but my own."

"Fair enough." Clinter revved his engine to the redline once again, holding it there for at least five deafening seconds before letting it fall back to idle. He reached into an inside pocket of his leather jacket and pulled out what appeared to be a business card. It had no name or address on it, however, just a phone number. He handed it to Gurney. "My cell. Always with me. Let me know anything you think I might need to know. Secrets create collisions. Here's hoping we don't collide."

Gurney slipped the card into his pocket. "A question before you go, Max. I have the impression you took a longer look than anyone else at the personal lives of the victims. I'm wondering what stuck in your mind."

"Stuck in my mind? Like what?"

"When you think of the victims or their families, is there any little oddity that bubbles to the surface—anything that might connect them all together?"

Clinter looked thoughtful, then recited the names in a kind of rapid rhythmic litany: "Mellani, Rotker, Sterne, Stone, Brewster, Blum." The thoughtful look deepened into a frown. "Plenty of oddities. Connections are more elusive. I spent weeks, years on the Internet. Followed names to news stories, news stories to more names, organizations, companies, back and forth, one thing leading to ten other things. Bruno Mellani and Harold Blum went to the same high school in Brooklyn, different years. Ian Sterne's son had a girlfriend who was one of the victims of the White Mountain Strangler. She was a senior at Dartmouth at the very same time that Jimi Brewster was there as a freshman. Sharon Stone may once have shown a house to Roberta Rotker, whose Rottweilers came from a kennel in Williamstown two miles down the road from Dr. Brewster's estate. I could go on. But you get my point? Connections of a sort, with significance yet to be determined."

A cold gust swept across the pasture, bending the stiff, dry weeds.

Gurney stuffed his hands into his jacket pockets. "You never found a thread that connected them all?"

"Not a thing, except the fucking cars. Of course, I was the only one looking. I know what my colleagues were thinking: The cars are the obvious connection, so why look for a second connection?"

"But you think there is one, don't you?"

"I don't *think* there is. I'm sure there is. A bigger scheme that no one's figured out. But we're past that now."

"Past it?"

"The Shepherd's on the move. Setting me up. To finish me off. All coming to a head. So much for thinking and weighing and figuring. The time for thinking's behind us. It's time for combat. Got to go. Time's running out."

"One last question, Max: Does the statement 'Let the devil sleep' mean anything to you?"

"Not a thing." His eyes widened. "It's an eerie kind of saying, though, isn't it? Pushes one's mind in a peculiar direction. Where'd you hear it?"

"In a dark basement."

Clinter stared at Gurney for a long moment. "Sounds like a good place for it." He adjusted his black helmet, revved his engine, gave a small military salute, pivoted the bike in a rapid one-eighty, and made his way down the hill.

When bike and rider were out of sight, Gurney trudged back up to the house, mulling over the odd little "links" Clinter had found among the families. It brought to mind the six-degrees-of-separation concept and the related likelihood that any significant probing of people's lives might turn up a surprising number of places where their paths had crossed.

The elephant in the room continued to be, as Clinter had put it, "the fucking cars."

Back in the kitchen, Gurney had another cup of coffee. Madeleine came into the house through the mudroom and asked mildly, "Friend of yours?"

"Max Clinter." He began to relate what the man had told him, but he noticed the time on the clock. "Sorry, it's later than I thought. I need to be in Sasparilla at nine forty-five."

"And I'm on my way to the bathroom."

A few minutes later, he called in to her that he was leaving. She called out for him to be careful.

"Love you," he said.

"Love you," she said.

Five minutes after that, when he was about a mile down the mountain road, he saw a Priority Mail truck coming up toward him. There were only two other houses between that point and his own, both occupied mainly on weekends, meaning that the delivery was probably for him or for Madeleine. He pulled over and waved as he got out of his car.

The driver stopped, recognized him, retrieved a Priority envelope from the back of the truck, and handed it to him. After the exchange of a few commiserating words about the too-chilly spring, the driver departed and Gurney opened the envelope, which was addressed to him.

Inside the outer envelope was a plain manila envelope, which he also opened, extracting a single sheet of paper. He read:

> *Greed spreads in a family like septic blood in bathwater. It infects everyone it touches. Therefore the wives and children you hold up as objects of sorrow and pity shall also be cut down. The children of greed are evil, and evil are those whom they embrace. Therefore they, too, shall be cut down. Whomsoever you hold up for the fools of the world to console, they all shall be cut down, whether related by blood or by marriage to the children of greed.*
>
> *To consume the product of greed is to consume its stain. The fruit leaves its mark. The beneficiaries of greed bear the guilt of greed, and they must bear its punishment. They will die in the spotlight of your praise. Your praise shall be their undoing. Your pity is a poison. Your sympathy condemns them to death.*
>
> *Can you not see the truth? Have you gone blind?*
>
> *The world has gone mad. Greed masquerades as laudable*

*ambition. Wealth pretends to be proof of talent and worth. The channels of communication have fallen into the hands of monsters. The worst of the worst are exalted.*

*With devils in pulpits and angels ignored, it falls to the honest to punish what the mad world rewards.*

*These are the true and final words of the Good Shepherd.*

## Chapter 35

# Invitation to the Party

A s Gurney turned onto Route 7, the main road through Sasparilla, his phone rang. The ID said it was Kyle, but the voice was Kim's.

The guilt and anger of the previous day's call had been replaced by shock and fear. "Something came a minute ago by rush mail . . . from *him* . . . the Good Shepherd . . . It talks about people being cut down . . . people dying."

Gurney asked her to read it to him. He wanted to be sure it was the same message he'd received himself.

It was identical.

"What should we do?" she asked. "Should we call the police?"

Gurney told her that he'd received the same message and that he was only minutes away from a meeting at which he'd be passing it along to the state police and the FBI. But he did have a question for her. "How was the envelope addressed?"

"That's the scariest part." Her voice was trembly. "The outer envelope was addressed to Kyle here at his apartment, but there was a second envelope inside it that had *my* name on it—which means the Good Shepherd must know I'm here, that we're here together. How could he know that?"

When Meese's nasty phone message had prompted Madeleine to ask a similar question the night before, Gurney had dismissed the possibility of a physical tail. Now he wasn't so sure.

*"How could he know?"* Kim repeated, her voice rising.

"He might not actually know that you're there together. He might just believe that Kyle would have a way of reaching you, of getting the message to you." Even as he was saying this, he realized it didn't make a lot of sense, that he was mainly trying to calm her.

It didn't seem to be working. "Overnight mail means he wanted me to get it this morning. And he used both our names. *So he must know we're both here!*"

That logic was less than perfect, but Gurney wasn't about to debate it. For a moment he considered bringing the NYPD into the affair, if for no other reason than to get a uniform to pay them a visit, creating the illusion of protection. But the confusion, crossed wires, and need for explanations that would ensue outweighed the practical benefits. The bureaucratic bottom line was that there was no concrete evidence of an imminent threat to them, and involving the NYPD would likely start with an argument and end in a mess.

"Here's what I want you to do. I want you to stay in the apartment—both of you. Make sure the door is locked. Don't open it for anyone. I'll call you again after my meeting. In the meantime if there's any tangible threat—or any communication at all beyond the message you've already received—call me immediately. Okay?"

"Okay."

"Now, let me ask you about something else: Can you access the video record of your interview with Jimi Brewster?"

"Yes, sure. I have a copy right here on my iPod."

"With you?"

"Yes."

"In a format you can e-mail me?"

"Depends on how large a document your e-mail server will accept. I'll reduce the resolution to minimize the file size, and there shouldn't be any problem."

"Fine, just so long as I know what I'm looking at."

"You want me to send it right now?"

"Please."

"Can I ask why?"

"Jimi Brewster's name came up in another context. A conversation I had with Max Clinter. I'd like to get a better sense of who he is."

As Gurney ended the call, he was turning into the parking lot of New York State Police Zone Headquarters. He passed a row of trooper cruisers and pulled in next to a gleaming silver BMW 640i.

An eighty-five-thousand-dollar flash-and-dash vehicle would be a questionable choice for a civil servant, but for a high-flying consultant who was moving up in the world it could make sense. It hadn't occurred to him until then that Rebecca Holdenfield might be attending the meeting, but now he'd be willing to put even money on it. It was her kind of car.

He checked his watch. He was five minutes early. He could use the time to return Connie Clarke's call, with an honest excuse to keep the conversation short in case she actually picked up. As he was retrieving her number, one of the NYSP's black Crown Victorias pulled in beside him. Bullard was in the passenger seat, and Andy Clegg was driving.

Bullard motioned to Gurney to join them, pointing toward the big sedan's rear seat. He did as he was bidden, bringing his Priority Mail envelope with him.

Bullard began speaking like someone who'd carefully thought through what she wanted to say. "Good morning, Dave. Thanks for coming on short notice. Before we go inside, I wanted to make you aware of my position. As you know, BCI's Auburn unit is investigating the murder of Ruth Blum. The murder may or may not be related to the ten-year-old Good Shepherd case. We may be dealing with the same perp, or a copycat, or with some third option still undefined."

To Gurney there was no possibility of any "third option"—but he understood that Bullard wanted to establish the broadest rationale for retaining investigative control.

She went on. "I understand that there's an established theory of the original case, and I understand that you've been questioning it aggressively. I want you to know that I come to the table with an open mind. I have no vested interest in any particular version of the truth. I also have no interest in ego-driven pissing matches. My interest is in facts. I have a great fondness for them. I asked you to join us this morning because I sensed that you might share that fondness. Any questions?"

It all sounded as straightforward as Bullard's clear, forceful voice. But Gurney knew that the reality of the situation had another layer. He was pretty sure he'd been invited because Bullard had discovered, probably from Daker, that he'd gotten under Trout's skin—meaning that his unstated role was to complicate the chemistry of the meeting and keep Trout off balance. In short, he was there as a wild card in Bullard's hand.

"Any questions?" she repeated.

"Just one. I assume that Daker showed you the FBI profile of the Good Shepherd?"

"Yes."

"What do you think of it?"

"I'm not sure."

"Good."

"Pardon?"

"Sign of an open mind. Now, before we go in, I have a small bombshell for you." He opened the Priority envelope he'd been holding in his lap, then the inner envelope, and slid the message out. "This was delivered to me this morning. I've already handled it, but it would be better if no one else touched it."

Bullard and Clegg turned a little farther around in their seats to face him. He read the message aloud, slowly. He was struck again by its elegance—especially in the conclusion: *"With devils in pulpits and angels ignored, it falls to the honest to punish what the mad world rewards."* The problem was, it was an elegant expression of emotion that felt devoid of any emotion at all.

When he finished, he held it up for Bullard and Clegg to read for themselves. Bullard's expression was electric.

"This is the original?" she asked.

"One of two originals that I know of. The other one was received by Kim Corazon."

She blinked several times, rapidly—in a way that seemed a by-product of rapid thinking. "We'll make half a dozen copies when we go inside, then tag the original in an evidence bag for Albany forensics." Her eyes shifted to Gurney. "Why you?"

"Because I'm helping Kim Corazon? Because he wants to stop both of us?"

More blinking. She looked at Clegg. "The people alluded to in this message need to be alerted. Everyone we can identify that would fit his definition of the enemy." She looked back at Gurney. "Hold it up again so I can read it." She scanned down through the text. "It sounds like he may be threatening everyone in the families of the original victims, their children, and their children's families. We need names, addresses, phone numbers—fast. Who would have all that stuff?" She glanced at Clegg.

"There was some location and contact information in the files Daker showed us, but the question would be, how current is it?"

"Your most current source would be Kim Corazon," said Gurney. "She's been in touch with a lot of those people."

"Right. Good. Let's get inside and get some help on this. Our main concern here is to provide an appropriate alert to anyone who may be in danger, without creating a panic situation."

Bullard was first out of the car, leading the way into the headquarters building. Gurney recognized the aggressive stride of the kind of person who is totally energized by a crisis. As he was about to follow her through the heavy glass doors into the reception area, he caught sight of a dark SUV turning into the parking lot. The lean, expressionless face behind the wheel belonged to Agent Daker.

A reflection on the glass obscured the face of Daker's passenger. The result was that Gurney couldn't tell if Trout had seen him or, if he had, how unhappy it had made him.

## Chapter 36

# Ice Picks and Animals

Because of the turmoil generated by the Good Shepherd's message and the time required for the various initiatives that needed to be set in motion, their scheduled meeting began forty-five minutes late, with a rearranged agenda and burned-smelling coffee.

It was a typical windowless conference room with a pushpin corkboard affixed to one wall and a shiny whiteboard on the adjoining wall. The fluorescent lighting was both bright and bleak, a reminder of Paul Mellani's claustrophobic office. A plain rectangular conference table with six chairs occupied most of the space. A small table with an aluminum coffee urn, Styrofoam cups, plastic spoons, powdered creamer, and a nearly empty box of sugar packets stood in a corner. It was the kind of room in which Gurney had spent countless hours, and the reaction it produced never changed. Whenever he entered a room like that, he immediately wanted to leave it.

On one side of the table sat Daker, Trout, and Holdenfield. On the opposite side sat Clegg, Bullard, and Gurney. It was an arrangement suited to confrontation. On the table in front of each of them, Bullard had placed a photocopy of the Good Shepherd's new missive—which everyone had now read several times.

In front of Bullard herself, there was also a fat file folder—on top of which, to Gurney's surprise, was the summary he'd e-mailed her of his thoughts regarding the original case.

Bullard was seated directly across the table from Trout, whose hands where folded before him. "I appreciate your making the trip here," she said. "Beyond the obvious importance of this new communication, purportedly from the Good Shepherd, is there any-thing else top-of-mind that you'd like to address as we get started?"

Trout smiled blandly, turning his palms up in a traditional gesture of deference. "It's your turf, Lieutenant. I'm here to listen." Then he shot a less cordial glance at Gurney. "My only concern would be the inclusion of nonvetted personnel in an internal discussion of an inves-tigation in progress."

Bullard screwed up her face in bafflement. "Nonvetted?"

The bland smile returned. "Let me be more specific. I'm not refer-ring to Mr. Gurney's much-publicized past career in law enforcement, but to the unknown nature of his present entanglement with individu-als who could become subjects of this investigation."

"You mean Kim Corazon?"

"And her ex-boyfriend, to name just two that I'm aware of."

Interesting that he would know about Meese, thought Gurney. Two possible sources for that: Schiff in Syracuse and Kramden, the arson man, who had asked Kim about threats and enemies. Or Trout may have started snooping into Kim's life in other ways. But why? Another indication of his control mania? His hell-bent determination to circle the wagons?

Bullard was nodding thoughtfully, her gaze drifting to the blank whiteboard. "That's a reasonable concern. My own position is prob-ably less reasonable. More emotional. My feeling is that the perp is trying to push Dave Gurney away from the case, and that makes me want to pull him into it." Suddenly there was steel in her voice and in the strong lines of her face. "See, whatever the perp is *against*, that's what I'm *for*. I'm also willing to make some assumptions here about individual integrity—the integrity of every individual in this room."

Trout leaned back from the table. "Don't misunderstand me. I'm not questioning anyone's integrity."

"Sorry if I missed your point. A moment ago you used the word 'entanglement.' In my mind that word has definite connotations. But let's not get bogged down before we get started. My recommendation is that we review first what we know about the Blum homicide, then go on to a discussion of the message received this morning, as well as the nature of the relationship between this homicide and the murders that occurred in the spring of 2000."

"And, of course, the jurisdictional issue," added Trout.

"Of course. But we can address that only in light of the facts on the ground. So facts first."

A small smile came to Gurney's lips. The lieutenant struck him as tough, smart, clear, and practical—in the right proportions.

She continued. "Some of you may have seen the detailed CJIS Update Number Three we posted last night? In the event that you haven't, I have copies here." She removed several printouts from her folder and passed them around the table.

Gurney scanned quickly through his. It was a concise summary of the Blum crime-scene evidence and the preliminary forensic conclusions. He was pleased by the validation of the guesses he'd made at the site, as well as by the frowns forming on the faces of Trout and his companions.

After giving them time to absorb the information and its implications, Bullard underscored some key points, after which she asked if there were any questions.

Trout held up the CJIS report. "What significance are you attributing to this confusion over where the killer parked his car?"

"I think 'attempted deception' would be more accurate than 'confusion.'"

"Call it whatever you like. My question is, what significance does it have?"

"By itself not much, beyond indicating a certain level of caution. But combined with the Facebook message, I'd say it indicates an attempt to create a false narrative. Like the body being moved from the upstairs room where the attack took place to the entry hall where it was found."

Trout raised an eyebrow.

"Microscopic scrape marks from the heels of her shoes on the stair carpets, consistent with dragging," explained Bullard. "So we were being set up to buy into a version of the crime very different from what actually occurred."

Holdenfield spoke for the first time. "Why?"

Bullard smiled like a teacher with a student who finally asked the right question. "Well, had we swallowed the deception—the scenario of the killer pulling into the driveway, knocking on the front door, stabbing the victim when she opened it, and driving off into the night—we'd have ended up believing that the Facebook message was the victim's and that everything in it was true, including the description of the killer's vehicle. Plus that the killer was probably someone she didn't know."

Holdenfield looked honestly curious. "Why someone she didn't know?"

"Two reasons. First, the Facebook message indicates that it wasn't a vehicle she recognized. Second, the misleading position of the body conveys the false message that she never let him into the house—when in fact we know that she did."

"Pretty thin evidence for any of that," said Trout.

"We have evidence that he *was* in the house and that he made an effort to mislead us on that point. There are several reasons he might want to do that, but a big one could be to conceal the fact that the victim knew him and invited him in."

That seemed to take Trout by surprise. "You're claiming that Ruth Blum knew the Good Shepherd personally?"

"I'm claiming that certain elements of the crime scene demand we take that possibility seriously."

Trout looked at Daker, who shrugged as though he didn't think it mattered one way or the other. Then he looked at Holdenfield, who appeared to be thinking that it mattered a great deal.

Bullard leaned back in her chair and let the silence build before adding, "The false narrative constructed by the Good Shepherd around the Ruth Blum murder has me wondering about his original murders."

"Wondering?" Trout was agitated. "Wondering what?"

"Wondering if he had the same appetite for deception back then. What do you think, Agent Trout?"

Bullard, in her way, had dropped a small bombshell. It wasn't a *new* bombshell, of course. It was what Gurney had been muttering for a week and Clinter for the past ten years. But now, for the first time, it had been tossed onto the table not by an outsider but by a ranking investigator with an arguable right to pursue the case to its conclusion.

She appeared to be inviting Trout to soften his insistence that the essence of the case was summed up by the manifesto and the offender profile.

Unsurprisingly, he stalled and sniped. "You spoke earlier about the importance of facts. I'd like a lot more of those before offering any opinion. I'm in no rush to rethink the most analyzed case in modern criminology, just because someone tried to fool us about where he parked his car."

The sarcasm was a mistake. Gurney could see it in the set of Bullard's jaw and in the extra two seconds she held the man's gaze before she went on. She picked up her e-mail printout of Gurney's questions.

"Since you folks at the FBI have been at the center of all that analyzing, I'm hoping you can illuminate a few points for me. This business with the little animals? I'm sure you saw in our CJIS report that a two-inch plastic lion had been placed on the victim's mouth. What's your take on that?"

Trout turned toward Holdenfield. "Becca?"

Holdenfield smiled meaninglessly. "That's a speculative area. The source of the original animals—a Noah's Ark play set—suggests a religious significance. The Bible describes the flood as God's judgment on an evil world, just as the Good Shepherd's actions represent his own judgment on that world. Also, the Good Shepherd used only one of each pair of animals at each attack site. There may be an unconscious significance for him in breaking up the pairs that way. His way of 'culling the flock.' From a Freudian perspective, it might reflect a childhood desire to break up his parents' marriage, perhaps by killing one of them. I would emphasize again that this is speculative."

Bullard nodded slowly, as if absorbing a profound insight. "And the very big gun? From the Freudian perspective, that would be a very big penis?"

Holdenfield's expression became wary. "It's not quite that simple."

"Ah," said Bullard, "I was afraid of that. Just when I think I'm catching on . . ." She turned to Gurney. "What's your read on the big gun and the little animals?"

"I believe their purpose was to generate this conversation."

"Say that again?"

"My read on the gun and the animals is that they're purposeful distractions."

"Distractions from what?"

"From the essential pragmatism of the whole enterprise. They're designed to suggest an underlying layer of neurotic motivation, or even derangement."

"The Good Shepherd wants us to believe that he's deranged?"

"Under the surface rationale of a typical mission-driven killer, there's always a layer of neurotic or psychotic motivation. It's the unconscious source of the homicidal energy that drives the conscious 'mission.' Right, Rebecca?"

She ignored the question.

Gurney continued. "I believe that the killer is fully aware of all that. I believe that the gun and the animals were the final touches of a master manipulator. The profilers would expect to find things like that, so he provided them. They helped make the 'mission' concept believable. The one hypothesis the killer didn't want anyone to propose or pursue was that he was perfectly sane and that his crimes might have a purely practical motive. A traditional murder motive. Because that would have led the investigation in a completely different direction and probably would have exposed him fairly quickly."

Trout sighed impatiently, addressing himself to Bullard. "We've been through all this with Mr. Gurney before. And his assertions are still nothing more than assertions. They have no evidentiary basis. Frankly, the repetition is tiresome. The accepted hypothesis represents a totally coherent view of the case—the *only* rational, coherent view of the case that's ever been put forward." He picked up his copy of the new Good Shepherd message, gesturing with it. "Plus—this new communication is one hundred percent consistent with the original manifesto and offers a perfectly credible explanation for his attack on Harold Blum's widow."

"What do you think of it, Rebecca?" said Gurney, pointing to the paper in Trout's hand.

"I'd like some more time to study it, but right now I'd say with a reasonable level of professional certainty that it was composed by the same individual who composed the original document."

"What else?"

She pursed her lips, seemed to be weighing different ways of answering. "He's articulating the same obsessive resentment, which has now been aggravated by the TV airing of *The Orphans of Murder*. His new complaint, the motivating factor that triggered his attack on

Ruth Blum, is that *Orphans* is an intolerable glorification of despicable people."

"All of which makes sense," interjected Trout. "It reinforces everything we've been saying about the case from the very beginning."

Gurney ignored the interruption, remaining focused on Holdenfield. "How angry would you say he was?"

"What?"

"How angry was the man who wrote that?"

The question seemed to surprise her. She picked up her copy and reread it. "Well ... he employs frequent emotional language and images—'*blood ... evil ... stain ... guilt ... punishment ... death ... poison ... monsters*'—expressing a kind of biblical rage."

"Is it *rage* we're seeing in that document. Or a *depiction* of rage?"

There was a tiny twitch at the corner of her mouth. "The distinction being ... ?"

"I'm wondering if this is a furious man expressing his fury or a calm man writing what he imagines a furious man would write under these circumstances."

Trout broke in again. "What's the point of this?"

"It's pretty basic," said Gurney. "I'm wondering if Dr. Holdenfield, a very insightful psychotherapist, feels that the writer of this message was expressing an authentic emotion of his own, or was he, in a way, putting words in the mouth of a fictional character he'd invented—the so-called Good Shepherd."

Trout looked at Bullard. "Lieutenant, we can't spend the whole day on this kind of eccentric theorizing. This is your meeting. I'd urge you to exert some control over the agenda."

Gurney continued to hold the psychologist's gaze. "Simple question, Rebecca. What do you think?"

She took a long time before replying. "I'm not sure."

Gurney sensed, finally, some honesty in Holdenfield's eyes and in her answer.

Bullard looked troubled. "David, a couple of minutes ago, you used the phrase 'purely practical' in relation to the Good Shepherd. What kind of purely practical motive could prompt a killer to choose six victims whose main connection with one another is that they were driving extravagant cars?"

"Extravagant black Mercedes cars," corrected Gurney, more to himself than to her—*The Man with the Black Umbrella* coming once again to mind. Referring to the plot of a movie during the discussion of a real crime was risky, especially in unfriendly company, but Gurney decided to go ahead. He recounted how the snipers were stymied in their pursuit of the man with the umbrella when he was immersed in a crowd of people with similar umbrellas.

"What the hell's the connection between that story and what we're here to talk about?" It was Daker's first comment at the table.

Gurney smiled. "I don't know. I just have the feeling that there is one. I was hoping someone in the room might be perceptive enough to see it."

Trout rolled his eyes.

Bullard picked up the e-mail in which Gurney had listed his questions about the murders. Her eyes stopped halfway down the page, and she read aloud. " 'Were they all equally important?' " She looked around the table. "That strikes me as an interesting question in the context of the umbrella story."

"I don't see the relevance," said Daker.

Bullard's eyes were blinking again, as though clicking off possibilities. "Suppose not all the victims were primary targets."

"And the ones that weren't—what were they? *Mistakes?*" Trout's expression was incredulous.

Gurney had already explored that avenue with Hardwick, and it had led to scenarios too unlikely to take seriously. "Not mistakes," said Gurney. "But secondary, in some way."

"Secondary?" repeated Daker. "What the hell does that mean?"

"I don't know yet. It's still just a question."

Trout let his hands fall on the table with a bang. "I'll only say this once. There comes a time in every investigation when we have to stop questioning the basics and concentrate on the pursuit of the perpetrator."

"The problem here," responded Gurney, "is that no serious questioning process ever got started."

"Okay, okay," said Bullard, raising her hands in a double "Stop" gesture. "I want to talk about action steps."

She turned to Clegg, who was seated on her left. "Andy, give us a quick review of what's happening."

"Yes, ma'am." He pulled a slim digital device out of his jacket pocket, tapped a few keys, and studied the screen. "Tech team has released the crime scene for general access. Physical evidence bagged, tagged, and entered in the system. Computer transported to computer forensics. Latent prints processed through IAFIS. Prelim ME report in hand. Autopsy report and full tox screens in seventy-two hours. Site and victim photos entered in the system, ditto incident report. CJIS report, third update, in the system. Status of door-to-doors: forty-eight completed, projected total sixty-six by end of day. Initial verbatims available, summaries to come. Based on two eyewitness observations of a Humvee or a Hummer-style vehicle in the vicinity, DMV is compiling ownership lists of all similar vehicles registered in central New York State."

"Planned utilization of these lists being what?" asked Trout.

"A database against which we can run the names of any ID'd suspects, as they become available," said Clegg.

Trout looked skeptical but said nothing more.

Gurney was uncomfortable with the fact that he already had the answer Clegg was chasing. Normally he favored maximum openness. But in this instance he feared that disclosure would only create a distraction and waste valuable time by diverting attention toward Clinter. And Clinter, after all, couldn't be the Good Shepherd. He was peculiar. Possibly crazy. But evil? No, almost certainly not evil.

But he had another motive for silence, a less objective one. He didn't want to appear too familiar with Clinter, too allied with him, too much on his wavelength. He didn't want to be tarred by the association. Holdenfield had tossed that PTSD diagnosis into his lap during their lunch in Branville. At some point Max Clinter had also gotten a PTSD diagnosis. Gurney didn't like the echo effect.

Clegg was winding up his report. "Tire-tread impressions made in the parking lot of Lakeside Collision are being processed, photos have been sent to vehicle forensics for original equipment and aftermarket matches. We got a decent side-to-side double impression. Crossing our fingers for a unique axle-width measurement." He looked up from the screen of the device from which he'd been reading. "That's as much as I'm aware of at the moment, Lieutenant."

"Any promised callback time on the physical analysis of the Shepherd message—ink, paper, printer data, latents on the address form, inner envelope, et cetera?"

"They said they'd have a better idea within the next hour."

Bullard nodded. "And the outgoing notifications?"

"Just starting that process. We have a preliminary list of family members in the background materials provided by Agent Daker. I believe Ms. Corazon is being contacted now for her own list of current phone numbers, per Mr. Gurney's suggestion. Carly Madden in Public Information is helping to formulate an appropriate message."

"She understands the communications objective—*serious alert without panic*—and the importance of getting it just right?"

"She's been made aware of that."

"Good. I'd like to see the draft before the live calls. Let's move on that front ASAP."

Gurney's sense of the woman was firming up. She devoured stress like vitamins. Her job was probably her sole addiction. "ASAP" was almost certainly the way she wanted everything to happen. And adversaries should take care.

She looked around the table. "Questions?"

"You seem to have your fingers on a lot of buttons at the same time," said Trout.

"So what else is new?"

"What I'm saying is that there's a point beyond which we all need some help."

"No doubt. Feel free to call me if you ever find yourself in that position."

Trout laughed—a sound as warm and musical as a car starter with a dying battery. "I just wanted to remind you that we have some resources at the federal level that you may not have in Auburn or Sasparilla. And the fact is, the clearer the linkage between this new homicide and the old case becomes, the greater the institutional pressure will be on both of us to bring federal resources to the table."

"That might happen tomorrow. But today is today. One day at a time."

Trout smiled—a mechanical expression consistent with his laugh. "I'm not a philosopher, Lieutenant. Just a realist pointing out how things are and where this case is bound to end up. I suppose you can choose to ignore that, until the moment it occurs. But we do need to spell out some ground rules and lines of communication, starting now."

Bullard glanced at her watch. "Actually, what's starting now is a brief lunch break. Twelve noon on the dot. I suggest we reconvene at twelve forty-five to discuss those ground rules and lines of communication—and then do some actual work, ground rules permitting." Her sarcasm was softened by a smile. "The coffee and the snack machines in this building are pretty awful. Would you Albany folks like a recommendation for a local lunch place?"

"No need for that. We'll be fine," Trout answered.

Holdenfield looked pensive, restless, far from fine.

Daker looked like he felt nothing at all—beyond a general desire to liquidate all the troublemakers in the world, painfully, one by one.

Bullard and Gurney were seated in a horseshoe-shaped booth in a small Italian restaurant with a bar and three inescapable television screens.

They each had a small antipasto and were sharing a pizza. Clegg had remained at the unit to monitor progress on the multiple initiatives that had been put in motion. Bullard had been quiet since they'd arrived. She was segregating the hot peppers on the rim of her salad plate. Once she'd uncovered and moved the last of them, her gaze rose to Gurney's eyes. "So, Dave, tell me. What the hell are you up to?"

"Put a finer point on that question and I'll be happy to answer it."

She looked down at her salad, speared one of the hot peppers with her fork, popped it into her mouth, chewed it and swallowed it without a hint of discomfort. "I sense a lot of energy in your involvement. *A lot.* This is more than just a favor you're doing for some kid with a hot idea. So what is it? I need to know."

He smiled. "Did Daker by any chance tell you that RAM wants me to do a program of critical commentaries on failed police investigations?"

"Something like that."

"Well, I have no intention of doing it."

She gave him a long, appraising look. "Okay. Do you have any other financial or career interests in the current situation that you haven't told me about?"

"None."

"Okay. What is it, then? What's the attraction?"

"There's a hole in the case big enough to drive a truck through. Also big enough to keep me awake nights. And peculiar things have happened that I believe were designed to discourage Kim's pursuit of her project and to discourage my participation. I have a perverse reaction to efforts like that. Pushing me toward the door makes me want to stay in the room."

"I told you something similar about myself." She said this so evenly that it was hard to tell if it was meant as a token of comradeship or as a warning not to try to manipulate her. Before he could decide which it was, she continued. "But I have a feeling there's something else. Am I right?"

He was wondering how open he should be. "There's more. I'm reluctant to tell you what it is, because it makes me look silly, small, and resentful."

Bullard shrugged. "One of life's basic choices, isn't it? We can look hip, slick, and cool. Or we can tell the truth."

"When I first started looking into the Good Shepherd case for Kim Corazon, I asked Holdenfield if she thought Agent Trout would be willing to listen to my views on the case."

"And she said that he wouldn't, because you were no longer an active member of law enforcement?"

"Worse. 'You must be joking.' That's what she said. One little comment. One aggravating little comment. Must seem like a crazy reason for me to tighten my grip on this thing and refuse to let go."

"Of course it's a crazy reason. But at least now I know what's behind all the tenacity." She ate a second hot pepper. "Getting back to that hole in the case that keeps you awake nights. What questions do you find yourself struggling with at two A.M.?"

He didn't have to think long about the answer. "Three big ones. First, the time factor. Why did the murders start when they did, back in the spring of 2000? Second, what lines of inquiry were aborted, or never initiated, because of the arrival of the manifesto? Third, what made 'Killing the Greedy Rich' the right cover story to conceal whatever was really going on?"

Bullard raised a challenging eyebrow. "Assuming that something *was* going on other than 'Killing the Greedy Rich'—an assumption you're a hell of a lot more committed to than I am."

"It'll grow on you. As a matter of fact—"

*"The Good Shepherd is back!"* The unnerving aptness of the announcement from the television above the bar stopped Gurney in midsentence. One of RAM's melodramatic news anchors was sharing a split screen with a well-known gray-pompadoured evangelist, the Reverend Emmet Prunk.

"According to reliable sources, the dreaded upstate New York serial murderer is back. The monster is haunting the rural landscape once again. Ten years ago the Good Shepherd ended Harold Blum's life with a bullet in the head. Two nights ago the killer returned. Returned to the home of Harold's widow, Ruth. He entered her residence in the middle of the night and drove an ice pick through her heart." The man's overdone delivery was as attention-getting as it was repulsive. "This is so . . . so inhuman . . . so beyond the bounds . . . Sorry, folks, there are things in this world that just plain leave me speechless." He shook his head grimly and turned toward the other half of the split screen, as though the TV evangelist were actually sitting next to him in the studio. "Reverend Prunk, you always seem to have the right words, the right insight. Help us out. What's your perspective on this terrifying development?"

"Well, Dan, like any normal human being, I find that my feelings here run the gamut from horror to outrage. But I do believe that in God's economy there is a purpose in every event, however dreadful that event may seem to our merely human way of seeing. 'But, Reverend Prunk,' someone might ask me, 'what could be the purpose in this nightmare?' And I would say to him that in the demonstration of so much evil there is much to be learned about the nature of evil in our world today. This monster has no respect for his victims. They are chaff to be blown away in the wind of his willfulness. They are nothing. A wisp of smoke. A piece of dirt. This is the lesson the Lord has placed before our eyes. He is showing us the true nature of evil. To extinguish life, to blow it away like a wisp of smoke, to trample it like a piece of dirt, that is the essence of evil! This is the lesson the Lord raises up for the righteous to see in the deeds of the devil."

"Thank you, sir." The anchor turned back to the camera. "As always, wise words from the Reverend Emmet Prunk. And now some important information from the good people who make RAM News possible."

A sequence of loud, hyperactive commercials took the place of the talking heads.

"Jesus," muttered Gurney, looking across the table at Bullard.

She met his gaze. "Tell me again that you're not doing business with those people."

"I'm not doing business with those people."

She held his gaze a little longer, then made the kind of face she might make if one of the peppers were repeating on her. "Let's back up to your point about certain lines of inquiry being aborted by the arrival of the manifesto. Have you given any thought to what they might be?"

"The obvious stuff. To start with, cui bono? The simple question of who might have profited in a practical way from all six murders has to top the list of things that were never pursued once the manifesto got everyone pointed in the mission-killer direction."

"Okay, I hear you. What else?"

"A connection. Some background linkage among the victims."

"Other than the Mercedes thing?"

"Right."

She looked skeptical. "Problem with that is that it would make the cars secondary. If they weren't the primary criterion for the attacks, then they must have been coincidental. Hell of a coincidence, don't you think?"

Her objection was a direct echo of Jack Hardwick's. Gurney had had no answer for it then, and he still didn't.

"What else?" she asked.

"In-depth investigations of each individual case."

"What do you mean?"

"Once the serial pattern was evident, it dictated the nature of the investigation."

"Of course it did. How else——"

"I'm just listing paths not explored. I'm not saying they *should* have been explored—only that they weren't."

"Give me an example."

"If the murders had been investigated as individual crimes, the process would have been totally different. In any case of premeditated murder without an obvious motive or suspect, you know as well as I do what would happen. The exploration would begin with the victim's life and relationships—friends, lovers, enemies, criminal connections, criminal record, bad habits, bad marriages, ugly divorces, business conflicts, will and estate provisions, debts, financial pressures and opportunities. In other words, we'd root around in the victim's life looking for situations and people of interest. But in this case——"

"Yes, yes, of course, in this case none of that happened. If someone is driving around shooting through random Mercedes windows in the middle of the night, you don't spend time and money checking on each victim's personal problems."

"Obviously. A psychopathological pattern, especially with a simple trigger like a shiny black car, makes finding the psycho perp the sole focus. The victims are just generic components of the pattern."

She gave him a hard stare. "Tell me you're not suggesting that the Good Shepherd murders had six different motives arising from the individual lives of the six victims."

"That would be absurd, right?"

"Yes. Just as absurd as the idea of the six similar cars being coincidental."

"I can't argue with you on that."

"Okay, then. So much for the paths not taken. A little while ago, you mentioned the time factor as one of the questions on your restless mind. You have specific thoughts about that?"

"Nothing specific right now. Sometimes a close look at *when* something occurred can be a back door into understanding *why* it occurred. By the way, your reference to my restless nights reminded me of something I wanted to tell you. Paul Mellani, son of Bruno Mellani and a participant in Kim's *Orphans* project, happens to have a permit for a Desert Eagle pistol."

"When did he get it?"

"I don't have access to that information."

"Really?" She paused. "Speaking of your access to information, I believe Agent Trout has taken an interest in that subject."

"I know. He's wasting his time. But thank you for mentioning it."

"He's also taken an interest in your barn."

"How do you know that?"

"Daker told me that your barn burned down under suspicious circumstances, that an arson investigator found your gas can hidden somewhere, and that I should exercise appropriate caution in dealing with you."

"And what did *that* tell you?"

"That they don't like you very much."

"What a revelation!"

"Matthew Trout could be a troublesome enemy."

"Into each life a little rain must fall."

Bullard nodded, almost smiled.

Then she got on her phone. "Andy? I need you to track down some handgun permit information.... Paul Mellani.... Yes, the same one.... For a Desert Eagle.... I've been told he has one, but the big question is when did he get it.... The original permit date.... Right.... Thanks."

They ate silently for a while, finishing their antipasti and most of the pizza, as a series of promos for grotesque RAM reality shows blared from the restaurant's three TV screens.

One show was called *Roller Coaster,* and it apparently involved a contest in which four men and four women vied with one another to rack up the largest number of pounds lost or gained, or gained first and then lost, over a twenty-six-week period, during which they were forced to remain in one another's constant company. A previous winner had gone from 130 pounds up to 261 pounds and back down to 129 pounds, thus earning both the Double-Up and the Half-Down bonus awards.

As Gurney was wondering if America owned a special patent on media insanity or if the whole world had lost its collective mind, his phone rang with a text message from Kim, telling him to check his e-mail for the video file of her conversation with Jimi Brewster.

Seeing her name on his ID screen reminded him of another

logistics detail. He looked over at Bullard, who was gesturing to the
waiter to bring the bill. "I assume you'll want to run Kim Corazon's
copy of the Shepherd's new message through the Albany lab. What do
you want her to do with it?"

"Where is she now?"

"In my son's apartment in Manhattan."

She hesitated for a second or two, as if filing that fact for later
examination. "Have her bring it to the state police liaison office at
NYPD headquarters, One Police Plaza. When we get back to the unit,
I'll give you the routing instructions that need to go with it."

Gurney was about to slip his phone back into his pocket when it
occurred to him that Bullard might be interested in the Brewster video.

"By the way, Lieutenant, a while back Kim interviewed Jimi
Brewster, one of the so-called *Orphans*. He's the one who—"

She nodded. "The one who hated his surgeon father. I read about
him in the background pile Daker dumped on me."

"Right. Well, Kim just e-mailed me a video copy of her interview
with him. You want it?"

"Of course I want it. Can you forward it to me right now?"


When they returned to the conference room, Trout, Daker, and
Holdenfield were already at the table. Although Gurney and
Bullard were just a minute late, Trout shot a sour glance at his watch.

"Got somewhere else you need to be?" asked Gurney, his casual
tone and bland smile providing only thin cover for a dangerous level
of hostility.

Trout chose not to answer, not even to look up, probing instead
with a fingernail for a speck of something between his front teeth.

As soon as Bullard and Gurney had taken their seats, Clegg entered
the room and placed a sheet of paper before the lieutenant, which she
scanned with a curious frown. "Does this mean you've started making
the warning calls?"

"Initial calls to establish contact," said Clegg, "to find out quickly
who's reachable and who isn't. We're telling live contacts we'll be getting back to them within the hour with information related to the case.
With our voice-mail contacts, we're asking for callbacks."

Bullard nodded, her eyes running down the sheet again. "According to this you've spoken directly to Ruth Blum's sister en route from Oregon to Aurora, to Larry Sterne in Stone Ridge, and to Jimi Brewster in Turnwell. What about the rest of the people on this list?"

"Callback requests have been left on the voice mails of Eric Stone, Roberta Rotker, and Paul Mellani."

"Do we have their e-mail addresses?"

"I believe Kim Corazon supplied them for everyone on her contact list."

"Then follow up your voice mails immediately with e-mails. Anyone we don't hear back from within the next half hour, we follow up again. Tell Carly she's got fifteen minutes to give me a draft. If we don't get a response to the second message, we need to dispatch troopers to each physical address."

After Clegg hurried out of the room, Bullard took a deep breath, sat back in her chair, and gazed thoughtfully at Trout. "Getting back to more difficult questions, do you have any ideas regarding the motive behind Ruth Blum's murder?"

"It's what I said before. Just look at the Shepherd's message."

"I have it memorized."

"Then you know the motive as well as I do. The debut of *The Orphans of Murder* on RAM the other night hit his most sensitive nerve and brought the whole kill-the-rich mission back to life."

"Dr. Holdenfield? You agree with that?"

Rebecca nodded stiffly. "In general, yes. More specifically, I'd say that the TV program brought his *resentment* back to life. It broke whatever dam had been holding the emotion in check for the past ten years. Then the rage began to flow again into his social-injustice fixation, and the murder was the result."

"Interesting way of seeing it," said Bullard. "Dave? How do you see it?"

"Cool, calculated, risk-averse—the opposite of Rebecca's description. Zero rage. Total rationality."

"And the totally rational motive for killing Ruth Blum would be . . . ?"

"To stop the work being done on *Orphans*, because it posed a threat to him."

"That threat being . . . ?"

"Either something that Kim might discover as she continued the interviewing process or something that a viewer might realize while watching the series on TV."

Bullard's skepticism returned. "You mean a link that might connect the victims? Other than their cars? We just discussed the problem with—"

"Maybe it's not a 'link' per se. Kim's stated goal—widely advertised—was to *reveal the effects of murder on the lives of the living.* Maybe there's something in the current lives of those families that the killer doesn't want revealed—something that might point to his identity."

Trout yawned.

Perhaps if he hadn't, Gurney wouldn't have felt compelled to add a final possibility. "Or maybe the murder, combined with the explanatory message, is an effort to make sure that everyone keeps thinking about the Good Shepherd attacks in the same old way. Maybe it's an effort to head off the possibility of someone finally launching the kind of investigation that should have been conducted at the time."

There was fury in Trout's eyes. "What the hell do you know about what should have been done at the time?"

"What seems clear is that you viewed the case exactly the way the Good Shepherd wanted you to, and you acted accordingly."

Trout stood up abruptly. "Lieutenant Bullard, as of now this case is coming under federal control. The chaos and crackpot theories you're encouraging here don't give me any alternative." He pointed at Gurney. "This man is here at your invitation. He has no official standing. He has repeatedly voiced a stunning disrespect for the Bureau. He may very well become the central figure in a felony arson case. He may also be the recipient of illegally leaked materials from FBI and BCI files. He has suffered traumatic brain injury and may have physical and psychological impairments to his perception and judgment. I refuse to waste any more time debating anything with him, or in his presence. I'll be speaking to your Major Forbes about the realignment of investigatory responsibility."

Daker stood up next to Trout. He looked pleased.

"Sorry you feel that way," said Bullard calmly. "My purpose in airing contrasting points of view was to test their relative strengths. You don't think my purpose was achieved?"

"It's been a waste of time."

"Trout's going to be famous," said Gurney with a chilly grin. Everyone looked at him. "He's going to go down in FBI history as the only supervising agent who ever took control of the same case twice and managed to screw it up twice."

There were no farewells, no handshakes.

Thirty seconds later Gurney and Bullard were alone in the room.

"How sure are you?" she asked. "How sure are you that you're right and everybody else is wrong?"

"About ninety-five percent."

No sooner did he hear his own words than a profound doubt swept through him. To be that sure of anything in these shadowy circumstances suddenly seemed like manic overconfidence.

He was about to ask her how soon she expected actual control of the process to move to the FBI regional office when Clegg appeared in the doorway. His eyes were wide with the kind of distressed urgency you saw only on the faces of young cops.

Bullard looked up. "Yes, Andy?"

"Another murder. Eric Stone. Just inside his front door. Ice pick to the heart. A little plastic zebra on his lips."

## Chapter 37

# Willing to Kill

"Oh, God!" said Madeleine, wincing. "Who found him like that?"

She was standing at the sink island, a half-drained colander of noodles in her hands. Gurney was sitting on a high stool across from her. He'd been relating the low points, difficulties, and conflicts of his day—something that didn't come naturally to him. Never had. He blamed it on his genes. His father had never admitted to being disturbed by anything, never admitted to experiencing fear or anger or confusion. "Speech is silver, but silence is golden" was his father's favorite aphorism. In fact, until Gurney learned different in high school, he thought that was the famous "golden rule."

His first instinct was still to say nothing about anything he felt. But lately he'd been trying to make small advances against this life-long habit. His injuries last autumn had diminished his tolerance for stress, and he'd discovered that sharing some of his thoughts and feelings with Madeleine seemed to help, seemed to relieve the pressure.

So he sat on the stool by the sink, feeling awkward, narrating the day's disturbances, answering her questions as best he could.

"One of his customers found him. Stone made a living as a specialty baker for some local inns and B&Bs. One of the inn owners came by to pick up an order of cookies. Gingersnaps. She noticed that the front door wasn't completely closed. When Stone didn't answer her knocking, she opened the door herself. And there he was. Just like Ruth Blum. On his back in the entry hall. With the handle of an ice pick protruding just below his sternum."

"God, how awful! What did she do?"

"Apparently called the police."

Madeleine shook her head slowly, then blinked, looking surprised to find herself still holding the colander. She emptied the steaming noodles into a serving platter. "That was the end of your day in Sasparilla?"

"Pretty much."

She went to the stove and got a pan in which she'd been sautéing asparagus and mushrooms. She tipped the mixture onto the noodles and put the empty pan in the sink. "The confrontation you were telling me about with that Trout person—how concerned are you?"

"I'm not sure."

"He sounds like an officious ass."

"Oh, there's no doubt about that."

"But you're worried that he might be a dangerous ass?"

"That's one way of putting it."

She brought the noodle-asparagus-mushroom platter to the table, then got plates and silverware. "This is all I cooked tonight. If you want to add meat, there are some leftover meatballs in the fridge."

"This is fine."

"Because there are plenty of meatballs, and—"

"Really, this is fine. Perfect. By the way, I forgot to mention, I suggested to Kyle that he and Kim come back up here for a couple of days."

"When?"

"Now. Starting tonight."

"I mean when did you suggest it?"

"I called them on my way home from Sasparilla. The fact that they got that message in the mail means the sender knows where Kyle lives. So I thought it might be safer—"

Madeleine frowned. "The 'sender' also knows where *we* live."

"It just . . . feels better to have them up here. Strength in numbers, maybe?"

They ate in silence for several minutes.

Then Madeleine put down her fork, her food only half finished, and gave her plate a small nudge toward the center of the table.

Gurney looked at her. "Is something wrong?"

" 'Is something wrong?' " She stared at him incredulously. "Did you really ask me that?"

"No, I mean . . . Christ, I don't know what I mean."

"It seems that all hell's breaking loose," she said. "Quite literally."

"I don't disagree."

"So what's your plan?"

She'd asked him the same question after the barn burned down. It was more unsettling now, because the situation had deteriorated so rapidly. People were dying, with ice picks rammed through their hearts. The FBI team seemed more intent on vilifying him and protecting themselves than discovering the truth. Holdenfield had insidiously undercut him with the "traumatic brain injury" and "psychological impairment" ammunition she'd fed to Trout. Bullard might be a semi-ally at the moment, but Gurney knew how quickly that alliance would evaporate if she decided it was in her interest to make peace with Trout.

But that wasn't all. Beneath and beyond the tangle of ugly specifics and concrete threats, he had a sense of accelerating evil, the feeling of a faceless doom descending on him, on Kim, on Kyle, on Madeleine. Whatever devil that little recording in the basement had warned him to let sleep was awake and abroad in the land. And all Gurney had as a "plan" was his determination to keep studying the puzzle pieces, to keep searching for the hidden picture, to keep poking at the official house of cards until it collapsed—or until its defenders succeeded in dragging him away.

"I have no plan," he said. "But if you have the time, there's something I'd like you to look at with me."

She glanced up at the big Regulator clock on the wall. "I have about an hour, maybe a little less. We have yet another meeting at the clinic. What do you want me to look at?"

He led her into the den, and as he downloaded the Jimi Brewster video file that Kim had sent to him, he explained what little he knew of it.

They settled into their chairs in front of the computer screen.

The video itself began with a segment that appeared to have been shot from the passenger seat of Kim's car as it approached a roadside sign in a snowbank announcing entry into Turnwell, the virtually nonexistent northern Catskills village where Jimi Brewster picked up his mail.

His actual residence turned out to be far up into the hills, away from the bleak cluster of tumbledown homes and abandoned stores that made up the village itself. The only active establishments appeared to be a bar with a filthy front window, a gas station with one pump, and a post office in a cinder-block building the size of a one-car garage.

Kim's car—and video—proceeded up a rutted road with snowbanks on either side, separating it from more tumbledown buildings and trees that seemed long dead rather than just seasonally leafless. Absorbing this, Gurney was struck that Turnwell represented a country environment that was as far removed from Williamstown, where Jimi's father had lived, as the dark side of the moon. He wondered if the cultural and aesthetic distance constituted an intentional statement.

The question was increasingly on his mind as the video proceeded.

Also, the question of who was wielding the camera. Presumably Robby Meese, a fact that would place this visit to Jimi Brewster sometime prior to the breakup.

The car slowed as it approached a small house on the right. The house and the bleak property surrounding it showed an aggressive disregard for appearances. Nothing, from the posts supporting the sagging roof over the tilting porch to the door of the adjoining outhouse, was set at a right angle to anything else. In Gurney's experience a blatant disregard for the ninety-degree concept was usually an indication of poverty, physical incapacity, depression, or a cognitive disorder.

The man who emerged from the shabby front door onto the porch was slim and nervous-looking, with darting eyes. He was wearing black jeans and a T-shirt of the same orangey color as his short hair and close-cropped beard.

His having been a freshman in college twenty years earlier would make him at least thirty-seven, but he looked a decade younger. The CHALLENGE EVERYTHING aphorism printed in bold letters on the front of his shirt lent support to the image of youthfulness.

"Come in," he said, waving his guests impatiently toward the door. "It's fucking freezing out here."

The camera followed him inside. The back of his shirt proclaimed, AUTHORITY SUCKS.

The interior of the house was as uninviting as the outside. The furniture in the small front room was minimal and worn-looking. There was a colorless couch against one wall and a small rectangular table pushed against the opposite wall with a folding chair on each of its exposed sides.

There was a closed door on each side of the couch. A door in the rear of the room provided a glimpse of a narrow kitchen. The light was coming primarily from a wide window over the table.

As the camera panned around the cramped space, Kim's voice could be heard. "Robby, turn that off until we get settled." The camera continued to run, zooming in slowly on the slight, red-haired man, who was shifting his weight from foot to foot with a twitchy energy. It was hard to tell whether he was smiling or grimacing.

"Robby. The camera. Off. *Please.*" Despite Kim's peremptory tone, the video continued for at least ten seconds more before fading to black.

When the picture and sound resumed, Kim and Jimi Brewster were sitting across from each other at the table. The picture angle and framing suggested that Meese was probably operating the camera from somewhere on the couch.

"All right," said Kim with the kind of enthusiasm Gurney remembered seeing in her the day he met her. "Let's get right into it. I want to say again, Jimi, how much I appreciate your willingness to take part in this documentary project. By the way, would you prefer that I call you Jimi or Mr. Brewster?"

He shook his head—a small, jerky movement. "Doesn't matter. Whatever." He began drumming his fingernails lightly in a staccato rhythm on the tabletop.

"Okay. If it's all the same to you, I'll call you Jimi. As I explained while we had the camera turned off, this conversation we're having now is a preliminary run-through of some questions I'll be asking you at a future date in a more formal—"

He stopped his drumming abruptly and broke in. "Do you think I killed him?"

"Excuse me?"

"That's what everyone secretly wonders."

"I'm sorry, Jimi, but I'm not following—"

Again he interrupted her. "But if I killed him, then I must have killed them all. Which is why they couldn't arrest me, because I have an alibi for the first four."

"I'm lost here, Jimi. I never thought that you killed—"

"I wish I had."

Kim paused, looked stunned. "You wish . . . that you'd killed your father?"

"And all the others. Do you think I look like the Good Shepherd?"

"What?"

"I mean, like the way you imagine the Good Shepherd would look?"

"I never . . . I never really pictured him."

Brewster started drumming his fingernails again. "Because he did everything in the dark?"

"The dark? No, I just . . . I just never pictured him, I don't know why."

"Do you think he's a monster?"

"Physically . . . a monster?"

"Physically, mentally, spiritually—any way, every way, whatever way. Do you think he's a monster?"

"He did kill six people."

"Six monsters. Which makes him a hero, right?"

"Why do you think that all his victims were monsters?"

During this dialogue the camera had been zooming in very gradually, like an intruder on tiptoes, as if to explore the slightest tic or wrinkle in their faces.

Jimi Brewster's eyelids were quivering without quite blinking. "Easy. You piss away a hundred thousand dollars for a car—a fucking *car*—you are, de facto, an evil piece of shit." His voice was intense and accusatory and seemed, like everything else about him, less mature than his chronological years. He looked and sounded more like a troubled member of a high-school chess club than a man in his late thirties.

"An evil piece of shit? Is that the way you felt about your father?"

"The great surgeon? The fuckface money-grubbing piece-of-shit surgeon?"

"Your father. You still hate him as much now as you did back then?"

"Is my mother still as dead now as she was back then?"

"Sorry?"

"My mother killed herself with sleeping pills he prescribed for her. The great genius surgeon. Who got his genius head blown off. You want to hear a secret? When they called me to tell me, I made them repeat it three times. They thought I was in a state of shock. I wasn't. I was in a state of such pure joy that I wanted to make sure I wasn't dreaming. I wanted to hear the news again and again. It was the happiest day of my life." Brewster paused, radiating excitement, fixated on Kim's face.

"Aha!" he cried. "There it is! I can see it in your eyes!"

"See what?"

"The big question."

"What big question?"

"Everybody's big question: Could Jimi Brewster be the Good Shepherd?"

"As I said before, that idea never occurred to me."

"But it's there now. Don't lie. You're thinking, 'All that hate. Was it enough hate to blow away six pieces of shit?' "

"You said you had an alibi. If you had an alibi——"

He interrupted her. "Do you believe that some people can be physically in one place and spiritually someplace else?"

"I . . . I'm not sure what that means."

"There are Indian yogis that people have reported seeing in two different places at the same time. Time and space may not be what we think they are. I seem to be here, but I might also be somewhere else."

"Sorry, Jimi, I don't really——"

"Every night, in my mind, I drive around on dark roads, looking for genius doctors—pill pushers, robotic shits—and when I see one in his shiny shit car, I aim my gun at him, leveling the gun sight midway between his temple and his ear. I squeeze the trigger. There's a blast of light from heaven—the white light of truth and death—and half his fucking head is gone!"

The pace and loudness of the fingernail drumming increased.

The camera zoomed in on Brewster's face. He was staring wildly across at Kim, seemingly awaiting her reaction, gnawing at his lower lip. The camera zoomed out again to include them both in the frame.

Instead of reacting directly, she took a deep breath and changed the subject. "You went to college?"

He seemed taken aback, disappointed. "Yes."

"Where?"

"Dartmouth."

"What was your major?"

His mouth widened in a little spasm that may have been a one-second smile. "Pre-med."

"I'm surprised."

"Why?"

"From what you've said about your feelings toward your father, I didn't think you'd want to follow in his footsteps."

"I didn't." This time his mouth spasm was more recognizably a smile, though hardly a warm one. "I quit a month before graduation."

Kim frowned. "Just to disappoint him?"

"Just to see if he knew I existed."

"Did he?"

"Not really. All he said was that it was stupid of me to quit. Like he might have said it was stupid of me to have left my car window open in the rain. He wasn't even angry. He didn't care enough to be angry. He was so fucking calm about everything. You should have seen how fucking calm he was at my mother's funeral."

"That was a lot of his money you wasted by not graduating. Did he care about that?"

"He spent eight hours a day in the operating room, five days a week. The son of a bitch could make enough money in two weeks to pay for my four years at Dartmouth. My room, board, and tuition was a fucking flyspeck in his life. Like my mother was. Like I was. He drove cars that meant more to him than we did."

Kim said nothing. She raised her interlocked fingers and pressed them against her lips, closing her eyes, as though trying to stifle some unruly emotion. The silence went on for a long time. She cleared her throat before speaking again. "How do you live?"

He burst out in a harsh laugh. "How does anyone live?"

"I mean, how do you earn a living?"

"Is that some kind of ironic point you're trying to make?"

"I don't understand."

"You're thinking that I live off the money he left me. You're thinking that his money, which I pretend to hate, is actually supporting me. You're thinking, 'What a creepy little hypocrite!' You're thinking I'm exactly like him, that all I ever wanted was the fucking money."

"I wasn't thinking any of those things. It was just an innocent question."

He let out another harsh laugh. "A TV reporter with an innocent question? That's like a fucking devil with a heart of gold. Or a surgeon with a soul. Yeah. Right. An innocent question."

"You can believe what you want about it, Jimi. Does it have an answer?"

"Ah. *Now* I see what this is about. You want to know how we all made out. Our inheritances. How much we got. Is that what you want to know?"

"I want to know whatever you want to tell me."

"You mean, whatever I want to tell you about the money. Because that's what your fucking TV audience would want to know about. Financial pornography. Okay. Fine. The fucking money. The majorly screwed one was the pathetic accountant, whose sister got everything because of her fucked-up kids. Then there was the flaming baker, who mainly inherited his big blond mama's debts. The sweet little lawyer's wife did okay, ended up with two or three mil, mainly because her husband had a shitload of term insurance. This is the kind of crap they shared in their fucking support group. This is the kind of crap you want to know about?"

"Whatever you want to tell me."

"Right. Sure. Fine. Larry Sterne ended up with his father's medical-dental beauty factory, which I'm sure is worth millions. Roberta, the scary lady with the scary dogs, got her whore-fucking father's multimillion-dollar toilet business. And of course there's me. My greedy shit of a father had a brokerage account at Fidelity that was worth a little over twelve million dollars when he bit the bullet. And in case your truth-seeking TV audience wants the latest update, that brokerage account, now in my name, is worth around seventeen million. Which obviously raises a question in your mind: 'If little Jimi

Brewster has such a fucking pile of money, why's he living in this fucking dump?' The answer is simple. Can you guess what it is?"

"No, Jimi, I can't."

"Oh, I think you could if you tried, but I'll tell you. I'm saving every cent of it to give to the Good Shepherd, if they ever catch him."

"You want to give your father's money to the man who killed him?"

"Every bloody cent. It should make a nice legal defense fund, don't you think?"

## Chapter 38

# The White Mountain Strangler

The video continued for another ten or fifteen minutes, but nothing else was said that approached in impact the stated plan for Dr. James Brewster's estate. After a brief discussion of the source of current income that Jimi relied on to pay his bills—a small website-design and electronics-consulting business—the interview gradually petered out. The video ended with a serious-looking Kim saying good-bye to Jimi and promising to be in touch with him again shortly.

"Jesus," said Gurney, shutting down the computer and leaning back in his chair.

Madeleine sighed. "So full of guilt."

He looked at her curiously. "Guilt?"

"He hated his father, probably wished him dead. Maybe even wished someone would kill him. Then he *was* killed. Hard to escape from that."

"Even if he had nothing to do with it . . ." Gurney was thinking out loud.

"But he did, in a way. When his dream came true, there was no escaping the fact that it was *his* dream. He got what he'd hoped for."

"In that video I saw a lot more anger than guilt."

"Anger doesn't hurt as much as guilt."

"It's a choice?"

Madeleine gave him a long look before answering. "If you can stay focused on the fact that your father did such terrible things that he deserved to die, then you can stay angry at him forever, instead of feeling guilty for wishing him dead."

Gurney had an uneasy sense that she was telling him something not only about Jimi Brewster but about his own frozen relationship with his late father—a man who had ignored him as a child and whom he in turn ignored in later life. But that was a fraught area he had no desire to venture into now. The broad expanse of father-and-son issues was a swamp in which he could easily become mired.

Focus indeed was everything. So—more questions, more action. He headed out from the den to the kitchen to get his cell phone.

Lieutenant Bullard had had the Brewster video in her possession since lunchtime. Surely she would've been curious enough to have watched it by now. It was odd she hadn't called to discuss it. Or maybe not so odd, considering the shifting pressures of the situation. And the unstable politics. Might be worth a call to her, just to check the political pulse. Unless hanging back and waiting for her to initiate the call might send a better message.

He was saved from having to make the decision by the sight, through the kitchen window, of Kim's red Miata coming up the hill past the remnants of the barn—and, behind the Miata, Kyle on his BSA.

As they were approaching the cleared area by the house, the Miata jounced with a loud clunk into and out of a declivity formed by a collapsed groundhog burrow in the rough pasture lane. But when Kim emerged from the car after parking next to Gurney's Outback, her expression showed no awareness of the impact. As she walked toward the doorway where he was standing, it was clear that the rigid anxiety around her mouth and eyes arose from concerns deeper than a whack to her rear axle. He sensed a similar anxiety in the grim, exaggerated attention Kyle was giving to balancing his motorcycle on its kickstand.

When Kim came face-to-face with Gurney, she was biting her lip as if to keep from crying. "I'm sorry for all this nutty emotion."

"It's perfectly all right."

"I don't understand what's happening." She had the look of a frightened child seeking absolution for an offense too complex to grasp.

Kyle was standing behind her, his own distress apparent now in the tight set of his mouth.

Gurney smiled as warmly as he could. "Come into the house."

As they entered the kitchen from the mudroom hallway, Madeleine entered from the opposite hallway. She was wearing what Gurney called her "clinic suit"—dark brown tailored slacks and a beige jacket, an outfit far more subdued and "professional" than her preferred riot of tropical colors.

She smiled thinly at Kim and Kyle. "If you're hungry, there's stuff in the fridge and the pantry." She went to the sideboard and picked up the tote bag that served as her general carryall. It bore a logo consisting of a friendly-looking goat circled by the words SUPPORT LOCAL FARMING.

"I should be back in two hours," she said on her way out.

"Be careful," Gurney called after her.

He looked at Kim and Kyle. They were obviously tired, wired, and scared.

"How did he know?" Kim asked, a question apparently so much on her mind that she assumed that its meaning would be clear.

"You mean, how did the Shepherd know he could send you something at Kyle's address?"

She nodded rapidly. "I hate the idea that he was following us, watching us. It's too creepy." She began rubbing her arms as though trying to get warm.

"Not any creepier than that little recording, or the drops of blood in your kitchen, or the knife in your basement."

"But that was all Robby. Robby the asshole. But this . . . this is the killer . . . who killed Ruthie . . . and Eric . . . with ice picks! Oh, my God . . . Is he going to kill everyone I spoke to?"

"I hope not. But right now it might be a good idea to start the woodstove going. It gets pretty chilly in here when the sun goes down."

"I'll take care of it," said Kyle, sounding desperately eager to do something useful.

"Thanks. Kim, why don't you try to relax in the armchair closest to the stove. There's a wool blanket on the seat. I'll put on some coffee for us."

Ten minutes later Gurney was sitting with Kim and Kyle in the semicircle of chairs around the fire. The soothing smell of cherrywood, reddish yellow flames flickering in the belly of the iron stove, and steaming coffee mugs in their hands provided a small touch of reassurance, a hint that chaos might indeed have boundaries.

"I'm pretty confident that no one followed us down to the city," said Kyle. "And I know for sure that no one followed us back up here today."

"How can you say that?" Kim's question came across more as a plea for reassurance than as a challenge.

"Because I was behind you all the way, sometimes really close, sometimes way back. I kept checking. If anyone was tailing us, I would have seen them. And by the time we got off Route 17 at Roscoe, there was no traffic in sight at all."

Kyle's explanation seemed to lower Kim's fear level just a little. It raised other possibilities in Gurney's mind, which he decided to keep to himself, at least for the time being, since they would do no good for Kim's emotional state.

"You mentioned Robby Meese a few minutes ago," said Gurney. "I was wondering . . . how much contact did he have with Jimi Brewster?"

"Not very much."

"Wasn't he the cameraman for the video you sent me?"

"He was, but the Robby-Jimi chemistry was bad. Robby's insecurity had just started rearing its ugly head."

"How?"

"The more Robby was exposed to the people involved in my project, the hungrier he seemed to be for their approval. That's when I started seeing a side of him I hadn't seen before—a real suck-up, a money worshipper. I think Jimi saw it, too. And Jimi was so violently against all that."

"Who was he sucking up to?"

"Pretty much everybody. Eric Stone, until he found out that everything Eric owned was mortgaged for more than it was worth. Then Ruthie, who was vulnerable and had enough money to interest him." She shook her head. "Such a sleazy little bastard—and he hid it so well for the first few months I knew him."

Gurney waited quietly for her to continue, which she did, after taking a deep breath. "Of course, there was Roberta, who had tons of money from her father's plumbing business. She was more intimidating than vulnerable, but he never stopped calling her. And there was Larry, also with scads of money, from his big cosmetic-dentistry practice. But I think Larry saw through Robby, saw how desperate he was for attention, maybe even felt sorry for him. Why are we talking about this? Robby didn't kill Ruthie or Eric. He's not capable of it. He's a creep, but not that kind of creep. So what difference does any of this make?"

Gurney didn't have an answer, but he was saved from having to admit it by the ringing of his phone on the sideboard. He hoped it would be Lieutenant Bullard with her reactions to the Brewster video. He glanced at the ID screen.

It was Hardwick. "Davey boy, I don't know if you are aware of this, but you have managed to turn yourself into a giant fart in the elevator."

"Is someone complaining?"

"Complaining? If tying a class-A felony around your neck and dropping you into the criminal-justice wood chipper is a form of complaining, then yeah, I'd say someone's complaining."

"Trout's actually pursuing the barn thing?"

"BCI arson unit has nominal control, but the FBI regional office is expressing serious interest. They're offering any help that might be needed to look into your financial life, find out if you might be in any tight situations that would make fire-insurance money attractive—gambling problems, mortgage problems, health problems, girlfriend problems."

"Son of a bitch," muttered Gurney. He began pacing around the dining table.

"Fuck did you expect? You threaten to pull the man's pants down in public, you're gonna get a reaction."

"I'm not surprised at the reaction, just at how fast I'm running out of time."

"Speaking of which, apart from pissing off everyone in the world, are you actually making any progress with your grand exposé of the hidden truth?"

"You say that like I'm searching for something that isn't there."

"Didn't say that. Just wondering if you're any closer to whatever the hell *is* there."

"I won't know till I get there. Meantime, what do you know about the White Mountain Strangler?"

There was brief silence. "Ancient history, right? Fifteen years ago? New Hampshire?"

"More like twenty years ago. In and around the town of Hanover."

"Right. It's sort of coming back now. Five or six women strangled with silk scarves, relatively short time frame. Why?"

"One of the strangler's victims was the girlfriend of the son of one of the eventual victims of the Good Shepherd. She was a senior at Dartmouth. And it just so happens that the son of another Good Shepherd victim was there at the same time, as a freshman."

"Huh? Girlfriend of . . . son of . . . victim of . . . senior . . . freshman . . . ? Who the hell are we talking about?"

"A Dartmouth senior, who happened to be a girlfriend of Larry Sterne, was killed by the strangler while Jimi Brewster was at Dartmouth as a freshman."

There was another silence. Gurney could almost picture little lights flashing in Hardwick's mental calculator. Eventually the man cleared his throat. "Am I supposed to find some significance in that? I mean, so fucking what? We've got two northeastern families who each lose a family member to a serial shooter in the year 2000. And it so happens that ten years earlier, in 1990, the son of one of those eventual victims was attending a large Ivy League institution when a friend of the son of another eventual victim was murdered by a serial strangler. I'll admit it has a bizarre ring to it, but I think a lot of simple coincidences can be made to sound bizarre. I just don't see what it could mean. Are you imagining that Jimi Brewster was the White Mountain Strangler?"

"I have no reason to. But just to get the question out of my mind, can you poke around in your databases—maybe the old CJIS reports, if they can still be accessed—and get the basic facts?"

"Like what?"

"To begin with—more details of the MO, victim profile, open leads, anything that might suggest a connection to Brewster."

"To begin with?"

"Well, eventually we might want to track down the CIO who ran the case and get into it a little deeper, find out if Brewster's name ever came up during the investigation."

This produced the longest silence of all.

"You there, Jack?"

"I'm here. Contemplating what a fucking incredible pain in the ass these little requests of yours are getting to be."

"I know."

"Is there any end in sight?"

"Like I said before, it's obvious that I'm running out of time. So yes, the end is in sight. One way or the other. I have maybe one more day."

"To do what?"

"To figure it all out. Or get buried under it for good."

Another silence, not quite as long.

Hardwick sneezed, then blew his nose. "The Good Shepherd case has been around for ten years. You plan to solve it in the next twenty-four hours?"

"I don't think I have any other options left. By the way, Jimi Brewster told Kim that he had an alibi for the Good Shepherd murders. You happen to know what it was?"

"Hard to forget that one. The Brewster murder was the last next-of-kin notification BCI made in the case. The doctor was shot in Massachusetts, but his son resided here, so we got the notification job—before the FBI took control of what then became an interstate investigation."

"What made it hard to forget?"

"The fact that Jimi's alibi sounded more like a motive—at least in the case of his father. Jimi was in county lockup on the dates of the first four attacks because he couldn't make bail on an LSD-possession charge and his father refused to help—let him sit in a cell for a couple of weeks. Jimi finally got some ex-girlfriend to come up with the bail money, and he was released—seething with anger—about three hours before his father was killed."

"Was he ever considered a suspect?"

"Not really. The MO on Dr. Brewster was a perfect match with the others. And Jimi couldn't have copied it, because at that point none of the details had been publicized."

"So we can forget about Jimi."

"Seems so. Too bad, in a way. He could have fit nicely into one of those possibilities on that list of yours."

"What do you mean?"

"That question you had about whether all the Good Shepherd victims were equally important. Well, if there was some way Jimi could have killed them all, his father would have been the one that mattered the most, and the others would have been like some kind of emotional spillover—people who drove his father's kind of car, which might have made them equally despicable, equally killable in his warped little mind. Duplicate targets. Guilt by association." He paused. "Oh, fuck that. What am I talking about? That's all psychobabble."

# Chapter 39

# Blood and Shadows

When she got home from her clinic meeting, exhausted and indignant, Madeleine seemed to be on her own wavelength. After a few comments about the miseries built into bureaucracies, she headed for bed, *War and Peace* tucked under her arm.

Shortly after that, Kim said something about wanting to be fresh and rested for the following day's meeting with Rudy Getz, said good night, and went upstairs.

Then Kyle followed.

When Gurney heard Madeleine click off her reading light, he closed up the woodstove, checked that the doors and windows were locked, washed a few glasses that had been left in the sink, found himself yawning, and decided it was time to go to bed himself.

As weary and overloaded as he felt, however, going to bed was a very different thing from going to sleep. The main effect of lying there in the dark was to create a limitless space in which the elements of the Good Shepherd case could whirl around, untethered to the real world.

His feet were sweating and cold at the same time. He wanted to put on warm socks but couldn't muster the motivation to get out of bed. As he gazed gloomily out the large, curtainless window nearest him, it struck him that the silver moonlight was covering the high pasture like the phosphorescence of a dead fish.

Restlessness finally forced him to get up and get dressed. He went out and sat in one of the armchairs near the woodstove. The woodstove at least felt pleasantly warm. A scattering of red embers gleamed on the grate. Sitting up seemed to offer a more stable geometry for his thoughts, a firmer position from which he could approach the case.

What did he know for sure?

He knew that the Good Shepherd was intelligent, unflappable under pressure, and risk-averse. Thorough in his planning, meticulous in his execution. He was absolutely indifferent to human life. He was hell-bent on keeping *The Orphans of Murder* from proceeding. He was equally adept with a cannon-size handgun and an intimate ice pick.

Risk aversion was the characteristic that Gurney kept coming back to. Could that be the key? It seemed to underlie so many aspects of the case. For example, the patient scouting of ideal locations for his attacks, the exclusive choice of left-hand curves to minimize the chance of post-shot collisions, the costly disposal of each weapon after a single use, the preference for inconspicuousness over convenience in the choice of the parking spot for the Blum murder, and the recurrent investment of time and thought in the creation of elaborate smoke screens—from the manifesto itself to the forged posting on Ruth's Facebook page.

This was a man determined to shield himself at any cost.

At any cost in time, money, and other people's lives.

That raised an interesting question. What other safety-ensuring, risk-minimizing tactics might he have employed in addition to those that had already come to light? Or, put another way, what other risks might he have faced in his homicidal endeavors, and how might he have decided to cope with them?

Gurney needed to put himself in the Good Shepherd's shoes.

He asked himself what possibilities he'd be most concerned about if he were planning to shoot someone in a car at night on a lonely road. One concern came immediately to mind: *What if he missed?* And what if the intended victim caught a glimpse of his license plate? It probably wouldn't happen, but it was a realistic enough possibility to worry a serious risk avoider.

Professional criminals often used stolen cars on their jobs, but the danger of keeping and driving a stolen car for three weeks, long after it would have been reported and entered in law-enforcement databases, seemed an unlikely strategy for minimizing risk. Alternatively, stealing a fresh car for each attack would create another kind of exposure. Not a scenario that the Good Shepherd would be comfortable with.

So what would he do?

Perhaps partially obscure the plate number with the application of a bit of mud? True, an obscured plate was a ticketable infraction, but so what? That risk was inconsequential in comparison to the risk that would be eliminated.

What else might the Good Shepherd worry about?

Gurney found himself staring at the embers on the woodstove grate, his mind refusing to focus. He rose from his chair, switched on the floor lamp, and went over to the sink island to make himself a cup of coffee. He'd long ago discovered that one way to get to a solution was to step away from the problem and go on to something else. The brain, relieved of the pressure to move in a particular channel, often finds its own way. As one of his born-and-bred Delaware County neighbors had once said, "The beagle can't catch the rabbit till you let him off the leash."

So on to something else. Or back to something else.

Back to the discomfort he'd felt when Kyle was insisting that no one had followed him and Kim to the city or back to Walnut Crossing. Gurney had seen no point in sharing his discomfort at the time, but now he needed to resolve the question that had been troubling him. He got the three flashlights out of the sideboard drawer, tried each one, and selected the one whose batteries seemed the least drained. Then he went to the mudroom, put on his paint-spattered barn jacket, turned on the light by the side door, and stepped outside.

It was cold now, not merely chilly. He got down on the frozen grass in front of Kim's car to check the clearance between the undercarriage and the ground. It wasn't sufficient for what he had in mind, so he went back into the house for her keys.

He found them in her bag on the coffee table by the fireplace.

Back outside, he went to the tractor shed and got the pair of inclined metal ramps that he normally used for elevating the riding mower when the blades needed changing. He placed the ramps in front of the Miata, then drove it gently forward and upward until the front end was an extra eight inches or so off the ground. Then he set the brake and returned to his position on the frozen grass. Lying on his back, he wriggled under the raised car with his flashlight.

It didn't take long to find what he'd suspected and feared might be there. It was a black metal box not much larger than a pack of cigarettes, held by a magnet to one of the forward frame components. A wire emerging from the box ran upward in the direction of the car's battery.

He wriggled out from under the car, backed it down off the ramps, went into the house, and replaced Kim's keys in her bag.

He had some thinking to do. The discovery of a GPS location transmitter on the Miata was not exactly a game changer, but it certainly added a disturbing new dimension. And it demanded a decision: to leave it there or not.

As he began working his way through the implications of each option, a backlog of other issues kept intruding. He decided to get rid of them, at least temporarily, with a phone call.

It was 11:30 P.M., and the chances of Hardwick's picking up were slim, but leaving a message would serve Gurney's mind-clearing purposes. As expected, the call went to voice mail.

"Hey, Jack, more pain-in-the-ass questions for you. Is there an easily accessible state database of ten-year-old traffic citations? Specifically, I'm wondering about obscured-plate citations issued in the upstate counties during the period of the Good Shepherd murders. Also, any progress yet with the White Mountain Strangler details?"

After he ended the call, he went back to pondering the GPS-locator situation. The fact that it was hardwired to the car's electrical system meant that, unlike a battery system with a limited transmission life, it could have been installed quite some time ago and still be operational. The installation questions were *when?*, *why?*, and *by whom?* No doubt it was the same person who was monitoring the bugs in Kim's apartment. It could be her obsessed ex-boyfriend stalker, but Gurney had a feeling the situation might be more complicated than that.

In fact, it was entirely possible that . . .

He went to the mudroom, put his barn jacket back on, and went out again to the parking area.

He moved the ramps from the front of the Miata to the front of the Outback. Having forgotten his keys and flashlight, he returned to the house and got them, then started his car and repeated the earlier process.

Half expecting to find a similar tracking device, he searched the front undercarriage thoroughly, but he found nothing. He opened the hood and searched the engine compartment. Still nothing. He traced the battery wiring to its various connections and found nothing out of place.

As a final bit of reassurance, he moved the ramps around from the front to the back and reversed the car up onto them. He slid under the elevated rear end with his flashlight.

And there it was. A second black box, slightly larger than the first to accommodate a battery, was magnetized to the top of one of the rear bumper supports. The brand and general specs printed on the side of the device indicated it was from the same manufacturer and functionally equivalent to the one on Kim's car, except for the power source.

The reason for the difference could have a number of explanations, but an obvious one was the different installation time required—at least half an hour for the wired version and virtually no time at all for the battery version. All things being equal, wired power was preferable—which suggested that whoever had installed them might have had more extended access to Kim's car than to the Outback. Which, of course, brought Meese again to mind.

It was after midnight now, but sleep was out of the question. Gurney got a notepad and pen from his desk in the den and spent some cramped time under each car, copying down the information printed on the trackers so he could look up their performance parameters on the manufacturer's website. GPS-based trackers all worked pretty much the same way, transmitting location coordinates that could be displayed as an icon on a map, viewable through appropriate software on virtually any computer with an Internet connection. The cost variability among the commercially available systems related to range, positional precision, software sophistication, and real-time accuracy. The technology had become, even at high levels of performance, fairly inexpensive—and therefore accessible to just about anyone who wanted it.

As he was pulling himself out from under the Miata for the second time that night, Gurney felt a vibration on his right hip, which startled him. He instinctively linked it to what he was doing, thinking it was somehow caused by the GPS device. A moment later he realized it was his phone, which he'd earlier set on vibrate to avoid waking anyone in the house if and when Hardwick got back to him.

As he scrambled to his feet, he pulled the phone from his pocket and saw Hardwick's name on the ID screen.

"That was fast," said Gurney.

"Fast? The hell are you talking about?"

"Fast answers to my questions."

"What questions?"

"The ones I left on your voice mail."

"I don't check my voice mail in the middle of the night. That's not why I'm calling you."

Gurney had a sickening premonition. Or maybe he just knew the shifting tones of Hardwick's voice well enough to recognize the sound of death. He waited for the announcement.

"Lila Sterne. Wife of the dentist. On the floor, inside their front door. Ice pick to the heart. That makes three current, plus the six oldies. Total of nine. No end in sight. Thought you'd want to know. Didn't think anyone else at this point would bother to tell you."

"Jesus Christ. Sunday, Monday, Tuesday. One every night."

"So who's next? Any bets on Wednesday's ice pick?" Hardwick's tone had shifted again—this time into the cynical register that went through Gurney like nails on a blackboard.

He understood the basic police need for detachment and black humor, but Hardwick always seemed to go beyond the necessary. That excess was the surface reason for Gurney's reaction, but he knew there was something deeper, something in that tone that reminded him of his father.

"Thanks for the information, Jack."

"Hey, what are friends for, right?"

Gurney went into the house and stood in the middle of the kitchen, trying to absorb all the data encountered in the past hour. He stood at the sideboard. With the kitchen lights on, he couldn't see out the window. So he turned them off. The moon was just a fraction shy of full—a ball with one slightly flattened side. The moonlight was bright enough to give the grass a gray sheen and the trees at the edge of the pasture distinct black shadows. Gurney squinted and thought he could just make out the drooping branches of the hemlocks.

Then he thought he saw something moving. He held his breath, leaning over closer to the window. As he leaned forward on the top of the sideboard, he uttered a sharp yelp at a stabbing pain that shot up through his right wrist. He knew, even before he saw the damage, that he'd carelessly pressed his hand down on the razor-edged head of the arrow that had been lying there for a week, and it had sliced deeply into the flesh. By the time he got the light back on, blood was pooling in his upturned palm and dripping between his fingers onto the floor.

## Chapter 40

# Facing Facts

Unable to sleep despite his total exhaustion, Gurney was sitting in semidarkness at the breakfast table, gazing out at the eastern ridge. Dawn was spreading like a sick pallor across the sky—a fair reflection of his state of mind.

Earlier, awakened by his cry of pain, Madeleine had driven him to the emergency room of Walnut Crossing's minimal hospital.

She'd stayed with him through a four-hour process that could have been completed in less than an hour if three ambulances hadn't arrived with the battered survivors of an unlikely accident in which a drunk driver had knocked down a billboard that acted as a ramp that launched a speeding motorcycle that landed on the hood of a car coming from the opposite direction. At least that was the story the EMS and ER people were telling and retelling each other outside the cubicle where Gurney had waited to be stitched and bandaged.

It had been his second visit to a hospital in less than a week, which in itself was troubling.

He'd been aware of Madeleine's worried glances in his direction on their way there, in the waiting area, and on the way home, but they'd hardly spoken. When they had, it was mainly about how his hand felt or about the need to either get rid of the damn arrow or at least keep it in a safer place.

There were other things he could have spoken to her about, perhaps that he should have spoken about. The tracker he'd found on Kim's car. The tracker on his own car. The third ice-pick murder. But he didn't say a word about any of those things.

The reason for his silence, he told himself, was that telling her would only upset her. But a small voice in the back of his head told him otherwise—that his real reason was to avoid debate, to keep his options open. He told himself that the concealment would be temporary, therefore not a matter of truth, only of timing.

When they got home, half an hour before dawn, she went to bed with the same concerned look that had crossed her face so many times that night.

Too agitated to doze off, he sat at the table, wrestling with the implications of the things he didn't want to talk about, especially the growing string of murders.

Of all the ways that killers end up being caught, few apply to killers who are intelligent and disciplined. And the Good Shepherd might be the smartest and most disciplined of all.

The only reasonable chance of identifying him would be through a massive coordinated law-enforcement effort. It would require reevaluating every piece of data from the original case. Overwhelming manpower. A mandate to start over with a clean slate. But in the current atmosphere, there was no way that was going to happen. Neither the FBI nor BCI would be able to step far enough outside the box. It was a box they'd built themselves, a box they'd been reinforcing for ten years.

So what was he supposed to do?

Ostracized and demonized, with a possible felony charge hanging over him and a PTSD label slapped on his forehead, what the hell *could* he do?

Nothing came to mind.

Nothing but an irritatingly simplistic aphorism.

You play the hand you've been dealt.

What the hell was in that hand anyway?

He concluded that most of his cards were garbage. Or unplayable with the near-zero resources at his disposal.

But he had to admit that he did have one wild card.

It might be worth something, or it might be worth nothing.

•  •  •

The sun rose behind a morning haze. It was still low in the sky when the house phone rang. Gurney got up from the table and went into the den to answer it. It was someone from the clinic, asking for Madeleine.

As he was about to take the handset to her in the bedroom, she appeared at the den door in her pajamas, extending her hand for it as though it were a call she'd been expecting.

She glanced at the ID screen before she spoke—in a pleasantly professional tone that contrasted with the sleepy look on her face. "Good morning, this is Madeleine."

She then listened quietly to what was evidently a long explanation of something—during which Gurney returned to the kitchen and put on a fresh pot of coffee.

He heard her voice again only briefly toward the end of the call, and only a few of her words clearly. It sounded to him as if she was agreeing to do something. A few moments later, she appeared at the kitchen doorway, regarding him with the previous night's worry back in her eyes.

"How's your hand?"

The lidocaine nerve block they'd given him prior to his nine stitches had worn off, and the lower half of his palm was throbbing.

"Not too bad," he said. "What are they asking you to do now?"

She ignored the question. "You should be keeping it elevated. Like the doctor said."

"Right." He raised his hand a few inches above the sink island, where he was waiting for the coffee to brew. "Did they have another suicide?" he asked, rather too jokily.

"Carol Quilty resigned last night. They need someone to fill in today."

"What time?"

"As soon as I can get there. I'm going to take a shower, have a piece of toast, and off I go. Will you be all right here alone?"

"Of course."

She frowned and pointed at his hand. "Higher."

He raised it to eye level.

She sighed, gave him a silly little "attaboy" wink, and headed for the shower.

He marveled for the thousandth time at her innate cheerfulness, her perennial ability to accept the reality of whatever had been placed in front of her and address it with an attitude far more positive than his own.

She faced life as it was and did the best she could.

She played the hand she'd been dealt.

Which made him think again about his wild card.

Whatever it might be worth, he needed to do something with it soon. He had to play it before the game was over.

He had the sinking feeling that it might not be worth a damn thing. But there was only one way to find out.

His "wild card" was his access to the eavesdropping equipment that had been installed in Kim's apartment. Perhaps by the Good Shepherd, who perhaps was still monitoring its transmissions. If both of those assumptions were valid—and both were big ifs—that equipment could provide a channel of communication. A way of talking to the killer. An opportunity to send a message.

But what kind of message should it be?

It was a simple question—with an unlimited number of answers.

All he had to do was figure out the right one.

Shortly after Madeleine left for the clinic, the den phone rang again. The ID announced it was Hardwick. The raspy voice said, "Check the *Manchester Union Leader*'s online archives. They did a series on the White Mountain Strangler case back in '91. Betcha find a shitload of what you want. Gotta go piss. Take care."

The man certainly had his ways of saying good-bye.

Gurney went to his computer and spent an hour wading through the online archives not only of the *Union Leader* but of other New England papers that had reported extensively on the Strangler's crimes.

There had been five attacks in two months, all fatal. All the victims were women, and all had been strangled with white silk scarves, which were left knotted around their necks. The common factors among the victims were more circumstantial than personal. Three of the women had lived alone, and they had been killed in their homes. The two others worked late in isolated environments. One had been killed in an unlit parking area behind a crafts store she managed, the other in a similar area behind her own small flower shop. All five attacks occurred within a ten-mile radius of Hanover, home of Dartmouth College.

Although a sexual motive is often present in the serial strangulation of women, there were no signs of rape or other abuse. And the "victim profile" struck Gurney as odd. In fact, there really wasn't any. The only physical factor the women appeared to have in common was that they were all fairly small. But they looked nothing alike. Their hairstyles and clothing styles were quite diverse. They represented a curious socioeconomic mix—a Dartmouth student (Larry Sterne's girlfriend at the time), two shopkeepers, a part-time cafeteria aide in a local grammar school, and a psychiatrist. They ranged in age from twenty-one to seventy-one. The Dartmouth student was a blond WASP. The retired psychiatrist was a gray-haired African-American. Gurney had rarely seen such variation among the victims of a serial killer. It was hard to discern in these women the killer's fixation—the obsession that had motivated him.

As he was pondering the peculiarities of the case, he heard the upstairs shower running. A little while after that, Kim appeared at the den doorway with a terribly anxious expression.

"Good morning," said Gurney, closing down his computer search.

"I'm so sorry for getting you into this," she said, close to tears.

"It's what I used to do for a living."

"When you did it for a living, no one burned down your barn."

"We don't know for sure that the barn has anything to do with the case. It might have been some—"

"Oh, my God," she broke in, "what happened to your hand?"

"The arrow that I left on the sideboard—I leaned my hand on it in the dark last night."

"Oh, my God," she repeated, wincing.

Kyle appeared in the hallway behind her. "Morning, Dad, how are—" He stopped when he saw the bandage. "What happened?"

"Nothing much. Looks worse than it is. Want some breakfast?"

"He cut it on that nasty arrow thing," said Kim.

"Jeez, that thing's like a razor," said Kyle.

Gurney stood up from his desk. "Come on," he said, "we'll have some eggs, toast, coffee."

He was trying to sound normal. But even as he smiled casually and led the way out to the kitchen table, the question of what to say about the latest murder or about the GPS trackers began to fill his mind. Did he really have a right to keep all that to himself? And why was he doing it?

Doubts about his own motivations had always been the principal termites undermining whatever peace of mind he was temporarily able to achieve. He tried to force his attention back to the mundane details of breakfast. "How about starting with some orange juice?"

Apart from a few isolated comments, breakfast was a quiet affair, almost awkwardly so. As soon as they'd finished eating, Kim, in her transparent eagerness to occupy herself with something, insisted on clearing the table and washing the dishes. Kyle absorbed himself in checking his text messages, appearing to go through all of them at least twice.

In the silence, Gurney's mind went back to the crucial question of how to play his wild card. He had only one chance to get it right. He had an almost physical sense of time running out.

He envisioned an endgame in which he would finally confront the Good Shepherd. An endgame in which the puzzle pieces would snap together. An endgame that would prove that his contrary view was the product of a sound mind and not the fantasy of a damaged cop whose best days were behind him.

He didn't have time to question the rationality of this goal—or the likelihood of his success. All he could do now was focus on how to bring about the confrontation. And where.

Deciding *where* would be easy.

*How* would be the challenge.

When the phone rang, it brought him back to the present, sitting at the table, which was now in the full light of the morning sun. He was surprised to see that while he'd been lost in his thoughts, Kim and Kyle had retreated to the armchairs at the far end of the room and that Kyle had started a small fire in the woodstove.

He went to the den to take the call.

"Good morning, Connie."

"David?" She sounded surprised to have reached him.

"I'm here."

"In the eye of the storm?"

"Feels that way."

"I bet it does." Her voice was edgy and energetic. Connie always sounded as though she were on uppers. "Which way is the wind blowing at the moment?"

"Sorry?"

"Is my daughter hanging in or heading for the exit?"

"She tells me she's determined to drop the project."

"Because of the intensity?"

"Intensity?"

"The ice-pick murders, rebirth of the Shepherd, panic in the streets. That's what's scaring her off?"

"The people who were murdered were people she cared about."

"Journalism isn't for the faint of heart. Never was, never will be."

"She also has the feeling that her idea for a serious emotional documentary is being converted into a sleazy RAM soap opera."

"Oh, for shit's sake, David, we live in a capitalist society."

"Meaning . . . ?"

"Meaning the media business is—surprise, surprise—a business. Nuance is nice, but drama is what sells."

"Maybe you ought to be having this conversation with her rather than with me."

"Like hell I should. She and I are oil and water. But, like I told you before, she looks up to you. She'll listen to you."

"What do you want me to tell her? That RAM is a noble enterprise, that Rudy Getz is a prince?"

"From what I hear on the street, Rudy is a shit. But he's a smart shit. The world is the world. Some of us face it, some of us don't. I hope she thinks twice about bailing out."

"Bailing out in this case might not be such a bad idea."

There was a silence—not a common thing in a conversation with Connie Clarke. When she spoke again, her voice was lower. "You don't know what that could lead to. Her decision to go to journalism school, to get a degree, to pursue this idea of hers, to build a media career for herself—it's all been such a lifesaver, such a salvation from where she was before."

"Where was that?"

There was another silence. "The ambitious, focused young woman you're seeing now is kind of a miracle. The way she was a few years ago had me scared—the way she was when she *bailed out* of normal life after her father disappeared. When she was in her teens, she was adrift. She didn't want to do anything, wasn't interested in anything. There were times she'd be okay, and then she'd sink back into a dark hole. This journalism thing—particularly this *Orphans* project—has provided some direction. It's given her a life. I'd rather not think where 'bailing out' might lead."

"Do you want to talk to her?"

"She's *there*? In your house?"

"Yes. Long story."

"There, now, in the same room with you?"

"In another room, with my son."

"Your son?"

"Another long story."

"I see. Well . . . I'd love to hear that story when you have time to tell it to me."

"Be happy to. Maybe in another day or two. Things are a little complicated right now."

"I gather. In the meantime please remember what I said."

"I'd better go now."

"Okay, but . . . do what you can, David. *Please.* Don't let her self-destruct."

When the call ended, he stood at the den window, staring out at the ridge without really seeing it. How the hell was anyone supposed to keep anyone else from self-destructing?

A fresh surge of throbbing in the heel of his hand interrupted his train of thought. He raised the hand, resting it against the window sash, and the pain faded. He looked at the clock on the desk. In less than an hour, he and Kim would have to leave for their meeting with Rudy Getz.

But right now he had more pressing issues to resolve.

The wild card. The opportunity to send a message to the killer.

What should the message be?

An invitation?

To come where? To do what? For what reason?

What might the Shepherd want?

One thing the Shepherd always seemed to want was security.

Perhaps Gurney could offer him an opportunity to eliminate some element of risk in his life.

Perhaps an opportunity to eliminate an adversary.

Yes. That would do nicely.

An opportunity to kill someone troublesome.

And Gurney knew the place for it. The perfect place for a murder.

He opened the desk drawer and took out a business card that had no name on it, just a cell number.

He took out his phone and made the call. It went into voice mail. There was no salutation, no identification, just a brusque command: "State your purpose."

"It's Dave Gurney. An urgent matter. Call me."

The response came less than a minute later. "Maximilian Clinter here. What's up, laddie?" The brogue was present in full force.

"I have a request. I have to do something, and I need a special place to do it."

"Well, well, well. Something major?"

"Yes."

"How major exactly?"

"As major as it gets."

"As major as it gets. Well, well. That can only mean one thing. Am I right?"

"I'm not a mind reader, Max."

"I am."

"Then you don't have to ask me any questions."

"It's not a question, just a request for confirmation."

"I'm confirming that it's major, and I'm asking for the use of your cabin for one night."

"Care to provide some details?"

"I haven't figured them out yet."

"The basic idea, then."

"I'd rather not."

"I have a right to know."

"I'm going to invite someone to join me there."

"The man himself?"

Gurney made no reply.

"Bloody hell! Is it the truth? You found him?"

"Actually, I want him to find me."

"In my cabin?"

"Yes."

"Why would he want to come there?"

"Possibly to kill me, if I can give him a good enough reason."

"I see. You plan to spend the night in my cabin in the middle of Hogmarrow Swamp, in the hope of getting a midnight visit from a man with a good reason to kill you. Do I have this right?"

"More or less."

"And what's the happy ending? A split second before you get your head blown off, I drop out of the sky to save you, like fucking Batman?"

"No."

"No?"

"I save myself. Or I don't."

"What are you, a one-man army?"

"It's too damn iffy for anyone else to be involved."

"I should be part of it."

Gurney gazed unseeingly out the den window, contemplating the wobbly stack of assumptions under his so-called plan. Going it alone would be risky as hell. But bringing in backup, especially someone like Clinter, would be riskier. "Sorry. My way or no way."

Clinter's voice exploded. "You're talking about the fucker who fucked up my life! The fucker I live to kill! The fucker I want to feed to a dog! And you're telling me it has to be done *your* fucking way. *Your fucking way?* Are you out of your fucking mind?"

"I really don't know, Max. But I see a tiny window of opportunity to stop the Good Shepherd. Maybe stop him from killing Kim Corazon. Or my son. Or my wife. It's now or never, Max. My only chance. There are already too many variables, too many what-ifs. And one more person in the mix would be one more variable. Sorry, Max, I can't tolerate that. My way or no way."

There was a long silence.

"Okay." Clinter's voice was flat. No brogue. No feeling.

"Okay what?"

"Okay, you can use my house. When do you need it?"

"Sooner the better. Let's say tomorrow night. From dusk to dawn."

"Okay."

"But I absolutely need you to stay away."

"What if you end up needing help?"

"Who helped you in that little room in Buffalo?"

"Buffalo was different."

"Maybe not so different. Are there keys to the cabin doors?"

"No. My little vipers are the only locks I've ever needed."

"Your rumored rattlesnakes?" Gurney recalled that odd tidbit from his visit to Clinter's cabin the previous week. It seemed like a month ago.

"Rumors can be stronger than facts, laddie. Never underestimate the power of the human mind. A snake in the brain is worth two in the bush." The brogue was creeping back in.

## Chapter 41

# The Devil's Accomplice

Shortly before eleven that morning, Kyle settled down with Gurney's computer, printer, and a USB cable and began transferring PDF files from his BlackBerry. A classmate was keeping him up to date with lecture summaries and assignments, reducing any pressure he might be feeling to return to the city. Kyle explained that his side job was also doable via e-mail, at least temporarily.

At eleven sharp, Gurney and Kim left for their twelve-thirty meeting with Getz. They took the Miata, with Kim driving. Gurney hoped, as a passenger, he might to be able to devote some serious thought to his notion of luring the Shepherd to Max Clinter's cabin. And, with a little luck, he might be able to grab a catnap.

With some crimes, figuring out the motive could lead you to the perp. With other crimes, identifying the perp could lead you to the motive. In the current situation, there wasn't enough time for either approach. The only hope was to get the perp to identify himself. Which sounded like an impossible challenge. How do you ensnare a man who has a hawk's eye for snares?

When they were halfway to Ashokan Heights on Route 28, Gurney finally sank into his desperately needed nap. It ended twenty-five minutes later, when Kim woke him on Falcon's Nest Lane, a mile from Getz's house.

"Dave?"

"Yes?"

"What do you think I should do?" She was looking straight ahead as she spoke.

"That's a big question," he said vaguely. "If you decide to back away from RAM, is there a Plan B?"

"Why do I need a Plan B?"

Before he could come up with an answer, the car reached the imposing entrance to Getz's driveway. Kim drove between the stone pillars into the tunnel of arching rhododendrons that led to the house.

Getting out of the car, they were greeted by the thumping reverberation of a helicopter rotor. It grew steadily louder as they stood looking up through the surrounding trees for the source. Soon it seemed so close that Gurney could feel it as much as hear it. He didn't see the craft itself, which had been approaching from a direction blocked from his field of vision by the façade of the house, until it was about to touch down on the roof. Caught briefly in the direct downwash of the rotors, Kim's hair was blown wildly around her face.

When the air was again still, she reached into her shoulder bag and took out a small brush. She neatened her hair, straightened her blazer, and gave Gurney a small smile. They climbed the cantilevered steps to the door, and Gurney knocked.

There was no response. He tried again. After they'd waited another half minute or so, as he was about to knock a third time, one of the doors opened.

Rudy Getz's mouth was stretched into something like a grin. His hooded eyes were gleaming in a way that made him look high. He was wearing black jeans and a black T-shirt, as he had been on their previous visit, but the white linen sport jacket had been replaced by a pale lavender one. "Hey, good to see you! Good timing! I like that. Come in, come in."

The modernistic interior with its cold metal-and-glass furniture was as Gurney remembered it. Getz was snapping his fingers as though his level of nervous energy demanded it. He pointed to the same oval, acrylic coffee table and cluster of chairs where they'd had their first meeting. "Grab a seat. Time for a drink. Love helicopters, love 'em to death. RAM's got a fleet of them. We're famous for it. The Ramcopters. Every major news event, a Ramcopter is always the first one there. Really big event, we send two. No one else has the resources to send two. Point of pride. But whenever I go up, I always land thirsty. Join me in a drink?"

LET THE DEVIL SLEEP

Before Gurney or Kim could answer, Getz put two fingers to his lips and whistled—a loud, sharp note that outdoors would have been audible at five hundred yards. Almost immediately the Rollerblader entered from a doorway on the far side of the room. Gurney recognized the skates, the black leotard stretched over the eye-catching body, the deep blue gel-spiked hair, the eyes as blue and shocking as the hair.

"You ever have Stoli Elit?" asked Getz.

"I'll just have a glass of water, if that's okay," said Kim.

"You, Detective Gurney?"

"Water."

"Too bad. Stoli Elit is really special. Costs a fortune." He looked at the Rollerblader. "Claudia, sweetheart, bring me three fingers, neat." He held up three fingers horizontally, to show her how much he wanted in his glass.

She pivoted on the tips of her skates and glided out through the far doorway.

"So we're all here. Let's sit down and talk." Getz motioned again to the chairs.

Kim and Gurney sat on one side of the table, Getz on the other side.

Claudia came gliding back and placed a glass in front of Getz. He picked it up, sipped some clear liquid from it, and smiled. "Perfect."

She gave Gurney an appraising glance and again disappeared through the far doorway.

"Okay," said Getz. "Business." He set his gleaming eyes on Kim. "Sweetheart, I know you got stuff you want to say. Let's get that out of the way first. Talk to me."

Kim looked lost for a moment before speaking. "I don't know what to say—other than that I'm horrified. Horrified by what's happened. I feel responsible. These people who were killed—they were killed because of me. Because of *The Orphans of Murder*. It has to be stopped. Ended."

Getz stared at her. "That's it?" He seemed taken aback, as though he'd been auditioning an actress who stopped speaking after her first line.

"That and the whole tone of the program. It wasn't what I was expecting. The way it was edited, that hokey opening on the dark country road, the so-called experts who were asked for their opinions—to be honest, I thought it was trashy."

"Trashy?"

"Bottom line, I want the series canceled."

"Bottom line, you want it canceled? That's pretty funny."

"Funny?"

"Yeah. Funny. You sure you don't want a drink?"

"I did ask for water."

"You did. That's the truth." Getz pointed a forefinger at her as if it were the barrel of a gun and grinned. Then he picked up his vodka and downed it in two long swallows. "Okay, let's get some facts on the table. A small housekeeping detail first. You really need to check your contract, sweetheart, so you'll have a clearer understanding of the basics—like who owns what, who makes what decisions, who gets to cancel things. Et cetera. But this is no time to get bogged down in legalities. We have bigger issues to talk about. Let me tell you a few things about RAM that—"

"Are you telling me you won't cancel it?"

"Please. Let me give you some context here. Without context we can't make good decisions. Please. Allow me to finish. I was starting to say there are a few things about RAM you may not know. Such as, we have more number-one shows running than any other cable or broadcast network. We have the highest—"

"I don't care."

"Please. Allow me to speak. These are facts you may not be aware of. We have the highest total audience figures in the business. Every year the numbers get better. Our parent company is the largest media company in the world, and we are their most profitable division. Next year we'll be even more profitable."

"I don't see the relevance of this."

"Please. Listen. We understand programming. We understand audiences. Bottom line? You want to talk bottom line? Bottom line is, we know what we're doing and we do it better than anyone. You had a program idea. We're turning that idea into gold. Media alchemy. That's what we do. Turn ideas into gold. You understand?"

Kim leaned forward, her voice rising. "What I understand is that people have gotten killed because of this program."

"How many people?"

"What?"

"Do you know how many people die on this planet every day? How many millions?"

Kim stared at him, momentarily speechless.

Gurney took the opportunity to ask casually, "Will the new murders boost your ratings?"

Getz flashed another grin. "You want the truth? The ratings will shoot through the roof. We'll run news specials, Second Amendment debates, maybe even a spin-off series. Remember the project I offered you? *In the Absence of Justice*—a hard-nosed review of unsolved cases? That could be a hot one. That's still very much on the table, Detective. *The Orphans of Murder* could have real legs. A franchise. Media alchemy."

Kim's hands were balled into fists. "That's so . . . so ugly."

"You know what it is, sweetheart? It's human nature."

Her eyes blazed. "It sounds to me like ugliness and greed."

"Right. Like I said. Human nature."

"That's not human nature! That's trash!"

"Let me tell you something. The human animal is just another primate. Maybe even the ugliest and stupidest one. That's the real truth. And I'm a realist. I didn't create the fucking zoo. I just make a living in it. You know what I do? I feed the animals."

Kim rose from her chair. "I'm done here. I'm leaving."

"You'll miss a nice sushi lunch."

"I'm not hungry. I need to leave here. Now."

She began walking in the direction of the front door. Gurney got up without comment and followed her. Getz stayed where he was.

He called after them as they neared the door. "Before you folks leave, I'd like to run something by you. We're trying to pick a new slogan. We've narrowed it down to two. The first is 'RAM News: The Mind and Heart of Freedom.' The second is 'RAM News: Nothing but the Truth.' Which one rings your bell?"

Shaking her head, Kim opened the front door and exited as quickly as she could.

Gurney looked back at the man who was still sitting at the acrylic table.

He was picking bits of invisible lint off his pale lavender jacket.

## Chapter 42

# Long Shot

Coming down the switchback road through the pine forest that separated Getz's hilltop estate from the main road, Kim drove wildly enough to distract Gurney from his thoughts about the RAM executive and his slimy media enterprise.

The second time the car skidded sideways onto the narrow shoulder, he offered to take the wheel. She refused, but she did lower her speed.

"I can't believe this," she said, shaking her head. "I was trying to create something good. Something true. And look what it's turned into. A horrible mess. God, how stupid I am! How stupidly naïve!"

Gurney looked over at her. Her conservative blue blazer, her unadorned white blouse, her almost severely simple hairstyle suddenly had the appearance of an adult's costume worn by a child.

"What am I going to do?" She asked the question in such a small voice that he barely heard it. "Suppose the Shepherd keeps killing people. That warning—'Let the devil sleep'—that was meant for me. But I ignored it. That makes every new murder my fault. How can we stop Getz from going ahead with this horrible thing?"

"I don't think we can stop Getz."

"Oh, God . . ."

"But there might be a way to stop the Shepherd."

"How?"

"It's kind of a long shot."

"Anything is better than nothing."

"I may need your help."

She turned to him. "I'll do anything. Tell me. Whatever it is, I'll—"

The car was drifting rapidly toward the guardrail.

"Jesus!" cried Gurney. "Watch the road!"

"Sorry. Sorry. But please—anything you want me to do, just tell me."

He wondered about the wisdom of discussing it while she was driving. But he didn't have the luxury of waiting. Time was the resource he was running out of quickest. He hoped his doubts and fears wouldn't come through in a way that made his thinking sound as shaky to her as it had to Clinter. "This is all based on two things I believe about the Good Shepherd. First, he'll gladly kill anyone who poses a threat to him, as long as he feels he can do it safely. Second, he has good reason to consider my interest in the case a threat."

"So what do we do?"

"We take advantage of the bugging system in your apartment to allow him to overhear certain things—things that will motivate him to take action in a way that will expose him."

"You think it's the Good Shepherd who's been eavesdropping on me? Not Robby?"

"It *could* be Robby. But my money would be on the Shepherd."

She appeared troubled by this idea but then nodded gamely. "Okay. What are we going to say for him to overhear?"

"I want him to know that I'll be in a very isolated place, in a very vulnerable position. I want him to believe that the situation offers him a unique chance to get rid of me and Max Clinter—that he *needs* to get rid of us, and there'll never be a better time to do it."

"So we're going to sit in my apartment and you're going to say stuff to me in the hope that he's listening?"

"Or that he'll be listening later. My guess is he's recording the transmissions from those bugs on a voice-activated device that he probably checks once or twice a day. As for 'saying stuff,' the way we disclose the information will need to be subtler than my just telling it to you. There needs to be a cover story, an emotional dynamic, a reason we're in the apartment, some tension. Ordinary, sloppy reality. He has to be made to feel that he's hearing things he's not supposed to be hearing."

• • •

When they arrived at Gurney's farmhouse a little after three, Kyle was in the den at the computer, surrounded by printouts, a BlackBerry, an iPhone, and an iPad. He greeted them without looking away from the screen, which was filled by some sort of spreadsheet. "Hey, folks. Welcome back. Be right with you. I'm closing this down."

There was no sign of Madeleine, who presumably was still at the clinic. While Kim went upstairs to change out of her business clothes, Gurney checked the landline's voice mail. No messages. He used the bathroom, then went out to the kitchen. Remembering that he hadn't had any lunch, he opened the refrigerator.

A minute or two later, when Kim came back downstairs, he was still staring at the shelves without really seeing anything. His mind was elsewhere—trying to get a grip on the elements of the drama he and Kim would be staging that evening, the drama on which so much depended.

Her arrival in the kitchen in a pair of jeans and a loose sweatshirt brought him back to the present.

"You want something to eat?" he asked.

"No thanks."

Kyle entered the room behind her. "I guess you guys heard the news."

Kim's expression froze. "What news?"

"Another murder—the wife of one of the people you were talking to. Lila Sterne."

"Oh, God, no!" Kim grabbed the edge of the sink island.

"This was on the radio?" asked Gurney.

"On the Internet. Google News."

"What did they say? Any details?"

"Just that she'd been stabbed to death with an ice pick sometime last night. 'Police are at the scene, investigation ongoing. Monster on the loose.' A lot of drama, not a lot of facts."

"Shit," Gurney muttered. Hearing the news a second time some-how made it worse, deepening his sense of the situation accelerating out of control.

Kim looked lost.

Gurney went over to her, put his arms around her. She hugged him with a fierceness that startled him. When she released him, she took a deep breath and stepped back.

"I'm okay," she said, answering his unasked question.

"Good. Because later we both need to be fully functional."

"I know."

Kyle frowned. "Fully functional? For what?"

Gurney explained as calmly and reasonably as he could his general objective and its reliance on the eavesdropping equipment in Kim's apartment. He was conscious of trying to make it sound like a more coherent strategy than it really was. He wondered whom he was trying to convince—Kyle or himself.

"Tonight?" said Kyle incredulously. "You plan on doing this tonight?"

"Actually," said Gurney, feeling again the terrible pressure of time closing in on him, "we should be leaving for Syracuse as soon as we can."

Kyle looked very worried. "Are you guys . . . prepared? I mean, this sounds like a huge deal. Do you have any idea what you're actually going to be saying—what it is you want the Shepherd to overhear?"

Gurney tried again for a tone of reassurance. "The way I see it—and I admit that a lot will have to be improvised as we go along—we show up at Kim's apartment in the middle of discussing the meeting we had today with Rudy Getz. Kim is telling me she wants to end the *Orphans* series on RAM. I'm arguing that maybe she shouldn't be so quick to turn her back on it."

"Wait a minute," said Kyle. "Why would you say that?"

"I want the Shepherd to see *me* as the primary threat to him, not Kim. I want him to believe that she wants the series to be canceled and that I might get in the way of that decision."

"That's it? That's the plan?"

"No, there's more. What I'm thinking is that in the middle of this discussion we're having about *The Orphans of Murder*, I get a phone call. A phone call supposedly from Max Clinter. And anyone listening to my side of the call—which is all that the bugs would be capable of picking up—will be given the impression that Max has discovered some information pointing to the identity of the Good Shepherd. Maybe some information that fits in with a few things I've discovered myself. The takeaway will be that Max and I are pretty sure who the Shepherd is and we're getting together at his cabin tomorrow night to compare notes and work out our next steps."

Kyle was quiet for a long minute. "So . . . the idea is that he'll . . . what? Come to Clinter's cabin to . . . to try to kill you?"

"If I handle it right, he'll see it as a low-risk way of eliminating a major threat."

"And you guys . . ." He looked back and forth between Gurney and Kim. "You guys are going to . . . just make all this up as you go along?"

"At this point it's the only way." Gurney looked up at the clock on the wall. "We have to get going."

Kim looked terrified. "I need my bag."

When Gurney heard her footsteps going up the stairs, he turned to Kyle. "I want to show you something." He led Kyle into the master bedroom and pulled out the bottom drawer of his bureau. "I don't know what time I'll be home tonight. In the event that anything unexpected happens—or any unwanted visitor arrives—I want you to know this is here."

Kyle looked down into the open drawer. It contained a short-barrel twelve-gauge shotgun and a box of shells.

## Chapter 43

# Talking to the Shepherd

Gurney and Kim drove to Syracuse in separate cars. With so much yet to be determined, maximum flexibility seemed wise.

Standing in front of the shabby little house that Kim's apartment formed half of, Gurney went over the plan with her again. As he did so, its ad-hoc flimsiness seemed increasingly evident. In fact, it was hardly a "plan" at all—more like some ill-conceived theatrical improvisation. But he couldn't let his growing doubts show, couldn't let them infect Kim. Any more anxiety would paralyze her. And for better or worse, this hollow little scheme of his was all they had.

He concluded by saying, with the most confident smile he could muster, "Whatever I say to you up in your apartment, just react as though you really believe it. Stay as close to your real feelings as you can. Just relax and react. Okay?"

"I guess."

"And just one more thing. Have your cell phone handy and ready to use. At some point I'll signal you to call my number to make my phone ring, and then I'll go through my fake conversation with Clinter. Whatever facts have to be invented, I'll invent them. Afterwards, you just play yourself. React the way you normally would. That's all there is to it." He gave her a wink and a thumbs-up. Then he wished he hadn't. He was embarrassed by the phony bravado.

She swallowed hard, opened the door into the tiny vestibule, then unlocked the door of her apartment. She led him down the narrow hall to the living room. He looked around at the futon couch, the cheap coffee table, the pair of worn armchairs, each partnered with a flimsy floor lamp. It was all as he remembered it, right down to the dirt-colored rug that was frayed in the middle.

"Go ahead, have a seat, Dave. I'll just be a minute," said Kim, her voice only slightly strained, as it might be from a difficult day. She walked down the hall and disappeared into the bathroom, closing the door loudly.

He paced around the room, cleared his throat a few times, sat down noisily on the couch. A few minutes later, she returned. They both laid their cell phones on the table.

"So . . . can I offer you a drink or something?"

"I *am* thirsty. What do you have?"

"Anything you want."

"Uh, maybe just some juice or something. If you have it."

"I think I can manage that. Give me a sec." She went back down the hall to the kitchen. He heard glasses banging against each other, the sink tap going on and off.

She returned with two empty water glasses. She handed him one, clinked hers against it, and said, "Cheers." She sat down on the couch, turning sideways to face him.

"Cheers to you, too. I see you're drinking wine. Something to make you feel better about the RAM deal."

She let out a loud sigh. "That whole situation is a nightmare."

Gurney cleared his throat. "Television is television, I guess."

"You saying I should be thrilled to work with Rudy, the slimebag?"

"Not necessarily thrilled," said Gurney. "But there *is* your future to think about."

"I'm not sure I want that kind of future. Why?" she said with a half-jesting edge in her voice. "Are you interested in chasing that opportunity Getz dangled to host your own show?"

"Not in this lifetime, at least not the way he described it," said Dave. He coughed, cleared his throat. "Any chance I can get a refill?" As he spoke, he pointed at her cell phone.

She nodded and picked it up. "You *are* thirsty." She stood noisily, giving her glass a sharp whack with her hand, knocking it over. "Shit! What a mess!" She stomped out of the room.

The glass was empty, there was no mess, but anyone listening in would be picturing one of those awkward moments in unrehearsed real life. Gurney smiled. The young lady had real talent.

A few moments later his phone rang. He picked it up and began his fictitious conversation.

"Max? . . . Sure, go ahead. . . . What do you mean? . . . Why are you asking? . . . What? . . . You're serious? . . . Yes, yes, of course. . . . Right. . . . No, no, the Facebook message was a fake. . . . Ah, good point. . . . How sure are you? . . . Look, what you're saying makes perfect sense, but that ID needs to be nailed down—I mean nailed down one hundred percent, no loose ends. . . . That's absolutely incredible, but, Jesus Christ, I think you're right. . . . Sure. . . . When? . . . Yeah, I'll bring everything. . . . All right. . . . Yeah. . . . Be very careful. . . . Midnight tomorrow night. . . . Absolutely!"

Gurney went through the motions of pressing the button to end the call, then laid his phone on the table.

Kim came back into the room. "Here's your refill," she said, as though she were handing him a glass. "Who was that call from? You look pretty excited about something."

"That was Max Clinter. It seems that the Good Shepherd finally made a major mistake—in addition to the ones at Ruth Blum's and at the auto-body shop up the road. Those I already knew about, but Max just made another discovery, and . . . now we know who he is."

"Oh, my God! You've identified the Good Shepherd?"

"Yes. At least I'm about ninety percent sure. But I want to make it a hundred percent. It's too big a thing for there to be any open question."

"Who is it? Tell me!"

"Not yet."

"What do you mean, *not yet*?"

"I can't take any chance of being wrong about it. Way too much at stake. I'm getting together with Clinter tomorrow night at his cabin. He has something I need to look at. If it matches what I've got, it'll close the loop—and the Shepherd is history."

"Why do you have to wait till tomorrow night? Why not right now?"

"Clinter's been staying out of the area ever since he got a text message from the Shepherd tricking him into driving around Ruth's neighborhood in Aurora. He got spooked. Doesn't even want to be in Cayuga County in the daylight. He said midnight tomorrow was the soonest he could get to his cabin."

"Jeez, I can't believe this! I can't believe you know who the Shepherd is and you won't tell me!" She sounded frightened, almost pathetic.

"It's safer this way." He waited a couple beats, as if mulling something. "I think, for now, you should check in to a hotel. Keep a low profile. Why don't you pack a few things in an overnight bag, then let's get out of here."

## Chapter 44

# Assessment

They didn't speak again until their cars were parked in the lot of one of the big chain hotels on the I-88 service road.

It was nearly seven-thirty, and the late-March dusk had turned into night. The lot's stark lights had come on, creating a visual atmosphere that was neither darkness nor daylight—perhaps what daylight might be like on a planet whose sun was a chilly blue and all the colors were faded and cold.

Kim had joined Gurney in the front seat of the Outback to discuss their "performance" and its potential impact on its presumed audience. Kim was the first to raise a practical question. "Do you think the Shepherd will swallow the bait?"

"Bottom line, yes. He may be suspicious. He's probably the kind of person who's suspicious of everything. But he'll have to do something. And to do something, he'll have to show up. In the scenario we laid out, the risk of doing nothing would be bigger than the risk of taking action. He'll understand that. He's a very logical guy."

"So you think we did okay?"

"You did more than okay. You seemed very much yourself. Now, listen to me: Spend tonight in this hotel. Don't open your door for *anyone*. Not under any circumstances. If anyone tries to persuade you to open the door, you get security on the phone immediately. Okay? Call me in the morning."

"Are we ever going to be safe?"

Gurney smiled. "I think so. I'm hoping we'll all be perfectly safe after tomorrow night."

Kim was biting her lower lip. "What are you going to do?"

Gurney leaned back, gazing out at the parking lot's bilious lighting. "My plan is to let the Good Shepherd step forward and hang himself. But that's tomorrow night. Tonight the plan is to go home, go to bed, and get the sleep I haven't gotten for two days."

Kim nodded. "Okay." She paused. "Well, I'd better get myself a room." She picked up her shoulder bag, got out of the car, and went into the hotel.

After watching Kim disappear into the hotel lobby, Gurney got out of his car, walked around to the rear, lay down on his back, and reached underneath. Without much trouble, he managed to remove the GPS tracker from the bumper support. Back in his seat, he opened the device with a small screwdriver and disconnected its battery.

From now until the final confrontation, he wanted to keep his location to himself.

## Chapter 45

# The Devil's Disciple

The Lord giveth. The Lord taketh away.

That night Gurney got seven uninterrupted hours of desperately needed sleep. The next morning, however, he awoke with a feeling of dread—a nameless fear that was only partly relieved by showering, dressing, and strapping on his Beretta.

At 8:00 A.M. he was gazing out the kitchen window, the sun a cool white disk in the morning haze. He was halfway through his first cup of coffee, waiting for it to have a positive effect. Madeleine was sitting at the breakfast table with her oatmeal, toast, and *War and Peace*.

"Were you up reading that all night?" he asked.

She blinked at the interruption, visibly confused and annoyed. *"What?"*

He shook his head. "Never mind. Sorry." It had been an ill-advised attempt at humor, hardly humor at all, based on his recollection that she'd been at the same table with the same book the previous evening when he'd come home from Syracuse and gone almost immediately to bed, giving her only the blandest summary of the drama he and Kim had acted out.

He finished his coffee and went to the pot for a second cup. As he was pouring it, Madeleine closed her book and slid it a few inches toward the center of the table.

"Maybe you shouldn't be drinking so much of that," she said.

"You're probably right." He filled his cup anyway but, in a peculiar concession to her concern, added only one sweetener packet to it instead of his usual two.

She continued to watch him. He had the impression that the worry in her expression took in larger issues than his caffeine consumption.

After he switched off the coffeemaker and went back to the window, she asked quietly, "Is there anything I can do for you?"

The question had a strange effect on him. It seemed so all-encompassing. Yet so simple.

"I don't think so." To his own ears, his answer sounded trite, inadequate.

"Well," she said, "let me know if you think of anything."

Her gentle tone made him feel even more inadequate. He tried to brighten his mood by changing the subject. "So what's on your agenda today?"

"The clinic, naturally. And I may not be home for dinner. I may go over to Betty's after work." She paused. "Is that all right?"

It was a question she often asked in a variety of contexts. It could be about going somewhere, or planting something in one of the flower beds, or a recipe decision. He always found it inexplicably irritating, and he invariably answered it the same way. "Of course it's all right." The exchange was always, as it was now, followed by a silence.

Madeleine reached for *War and Peace* and reopened it.

He took his coffee into the den, sat at the desk, and contemplated the uncertainties of the situation he'd be walking into that night, alone and largely unprepared, in Max Clinter's cabin.

Then a new thought—a new worry—came out of nowhere. He left his coffee in the den and went out to Madeleine's car.

Twenty minutes later he came back in, satisfied that his sudden fear was groundless and that her car was free of any unwanted electronic devices.

"What was that little trip all about?" she asked, peering at him over the top of her book as he passed through the kitchen on his way back to the den.

He decided he had no better option than to tell the truth. He told her what he'd been looking for and why—describing the discoveries he'd made on Kim's car as well as his own.

"Who do you think is responsible?" Her tone was even, but there was a tightness at the corners of her eyes.

"I'm not sure." The answer was technically true, but evasive.

"That Meese character?" she suggested, almost hopefully.

"Possibly."

"Or possibly the person who set fire to our barn? And booby-trapped Kim's stairs?"

"Possibly."

"Possibly the Good Shepherd himself?"

"Possibly."

She took a long, slow breath. "Does that mean he's been following you?"

"Not necessarily. Certainly not closely. I would have noticed. He may just want to know where I am."

"Why would he want to know that?"

"Risk management. Feeling of control. Natural desire to know where your enemy is at all times."

She stared at him, her mouth compressed into a straight line. It was plain that she could see another, more violent use for the information.

He was about to allay some of her fear by explaining that he'd already disconnected the tracker he'd found on his Outback, but he realized that would lead to the troublesome question of why he hadn't also disconnected the one on the Miata.

The answer, in reality, was simple. The Shepherd might believe that the battery version had run out of power, but it would strain credibility to have the hardwired version fail simultaneously. Gurney was reluctant to tell Madeleine this, however, because he knew how upset she'd be at the Shepherd's ability to track Kim for even one more day. There was a limit to how many conflicts he could deal with at once, and some triage was essential.

"So, Dad, are you going to tell us how it went?"

At the sound of Kyle's voice, Gurney turned to see his son entering the kitchen barefoot in jeans and a T-shirt, his hair wet from the shower.

"Pretty much like I said last night."

"Last night you didn't really say much at all."

"I guess I just wanted to get to bed. I was about to collapse. But it went smoothly enough. No glitches. I think the story we planted was believable."

"What now?"

There were limits to what Gurney wanted to say in front of Madeleine. The whole enterprise could easily end up sounding way too risky. He answered as matter-of-factly as he could. "Basically, I get into position and wait for him to walk into the trap."

Kyle looked skeptical. "Just like that?"

Gurney shrugged. Madeleine had stopped reading and was watching him.

Kyle persisted. "What were the magic words?"

"Pardon?"

"What did you guys actually say in your . . . your improvised scene . . . that's going to make this guy show up?"

"We created the impression that there might be a way he could get rid of me. It's hard to remember the precise—" His cell phone rang.

He looked at the ID screen and recognized Kim's number. He was grateful for the interruption. The gratitude lasted about three seconds. She sounded like she was hyperventilating.

"Kim? What's the matter?"

"God . . . God . . ."

"Kim?"

"Yes."

"What is it? What's the matter?"

"Robby. He's dead."

"What?"

"He's dead."

"Robby Meese is dead?"

"Yes."

"Where?"

"What?"

"Can you tell me where he is?"

"He's in my bed."

"What happened?"

"I don't know."

"How did he end up in your bed?"

"I don't know! He's just there! What should I do?"

"Are you in the apartment?"

"Yes. Can you come here?"

"Tell me what happened."

"I don't know what happened. I came here from the hotel this morning to get some more of my things. I went into the bedroom. I . . ."

"Kim?"

"Yes?"

"You went into the bedroom . . ."

"He's in there now. On my bed."

"How do you know he's dead?"

"He was lying on his face. I tried to roll him over, wake him up. There's the . . . the handle of something . . . sticking out of his chest."

Gurney's mind was racing, the puzzle pieces caught up in a whirlwind.

"Dave?"

"Yes, Kim?"

"Could you please come?"

"Listen to me, Kim. What you have to do right now is call 911."

"Can you come?"

"Kim, my being there won't help. You have to call 911. You have to do it right now. That's the most important thing. Do you understand?"

"Yes. But I wish you were here. Please."

"I know. But I'm going to hang up now, so you can make that 911 call. After you describe the situation to the dispatcher, call me back. You understand?"

"Yes."

When Gurney broke the connection, Kyle and Madeleine were staring at him. Five minutes later, as he was still recounting the call to them in as much detail as he could, Kim called back.

"The dispatcher said the police are on their way." Her voice sounded more controlled.

"Are you okay?"

"I guess. I don't know. There's a suicide note."

"Say that again."

"A suicide note. From Robby. On my computer."

"You checked your computer?"

"I just saw it. It's right here on the screen. In front of me. It was turned on."

"You're sure it's a suicide note?"

"Of course I'm sure. What else could it be?"

"What does it say?"

"It's awful."

"What does it say?"

"I don't want to read it out loud. I can't." She sounded like she was taking deep breaths.

"Please, Kim, try to read it to me. It's important."

"Do I really have to read it? It's really awful."

"Try. Please."

"Okay. I'll try. Okay." She read in a trembling voice, " 'The human race disgusts me. You disgust me. You and Gurney together disgust me. Life is disgusting. I hope someday you see the truth and it kills you. This is the last will of Robert Montague.' That's it. That's all it says. When the police come, what should I tell them?"

"Just answer their questions."

"Should I tell them about last night?"

"Answer their questions concisely and truthfully." He paused, searching for the right words. "I wouldn't volunteer a lot of stuff that would just muddy the picture."

"Is it all right to say you were here?"

"Yes. They'll want to know if you were in the apartment, when you came, when you left, and whether anyone was there with you. You can tell them we were there, that we were discussing your RAM project. I don't think it would be helpful to distract them with extraneous details about Max Clinter or his house. The thing is, you need to tell the truth, you can't lie—but you're not required to spew out unasked-for details. You understand what I'm saying?"

"I think so. Should I tell them I spent last night at a hotel?"

"Definitely. They'll want to know where you were, and you need to be truthful. If I were you, and my apartment had been entered mysteriously on a number of occasions, and the local police hadn't responded adequately, I wouldn't want to be sleeping there. I'd feel safer in a hotel, or in Walnut Crossing, or in a friend's apartment in Manhattan. By the way, did you leave the hotel at all during the night?"

"No, of course not. But suppose—" There was a loud knocking sound in the background. "The police are here. I'd better go. Call you later."

After the call ended, Gurney stood where he was, in the middle of the room, trying to get a firm hold on the facts, the implications, the immediate imperatives. He felt like a man juggling half a dozen oranges who'd just been tossed a watermelon.

A watermelon loaded with nitroglycerin.

## Chapter 46

# No Other Way

"Suicide?" said Kyle.

"I doubt it," said Gurney. "He wasn't the type. And even if he was, homicide would still make more sense."

"You think the Syracuse cops are good enough to figure out what really happened?"

"Maybe with a little help." He spent a few seconds weighing his options, then took out his phone and entered Hardwick's number.

The call was picked up on the first ring. "Seren-fucking-dipity!" said the rough voice.

"Beg pardon?"

"I was in the act of reaching for the phone to call you, and here you are. Don't tell me that ain't fucking-dipity."

"Whatever you say, Jack. The reason I'm calling is that I know something that could be of value to BCI, and you may be the only BCI person willing to talk to me."

"Yeah, well, after I give you a certain piece of news, you may not give a fuck about—"

"Listen to me. Robby Meese is dead."

"Dead? Dead, meaning whacked?"

"I'd say so, although it's been set up as a suicide."

"BCI is not yet aware of this corpse?"

"The Syracuse city police know about it. So you guys will find out soon enough. But that's not the issue. Whoever ends up being responsible for the forensics, I want to make sure they take a close look at the computer keyboard that was used to type the purported suicide note.

The smudges on the keys are likely to be very similar to those found on Ruth Blum's computer."

Hardwick paused as though he were trying to understand this. "Where is this corpse?"

"In Kim Corazon's apartment."

A longer pause. "The latex-glove smudges on Blum's keyboard were caused by someone trying to type something in a way that would preserve her fingerprints on the keys, to make it look like she typed it. Right?"

"Right."

"How does that work here? The preserved fingerprints on Corazon's keyboard would be hers, not Meese's. How would that make it look like he typed the note?"

"The killer could have asked Meese to type something else—an e-mail, who knows what—before he killed him. Then, with Meese's prints on the keys, the killer put on gloves and typed the suicide note."

"So what do you want me to do with this big insight?"

"When you see the CJIS homicide report on Meese, which with any luck will mention the computer note, it might suddenly occur to you—because of the Kim Corazon connection to Ruth Blum—that the computer keyboard imprints ought to be compared. You might want to mention it to Bullard over in Auburn. And to a Detective James Schiff in Syracuse."

"You don't want to do this yourself?"

"My name is not magic at the moment. Any suggestion from me will end up at the bottom of the pile, if it makes it into the pile at all."

Hardwick exploded in a hacking cough. Or it might have been a laugh. "Man, you don't know how fucking true that is, which is why I was about to call you. The arson unit has decided to bring you in for questioning. As a suspect."

"When?"

"Most likely tomorrow morning. Conceivably as early as this afternoon. Thought I'd mention it, in case you'd prefer not to be home."

"Okay, Jack. Thank you. I'll sign off now. Got a few things I need to do."

"Watch your ass, kemosabe. Posse's gettin' ugly."

When Gurney ended the call, he was standing in the middle of the long room. Madeleine and Kyle were sitting at the table. Kyle was gazing at him in frank amazement. "That's incredible—that thing with the gloves on the keyboard? Wow. How'd you figure that out?"

"I'm only guessing. I may not have figured anything out. But another problem's heating up. The arson-unit idiots are being pressured by the fed idiots to question me about the barn."

Kyle looked incensed. "Isn't that what that jerk Kramden did when he was here?"

"Kramden took my statement as a witness. Now they want to question me as a suspect."

Madeleine appeared nonplussed.

"A suspect?" cried Kyle. "Are they completely out of their fucking minds?"

"That's not all," said Gurney. "One or more law-enforcement agencies may want to question me about Robby Meese's death, since I was in Kim's apartment last evening. So I think it would be best if I weren't here. Homicide interviews can go on for a long time, and I have an appointment tonight I wouldn't want to miss."

Kyle looked angry, stressed, helpless. He walked to the far end of the room and stared into the cold woodstove, shaking his head.

Madeleine's gaze was fixed on Gurney. "Where will you go?"

"Clinter's cabin."

"And tonight . . . ?"

"I'll wait, watch, listen. See who shows up. Play it by ear."

"The calm way you talk about it is really frightening."

"Why?"

"The way you understate everything—when everything is at stake."

"I don't like drama."

There was a silence between them, broken by the sound of cawing in the distance. In the lower pasture, three flapping crows rose from the stubbled grass, climbing in a loose arc to the tops of the hemlocks on the far side of the pond.

Madeleine was taking long, slow breaths. "What if the Good Shepherd walks in with a gun and shoots you?"

"Don't worry. That won't happen."

"Don't worry? *Don't worry?* Did you really say that?"

"What I meant was, there may not be as much to worry about as you think."

"How do you know that?"

"If he's checking those bugs, he heard me say that Max and I are meeting at the cabin at midnight tonight. The most reasonable thing for him to do would be to show up a couple of hours ahead of us, decide on the most advantageous location, get his vehicle and himself out of sight, and wait. I think he'll find the prospect attractive. He has a lot of experience shooting people at night in remote rural settings. In fact, he's very good at it. He'd see the whole opportunity as low risk, high reward. And he'll find the familiar elements of darkness and isolation encouraging—almost like a comfort zone."

"Only if his mind works the way you think it does."

"He's an extremely rational man."

"Rational?"

"Extremely—to the exclusion of any empathetic feelings at all. Which is what makes him a monster, a complete sociopath. But it also makes him easy to understand. His mind is a pure risk-reward calculator, and calculators are predictable."

Madeleine stared at him as though he were speaking not just another language but a language from another planet.

Kyle's uncertain voice came from the far end of the room, where he was still standing by the woodstove. "So your idea is basically to show up first? So you'll be there waiting for him, instead of him being there waiting for you?"

"Something like that. It's really pretty simple."

"How sure are you about . . . all this?"

"Sure enough to go ahead with it."

In a way it was true. But a more honest answer might have included the fact that it was all relative—his breathing space was almost gone, standing still was not an option, and he couldn't think of any other way forward.

Madeleine got up from the table and took her cold oatmeal and unfinished toast to the sink. She stared at the faucet for a while without touching it, her eyes full of dread. Then, glancing up with a strained little smile, she said, "It looks lovely out. I'm going for a walk."

"Aren't you working at the clinic today?" asked Gurney.

"I don't have to be there till ten-thirty. Plenty of time. Too nice a morning to stay in the house."

She went to the bedroom, and two minutes later she emerged in a wild assortment of colors: lavender fleece pants, a pink nylon jacket, and a red beret.

"I'll be down near the pond," she said. "I'll see you before you go."

## Chapter 47

# An Angel Departing

K yle came over and sat at the table with Gurney. "Do you think she's all right?"

"Sure. I mean . . . obviously she's . . . I'm sure she's okay. Being outside always seems to help her. Walking does something for her. Something good."

Kyle nodded. "What should I do?"

It sounded like the biggest possible question a young man could ask his father. Thinking of it that way made Gurney smile. "Keep an eye on things." He paused. "How's your work going? And your school stuff?"

"E-mail is magic."

"Good. I feel bad about this. I've dragged you into some-thing . . . created a problem in your life where there shouldn't have been any . . . created a danger. That's not something . . . a parent . . ." His voice trailed off. He looked out through the glass doors, looked to see if the crows were still perched on the hemlocks.

"You didn't create the danger, Dad. You're the one who's taking care of it."

"Right. Well . . . I'd better get ready. I don't want to find myself hung up with this arson nonsense when I need to be somewhere else."

"You want me to do anything?"

"Like I said, just keep an eye on things. And you . . . you know where the . . ." Gurney gestured toward the bedroom.

"Where the shotgun is. Yep. No problem."

"By tomorrow morning, with a little luck, everything should be okay." On that note, which had an emptier ring than he would have liked, Gurney left the room.

There really wasn't much for him to do before setting out. He checked to make sure his phone was adequately charged. He checked the action of his Beretta and the security of his ankle holster. He went to his desk and got out the folder of information Kim had given him during their first meeting, and he added to it the printouts of the reports Hardwick had e-mailed him. He had quite a few hours left before any kind of confrontation would occur, and he planned to review once again all the facts in his possession.

When he came back out to the kitchen, Kyle was standing by the table, plainly too anxious to sit.

"Okay, son, I'd better be going."

"Right, then. See you later." Kyle raised his hand in a determinedly casual gesture—something between a wave and a salute.

"Right. See you later."

Gurney went out quickly to his car, grabbing his jacket from the mudroom on his way. He was hardly aware of driving down the pasture lane, until he reached the place by the pond where the grassy surface merged into the gravel of the town road. At that moment he caught sight of Madeleine.

She was standing by a tall birch on the uphill verge of the pond, her eyes closed, her face raised to the sun. He stopped the car, got out, and walked toward her. He wanted to say good-bye, say that he'd be home before morning.

She opened her eyes slowly and smiled at him. "Isn't it amazing?"

"What?"

"The air."

"Oh. Yes, very nice. I was just on my way, and I thought——"

Her smile caught him off balance. It was so . . . so intensely full of . . . what? Not sadness, exactly. Something else.

Whatever it was, it was in her voice as well. "Just stop for a bit," she said, "and feel the air on your face."

For a moment—a few seconds, a minute perhaps, he wasn't sure—he was transfixed.

"Isn't it amazing?" she said again, so softly that the words seemed to be a part of the air she was describing.

"I have to go," he said. "I have to go before——"

She stopped him. "I know. I know you do. Be careful." She put her hand on his cheek. "I love you."

"Oh, God." He stared at her. "I'm afraid, Maddie. I've always been able to figure things out. I hope to God I know what I'm doing. It's all I can do."

She placed her fingers gently on his lips. "You'll be brilliant."

He didn't remember walking to his car, or getting into it.

What he remembered was looking back, seeing her standing on the high ground above the birch, radiant in the sunlight in her profusion of colors, waving to him, smiling with a poignancy beyond his understanding.

## Chapter 48

# The One That Mattered

The countryside between Walnut Crossing and Cayuga County presented one classic bucolic vista after another—small farms, vineyards, and rolling cornfields, interspersed with hardwood copses. But Gurney hardly noticed. His mind was on his destination—a stark little cabin in a black-water bog—and what might happen there that night.

It wasn't yet noon when he arrived. He decided not to go into the property right away. Instead he drove slowly past the dirt entry road with its skeleton sentinel and sagging aluminum gate. The gate was open, but its very openness appeared more ominous than inviting.

He proceeded a mile or so, then made a U-turn. Halfway back to Clinter's forbidding driveway, he saw a large, decrepit barn in the middle of a weed-choked field. The roof was sagging dramatically. Quite a few boards were missing from the siding, as was one of the double doors. There was no farmhouse in sight—only a disheveled foundation that might once have supported one.

Gurney was curious. As soon as he came to what he suspected had formerly been the entrance, he drove slowly up into the field, all the way to the front of the barn. It was dark inside, and he had to switch on his headlights to get a sense of the interior. The floor was concrete, and there was a long open passageway extending from the front clear through to the shadowy back of the building. It was filthy, with decaying hay everywhere, but otherwise it was empty.

He made a decision. He drove slowly into the barn—as far as he could into its dark recesses. Then he took his file of *Orphans* data and police reports, got out of the car, and locked the doors. It was exactly noon. He was going to have a long wait, but he was prepared to make good use of it.

He proceeded on foot down through the tangled field and along the road to Clinter's driveway. Walking in along the narrow causeway that traversed the beaver pond and adjacent swamp, Gurney was struck again by the godforsaken loneliness of the place.

As promised, the front door of the cabin was unlocked. The interior, which seemed to consist of one large room, had the musty smell of a place whose windows are rarely opened. The log walls contributed another smell, woody and acidic. The furniture looked like it had come from a store specializing in the "rustic" style. It was a man's environment. A hunter's environment.

There was a stove, a sink, and a refrigerator against one wall; a long table with three chairs against the adjacent wall; a low single bed against another wall. The floor was made of dark-stained pine boards. The outline of what appeared to be a trapdoor in the floor caught Gurney's eye. There was a finger hole drilled near one edge, presumably as a way of lifting it open. Out of curiosity, Gurney tried it, but it wouldn't budge. Presumably, at some time in the past, it had been sealed shut. Or, knowing Clinter, there might be a concealed lock somewhere. Perhaps that's where he stored the "collectible" guns he sold to other "collectors" without the need for a federal firearms license.

There was a window that provided some illumination over the long table, as well as a view of the path outside. Gurney settled down there in one of the three chairs and tried to arrange his thick handful of papers in a practical sequence for the hours ahead. After making a few piles, shifting items from pile to pile, and moving the piles into various orders of priority, he abandoned his efforts at organization and decided to start wherever he felt like starting.

Steeling himself, he picked up the sheaf of ten-year-old autopsy photos and chose the ones that documented the head wounds. Once again he found them horrific—the way the massive traumas distorted the facial features of the victims into grotesque facsimiles of living emotions. Once again the gross violation of their personal dignity outraged him, renewing his resolution to give them the respect they deserved—to restore, by bringing their killer to justice, the dignity that had been stolen from them.

That sense of resolution felt good. It felt purposeful, uncomplicated, energizing. But the good feeling soon began to fade.

As he looked around the room—this cold, uninviting, impersonal room that served as a man's home—he was struck by the smallness of Max Clinter's world. He couldn't be sure what Clinter's life had been like prior to his encounter with the Good Shepherd, but surely it had withered and contracted in the years since. This cabin, this little box perched on a mound of earth in the middle of a bog in the middle of nowhere, was the den of a hermit. Clinter was a deeply isolated human being, driven by his demons, by his fantasies, by his hunger for revenge. Clinter was Ahab. A wounded, obsessed Ahab. Instead of roaming the sea, he was Ahab lurking in the wilderness. Ahab with guns instead of harpoons. He was locked in his own quest, envisioning nothing but the culmination of his own furious mission, hearing nothing but the voices in his own mind.

The man was utterly alone.

The truth of it, the force of it, brought Gurney to the verge of tears.

Then he realized that the tears weren't for Max.

They were for himself.

And it was then that the image of Madeleine came to him. The recollection of Madeleine standing on the little rise beyond the birch. On the little rise between the pond and the woods. Standing there, waving good-bye to him. Standing in that wild burst of color and light, waving, smiling. Smiling with an emotion that was far beyond him. An emotion beyond words.

It was like the end of a film. A film about a man who had been given a great gift, an angel to lovingly light his way, an angel who could have shown him everything, led him everywhere, had he only been willing to look and to listen and to follow. But the man had been too busy, too absorbed in too many things, too absorbed by the darkness that challenged and fascinated him, too absorbed by himself. And finally the angel was called away, because she had done all she could do for him, all that he was willing to allow done. She loved him, knew all there was to know of him, loved him and accepted him exactly the way he was, wished him all the love and light and happiness he was capable of accepting, wished him all the best of everything forever. But now it was time for her to go. And the film ended with the angel smiling, smiling with all the love in the world, as she disappeared into the sunlight.

Gurney lowered his head, biting his lip. Tears rolled down his cheeks. And he began to sob. At the imagined film. At the truth of his own life.

It was ridiculous, he thought, an hour later. It was absurd. Self-indulgent, over-the-top, hyperemotional nonsense. When he had time, he'd look at it more carefully, figure out what actually triggered his childish little breakdown. Obviously he'd been feeling vulnerable. The political dynamics of the case had isolated him, his imperfect recovery from his gunshot wounds had left him frustrated and touchy. And no doubt there were deeper issues, echoes of childhood insecurities, fears, and so forth. He would definitely have to take a closer look. But right now . . .

Right now he needed to make the best use of the time that was available to him. He needed to prepare himself for whatever confrontation might emerge from the process he and Kim had set in motion.

He began shuffling through the papers on the table, reading everything from summaries of the original incident reports to Kim's status notes on her initial contacts with the families, from the Offender Profile generated by the FBI to the full text of the Good Shepherd's Memorandum of Intent.

He read through all of it. Carefully, as though he were reading it for the first time. With frequent glances out the window at the causeway path and occasional trips around the room to check the other windows, the task consumed over two hours. And then he went through it all over again.

By the time he finished his second pass, the sun had gone down. He was fatigued from reading and stiff from sitting. He got up from the table, stretched, withdrew the Beretta from his ankle holster, and stepped out through the front door. The cloudless sky was in that stage of dusk in which the blue is fading to gray. Somewhere out in the beaver pond, there was a loud splash. And then another. And another. And then compete silence.

The quiet brought with it a feeling of tension. Gurney slowly circled the cabin. It all appeared unchanged from what he remembered from his earlier visit—except that the Humvee that had been parked out in back of the picnic table was gone. When he came around to the front, he went back inside, closing the door behind him but leaving it unlatched.

In just the three or four minutes he'd been outside, the light level had fallen noticeably. He returned to the table, laid the Beretta down within easy reach, and selected from the piles of papers his own list of questions about the case. The one that caught his attention was the same one Bullard had alluded to in Sasparilla and Hardwick had mentioned on the phone in connection with a hypothetical pair of motives Jimi Brewster might have had for killing not only his father but the other five victims.

Hardwick theorized that Jimi could have killed his father out of pure hatred for him and the materialistic priorities embodied in his choice of car, and killed the other five because they, with their similar cars, were just like his father. In that way there would have been one primary and five secondary victims.

However, although there was something tantalizing about the theory, it didn't really jibe with Gurney's knowledge of pathological killers. They tended to kill either the primary object of their hatred *or* a series of substitutes, not both. So the primary-secondary motivation structure didn't quite . . .

Or did it?

Suppose . . .

Suppose the killer did have one primary target. One person he wanted to kill. And suppose he killed the five others not because they reminded him of the primary—*but because they would remind the police of the primary.*

Suppose he killed those other five people simply to create the impression of a different kind of crime. At the very least, those extra victims would clutter the field so thoroughly that it would make it impossible for the police, or anyone else, to see clearly who among the six the primary really was. And, of course, the way the Good Shepherd murder scheme had been engineered, the police would never even get to the point of asking that question.

Why would it occur to them that the six were really the sum of one and five? Why would they even start down that road? Especially if they had, from the very beginning, a solid theory of the case that made all six targets equally important. Especially if they'd received a mission killer's manifesto that made all the murders make equal sense. A manifesto that explained everything. A manifesto so cleverly constructed and so reflective of the details of the crimes that the best and the brightest swallowed it whole.

Gurney had the feeling that finally he might be seeing something clearly—a sense that the fog was starting to lift. It was his first vision of the case that seemed, at least at first glance, coherent.

As with most of the insights in his career, his immediate thought was that it should have occurred to him sooner. After all, this way of looking at the murders was only a small turn of the dial from Madeleine's description of that pivotal scene in *The Man with the Black Umbrella*. But sometimes a millimeter makes all the difference.

On the other hand, not every idea that feels right is right. Gurney knew from experience how dangerously easy it is to overlook logical flaws in one's thinking. When the product of one's own mind is the subject, objectivity is an illusion. We all believe we have an open mind, but no one really does. A devil's-advocate process is essential.

His first choice for devil's advocacy was Hardwick. He took out his phone and placed the call. When it went to voice mail, he left a brief message. "Hey, Jack. I have a slant on the case that I'd like your reaction to. Call me."

He checked to make sure his phone was still set on vibrate. He wasn't sure what the night had in store for him, but in the scenarios he imagined, a ringing phone could be a problem.

His next devil's-advocate choice was Lieutenant Bullard. He didn't know where she stood at this point, but the need he felt for feedback outweighed his concern about the politics. Besides, if his insight into the case was correct, it could tilt the politics back in his favor. That call also went into voice mail, and he left essentially the same message for her that he'd left for Hardwick.

Not knowing when Hardwick or Bullard might get back to him and still wanting to expose his new perspective to a live listener, he decided, with mixed feelings, to call Clinter. After the third ring, the man himself answered.

"Hey, laddie, trouble on your big night? You calling for help?"

"No trouble. Just an idea I want to bounce off you. Might have holes in it, or it might be significant."

"I'm all ears."

It suddenly struck Gurney that there was a sizable psychic overlap between Clinter and Hardwick. Clinter was Hardwick gone over the edge. The thought, strangely, made him both more and less comfortable.

Gurney explained his idea. Twice.

There was no response. As he waited, he gazed out the window at the broad, marshy pond. The full moon had risen, giving the dead trees looming above the marsh grass an eerie presence. "You there, Max?"

"I'm absorbing, laddie, absorbing. I find no fatal fault with what you say. It does, of course, raise questions."

"Of course."

"To be sure I understand, you're saying that only one of the murders mattered?"

"Correct."

"And the other five were protective cover?"

"Correct."

"And none of the murders had a damn thing to do with the ills of society?"

"Correct."

"And the fancy cars were targeted . . . why?"

"Maybe because the one victim that mattered drove one. A big, black, expensive Mercedes. Maybe that's where the whole concept came from."

"And the other five people were shot essentially at random? Shot because they had the same kind of car? To make it look like there was a pattern."

"Correct. I don't think the killer knew or cared anything about the other victims."

"Which would make him a rather chilly fucker, wouldn't it?"

"Correct."

"So now the big question: Which victim was the one that mattered?"

"When I meet the Good Shepherd, I'll ask him."

"And you think that'll happen tonight?" Clinter's voice was pulsing with excitement.

"Max, *you have to stay away.* It's a fragile thing I'm putting together."

"Understood, laddie. One more question, though: How does your theory of the old murders explain the current ones?"

"That's simple. The Good Shepherd is trying keep us from realizing that the original six victims were the sum of one and five. Somehow *The Orphans of Murder* has the potential to expose that secret—possibly by pointing in some way to the one that mattered. He's killing people to keep that from happening."

"A very desperate man."

"More practical than desperate."

"Christ, Gurney, he's murdered three people in three days, according to the news."

"Right. I just don't think that desperation has much to do with it. I don't believe the Shepherd regards murder as that big a deal. It's simply an action he takes whenever it seems advantageous. Whenever he feels that killing someone will remove more risk from his life than it will create. I don't think desperation enters into—"

A call-waiting signal stopped Gurney in midsentence. He checked the ID. "Max, I have to go. I've got Lieutenant Bullard from BCI trying to get through. And, Max? Stay away from here tonight. Please."

Gurney glanced out the window. The weird black-and-silver landscape raised gooseflesh on his arms. He was standing in a shaft of moonlight that crossed the center of the room, projecting an image of the window, along with his own shadow, on the far wall above the bed.

He pressed TALK to take the waiting call. "Thank you for getting back to me, Lieutenant. I appreciate it. I think I may have some—" He never finished the sentence.

There was a stunning explosion. A white flash accompanied by a deafening blast. And a terrific impact to Gurney's hand.

He staggered back against the table, unsure for several seconds what had happened. His right hand was numb. There was a stinging ache in his wrist.

Fearing what he might see, he held his hand up in the moonlight, turning it slowly. All the fingers were there, but he was holding only a small piece of the phone. He looked around the room, searching futilely in the darkness for other areas of damage.

The first explanation that occurred to him was that his phone had exploded. His mind raced around the edges of that improbability, trying to imagine a way it could have been set up, a time when the phone might have been accessible to someone capable of that kind of sabotage, how a miniature explosive device could have been inserted and then triggered.

But that wasn't just improbable, it was impossible. The concussive impact, the sheer force of the explosion, put its source beyond anything he could conceive of being fitted into a functioning phone. A dummy phone, perhaps, built for the purpose, but not the phone on which he'd just been speaking.

Then he smelled ordinary cartridge gunpowder.

So it wasn't a sophisticated mini-bomb. It was a muzzle blast.

However, it was a muzzle blast far too loud for any normal handgun—which was why he hadn't reached the right conclusion immediately.

But he did know at least one handgun that could produce a report of that magnitude.

And at least one individual with the accuracy and steadiness of hand required to put a bullet through a cell phone by moonlight.

His next thought was that the shooter must have fired into the room through one of the windows, and he instinctively dropped to a crouch, peering up at the window over the table. However, it was still closed and the panes illumined by the moonlight were unbroken. Meaning the shot must have come from one of the rear windows. But given the position of his body at the moment of impact, it was hard to see how the bullet could have reached the phone in his hand without passing through his shoulder.

So how . . . ?

The answer arrived with a small shiver.

The shot hadn't come from outside the cabin.
Someone was there, in the room, with him.
The realization came to him by sound rather than sight.
The sound of breathing.
Just a few feet away.
Slow, relaxed breathing.

*Chapter 49*

# An Extremely Rational Man

A s Gurney looked in the direction from which the sound was coming, he saw, interrupting the strip of silvery light across the cabin floor, a dark rectangle where the trapdoor had been opened. On the far side of the opening, there was just enough faintly reflected moonlight to suggest the presence of a standing figure.

A hoarse whisper confirmed the impression. "Sit at the table, Detective. Put your hands on top of your head."

Gurney quietly followed the instructions.

"I have some questions. You must answer them quickly. Do you understand?"

"I understand."

"If the answer is not quick, I will assume it's a lie. Do you understand?"

"Yes."

"Good. First question: Is Clinter coming here?"

"I don't know."

"You just told him on the phone not to come."

"That's right."

"Do you expect him to come anyway?"

"He may. I don't know. He's not a predictable man."

"That's true. You must keep telling me the truth. The truth will keep you alive. You understand?"

"Yes." Gurney sounded perfectly calm, as he often did in extreme situations. But inside, at that moment, he was full of fear and fury.

Fear of the situation he'd walked into and fury at the arrogant miscalculation that had put him there.

He'd assumed that the Good Shepherd would conform to the timing he'd spelled out in his scene with Kim and that the man would show up at the cabin two or three hours before Clinter and Gurney's supposed midnight meeting. In the welter of facts and twists and what-ifs swirling around in his head, he'd failed to consider the obvious possibility that the Shepherd might show up much earlier than that—maybe a good twelve hours earlier.

What the hell had he been thinking? That the Shepherd was a logical man and the logical time to arrive would be a few hours before midnight. And therefore that's what would happen, issue resolved, on to the next point? Jesus, how fucking stupid! He told himself he was only human, and humans make mistakes. But that didn't take the bitter edge off his making such a deadly one.

The throaty, half-vocalized whisper grew louder. "It was your hope to trick me into coming here? To somehow take me by surprise?"

The aptness of the question was unnerving. "Yes."

"The truth. Good. It keeps you alive. So, now, your phone call to Clinter. You believe what you told him?"

"About the killings?"

"Of course about the killings."

"Yes, I do."

For several seconds all Gurney heard was the sound of his questioner's breathing—followed by a question so softly uttered it was barely louder than the breathing itself. "What other thoughts do you have?"

"My only thought right now is, are you going to shoot me?"

"Of course. But the more truth you tell me, the longer you live. Simple. You understand?"

"Yes."

"Good. Now tell me all your thoughts about the killings. Your true thoughts."

"My thoughts are mostly questions."

"What questions?"

Gurney wondered if the hoarse whisper was a vocal impairment or a way of concealing the Good Shepherd's real voice. He suspected the latter. The implications of that were interesting, but he had to focus now on the immediate need to stay alive.

"I wonder how many other people you've killed, besides the ones we know about. Possibly quite a few. Am I right about that?"

"Of course."

Gurney was startled by the frankness of the answer and felt a fleeting moment of hope that the man could be engaged in a kind of dialogue—that his pride might drive him to boast of things he'd done. After all, sociopaths did have egos and enjoyed living in the echo chamber of their own narratives of power and ruthlessness. Perhaps he could get the man talking about himself, and thus stretch the window of opportunity for outside intervention.

But then the coin of hope flipped to its opposite side, and Gurney saw the clear implication of the man's willingness to speak: It carried no risk, because Gurney would soon be dead.

The whisper became a parody of gentleness. "What else do you wonder about?"

"I wonder about Robby Meese and your relationship with him. I wonder how much he did on his own and how much you encouraged him to do. I wonder why you killed him when you did. I wonder if you thought his so-called suicide would be believed."

"What else?"

"I wonder if you were really trying to put Max Clinter in the frame for Ruth Blum's murder or if you were just playing a silly game."

"What else?"

"I wonder if you thought your message on Ruth's Facebook page would be believed."

"What else?"

"I wonder about my barn." Gurney was trying to string out the interchange as long as he could, with as many pauses as he could insert. The longer it lasted, the better—in every way.

"Keep talking, Detective."

"I wonder about the GPS locators on the cars. I wonder if the one on Kim's car was your idea or Robby's. Robby the stalker."

"What else?"

"Some of the things you've done are very clever, and some are very stupid. I wonder if you know which is which."

"Provocation is pointless, Detective. Have you come to the end of your thoughts?"

"I wonder about the White Mountain Strangler. Such an odd case. Are you familiar with it? It has certain interesting features."

There was a long silence. Time equaled hope. Time gave Gurney the space to think, perhaps even a chance to get to his gun on the table behind him.

When the Shepherd spoke again, the purr was syrupy. "Any final thoughts?"

"Just one more. How could someone so smart make such a colossal mistake at Lakeside Collision?"

There was a long silence. An alarming silence that could mean anything. Perhaps the Good Shepherd had finally been jarred off balance. Or perhaps his finger was tightening on the trigger. A tremor ran through Gurney's stomach.

"What are you talking about?"

"You'll find out soon enough."

"I want to know now." There was a new intensity in the whisper, along with the glint of something moving in the shaft of moonlight.

Gurney caught his first glimpse of the barrel of a huge silver-plated pistol, no more than six feet away.

"Now," the man repeated. "Tell me about Lakeside Collision."

"You left some identification there."

"I don't carry identification."

"That night you did."

"Tell me exactly what it was. Tell me right now."

The way Gurney saw the situation, there was no good answer, no answer likely to save him. There was certainly no way that revealing the tire-track discovery would result in a reprieve. And begging for his life would be worse than useless. There was only one option that offered him even a glimmer of staying alive for as much as another minute: stonewalling, refusing to divulge anything more.

Gurney tried to keep his voice from shaking as he spoke.

"You left the solution to the puzzle in the parking lot of Lakeside Collision."

"I don't like riddles. You have three seconds to answer my question."

"One." He raised his pistol slowly toward Gurney's face.

"Two." The barrel glinted in the shaft of moonlight.

"Three." He pulled the trigger.

## Chapter 50

# Apocalypse

Gurney's reflexive jerk away from the flash and the deafening blast would have sent his chair toppling over backward if it weren't for the edge of the table. For a minute he couldn't see anything, and all he could hear was the harsh, ringing echo of the gunshot.

He felt some wetness on the left side of his neck, a slight trickle. He put his hand to the side of his face, felt more wetness on his earlobe. As he moved his fingers higher, he discovered a searing, stinging spot at the very top of the ear—the source of the blood.

"Put your hands back on top of your head. Now." The whispery voice seemed far away, lost in the reverberation in his ears.

But he did his best to comply.

"You hear me, yes?" said the distant, muffled voice.

"Yes," said Gurney.

"Good. Listen carefully. I will ask you my question again. You must answer it. I am a good judge of what is true and what is not. If I hear truth, we go on, harmlessly. Just a nice conversation, you know? But if I hear a lie, I pull the trigger again. Clear?"

"Yes."

"Each time I hear a lie, you lose something. Next time not just a little nick from your ear. You lose more important things. You understand?"

"I understand." Gurney's eyesight was starting to recover from the muzzle flash, and he could again make out a dim swath of moonlight across the middle of the room.

"Good. I want to know everything about this so-called mistake at Lakeside Collision. No riddles. Pure truth." In the moonlight the silver-plated pistol barrel gradually descended until it was aligned with Gurney's right ankle.

He gritted his teeth to keep from trembling at the thought of what a Desert Eagle slug would do to that joint. The immediate loss of his foot would be bad enough. But the arterial bleeding would be the real problem. And telling the truth or not, in response to this or any subsequent question, was not the lever that would control the outcome. The lever was the Good Shepherd's sense of personal security. And that lever could now move in only one direction. Because there was no possible scenario in which Gurney alive could pose a lesser risk to the Good Shepherd than Gurney dead.

The only variable yet to be determined was how many body parts would be severed before he bled to death. Before he bled to death, alone, on the floor of Max Clinter's cabin, in the middle of a swamp, in the middle of nowhere.

He closed his eyes and saw Madeleine on the hillside.

In fuchsia, violet, pink, blue, orange, scarlet . . . all shimmering in the sunlight.

He walked toward her, through grass that was as green as every living thing and smelled as sweet as heaven must smell.

She put her fingers lightly on his lips and smiled.

"You'll be brilliant," she said. "Absolutely brilliant."

And a moment later he was dead.

O r so he thought.

Through his closed eyelids, he sensed a sudden illumination. It was accompanied by the sound of distant music rising through the ringing in his ears, and, above and through it all, the throbbing of a great drum.

And then he heard the voice.

The voice that brought him back to the cabin in the swamp in the middle of nowhere. A voice amplified mightily by a bullhorn.

"POLICE . . . NEW YORK STATE POLICE . . . PUT DOWN YOUR WEAPONS . . . PUT DOWN YOUR WEAPONS AND OPEN THE DOOR . . . DO IT NOW . . . PUT DOWN YOUR WEAPONS

AND OPEN THE DOOR . . . THIS IS THE NEW YORK STATE POLICE . . . PUT DOWN YOUR WEAPONS AND OPEN THE DOOR."

Gurney opened his eyes. Instead of moonlight, a spotlight was shining in the window. He looked across the room at where his formidable, invisible captor had been standing ninja-like in the darkness. In his place was a man of average stature in brown slacks and a tan cardigan, with one hand raised to shield his eyes from the glare. It was hard for Gurney to associate this modest figure with the homicidal monster of his imagination. But in the man's other hand was the undeniable link to the monster: a gleaming .50-caliber Desert Eagle pistol. The pistol responsible for the blood still trickling down the side of Gurney's neck, the acrid smell of gunpowder in the room, the ringing in his ears.

The gun that had come so close to ending his life.

The man turned a little away from the spotlight and calmly lowered the hand he'd been holding in front of his eyes, revealing an impassive, unlined face. It was a face without distinction, without strong emotions, without any particularly prominent feature. It was a balanced, ordinary face. A face that was essentially forgettable.

Yet Gurney knew he had seen it before.

When he was finally able to place it, when he could finally attach a name to it, his first reaction was to think he must be mistaken. He blinked several times, trying to wrap his mind around the identity of the man facing him. He was having a hard time uniting that inoffensive, quiet identity with the words and actions of the Good Shepherd. Especially one of those actions.

But as his certainty increased and he was sure there was no mistake, he could almost feel the puzzle pieces being jarred into new positions, shifting into more interesting relationships, clicking together.

Larry Sterne gazed back at him, his expression more thoughtful than fearful. Larry Sterne who had reminded him of Mister Rogers. Larry Sterne, the soft-spoken dentist. Larry Sterne, the serene dental-medical entrepreneur. Larry Sterne, the son of Ian Sterne, who'd built a multimillion-dollar beauty-bestowing empire.

Larry Sterne, the son of Ian Sterne, who'd invited a lovely young Russian pianist to share his Woodstock home. And almost certainly his bed. And, potentially, a place in his will.

Dear God, was that what this was all about?

Had Larry Sterne simply been securing his inheritance?

Protecting his financial future from his father's unpredictable affections?

It was, of course, a substantial inheritance. An inheritance worth worrying about. A money machine, in fact. Not something one would want to lose.

Had the calm and gentle Larry been avoiding, through the simple expedient of killing his father, any risk of that money machine ending up in the hands of the lovely young Russian pianist? And then, by cluttering the landscape with five additional bodies, had he simply been avoiding any risk of the police asking what would have been their first question if Ian Sterne had been the only victim—the damning question that would have led them straight to Larry:

Cui bono?

In the weird combination of moonlight and shifting floodlights shining through the window, Gurney could see that Sterne's grip on his gun was still firm and steady, but the man's eyes were unmistakably focused on a world of diminishing options. It was hard to identify the emotion in those eyes. Was it terror? Rage? The fierce determination of the proverbial cornered rat? Or was it just that the icy calculator had gone into overdrive—giving the man's racing mental processes a frantic appearance?

Gurney concluded that he was in the presence of an essentially heartless, mechanical process. The same heartless, mechanical process that had been responsible for . . . how many deaths?

*How many deaths?* That was the question that brought the White Mountain Strangler case into sudden focus. It fit the pattern—the pattern of a case in which one murder mattered, a murder hidden by others that didn't matter at all—all tied together in a psycho-killer package with a white silk scarf. Gurney wondered, what had Larry's girlfriend done to make her life an inconvenience to him? Perhaps she'd gotten pregnant? Or perhaps it wasn't anything that serious. For a man like Larry—the White Mountain Strangler, the Good Shepherd—murder did not require a serious cause. It required only the prospect of producing a benefit greater than its cost.

The words of the RAM evangelist came back to Gurney with a

chill: To extinguish life, to blow it away like a wisp of smoke, to trample it like a piece of dirt, that is the essence of evil.

Outside, out past the beaver pond, a pulsing siren was turned on for
five seconds, then off. The previous bullhorn announcement was then
repeated at full volume.

Gurney turned in his chair and peered out the front window. Powerful spotlights were illuminating the property from the far side of the
causeway. He realized that the sound of the siren was what he must
have heard earlier. In the intensity of his emotional confusion, with the
pistol blast still ringing in his ears, it was the sound he'd taken for music.
And then he'd heard what was no doubt the sound he'd imagined to be
a great drumbeat—which he now recognized as the thumping rotor of
a circling helicopter. A helicopter that was sweeping its airborne searchlight back and forth over the cabin, over the tangled swamp grass, over
the stark tree trunks sticking up out of the black water.

Gurney turned to Sterne. He had two questions vying with each
other at the top of his list of forty or fifty. The first was the most urgent.

"What are you going to do now, Larry?"

"Proceed as reasonably as possible."

The answer, in all its rational tranquillity, couldn't have sounded
crazier.

"Meaning what, exactly?"

"Surrender. Play the game. Prevail."

Gurney's fear was that he was witnessing the calm before the
storm—that the sweet light of reason and surrender was about to
explode in a lunatic bloodbath.

"Prevail?"

"I always have. I always will."

"But you do . . . intend to surrender?"

"Of course." Sterne smiled, as though he were trying to soothe
a kindergartner's fear of getting on the bus. "What were you thinking? That I'd take you hostage, use you as a human shield to make my
escape?"

"It's been done."

"Not by me, not with you." He appeared genuinely amused. "Be
realistic, Detective. What kind of shield would you make? From what
I hear, your professional colleagues would be delighted to have an

opportunity to shoot you. I'd be better off shielding myself with a sack of potatoes."

Gurney was speechless at the man's composure. Was he totally insane? "You're pretty cheery for a guy whose case could end the state moratorium on executions. I hear that lethal injections aren't very pleasant." Even as he was saying this, frustrated by Sterne's attitude, he realized how dangerous and inadvisable a comment it was.

Apparently he need not have worried. Sterne just shook his head. "Don't be silly, Detective. Morons with third-rate lawyers have managed to put off their executions for twenty years or more. I can do better than that. Much better. I have money. A lot of money. I have connections both visible and invisible. Most important of all, I know how the legal system works. How it *really* works. And I have something of great value to offer that system. Something to trade, shall we say." He was radiating a composure that fell somewhere between yogic peace and madness.

"What do you have?"

"Knowledge."

"Of?"

"Certain unsolved cases."

Outside, five seconds of a pulsing police siren preceded another bullhorn announcement. The wording had become more urgent. "THIS IS THE STATE POLICE...PUT DOWN YOUR WEAPONS NOW...OPEN THE DOOR NOW...DO IT NOW...PUT DOWN YOUR WEAPONS IMMEDIATELY AND OPEN THE DOOR...OPEN THE DOOR NOW."

"Unsolved cases...such as?"

"You were wondering a few minutes ago how many people I might have killed—how many more than you've already counted."

The thudding roar of the helicopter was growing louder above the cabin, its searchlight brighter. Sterne seemed oblivious to it. His attention was entirely on Gurney, who in turn was trying to analyze and respond to the latest twist in what was becoming one of the most unsettling cases of his career.

"I don't follow the logic, Larry. If they can hang the Good Shepherd murders on you—"

"Big if, by the way."

"Okay, big if. But if they can, I don't see how you get much lever-age out of confessing to a couple more."

Sterne smiled his transcendental smile. "I see what you're doing. You're ridiculing my offer to get me to show my hand. Silly little ploy. But that's all right. No secrets among friends. Let me ask you a hypo-thetical question: How important would it be to a state police agency to clear—again, quite hypothetically—twenty or maybe thirty unsolved cases?"

Gurney was disheartened. Larry Sterne was either flat-out delu-sional or an impulsive liar with the kind of megalomania that told him he could make up anything and make people believe it.

Sterne seemed to sense Gurney's skepticism. His reaction was to double down. "I'm thinking that there should be some leverage in put-ting thirty cases in the 'solved' file. Dramatically improving depart-ment statistics. Providing closure for the families. If thirty isn't a big enough number, we might even be able to offer forty. Whatever it takes to make the kind of deal I have in mind."

"What kind of deal would that be, Larry?"

"Nothing unreasonable. I think you'll find me the most reasonable man you've ever met. No need to get into the specifics at this point. All I'm talking about is an imprisonment with certain fundamental ame-nities. A comfortable cell of my own. Basic conveniences. The relax-ation of only the most unnecessary rules. I wouldn't ask for anything that men of goodwill couldn't easily negotiate."

"And in return for that, you'd be willing to confess to twenty or thirty or forty unsolved murders? With full corroborative details on motive and method?"

"Hypothetically."

The bullhorn announced, "THIS IS YOUR LAST CHANCE TO PUT DOWN YOUR WEAPONS AND OPEN THE DOOR. YOU MUST DO IT NOW."

Gurney tried a wild swing from another direction. "Including the White Mountain Strangler case?"

"Hypothetically."

"And the number of victims is as high as it is because the basic method was always the same—to kill five or six people each time, to obscure the motive for the one that mattered?"

"Hypothetically."

"I see. But there's a question I'd like to clear up—just to be sure I understand the risk calculation driving the MO. Wouldn't it be reasonable to assume that one well-planned murder would pose less chance of exposure than five or six?"

"The answer to that is no. However well planned one murder may be, it still focuses attention on that one victim and the consequences of that one death. There is no escape from the singularity of the event. However, the additional murders remove virtually all risk that the central murder will receive the focus it requires—and they create virtually no additional risk. Murderers are caught primarily because of their connections with their victims. If there are no connections . . . well, I'm sure you understand the concept."

"And the cost—the lives ended—that never concerned you?"

Sterne said nothing. His bland smile said it all.

Gurney wondered how long it would take a tough state prison to wipe it off his face.

The smile widened, as Sterne again seemed to sense Gurney's train of thought. "I'm actually looking forward to my interactions with the penal system and its population. I'm a positive thinker, Detective. I embrace the reality that's been placed in front of me. A penitentiary is a new world to conquer. I have an ability to attract people who can be of use. You seem to have noted my success with Robby Meese. Think about that. Penal institutions are full of Robby Meeses—susceptible young men looking for a father figure, for someone who understands them, someone who's on their side, who can channel their energies, their fears, their resentments. Think about it, Detective. With appropriate guidance, young men like that could become a kind of palace guard. It's an exciting prospect, one I've had occasion to think about many times over the years. In short, I believe that prison life will be quite manageable. I might even become a bit of a celebrity. I have a feeling I may become the darling of the psychological community all over again—as they try to rehabilitate themselves with profound new insights into the true story of the Good Shepherd. And don't forget the books. Authorized and unauthorized biographies. RAM specials. And you know something? I may end up a lot better off than you in the long run. You've earned yourself more enemies on the outside than I'll have on the inside. Not such a great victory for you, when you think about it. I can pay people to watch my back. People who are very good at that sort of thing. But how about your back? If I were you, I'd be concerned."

"PUT DOWN YOUR WEAPONS AND OPEN THE DOOR NOW."

Gurney stared across the room at the plain little man in the tan cardigan. "Tell me something, Larry. Do you have any regrets at all?"

He looked surprised. "Of course not. Everything I did makes perfect sense."

"Including Lila?"

"Pardon?"

"Including killing your wife, Lila?"

"What about it?"

"That made perfect sense, too?"

"Of course. Or I wouldn't have done it—hypothetically speaking. Actually, we had more of a business arrangement than a traditional marriage. Lila was a sexual athlete of high refinement. But that's another story." He produced a small, speculative smile. "Might make an exciting film."

He walked past Gurney to the front door, opened it, and tossed the big pistol out onto the grass.

"OPEN YOUR HANDS ... RAISE THEM ABOVE YOUR HEAD ... WALK FORWARD SLOWLY."

Sterne raised his hands and stepped out of the cabin. As he walked toward the causeway path, the helicopter searchlight fastened on him. A vehicle at the far end of the causeway—with headlights, fog lights, and two spotlights all on—began to move forward.

That was odd. In conditions like this, you'd want to maintain your position and let the perp come to you. To a preselected spot where you and your backup team could most safely control the situation.

Speaking of which, where the hell *was* the backup team? In the chopper hovering over the cabin? No team leader in his right mind would handle it that way.

There were a number of spotlights set up out there, but no other headlights. No trooper cruisers. Christ, if there was one, there ought to be a dozen.

Gurney picked up his Beretta off the table and watched from the window.

It was hard to see much of the vehicle creeping forward on the causeway, with all its lights pointing straight ahead. But one thing was evident: The position of the headlights made it too wide to be a cruiser. The NYSP did have a variety of SUVs—but the thing on the causeway was too wide to be any of them.

It was, however, just wide enough to be Clinter's Humvee.

Meaning that the chopper overhead wasn't NYSP either.

*What the fuck?*

Sterne was out on the causeway now, hands still raised, about twenty feet from the approaching vehicle.

Gurney stepped out of the cabin, holding the Beretta in his jacket pocket, and looked up. Despite the downward glare of the chopper's searchlight, he easily recognized the giant RAM logo on its belly.

The searchlight swept along the causeway, first illuminating Sterne, then the vehicle in front of him—which did in fact appear to be Clinter's Humvee. There was something mounted on the hood. Maybe some kind of weapon? The chopper's light swept out over the water, back over the cabin, and back toward the causeway.

What the hell was going on out there? What was Clinter up to?

The answer came with a hideous shock. From the contraption on the hood, a stream of fire shot forward, instantly engulfing Sterne from head to foot in a billowing orange blaze. The man began reeling, shrieking. The helicopter made a steep pivot, coming down closer, but the rotor downdraft intensified the swirling flames, and the craft swung away, rising steeply.

Gurney sprinted from the cabin out onto the causeway path. But by the time he got close to Sterne, the man had already crumpled to the ground, blessedly unconscious, engulfed in a fire raging with the blinding heat of homemade napalm.

When Gurney looked up from the burning body, Max Clinter was standing next to the open door of the Humvee in his camouflage uniform and snakeskin boots. His lips were drawn back and his teeth bared. He was holding a machine gun of the sort Gurney had seen only in old war movies, and then only set on a supporting base. It appeared too large, too heavy, for a man to carry, but Clinter seemed unaware of its weight as he took several long strides away from the Humvee and raised the huge gun's muzzle toward the sky.

The angle of the weapon and the insane ferocity in Clinter's eyes created a momentary impression that the man was about to assault the moon itself. But then the muzzle moved steadily toward the RAM helicopter, whose roaring downdraft was turning the placid surface of the pond into a mass of vibrating ripples.

As soon as Gurney realized Clinter's objective, he screamed, "Max! No!"

But Clinter was beyond reach, beyond listening, beyond stopping. He set his feet wide apart and, shouting something Gurney could not decipher in the din, began to fire.

At first the stream of bullets seemed to have no effect. Then the helicopter lurched sideways and started to descend in small, swooping arcs. Max kept firing. Gurney was trying to get to him, but the blaze spreading out from Sterne's body was blocking the way. The heat and the stench of burning flesh were horrendous.

Then, with an abrupt shudder, the helicopter pitched ninety degrees over onto its side, exploded into flames, and smashed down onto the causeway behind the Humvee. There was a second explosion and then a third, as Clinter's vehicle was enveloped in the conflagration. Clinter seemed not to notice that he had been caught in a spray of burning fuel.

Gurney jumped into the pond to get around Sterne's body, lurching through the waist-high water with the bottom slime sucking at his feet. By the time he'd scrambled back up onto the causeway, half crawling, half stumbling toward Clinter, the man's clothes and hair were in flames. Still gripping the machine gun, Clinter began to run wildly in the direction of the cabin, the air from his rapid movement feeding the fire that was consuming him. Gurney propelled himself forward, trying to drive him off the path and into the pond, but they fell together on the ground just short of the water's edge with the huge gun between them, spraying bullets out into the night.

# Chapter 51

# Grace

Late the next morning, Gurney was still in an emergency-room bed in a room off the main ER area in Ithaca's municipal hospital. Although the ER personnel had been relatively sure that his condition was not serious—mostly first-degree and a few second-degree burns—Madeleine had insisted upon her arrival that the on-call dermatologist be summoned.

Now that the dermatologist, who looked to them like a child playing a doctor in a school play, had come and gone, confirming the existing diagnosis, they were waiting for some insurance confusion to be sorted out and paperwork to be completed. Someone's computer system was down—it wasn't quite clear whose—and they'd been cheerily advised that the whole process might take a while.

Kyle, who had accompanied Madeleine to the hospital, was roaming between Gurney's room and the waiting room, the gift shop and the cafeteria, the nurses' station and the parking lot. It was clear that he wanted to be there, and equally clear that he was frustrated by the lack of anything useful to do. He'd been in and out of Gurney's little room numerous times that morning. After several awkward beginnings, he finally managed to make a request he said had been on his mind ever since Madeleine had mentioned to him that Gurney's old motorcycle helmet was stored away in their attic.

"You know, Dad, our heads are about the same size. I wonder . . . if it would be okay . . . I mean . . . I was wondering if could I have your helmet?"

"Sure, absolutely. I'll give it to you when we get back to the house."

Gurney smiled at the thought that Kyle apparently had inherited his father's roundabout way of expressing affection.

"Thanks, Dad. That's great. Wow. Thanks."

Kim had called—twice—to find out how Gurney was, to apologize for not being able to come to the hospital, to thank him profusely for risking his life to confront the Shepherd, and to let him know she'd been interviewed at length the previous day by Detective Schiff in connection with the Robby Meese homicide. She'd explained that she'd been *appropriately* cooperative. However, when Schiff had been joined that morning by Agent Trout of the FBI to reinterview her in light of the fiery drama at Max Clinter's, she'd decided it would be wise to have an attorney present—putting that new interview temporarily on hold.

Hardwick strode into Gurney's room a minute before noon. After giving Madeleine a grin and a reassuring wink, he gave Gurney a frowning once-over and burst into laughter—more of a rhythmic growling than an expression of merriment. "Jesus, man, what the hell did you do to your eyebrows?"

"I decided to burn them off and start over."

"Did you also decide to turn your face into a fucking pomegranate?"

"Nice of you to drop by, Jack. I need the encouragement."

"Christ, on the TV you look like James Bond. Here you look like—"

"What do you mean, on TV?"

"Don't tell me you haven't seen it."

"Seen what?"

"Jesus, Mary, and Joseph. The man instigates the Third World War and pleads ignorance. The whole damn thing from last night has been running on RAM News all morning. Sterne coming out of the cabin. That bloody flame-thrower mounted on Maxie's hood. Sterne being incinerated. Maxie machine-gunning the Ramcopter out of the sky. Your heroic self charging out into the night to risk your life. The Ramcopter crash—followed by what the talking RAM heads keep calling 'the horrible tragic fireball.' It's one hell of a show, Davey boy."

"Hold on a second, Jack. The helicopter got shot down. So where did the footage of the crash come from?"

"The fuckers had two choppers out there. One Ramcopter went down, the other Ramcopter just moved into position and kept filming.

Tragic fireballs are good for ratings. Especially with two people being burned to death in the process."

Gurney was grimacing, Max Clinter's fiery death still painfully vivid. "And this is on television?"

"Damn thing's been running all morning. Showbiz, my friend, it's fucking showbiz!"

"Those helicopters—how did they happen to be there to begin with?"

"Your friend Clinter gave RAM News a heads-up. Called earlier and told them that something really big was about to go down that night with the Good Shepherd, and they should position themselves in the area, ready to come swooping in. He called them again right before he made his move. Max always hated RAM for the nasty way they covered his original debacle with the Shepherd. Seems that shooting down the chopper was part of his plan."

As Gurney was absorbing this, Hardwick left the room and crossed a large open area to the nurses' station, where he interrupted a young woman working at a computer.

He returned with a triumphant gleam in his eye. "They've got a couple of TVs on rollers. The little peach with the big tits is gonna get us one. You should see this crap for yourself."

Madeleine sighed and closed her eyes.

"In the meantime, Sherlock, two questions: How the hell did Larry the dentist get so good with a gun?"

"My impression is that he had a passion for precision that was off the charts. People like that have a way of getting good at things."

"Too bad we can't bottle that and sell it to sane people. Second question, a bit more personal: Did you have any idea what you were walking into at Clinter's place?"

Gurney glanced at Madeleine. Her eyes were on him, waiting for his answer.

"I expected to meet the Shepherd. The disaster was unanticipated."

"You sure about that?"

"The hell does that mean?"

"Did you really believe that Clinter would stay away like you told him to?"

Gurney paused. "How did you know I told him to stay away?"

Hardwick parried the question with another question. "Why do you think he showed up when he did?"

That little mystery had been in the back of Gurney's own mind. The timing had been too perfect, relative to the nasty turn of events inside the cabin. The explanation now seemed obvious. "He bugged his own house?"

"Of course."

"And he had the receiver in the Humvee?"

"Yes."

"So he was listening in on my conversation with Larry Sterne?"

"Naturally."

"And his receiver recorded everything that was said in the cabin, including my phone call to him. And somewhere along the line, you guys got the recording—which is how you know that I told him to stay away. But the Humvee went up in flames, so how did you get—"

"We got it directly from the man himself. He e-mailed BCI the audio file just before he cranked up that flame-thrower of his. Seems he knew how the dance might end. It also seems that he wanted us to have something concrete that vindicated your view of the case."

Gurney felt a burst of gratitude to Clinter. Larry Sterne's comments and admissions would bury the "manifesto" fiction once and for all. "That's going to make a lot of people very unhappy."

Hardwick grinned. "Fuck 'em."

There was a long silence, during which Gurney realized that his involvement in the Good Shepherd case had essentially come to an end. The crime was solved. The danger was over.

A lot of people in law enforcement and forensic psychology would soon be engaged in an orgy of frantic finger-pointing, insisting that OPM—other people's mistakes—had led them astray. Gurney himself might, at some point after the dust had settled, receive some small recognition for his contribution. But recognition was a mixed blessing. It often had too high a price.

"By the way," said Hardwick, "Paul Mellani shot himself."

Gurney blinked. "What?"

"Shot himself with his Desert Eagle. Apparently a few days ago. Woman in the adjoining storefront yesterday afternoon reported getting a bad smell through the ventilation system."

"No doubt about its being a suicide?"

"None."

"Jesus."

Madeleine looked stricken. "Is that the poor man you talked to last week?"

"Yes." He turned to Hardwick. "Were you able to find out how long he'd owned the gun?"

"Less than a year."

"Jesus," said Gurney again, talking more to himself than to Hardwick. "Of all the possible weapons he could have used, why a Desert Eagle?"

Hardwick shrugged. "A Desert Eagle killed his father. Maybe he wanted to go the same way."

"He hated his father."

"Maybe that was the sin he had to atone for."

Gurney stared at Hardwick. Sometimes the man said the damnedest things.

"Speaking of fathers," said Gurney, "any trace at all of Emilio Corazon?"

"More than a trace."

"Huh?"

"When you have some time, you might want to think about how to handle this."

"Handle what?"

"Emilio Corazon is a late-stage alcoholic and heroin addict living in a Salvation Army shelter in Ventura, California. He panhandles to get money for booze and heroin. He's changed his name half a dozen times. He doesn't want to be found. He needs a liver transplant to stay alive, but he can't stay sober long enough to get on the list. He's getting dementia from the ammonia levels in his blood. The people at the shelter think he'll be dead in three months. Maybe sooner."

Gurney felt like he should say something.

But his mind was blank.

He felt empty.

Aching, sad, and empty.

"Mr. Gurney?"

He looked up. Lieutenant Bullard was standing in the doorway.

"Sorry if I'm interrupting something. I just . . . I just wanted to thank you . . . and make sure you were all right."

"Come in."

"No, no. I just . . ." She looked at Madeleine. "Are you Mrs. Gurney?"

"Yes, I am. And you . . . ?"

"Georgia Bullard. Your husband is a remarkable man. But of course you know that." She looked at Gurney. "Maybe, after all this gets sorted out, I was wondering, maybe I could treat you and your wife to lunch? I know a little Italian restaurant in Sasparilla."

Gurney laughed. "I look forward to it."

She backed away with a smile and a wave and, as suddenly as she'd appeared, was gone.

Gurney's mind returned to the fate of Emilio Corazon and the effect the news was likely to have on his daughter. He closed his eyes, leaning his head back against his pillow.

When he opened them, he wasn't sure how much time had passed. Hardwick was gone. Madeleine had moved her chair from the corner of the room to the side of his bed and was watching him. The scene reminded him of the all-too-similar end of the Perry case, when he had come so close to being killed, when he had suffered the physical damage that in some ways was still with him. And when he had emerged from the coma at the end of that experience, Madeleine was by his bed, waiting, watching.

For a moment, meeting her gaze, he was tempted to repeat that jokey cliché, *We have to stop meeting like this.* But somehow it didn't feel right, not really funny, not a joke he had a right to make.

An impish smile appeared on Madeleine's face. "Were you going to say something?"

He shook his head. Really just rocked it slightly from side to side on the pillow.

"Yes you were," she said. "Something silly. I could see it in your eyes." He laughed, then winced at the pain of the skin stretching around his mouth.

She put her hand on his. "Are you upset about Paul Mellani?"

"Yes."

"Because you're thinking you should have done something?"

"Maybe."

She nodded, gently rubbing the backs of his fingers. "It's too bad that the search for Kim's father didn't have a happier ending."

"Yes."

She pointed to his other hand, the bandaged one. "How's the arrowhead wound?"

He raised the hand from the bed and looked at it. "I'd forgotten about it."

"Good."

"Good?"

"I don't mean the injured hand. I mean the arrow. The great arrow *mystery*."

"You don't think it's a mystery?" he asked.

"Not a solvable one."

"So we should ignore it?"

"Yes." When he didn't appear convinced, she went on. "Isn't that just the way life is?"

"Full of inexplicable arrows falling out of the sky?"

"I mean, there'll always be things we don't have the time to understand perfectly."

It was the sort of statement that bothered Gurney. Not that it wasn't true. Of course it was true. But he felt that the *tenor* of it constituted an attack on the rational process. An attack on the way his own mind worked. Yet if ever there was an argument not worth getting into with Madeleine, that was it.

A young nurse came to the door, pushing ahead of her a TV on a rolling stand, but Gurney just shook his head and waved her away. RAM's "horrible tragic fireball" could wait.

"Did you understand Larry Sterne?" Madeleine asked.

"Maybe part of him. Not all of him. Sterne was . . . an unusual creature."

"It's nice to know there aren't a whole lot of them running around."

"He thought of himself as a thoroughly rational man. Thoroughly practical. A paragon of reason."

"Do you think he ever cared about anyone else?"

"No. Not a bit."

"Or trusted anyone?"

Gurney shook his head. " 'Trust' would not have been a meaning-ful concept to him. Not in the normal sense. He would have seen the willingness to trust as a form of weakness, an irrational flaw in others, a flaw that he could exploit. His relationships would have been based on exploitation and manipulation. He would have viewed other people as tools."

"So he was all alone, then."

"Yes. Completely alone."

"How dreadful."

Gurney almost said, *There but for the grace of God go I.* He knew how isolated he could become and hardly notice that it was happen-ing. How relationships could slip away like smoke in the breeze. How easily he could sink into himself. How natural and benign his isolating obsessions could seem.

He wanted to explain this to her, explain this peculiarity of his being. But then he got that feeling he sometimes got when he was near her—the feeling that she already knew what he was thinking without his having to say the words.

She looked into his eyes, squeezing his hand and holding it that way.

Then, for the first time ever, he got that same peculiar feeling, but in the opposite direction. He got the feeling that *he* already knew what *she* was thinking, without her having to say the words.

He could feel the words in her hand, see the words in her eyes.

She was telling him not to be afraid.

She was telling him to trust her, to believe in her love for him.

She was telling him that the grace on which he depended would always be with him.

In the profound peace that followed her silent words, he felt relieved of every care in the world. All was well. All was quiet. And then, somewhere in the far distance, there was a sound. It was so faint, so delicate, he wasn't sure whether he was hearing it or feeling it or imagining it. But he knew exactly what it was.

It was the distinctive lilting rhythm of Vivaldi's "Spring."

## *Acknowledgments*

Continuity itself is usually a good thing in business and professional relationships. And when that continuity involves truly talented, dedicated people it can be a delightful thing.

From the publication of my first novel, *Think of a Number*, through the second, *Shut Your Eyes Tight*, to the third, *Let the Devil Sleep*, I have had the privilege of working with the same extraordinary people—a superb agent, Molly Friedrich, her wonderful associate, Lucy Carson, and an unfailingly insightful editor, Rick Horgan.

Thank you, Rick. Thank you, Molly. Thank you, Lucy.

New from **John Verdon**

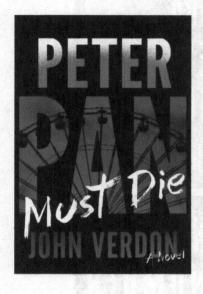

AVAILABLE WHEREVER BOOKS ARE SOLD

# Also by John Verdon

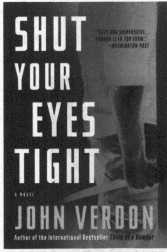

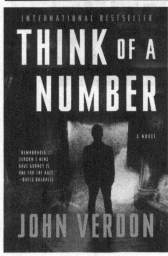